THE EDGE OF INNOCENCE

THE EDGE OF INNOCENCE

David P. Miraldi

978-0-9989189-1-4

For Leslee

INNOCENCE

The quality or state of being innocent; freedom from sin or moral wrong
Freedom from legal or specific wrong; guiltlessness
Simplicity; absence of guile or cunning; naiveté
Lack of knowledge or understanding
Harmlessness; innocuousness
Chastity

Source: Dictionary.com

Contents

INTRODUCTION

We were alone when the phone rang sometime after eleven p.m. that Friday night just before Christmas. With our parents out for the evening, my older brother and I were looking after ourselves, a freedom that we had just recently earned. He was twelve, and in a few weeks, I would be eleven. We had promised to put ourselves to bed more than an hour earlier, but here we were, still watching television. The garage was visible through the sunroom's windows, and we would have plenty of time to race up the stairs at the first sight of our parents' car. When I picked up the receiver, I expected to hear my mother's voice. Instead, I heard a man's voice that I did not recognize.

"Hey, is Ray there? I need to talk to him." His voice was gruff and impatient. I could hear people talking in the background.

"I'm sorry, he's not here right now," I replied, struggling not to sound tired.

"Well, I'm calling from the jail," he said. I could hear him mumble, "Damn it, he's not in." Then the line went dead.

I told my brother about the call.

"Well, that was really stupid. You just let some strange guy know that we're all alone right now," he said.

Spooked, we turned on extra lights, checked the locks, and went to bed. The next morning, I told my father that someone had phoned him from the jail. As an attorney, he occasionally had a client call him at home.

"Did he leave a name?" he asked.

"No. He just hung up on me," I answered.

"Probably nothing I would be interested in anyway," he replied.

That afternoon the two local newspapers reported the death of Florence Bennett and the arrest of her husband, Casper Bennett, on suspicion of murder. Mr. Bennett claimed to have found Mrs. Bennett partially clothed and dead in scalding water in their home's bathtub. The police believed that he had held his wife's head under the water and drowned her.

My father wondered if Bennett was our unknown caller from the night before. He had several times represented Bennett—first in two divorce proceedings and more recently in a collection matter. If Bennett had been the caller the night before, he did not call my father again. Instead, he hired a well-known and highly regarded criminal defense attorney, Lon Adams, to defend him.

At this time, in December of 1963, my father was a forty-four-year-old attorney, trying to build a successful law practice in his hometown of Lorain, Ohio, a city of seventy thousand, known for its steel mill and other manufacturing plants. Like almost everyone else whose life was interrupted by World War II, he started his professional career late, returning to Lorain in 1949 at the age of thirty. Almost immediately, he caught the eye of Lorain's city solicitor, John Pincura, who offered him the position of assistant city prosecutor. The following year he was appointed the Lorain city prosecutor and oversaw all the criminal cases in the city's municipal court.

The prosecutor position gave him needed experience but paid poorly. Because the city job was part-time, it theoretically allowed him to develop his own private practice. However, in the early years, my father's private practice struggled and provided little revenue.

In developing his private practice, my father often took chances with cash-strapped clients who were starting new businesses. As kids, we were amazed by the things my dad brought home in return for his legal services. The Bob Beck auto dealership regularly loaned us cars, including a chartreuse, big-finned Chevrolet that only a color-blind buyer might have considered. When a client's sporting goods business was struggling, the owner settled his account by giving my father enough equipment to outfit a baseball team—much to our delight and that of the neighborhood gang. Another time he loaded up the family car with carpentry tools and a power megaphone from a soon-to-be-shuttered hardware store. He joked that if we ever got lost in the woods, we could use the megaphone to summon "moose hunters to find us."

Although my father's private practice grew slowly, his rise as a successful prosecutor was quick. The municipal court trials occurred almost daily. He honed his courtroom skills on these small cases and became adept at cross-examining witnesses and connecting with jurors. Although he was a very effective city prosecutor, the small misdemeanor cases that he handled were not of much consequence, and his opponents were often only marginally prepared. It was an open question whether he would be successful when he tried larger cases against more skilled opponents in the county court.

In 1959 my father took the plunge and resigned as the city prosecutor in order to devote himself full-time to his private practice. He was now free to handle criminal defense matters, but rarely did so. Although he was in no position to be picky, he insisted that he didn't want his "waiting room filled with a bunch of lowlifes."

Occasionally, he would handle a criminal case, but only for those defendants who had never been in serious trouble before. A few months before the phone call from Casper Bennett, he had recently completed a highly charged public corruption trial of a local Republican officeholder. Despite my father's active role in local Democratic politics, he believed that the defendant was innocent and the charges were politically motivated. He took considerable flak from his fellow Democrats, especially after his client was acquitted. After the trial, I overheard him tell my mother that he would never handle another serious criminal case again.

He did not like the burden of preserving someone's liberty. He believed that if he did his job well, the jury would find his client not guilty. However, if he stumbled in any way, his client would be sentenced to prison. And he would blame himself—not the difficult facts of the case or something else that was beyond his control.

As it turned out, we had not heard the last from Casper Bennett. About a month before the trial, Bennett asked my father to serve with Lon Adams as part of his defense team. My father accepted, and over the next month, he closed his office to all other clients, dedicating himself to Bennett's defense.

When the trial began, both local newspapers covered it in great detail. I read the newspaper accounts and, like any kid, asked my dad the ultimate question.

"Did he do it, Dad?"

"He tells me that he didn't and he is quite forceful with his denials, but, of course, no one really knows," he replied.

****

Forty years later, I found part of my father's legal file pertaining to his defense of Bennett. He brought the file home sometime before he died in 1985 and my mom always kept it. When she moved to a retirement community in 1993, the file went with her and was stored in a closet. When she moved to a much smaller assisted-living unit in 2005, I found the file and took it home. There it sat for the next five years, until I decided to look at what my father had saved—notes from his closing argument, partial transcripts of two expert witnesses, legal research, a transcript of the preliminary hearing, a sensational magazine article from *True Police* about the case, and the defendant's lengthy, transcribed statement about his whereabouts on the night of his wife's death.

I, too, had become a lawyer, and had limited my practice to civil litigation, never once handling a felony criminal case. However, this case seemed to cast a spell on me, calling me to do more research and investigation.

In 2010, the problem was time. I had very little of it to devote to the project. And when I did, time had eliminated all the major players—Casper Bennett was dead, as were all of the attorneys involved in the case, the presiding judge, most of the critical witnesses, and the principal investigators from the Lorain police. The county prosecutor confirmed what I had expected; its file had been destroyed years ago. I located the trial's court reporter who told me that the trial had never been transcribed and his transcription notes were long gone. He remembered the trial and sent me an e-mail about his recollections. Feeling discouraged, I put the file away.

In 2015, I was close to retirement when the Bennett file beckoned me again. I was talking with a former client, a retired records custodian for the Lorain police, when an idea struck me. Was it possible that the Lorain police still had parts of its original investigation on the Bennett case? Making no promises, he agreed to check. A few weeks later, he called with the surprising news that the complete police file was intact and archived in the musty basement of the Lorain city hall. After I made a public records request, a wealth of information was in my hands: reports, witness statements, tests, scribbled notes, and photographs—a sizable cache of 155 pages. And there was new information: exculpatory evidence never shared with the defense and incriminating evidence never offered at trial for a variety of reasons. Buoyed by this fortunate find, I located and talked to the few remaining witnesses.

As I devoted more and more time to the project, I received some unexpected bonuses. As I did the research, the Lorain of my youth returned. And when I actually began writing the book, I found that my father, after a three-decade absence, once again took center stage in my life.

This book is very much about the police investigation of Florence Bennett's death on December 20, 1963, and the trial of her husband, Casper Bennett, four months later. However, I hope the book is more than that. As the story unwinds, I hope the reader will see how tenuous and elusive justice can be, even in a system as enlightened as our own. Ultimately, this story tests the boundaries of innocence and guilt.

Although I have described events that actually happened, involving people who really existed, this is a work of historical fiction and not one of nonfiction. Except for the testimony of two medical experts, there is no transcript of the trial. I had to imagine and re-create the dialogue, the thoughts, and the trial testimony of the principal players in this drama. Using detailed newspaper accounts, the police witness statements, the preliminary hearing transcript, and other sources, I have tried to tell this story accurately.

Did Casper Bennett kill Florence Bennett on December 20, 1963? Like my father, I will tell you that I do not know. However, I think the answer is clearer now than it was fifty-two years ago. For me, examining the case one more time was worth the journey—and I hope it will be for the reader as well.

THE EDGE OF INNOCENCE

PART 1: THE ARREST AND INVESTIGATION

CHAPTER 1

Sergeant Charles Springowski
December 20, 1963

On this Friday night, Lorain's downtown was alive with shoppers, and on its main street, Broadway, a constant parade of cars plodded past its retail stores. After the president's assassination a month earlier, no one seemed much interested in celebrating the Christmas holiday or buying gifts. Tonight, however, several of Lorain's major retailers were open until midnight and offered special promotions. Shoppers packed the sidewalk in front of Lynn's, where dresses were discounted by 50 percent, some as cheap as a dollar. Bargain hunters were also streaming to Lorain's only discount retailer, the Jupiter Store, where tinsel icicles were practically being given away at twenty-eight cents a package. The cars of those not yet shopping did a slow dance around downtown's central blocks, ready to pounce when a parking spot opened.

Two Lorain police detectives, Sergeant Charles Springowski and Sergeant Joseph Trifiletti, were killing time. Earlier that evening, they had knocked on a few doors looking for a witness, but the man had left town a few days earlier, and nobody had any idea where he was now. For most of their shift, the two detectives had driven up and down Broadway in an unmarked cruiser, joining the congestion.

"Let's get some coffee," Trifiletti suggested.

It was close to 9:25 when they parked the cruiser and walked into Sutter's. Despite the crowded streets, the restaurant itself was almost deserted and the waitress, a dumpy woman in her fifties, turned her back on them as soon as they entered. She quickly busied herself by wiping a table that was already clean.

"We only want a cup of coffee, Helen. We won't stay too long," Springowski told her. Helen ignored them. The detectives walked to a table about fifteen feet from the door, and as they sat down, Trifiletti spotted a crumpled *Lorain Journal* resting on a nearby chair.

Helen quickly returned with two cups of coffee. "You know, I was just about ready to lock the front door when you two bums walked in," she said. Springowski couldn't tell if she was actually angry at them or just feigning irritation to make them feel uncomfortable. Some of the coffee spilled into the saucers as she plopped them down onto the table.

"Hey, aren't we charming tonight?" Trifiletti asked. "Got some last-minute Christmas shopping to do tonight, Helen? Looks like the stores are open late."

"Gentlemen, I've had a long day and I don't want it to last one minute longer than it has to."

"Okay. Five minutes, maybe ten minutes tops, and we'll be gone," Trifiletti assured her, but Helen was already on her way back to the kitchen by the time he finished his sentence.

Trifiletti handed part of the newspaper to Springowski. "Here, check out the movies," Trifiletti said, knowing Springowski hadn't attended one in years.

"What junk are they showing down here tonight?" Springowski muttered to himself. Looking at the movie ads, Springowski was instantly amused. The Ohio Theater had a double feature—*Beach Party* and *Operation Bikini*, starring Frankie Avalon. Springowski wondered who would have scheduled this in December. At the Palace, the choice was not much better. Ray Milland was starring in *"X": The Man with the X-Ray Eyes.* Springowski read, "Suddenly . . . he could see thru clothes . . . and flesh . . . and walls!! He stripped souls as bare as bodies."

As a detective in the Lorain Police Department for over thirty years, Springowski could see how this "power" might come in handy, but then he quickly reconsidered. The crimes committed in Lorain usually didn't require a Sherlock Holmes to figure them out. Lorain had its drunks, prostitutes, gamblers, and small-time burglars, but not much more. And they left plenty of clues.

Lorain was a city of just under seventy thousand located on Lake Erie, about twenty-five miles west of Cleveland. More than half of its inhabitants were foreign-born or the first-generation children of immigrants. Poles, Italians, Slovenes, and Hungarians had come in large numbers at the turn of the century to work in the city's steel mill, shipyard, docks, and manufacturing plants. Now their children, people like Springowski, had moved out of the blue-collar jobs and into less physically demanding occupations. They were in business, law enforcement, banking, the building trades, and even the professions.

Springowski turned the page and his eye was drawn to a headline, "'Sister Mary' Indicted on Three Larceny Counts." Springowski knew all about this. He gestured to Trifiletti and pointed to the article. "Hey, here's an article about that *big* case you cracked a couple of weeks ago."

The article reported that a Lorain County grand jury had indicted a New York City gypsy who, posing as a nun, had taken about $10,000 from three Lorain women in a scheme known as a "pigeon drop." The gypsy told the women that all of their troubles stemmed from their paper money and offered to bless it. After blessing it, she switched the money with bundles of worthless paper. She was arrested when one victim invited her back to bless more money. That time, Trifiletti was waiting for her. Springowski shook his head. What was that gypsy woman thinking? Did she think she could really make that switch again? For that matter, what were any of these women thinking?

Springowski was continually amazed by what people believed they could get away with. Some people were undone by their greed. Others bragged to friends about their criminal exploits. However, in most situations, if the police banged on enough doors, they could find someone who saw something. Lorain's neighborhoods were static—most people lived in their homes for decades, and they knew their neighbors. When something or someone was out of place, someone else noticed it. Usually, it was an older couple or a widow. These people were always peering out of their windows or easily awakened by noises in the middle of the night.

"Hey, Dick Tracy, let's allow Helen to get home," Springowski told Trifiletti. "I would pay for the coffee, but, you know, my money's not been blessed by Sister Mary."

"Mine neither," said Trifiletti.

"Hey, Helen," Springowski yelled toward the kitchen, "thanks for the coffee." The two detectives left without paying.

As soon as they got back in their car, they heard the dispatcher on the radio. When they responded, the dispatcher sounded peeved.

"I've been trying to reach you guys for about ten minutes. Where have you been?"

"Just doing our job, Bonnie. We had to leave the cruiser for a few minutes," Springowski said as he cleared his throat. "What's up?"

"Hey, I need you to go to 1733 Long Avenue. A man called the operator to report that he'd found his wife unresponsive in the bathtub. The operator called the rescue squad and us. I sent Metelsky and Edwards there first. They called back and said the woman is dead. She apparently died in a bathtub and the bathwater's supposed to be scalding hot. The husband's hysterical and Metelsky wants some dicks there right away."

"We'll be there in five minutes," Springowski answered. "That's my old neighborhood, you know. You got more Polacks living there than in Warsaw."

"Yeah, I know. That's why I called you."

"You're sweet."

"Also 'cause you guys are the only two detectives I got workin' tonight," the dispatcher added.

"Hey, Bonnie, who made the call?"

"Casper Bennett, do you know him?"

"Oh yeah. Oh yeah. I know him."

Although Springowski was about twenty years older than Casper Bennett, he had known him since Casper was a teenager. Casper, like

Springowski, had connections to Lorain's old Polish neighborhood, which fanned out from Fifteenth and Long Avenue in central Lorain.

The neighborhood was anchored by the Polish Club and the massive Roman Catholic church, Nativity of the Blessed Virgin Mary, both yellow brick buildings that stood across the street from one another. Springowski could never understand why the Poles were so enamored with this yellow brick, a shade that reminded him of urine. Fortunately, the color scheme did not creep into nearby Pulaski Park, a tiny triangular park that displayed a statue of Casimir Pulaski, the Polish count who fought and died with the Americans during the Revolutionary War. A generation before, Lorain's Polish immigrants had erected this monument as if to blunt the hostility that the older, more established Lorain families felt toward the Poles and other immigrants who were overrunning their city.

Springowski knew that "Casper Bennett" was not Casper's given name. Like the Revolutionary War hero, he'd been christened Casimir. His last name was Bernatowicz, not Bennett. Casper, like his three younger brothers, went by Bennett, although none of the brothers had legally changed their last name.

The oldest of four children born to Polish immigrants, Casper Bennett had lived on Long Avenue for as long as Springowski could remember. Springowski had moved to Lorain from New York around 1930 when economic times were tough. At first he and his wife lived with his in-laws, and he scuffed around as a laborer and then as a meat cutter before hiring on with the Lorain Police Department in 1932.

Springowski had first met Casper when Casper was still in high school. Casper often hung around his father's auto repair shop and Springowski would talk to both of them whenever he dropped off a car there. For some reason, Springowski had always liked Casper, maybe because he first liked Casper's dad, a gruff man who was as hardworking as he was hard-drinking. Springowski watched as Casper rebelled as a teenager, playing the role of the wise guy who spent his days at the billiard rooms. Despite this, he believed that the young Casper was basically a good kid who would eventually find his way and buckle down.

However, Springowski was eventually disappointed by Casper's choices. A poor student, Casper dropped out of high school. When he had to support himself in his late teens, he opened a billiard room to go with the dozen or so that were already operating in Lorain. By all accounts, Casper was a hard worker, but he soon gained a reputation as a binge drinker who could not control his urge to drink.

Whenever Springowski and Casper met, Casper would greet him warmly and try to make him laugh. Despite his outward joviality, Springowski sensed that Casper was a troubled person. Besides his drinking binges, Casper had an unhappy marriage. His wife, Florence, was allegedly an alcoholic too, and their marriage was often in shambles. Casper was unfaithful and openly cavorted with a barmaid named Irene Miller.

Casper currently co-owned the B & M Grille on Fourteenth Street with Florence's uncle Frank Mishak. Springowski suspected that if the police ever targeted the B & M, they would uncover liquor law violations and gambling. The B & M attracted a younger crowd, almost exclusively male, including underage high school jocks who played pool there and, if things were slow, could buy a beer. But Casper had always skirted serious trouble with the law, and as Springowski headed toward Casper's house, he hoped to hell that Casper had nothing to do with his wife's death.

The two detectives parked outside the Bennett home—a small, white, two-story house with a tiny attic, probably built in the 1920s and squeezed in between two other almost identical-looking homes. Outside, a police cruiser and ambulance were parked, their oscillating lights still pulsing, adding an eerie glow to the neighborhood's outdoor Christmas decorations.

The front door was open, allowing Springowski and Trifiletti to enter. They followed the sound of voices coming from a second-floor bedroom.

Springowski could identify the voice of George Metelsky, one of the first two Lorain policemen to arrive at the scene. Metelsky's voice stopped in midsentence when Springowski entered the room and Springowski could sense relief in the other man's eyes. Metelsky had been talking to Casper Bennett and the two men initially blocked Springowski's view of the bed.

As Springowski got closer, he saw the dead woman draped diagonally, almost carelessly, across the bed, a flower-patterned bedspread thrown over her to hide her midsection and legs. Her chest was bare and her long brown hair, flecked with globs of displaced skin, was matted against her face. Her nightgown was bunched around her neck and her skin was a raw red. He pulled back the bedspread to view her legs and saw some slight bleeding about her ankles. The room was warm, the result of steam and too many people packed into the tiny space.

The two medics had placed an oxygen mask over her mouth, but none of them were working on the body. Trifiletti walked over to one of them. "Dead?" he asked.

"Yeah, and for some time. There was no pulse when we got here," one medic replied.

As soon as Casper saw Springowski, he rushed over to him. "I found her like that in the tub when I got home a few minutes ago." Casper was dressed in a white shirt, the sleeves rolled up from his wrists. He was about five feet nine inches tall and weighed close to two hundred pounds. "I couldn't get her out at first. The water was so damn hot. I just couldn't get a good grip. I think she slipped away from me five or six times. I finally got ahold of her under her armpits and dragged her here," Casper said, pointing to the bed.

Before Springowski could say anything, Casper looked over at his wife. "When I saw her in the tub, I said, 'Oh, Florence, what have you done to yourself?'"

"I'm sorry for you, Casper," Springowski responded. "You need to settle down. Okay? When you do, we'll have to ask you some questions. You understand that, right?"

As if the words did not register, Casper continued, "Before I left, I told her she needed to take a bath. I told her she was dirty. She'd been sick for about four days, but I told her I'd help her with a bath when I got back home. I didn't mean for her to take a bath by herself. She drinks too much and she keeps falling. My God, why did I tell her she was dirty?"

Springowski had been watching Bennett closely. As far as he could tell, Bennett was not faking the hysteria. He was talking fast and not listening to what others were saying to him. His eyes darted all around the room and he seemed truly distraught. "Okay, Casper. Just tell me a few things and I'll talk to you more at the station after I finish up here."

"Okay," Bennett said.

"When did you last see her alive?" Springowski asked, his tone gentle and fatherly.

"Around quarter to eight when I left to do some errands. I kissed her good-bye and told her I'd be home soon."

"When did you get back home?"

"About ten minutes before I called the rescue squad."

Bennett was listening to his questions and answering them appropriately. He seemed less agitated and Springowski was encouraged.

"What did you find when you got home?"

"She was kind of sitting up with her back against the spigots. You know, the faucet was running when I ran in and it was all steam in the bathroom. She was sitting up with her head slumped. I'm not sure if her head was in the water or not. I'm pretty sure that her legs were under the water. I turned the water off right away. Like I said, I couldn't get a good grip on her. The water was so hot, it was burning my hands."

Bennett held out his hands, first palm down and then palm up. The palm of his left hand was red and blistery. Springowski looked down at the tips of Bennett's fingers; some were taped or had Band-Aids on them. As if reading Springowski's mind, Bennett said, "I keep some of them taped for work so they don't crack open when I wash glasses all day long."

Before he could reply, Bennett continued, "I dragged her to the bed and I tried mouth-to-mouth breathing on her. After a couple of minutes of that, I could see she still wasn't breathing, so I called the operator for help." Bennett looked over at his wife and then at the medics, who were packing up their gear. Bennett continued to stare as one medic removed the oxygen mask from his wife's face.

Springowski quickly put his arm around Bennett and steered him away from the medic and the body. "That's enough for now, Casper. You need to get some treatment for those burns." Motioning to Metelsky's partner,

Springowski said, "Edwards, can you take Mr. Bennett downstairs while Trifiletti and I look around?" Turning to one of the medics, he said, "Can you check the burns on Mr. Bennett's hands, please?"

From the top of the stairs, Springowski watched the medics escort Casper into the dining room below. Springowski's mind flashed back thirty years and he was seated in that dining room, having supper with the Bernatowicz family. Across from him, a young Casper was telling a funny story, talking rapidly, gesturing with his hands, and trying to dominate the dinnertime conversation.

"Hey, Sarge, I need to talk to you," Metelsky said. Springowski hadn't noticed Metelsky walk over to him.

"Yeah, sure," Springowski replied. "I wanted to talk to you, too."

"Something just doesn't seem right here. How does a guy pull his wife out of the bathtub, drag her to this bed, and not get his shirt wet? Did you see his shirt? It was dry as a bone. It's clean, too. Wouldn't you expect to see some of that peeled skin on his clothes?"

Metelsky had joined the force just a few years earlier. Springowski thought Metelsky had a good head on his shoulders and liked him. He was the youngest of five children. His parents were Russian immigrants and his dad had died when Metelsky was just four years old, leaving his mother to raise and support all of them. Springowski knew Metelsky's mother, a woman who cleaned the offices of National Tube, the city's steel mill and largest employer. Springowski expected that Metelsky would work his way up the department's rungs just as he had.

Metelsky went on. "I also got a good look at his hands. The palm of his left hand is badly burned and so is the tip of his right little finger. The tops of his hands aren't burned at all. Now, how the hell does that happen? Does that fit with a guy who's trying to pull his wife out of a tub full of scalding water? Sergeant, something's not right here."

Springowski did not want to dismiss Metelsky's suggestion outright, but he simply could not picture Bennett murdering anyone. He'd need more than a dry shirt and a hand burn to be convinced of that. "I understand what you're saying, but it wouldn't take too long for his pants or his shirt to dry. I don't know what that burn pattern demonstrates, so let's hold off on any conclusions until we've looked around a bit. Show me what you found in the bathroom." Trifiletti was already in the bathroom when the other two men entered.

The bathroom was small, approximately six feet wide and nine feet long. It was dominated by an old five-foot-long porcelain bathtub supported by four tiny feet. The bathtub was hemmed in by a wall on one side and a toilet on the other. Springowski saw a wet towel on the floor directly in front of the toilet.

Springowski moved closer to the tub and peered in, blinking momentarily when he saw bits of skin and tufts of hair floating on the surface. The gray water filled the tub about halfway.

Looking at Metelsky, he asked, "Did you touch it?"

"Yeah. I had to pull my finger out almost immediately."

Springowski knew he had to put his finger in the water, too. *I'm getting too old for this*, he thought. At sixty-eight, he was the oldest member of the force and could have retired by now, but he still enjoyed working cases.

He gingerly slipped his left index finger into the water and held it there for several seconds before he, too, had to withdraw it. While he was rubbing his finger dry on his pant leg, Springowski looked at the tub's far edge, where the skin and nail from Florence Bennett's left thumb had come off in one big piece. "Oh my God," he said, mouthing the words to himself alone.

Then he saw blood on the far end of the tub, where Mrs. Bennett's feet would have been. That matched the lacerations that he had seen on both of her ankles. The room smelled of bubble bath and Springowski saw a broken bottle of it on the linoleum floor.

"Let's get a photographer over here," Springowski said. Looking at Metelsky, he asked, "Has the coroner been called?"

"I told the dispatcher to give him a call, so I'm assuming he's on his way," Metelsky said. "Do you need us for anything else?"

"No, go ahead and leave. We can take it from here," Springowski answered. Then, almost as an afterthought, he added, "Make sure Bennett is taken to the hospital for treatment of his burns. I don't care if you take him or if the rescue squad takes him."

About ten minutes later, Dr. Paul Kopsch, the county coroner, entered the house. By this time, Bennett, the first two policemen, and the rescue squad medics had all left. It was ten p.m.

The position of county coroner was an elected one and the coroner was not required to be a pathologist or an expert in forensic medicine. Dr. Kopsch had no such training and, in fact, was an anesthesiologist. However, Dr. Kopsch loved the excitement associated with police work and investigating suspicious deaths. Springowski knew him to be an intelligent, well-read man with diverse interests.

But there was also something of the eccentric in Dr. Kopsch. The man was fascinated with guns and had a collection of several hundred functioning firearms. Just two years before, he'd gone to an auction where almost everything at Crystal Beach, a defunct amusement park located in nearby Vermilion, was sold. Dr. Kopsch purchased the entire shooting gallery complete with targets and pump guns. Springowski had listened as Dr. Kopsch told him in great detail how he stood out in the rain with seven hundred people and outbid everyone for these items. What Dr. Kopsch did with the shooting gallery, Springowski never knew.

The Lorain police knew him well because Dr. Kopsch and another officer were developing a special bullet, one that would penetrate hard targets such as automobile doors and cinder blocks. Standard rounds, made largely of lead, often deformed and were ineffective when they struck these objects. Kopsch thought that if the police had a bullet that did not ricochet, the police could more effectively pursue fleeing subjects without endangering the public. Using a brass core and a Teflon tip, Kopsch developed a prototype that did just what he'd hoped. Springowski questioned whether this bullet was such a great thing. What would happen if it got into the hands of criminals?

Springowski took Dr. Kopsch to the bedroom where he bent over the body and began inspecting the burn pattern. Of medium height and build, Dr. Kopsch was about forty years old, and his hair was just beginning to gray. With his dark eyebrows and spectacles, he looked like a professor. He opened Florence's mouth with a metal probe and, using an examining light, looked down her throat. After an initial inspection of the entire body, he began to focus on the lower legs. He lifted them in order to examine both the front and back. He did this several times. Bored by this, Springowski and Trifiletti decided to go back into the bathroom and get another look.

A few minutes later, Dr. Kopsch appeared in the bathroom's doorway. "Come back over here, boys," he said to the two men, who were both older than he was. They walked back to the bedroom. "Look carefully at the lower legs." He stood out of the way and allowed Trifiletti and Springowski to look at the legs, although neither man lifted either of the limbs. "See anything unusual there?" he asked.

Springowski could see that the skin on the lower legs was not the raw red that it was on the rest of her body, but he decided to keep quiet. It was Trifiletti who answered for them. "They're not very burned."

"Not just that, they show no burns at all," Dr. Kopsch said as he pointed emphatically at the left shin. "She is burned on seventy-five percent of her body and nothing on the lower legs. That, gentlemen, is probably the most important finding here." Dr. Kopsch paused and looked expectantly at both detectives as if waiting for them to see the obvious. Neither man said anything.

Dr. Kopsch went on. "I think somebody was holding her head under the water. With her head under the water, her legs would pop up and extend over the side of the tub. That's why the legs are not burned. Where's the husband?"

This was not what Springowski wanted to hear. Trifiletti said, "He's at the hospital being treated for burns on his hands."

Dr. Kopsch's eyebrows lifted. "His hands are burned? He wasn't very careful, was he?"

"He says he burned them trying to get her out," Springowski said, keeping his tone even. Any cynicism here would throw him in with the lynching party.

"Oh, really. It would be interesting to know something about their marriage. You know, whether they were getting along or not," Dr. Kopsch said.

Trifiletti looked at Springowski, waiting for him to answer. Finally, Springowski replied, "The marriage was rocky from what I know. The husband has a girlfriend too." He immediately felt guilty. Had he just betrayed a confidence? Hell, no. The coroner had asked him a question and he knew the answer.

Dr. Kopsch's eyes lit up, but he said nothing. Instead, he walked back to the bathroom and touched the water in the tub and held his finger in it longer than Springowski had. Then he looked at the rest of the tub and immediately noticed the dried blood spots along one edge.

"There's dried blood on the edge of the bathtub that matches up pretty well with lacerations I found around her ankles. There's a broken bottle on the floor. If you ask me, it looks like she struggled," Dr. Kopsch said.

"That's what I think, too," Trifiletti volunteered.

"I assume you will arrest him tonight. Everything here points to a homicide, not an accident. This is not a difficult crime to solve. The husband did this one. No question here," Dr. Kopsch concluded.

Trifiletti said, "After he gets released from the hospital, we'll pick him up and take him back to the station and get as much out of him as we can. Springowski knows the family, so Bennett will talk to him. Then we'll arrest him."

Dr. Kopsch responded, "I'm going to look around the house for a little bit. I'll get someone to take the body to St. Joseph and the morgue. I'll have Dr. Chesner, my deputy, do the autopsy tomorrow. I don't expect that it will change anything."

Springowski had been questioning whether he was the right person to investigate this case, and now he wished some other detective had been on duty tonight. Then again, maybe it was better that he was there. Everyone else seemed to be going off half-cocked, while he seemed to be the only voice of reason. If Bennett drowned his wife, why use scalding water instead of warm or cold water? How could Bennett hold his wife's head under scalding water for several minutes when Springowski had only been able to keep his finger in it for a few seconds?

He was also troubled by Dr. Kopsch's quick analysis. How long had

Mrs. Bennett been dead? If alibi witnesses could verify Casper's absence from the house that evening, it would be critical to determine the exact time of the wife's death. Springowski thought that pathologists sometimes used a rectal thermometer to register a corpse's internal temperature in order to pinpoint the time of death. Had Dr. Kopsch done that? Springowski doubted it. Had Dr. Kopsch done everything possible to determine the time of death? Springowski doubted that, too.

Maybe he was just too close to this case to be objective. As he walked out of the house, Springowski wrestled with this thought. He had been on the force now for nearly thirty-two years, and in that time, he had never removed himself from any investigation. In the end, he decided he could be fair. He would stay on the case.

CHAPTER 2

Lon Adams

December 23, 1963

Lon Adams could hardly suppress his frustration as he sat slouched in an uncomfortable wooden chair across the table from his new client, Casper Bennett. Florence Bennett had died three days earlier and her husband had been arrested almost immediately. After picking him up from the emergency room around eleven p.m., Detectives Springowski and Trifiletti had questioned Bennett at the station and then arrested him on suspicion of murder.

Since then, Bennett had felt no need to hire an attorney. He seemingly repeated his story to any police officer who would listen (and plenty talked to him). Desperate to establish his alibi, Bennett had signed a statement two days after his wife's death. The police were interviewing everyone mentioned in the statement and searching for inconsistencies.

Bennett had also taken two lie detector tests. The first was inconclusive, while the second indicated that Bennett was lying about his wife's death. Fortunately for Bennett, lie detector results were not admissible at trial because they were deemed scientifically unreliable. Despite this, the lie detector results emboldened the Lorain police, who were now convinced that Bennett was a murderer, and they were determined to gather the evidence to convict him.

Adams was a tall, thin man just a year shy of sixty. He was the dean of Lorain County's criminal defense bar. With that distinction came the notoriety of defending people accused of the most heinous crimes. However, Adams did not limit his practice solely to criminal matters and accepted cases in domestic relations, personal injury, probate, and real estate.

Adams was not afraid to be different. Much to the amusement of his fellow attorneys, he recorded all client information and legal research on multiple note cards and brought them to hearings, stashed in his suit's breast pocket. Like a magician, he pulled them out at precise moments to respond to critical issues. At trial, Adams was more conventional and jotted down testimony and ideas on a yellow legal pad.

Lon Adams was a second-generation Lorain attorney. His father, Charles Adams, was a tenacious courtroom fighter who had died a few years before. By outward appearances, the two men were complete opposites. Unlike his tall and lean son, the elder Adams had been short, stocky, and built like a bulldog. In the courtroom, the father was known for his aggressive and pugnacious style, while his son was measured and patient, rarely agitated. In his conservative gray suits, Lon Adams resembled the distinguished British actor David Niven, while his tobacco-chewing, gun-packing father could have stepped out of a Laramie stagecoach.

However, both men were fierce individualists who disdained the government's intrusion into the lives of its citizens. As a result, the father and son shared one precept—the state had to prove a defendant's guilt beyond a reasonable doubt. No shortcuts. Everyone's freedom was protected when they forced the prosecutor to follow the strict dictates of the law. If a guilty man went free because the state failed to present enough evidence, then that was just the way it had to be.

At any first meeting, Adams needed to size up the client, and that included determining whether the client could pay his fees. Casper's brother, Chester, had already fronted $1,000 as an initial retainer, delivering the check to Adams earlier that day. Knowing that Bennett could afford him, Adams hoped he would like Bennett and believe his story. Over the years, Adams had learned that he could defend a paying client even if he did not believe him, but when he believed in his client's innocence, well, that was a real bonus.

Adams already knew some things about his new client. Twice before, Florence Bennett had hired Adams to bring divorce proceedings against Casper and claimed that Casper was an unfaithful, lying adulterer who verbally abused her and periodically slapped her around. Adams decided to put that information on the back burner for now. Women who wanted a divorce always exaggerated their husband's cruelty and infidelity, and Florence had seemed high-strung anyway. Both divorce proceedings did not go far, and during their course, he'd never met Casper. He would go into the interview with an open mind and judge the man for himself.

Adams's first impression of Bennett was not a positive one. His new client was looking down at his feet as he talked, never a good sign. "I just figured if I told 'em what happened, they'd let me go." As if Bennett could sense Adams's disapproval, he looked Adams in the eyes. "So help me God, I had nothing to do with Florence's death. I don't know how she fell in. I don't know why she turned the water on. I don't know why she didn't wait for me to help her take a bath. I don't got an answer for any of that. So why'd I talk to the police without an attorney? That's why. I figured if I cooperated, they'd realize I didn't do it."

Adams let Bennett's words sink in and did not respond. The man sounded sincere, but the words could have been rehearsed. God knew the guy had been in jail all weekend and had had plenty of time to practice those lines in his head.

Getting no response from Adams, Bennett continued, "Hell, Florence was drinking all the time. She was an alcoholic. She was taking sleeping pills, too. Another thing—I thought I could trust Charlie Springowski. He's known my family for years. You know my dad always fixed his car for him, sometimes for next to nothin'. How could Springowski do this to me? That's what I can't figure out."

Over the years, Adams had interviewed hundreds, perhaps thousands, of people accused of every kind of crime. They all insisted that they were innocent—and, of course, some were and some were not. He hoped that years of experience had taught him how to tell the difference. At this stage, Adams had not made up his mind about Bennett, but he certainly wanted to believe that this man had not drowned his wife.

"All right, let's talk about what happened on December twentieth. Why don't you start with when you got up and take me through the day, all the way to your arrest," Adams said as he rubbed his gray pencil mustache.

"Well, I always get up early because I have to open the bar at six thirty in the morning. I work there until five in the afternoon, when my partner gets there. On this Friday, I didn't go straight home. I called Irene Miller, who was working at the Sons of Italy, but she was busy and couldn't talk."

As soon as Adams heard the name Irene Miller, he struggled to remember how he knew it. Then it hit him. She was Casper's girlfriend, and, for Christ's sake, he had represented her in a proceeding against Casper too. How the hell did he find himself entangled in every legal squabble between Bennett and the women in his life?

Adams remembered Miller as a middle-aged barmaid who had been kicked around by life. Although she dressed neatly, she used tons of makeup and doused herself with industrial-strength perfume. Several years earlier, Miller had hired Adams because she had broken things off with Bennett and he wouldn't leave her alone. Casper phoned her at all hours, showed up at her doorstep, and demanded to see her. Adams had sent a letter to Bennett, warning him off, but Bennett had ignored the letter, forcing Adams to file a restraining order. Bennett and Miller had reconciled, if that is the right word for two adulterers who break up and resume their illicit relations. The restraining order became moot.

Adams returned his attention to Casper.

"So I drove around like I always do. You know, to unwind a bit. I drove down to Leavitt Road and by Lakeview Park. I'm not sure what time I got home, but it was probably between five thirty and six. Florence had been sick for the last four or five days from drinking too much. She wasn't feeling so good, so I asked her if she wanted some supper. I was going to warm up some leftovers. She said she didn't want any food, but she wanted two shots of whiskey. I initially told her no, but then I gave in and poured them for her. She went upstairs because she said she was tired and wanted to go to bed."

"Let me stop you there," Adams interrupted. "Had she been drinking before you got home?"

"I can't say for sure, but I think she had. She was drinking a lot over the last few weeks, so I would say she probably was drinking all day; but I wasn't home, so I didn't actually see her drink. There were empty bottles under the sink that I hadn't taken to the trash yet, so she could have finished a bottle and put it in the pile and I wouldn't know it."

Why was Bennett equivocating on this simple point? For Christ's sake, just say she was drinking all day, Adams thought.

"You know she was taking sleeping pills, too," Bennett added.

"What kind? Prescription stuff?" Adams asked, his eyes lighting up.

"No, not from a doctor. These were pills you could get at the drugstore."

"Okay, go on," Adams urged.

"I left the house around fifteen minutes to eight to run a few errands. I made sure she was in bed. I kissed her good-bye. She asked if I was going to stay out late and I said no. Oh yeah, I almost forgot, I told her that I would help her take a bath when I got back. She had been sick in bed for four or five days from drinking so much and I told her that she was dirty. I didn't say that to make her feel bad, just letting her know that we gotta deal with that later. I left through the back door. I didn't lock the door, you know, because Florence had gotten the locks changed a few weeks back and she hadn't given me a key."

Adams didn't want to interrupt Bennett—he wanted to hear the entire story and see how it flowed—but this was too much for him. "So why don't you have a key to your own house?" Adams demanded.

"Well, I'd been coming home late at night a few times, and she got really mad at me and she was just tryin' to teach me a lesson," Bennett replied. He shrugged his shoulders and gave Adams a half smile. Adams did not smile back.

"Go on," Adams said.

"Well, the first place I stopped was Don's Sohio on Twenty-First Street and Elyria Avenue. Ed Warner waited on me and filled the car with gas. I was giving away these small bottles of whiskey at the bar as Christmas presents, you know, so I gave two to Ed and told him to give one to Don and keep one for himself. I stopped somewhere and gave Irene Miller another phone call. She was busy waitressing at the Sons of Italy and she seemed a little irritated that I had called her again. So I drove down Broadway until I got to West Erie. I parked and went into Kingsley's Cigar Store. I bought the Elyria paper and the last edition of the *Cleveland Press*. I was heading home down Reid Avenue when I saw Joe Wasilewski around Fifteenth and Reid. He used to work at Runyan's and I know him from there."

Adams flinched when Bennett mentioned Runyan's because he knew the reputation of this "bookstore." In the front room, the store sold newspapers, girlie magazines, and books, while, behind a locked door in the back, bookies took bets on horse races and other sporting events. Was this alibi witness a former bookie? Adams groaned inwardly at the thought.

Bennett did not notice Adams's momentary inattention. "I waved to him and he waved back. And then I turned down Fourteenth Street to go by our bar, not to go in, but just to see how many cars were there and what kind of business we had that night. Then I got home, probably around ten minutes before I called for the rescue squad."

Adams was getting a sinking feeling about this alibi. Bennett had described a trip of three to four miles and activities that would take about five minutes each. Adams knew Bennett was leaving something out, maybe a lot of things out. What had this guy actually been doing for an hour and a half that evening? Trying to tie down the alibi, Adams asked, "So if you called the rescue squad around nine thirty, that means you got home around nine twenty?"

"Yeah, something like that. I don't know the exact time."

Adams did not like Bennett's breezy, almost careless response. Didn't this guy realize that his exact return time was a crucial piece of his alibi?

Undaunted, Bennett plowed on, "I came in through the back door and I seen there was a light on in the basement. At first I thought Florence was down there so I called to her. Then I remembered that I had taken some trays there to soak just before I'd gone out. I figured she was in bed so I went upstairs to check on her. As I passed the bathroom door, I heard the water running and I opened the door and that's when I seen her."

Bennett paused and then went on. "Her back was against the faucets and she was sittin' up with her head slumped forward. I'm not sure if her face was in the water or not. The lower part of her body and her feet were in the water. I yelled, 'Oh my God, Florence, what did you do?'"

Adams was no longer fidgeting with his mustache. He was studying Bennett's face, searching to see if he would look away or if his eyelids would flutter, but Bennett held his gaze.

"The water was pretty high, but I don't think it'd reached the overflow holes. I'm just not sure. I turned off the water and I don't know if it was just the hot that was on or whether the cold was on, too. It could've just been the hot faucet because the bathroom was all steamy. I reached to try and pull her out and the water was so hot, it was burning my hands."

Bennett's voice became agitated and he spoke more rapidly. "I tried a couple of times. She was slippery and the water was so hot, I couldn't keep my hands in the water for more than a few seconds. I was able to get ahold of her under her armpits and pulled her onto the bathroom floor. Then I dragged her into the bedroom where I was able to lift her onto the bed."

"Did you call the rescue squad at that point?" Adams asked.

"Well, no. My first thought was that she was not breathing and maybe I could give her that mouth-to-mouth breathing treatment. I just opened up her mouth with both hands and started blowing in and hoped that it'd start her breathing again. I did that for a couple of minutes and her chest would rise when I blew in, but she didn't start breathing on her own."

Adams thought it odd that Casper would attempt artificial respiration by himself. "Do you have any training in this, Casper?" Adams asked.

"No, not really. There's a fireman in the rescue squad, Murphy, who comes into the bar from time to time. He told me about bringing people back by doing it, and I asked him how to do it and he explained it to me. I figured I might have to use it on somebody in the bar someday. He says, you just pinch the nose, tilt back the head, and blow into the mouth. So that's what I done. But when I seen that it wasn't working and she wasn't breathing on her own, I got on the phone to the operator and told her to call the rescue squad for me. I turned on the front porch light and waited for them at the front door to make sure they came to the right house. As soon as I seen them, I opened the door and waved them in. I was pretty hysterical when they got there."

Bennett was looking at his hands as he paused in the story. When he started again, his voice became even more excited and his eyes seemed transfixed on something above Adams's head. "They go up to the bedroom and put an oxygen mask over her mouth and nose, and it's about now that I realize that my left hand is burned and part of my right. I just watch them, thinking that they can bring her back, and it seems like just a minute or so after they got there, two policemen were running up the steps and walked into the bedroom."

"Who were they?" Adams asked.

"I know lots of Lorain cops, but I don't know either of these two guys. They were young. Both of these guys were staring at Florence. You see, her nightgown was pulled up around her neck, all wet, and she just had her panties on. Florence was always such a private person and to see everyone looking at her, I could hardly stand it. I just wanted to tell them to look someplace else, but I kept my mouth shut. For Christ's sake, she was practically naked and I just kept thinking, *Oh my God, oh my God.*"

Adams sensed that Bennett was going to cry and the two sat in silence. While Casper fought to regain his composure, Adams thought again about Florence Bennett. When Florence first walked into his office, she was a well-groomed woman of forty, about five feet four inches tall, and of medium build. Adams thought that she had once been a handsome woman, but she looked ten years older than her stated age. She was nervous and rather soft-spoken at the beginning of the interview, but her voice became shrill when she described her husband.

She had wanted a divorce because she was tired of her husband's unfaithfulness. Casper was four years older than Florence and was having an affair with Irene Miller, who was a few years older than Casper. He had promised to give up this girlfriend several times, but he always broke his word. Worse yet, he was buying nice things for Irene. After he moved out of the house, he was taking her to places like Las Vegas and Hawaii, places Florence would have loved to visit. She'd had enough and wanted him completely out of her life.

Casper fought the divorce. As it dragged on, Casper became penitent and convinced Florence that he still loved her and would stay out of trouble. He moved back in with her and they dismissed the divorce action. A couple of years later, Casper began seeing Irene Miller again and moved into his own apartment. Florence filed for divorce a second time, and then Casper left Irene and returned to Florence once again, moving back to the Long Avenue home a few months before she died. Adams had meant to dismiss the second divorce action, but he just hadn't gotten around to it.

Adams knew that Florence was an alcoholic. Once she had come to his office very drunk. During the divorce proceedings, Casper's attorney claimed that Florence would go on weeklong binges, lock herself in the house like a recluse, and allow the place to turn into a trash heap. The attorney claimed that Casper became involved with Irene Miller only because he needed some female companionship, something he did not get at home. Adams did not believe that back then, but circumstances had changed. Who knew? Maybe it was true.

Adams said, "How much was Florence drinking around this time?"

"Lots," Bennett replied. "She only drank hard stuff and she could go through a fifth of whiskey or vodka in one day."

"You mentioned something about pills. What kind of pills are we talking about?" Adams asked.

"It was all over-the-counter medicines—aspirin, Alka-Seltzer, Sominex, and Sleep-eze," Bennett responded.

"Sominex. You mean that stuff that helps you sleep?" Adams asked.

"Yeah, that's the stuff. She would take them all the time to help her relax and get to sleep," Bennett said.

"Did she take any on the day she died?"

"Yes, she asked me for a couple and I gave 'em to her and then I hid the bottle in another room."

"So she took the sleeping pills with hard liquor?" Adams confirmed.

"Oh yeah. All the time," Bennett answered.

"Had she ever fallen before?" Adams asked, knowing it to be a critical question. If Florence had fallen before, a jury would be more likely to conclude that she'd fallen again, this time into the bathtub.

"She fell down a couple of times. One time she was drinking heavily and fell down the steps pretty bad and I had to take her to the hospital."

Adams interrupted, "When?"

"Just a couple of months ago. There'll be a record of it at St. Joe's and it should be in our family doctor's records, too."

"Besides you, Casper, who knew that she drank so much?" Adams asked.

"Lots of people. Workers who came to the house seen her drunk. The neighbors knew she drank. You can't keep that kind of thing a secret. Hell, years ago I tried to have her work at the bar. She drank so much on the job, we had to forget that idea," Bennett said. "You know I own the bar with her uncle Frank Mishak. Him and me hardly speak to each other anymore, but I think he'd tell you the same thing if you asked him."

"So, Casper, what do you think happened to Florence?" Adams asked.

"Well, Florence definitely had been drinking and had taken a few sleeping pills. Instead of waiting for me, she decided to take a bath by herself. She was weak from being sick and all her drinking. I figure she was just filling the tub with hot water and passed out or lost her balance and hit her head. She probably was knocked out and drowned. All I know is that I found her in the bathtub like that."

"Is it possible that she committed suicide?" Adams asked.

"No, no," Bennett replied without hesitation. "I've been thinking and thinking about this ever since I've been in jail. We was going to start over, the two of us. You know, we'd been talking about selling the bar and the house, taking the money and moving to Florida. She was kinda excited about this."

Adams was relieved that Bennett quickly rejected the suggestion of suicide. His response seemed both realistic and honest. If Casper and Florence were getting along better and planning a new life together in Florida,

Adams could use that to debunk the murder charge. Hell, the prosecution probably only had circumstantial evidence—no direct evidence linking Bennett to her death. If there was no enmity between the victim and the alleged murderer, how could the prosecution ever convince a jury that Casper had killed her? For the first time, Adams liked his chances. "Does anybody know that you two wanted to move to Florida?"

"Like I said, Frank Mishak and me don't talk about anything except the business, and even that, not very much. But he knows that I've been trying to sell my half of the bar for the last few months. My brother Chester also knew that Florence and me wanted to get out of here and move to Florida," Bennett replied.

This was exactly what Adams wanted to hear. He would have witnesses who would confirm the couple's recommitment to each another. Weighing his words carefully, Adams said, "Casper, here is what we need to do. You are entitled to a preliminary hearing. Most of the time, we just skip this because the prosecutor only has to prove that there's probable cause to believe that you committed a crime. Probable cause is really easy to show. It's almost no proof at all. But this time, we're not going to give them a free ride. We're going to force the prosecutor to bring in his witnesses to testify and tell us what he has to prove his case. My gut feeling is that he doesn't have much. At the very least, it forces him to show his hand, and that may be important later."

"Whatever you think, Mr. Adams," Bennett answered.

"I'll talk to you again before the preliminary hearing," Adams said. With that, he stood up, shook Casper's hand, and left.

CHAPTER 3

Sergeant William Solomon
December 21, 1963

Sergeant William Solomon could be intimidating. His fellow officers saw him as self-assured, even a little cocky. A no-nonsense guy, Solomon quickly formed opinions and stubbornly held them, regardless of later developments. He relished taking down the "bad guys" and enjoyed the power that went with his authority. He was big-boned and blunt, the quintessential tough cop.

Bill Solomon was the same age as Casper Bennett and both had attended Lorain High School until Casper dropped out during his junior year. Solomon knew Casper, not well, but enough to conclude that he was a bum. Like Bennett, Solomon was the oldest son of Eastern European immigrants. Solomon's parents were Hungarian, not Polish, and he'd grown up on East Thirty-Fourth Street, just beyond the smoke and grime of the steel mill where his father worked as a pipe bender. Solomon was employed full-time on the Lorain police force and moonlighted as a plumber during his off hours. Because of his plumbing background, Solomon believed he was uniquely qualified to investigate this bathtub drowning and uncover flaws in Bennett's story.

At the start of their shift, Solomon and Springowski met with two other officers, Sergeant Michael Kocak and Detective Roy Briggs, to divvy up tasks. Springowski asked Kocak and Briggs to track down the alibi witnesses, while Springowski and Solomon were to run tests on the bathtub and hot water heater, then look around the Bennett house. If they had time, Springowski and Solomon hoped to locate Casper's girlfriend, Irene Miller, and talk to her.

"I'm convinced this girlfriend knows what really happened. If we lean on her hard enough, she'll talk," Solomon said as they drove to the Bennett home. "She'll get scared if she thinks she might go to jail too. No woman wants her pretty face behind bars."

"Have you ever seen this pretty little face?" Springowski asked, raising his eyebrows. "Believe me, Irene Miller's nothin' to write home about. She's an over-the-hill barmaid who's got to be well over fifty."

"No, never seen her before. But if she's like most barmaids, she'll talk," Solomon responded. "Once you wind 'em up, they all talk."

The Bennett house was unlocked. The police had been unable to lock it because Casper did not have a key and did not know where Florence had hidden hers. Anyone could have come in and disturbed the crime scene. With Casper in jail, the police had taken their chances.

The two officers walked up the stairs and entered the bathroom. Although the water had been drained, the tub had a gray scum line about halfway up the tub. Florence's hair and skin were still stuck to the tub's side and bottom.

"So, does this line show how full the bathtub was last night?" Solomon asked, pointing to the scum line.

"Yeah, that's how full it was, and, believe me, that water was incredibly hot," Springowski confirmed.

"Did anyone bother to measure or mark the waterline before the tub was drained last night? You know there are lots of lazy slobs who never scrub out their bathtubs, and maybe that's what we're lookin' at right now."

"No, we didn't measure it, but this is how high the water was," Springowski said. Solomon didn't think Springowski sounded too confident, and he exhaled deeply, suppressing an urge to criticize the older detective. Instead, Solomon lightly kicked the outside of the tub in a few places.

Springowski was the first to break the silence. "You know, last night we're here with Casper, and the rescue squad is bandaging up his left hand.

He asks me if it's okay if he calls this girl he knows. I know he's seeing this Irene Miller woman, and I say no. A few minutes later, he says that he needs to talk to this woman. Again, I tell him he can't."

"Great guy. His wife is dead and he wants to talk to his girlfriend," Solomon said, momentarily forgetting his irritation about Springowski's failure to measure the waterline.

"But, you know, it just made me wonder if he killed his wife. I mean, would you call your girlfriend if you had just murdered your wife and the phone call's going to be overheard by the investigating detectives? To me, that's crazy. A murderer wouldn't do that," Springowski mused aloud.

"He would if he were a stupid son of a bitch, and Bennett is that," Solomon snapped, emphasizing the last two words. He wanted to say more, but, uncharacteristically, Solomon held his tongue. *What the hell is Springowski thinking?* he wondered.

Solomon turned on the hot water and let it run briefly. He did the same with the cold tap. "You turn on the hot water while I go down to the basement," Solomon commanded. "I want to check out the hot water heater, okay?"

Solomon saw that the house had a Hoffman Instantaneous Hot Water Heater, a model he knew well. When Springowski turned on the hot tap in the bathroom, gas ignited and heated the water in its copper coils. The longer the water ran, the hotter it became. However, the hot water heater had a safety thermostat that shut the gas off once the water reached 160 degrees. The gas would reignite and start heating the water again when the water temperature fell to 140.

Carrying a long thermometer that he had borrowed from a local plumber, Solomon went back upstairs. "Okay, let's see how hot the water is by the time it gets up here," Solomon said as he grabbed the hot tap.

"No, let's try to figure out what the temperature would be if a person was in the tub," Springowski suggested.

"Who the hell are you going to put in the tub?" Solomon asked. "It ain't going to be me, Charlie."

Springowski saw a rubber bath mat on the bottom of the tub. "Let's just hold this thing up a little ways from the faucets. I think that would be like a body breaking the water."

Solomon thought this was a stupid idea, but he kept this criticism to himself. "Okay. It's your show," he said.

Springowski held up the mat while Solomon turned on the hot water so that it flowed steadily. When the water reached the dirt line, Solomon took some readings. Near the faucets, the water was 158 degrees. In the center, it was 140, and about six inches from the end of the tub, it was just 120.

"That's interesting," Springowski said. "That's almost a forty-degree difference. Florence Bennett's lower legs would have been in water that was only a hundred and twenty degrees. That makes me wonder if that's why her lower legs weren't burned. You know, Kopsch made a big deal out of that. He thinks her legs popped out over the side of the tub while Casper held her head down. Kopsch—"

"Don't think too hard on this one," Solomon interrupted. "Wasn't there blood on the edge of the tub and the windowsill, and broken glass too? Come on, there was a struggle goin' on here last night. Christ, are you thinking Bennett didn't do it?"

"Hey, I'm not saying that. All I'm saying is that we just can't jump to conclusions. We got to do this thing right. You know, consider everything," Springowski said.

"Oh, really? I think you're goin' soft on me. That's what I'm thinking," Solomon said as he snatched the thermometer out of Springowski's hands.

"No, I'm not," Springowski shot back. "I just don't want to do a crappy investigation. That's all."

"No matter, we gotta test the overflow system next," Solomon said. "If the water'd been running for a long time, then water woulda flowed into that system and kept it from spilling onto the floor."

The men allowed the water to reach the overflow holes and spill into them. Within several minutes, they noticed water dripping down the outside of the tub and onto the floor. When Solomon took a closer look, he saw that the tub was corroded not only near one of the overflow holes but also where the overflow pipe connected to a drain.

"This baby's corroded too," he said, pointing to the overflow pipe. "Let's give it some time and see what kind of puddle develops." Unable to contain his excitement, Solomon stood up and rubbed his hands together.

Springowski wiped the water from the floor, and Solomon turned on the hot tap again. In one minute, a four-inch-diameter puddle had formed under the tub.

"Well, well," Solomon said. "The overflow's not workin'. You know what that means, right? If the water'd been runnin' for a long time before Bennett got home, then it would've triggered the overflow, and there would've been a really big puddle under this tub. So, Charlie, what did this floor look like last night?"

Springowski shuffled his feet and looked out the bathroom window before answering. "There was a towel between the tub and the toilet and it was pretty wet. As for puddles under the tub, all I can say is that it's possible."

"I'm not asking if it's possible. I'm asking about what you actually saw. Were there any puddles under the bathtub or not? That ain't a tough question."

"I didn't look under the tub. It didn't seem important then," Springowski said.

"Jesus, I can't believe you guys." For the second time, Solomon began to lightly kick the outside of the tub. After a few moments, he said, "Well, then, we'll have to check the photographs. I'm assuming somebody had enough brains to photograph under the tub," Solomon said.

Springowski hesitated. "I got Dan Turcus in to take pictures. I looked at them this morning. Several of them show the floor and the tub."

"That's not what I'm askin'. Did he take a picture under the tub?"

"I don't know."

"What do you mean you don't know?"

"I don't think he did," Springowski admitted.

"Shit," Solomon said. "I wish I'd been called out last night."

"Hey, if there had been a big puddle under the tub, Turcus would have taken a picture of it."

"Oh, really? Try saying that on the stand. Damn it, that photo should've been taken," Solomon said, shaking his head.

"Nobody saw any puddles of water on the floor and that's what everybody's going to say when they testify," Springowski said. "Calm down, Bill. Whether we have a photograph or not, nobody saw any water under the tub. End of story."

"Yeah, but did anyone actually look under the tub?" Solomon asked.

"There were four guys here last night. Nobody saw a puddle under the tub or coming out from under it. Don't worry. That's not going to be an issue," Springowski said.

Solomon walked out of the bathroom and paced in the hall for a minute. When he returned, he told Springowski, "We need to measure how much water it takes to reach the dirt line and the overflow pipes." The officers emptied the tub and then filled a gallon jug from the sink and kept adding water to the tub until the water reached those levels. It took twenty-five gallons to reach the dirt line and forty gallons to reach the overflow holes.

"How long would it take to fill the tub with twenty-five gallons?" Springowski asked.

"Depends on how open the tap is. It wouldn't be unusual for someone to turn it on so that water flowed at, let's say, three gallons a minute. That's a reasonable estimate," Solomon suggested.

As they began walking down the stairs, Solomon said, "You know Bennett's lawyer can't claim that the water'd been running for a long time. That's really, really big here. I mean, nobody can say she fell into that tub an hour or so before Casper got home. Because if she had, those leaks would've allowed water to spread all over the damn floor. So, if some fast-talking lawyer wants to tell a jury Mrs. Bennett fell into the tub, he'll have to say she fell in *just before* her husband got home." Solomon raised his eyebrows and smirked. "Nobody, I mean nobody, is going to buy that one."

Before they left, the two decided to search the house. In the cupboard under the kitchen sink, they found five empty bottles of Canadian Club whiskey. Behind the desk in the dining room, Solomon found a bottle of Four Roses that was almost empty.

"No question, somebody liked their booze," he called out to Springowski.

Solomon then went through the desk drawers. He found an unlocked strongbox that contained money, insurance policies, and other personal papers.

"Man, there's gotta be two grand in bills here," Solomon said. Under the money, he saw a whole slew of life insurance policies. "Lookee here, lookee here," Solomon exclaimed. "Must be more than a dozen life insurance policies on Florence Bennett." He quickly opened one up to see who was named as the beneficiary. "Casper is the beneficiary and I bet he is the beneficiary on all of these."

Solomon took the box into the kitchen and placed it on a table. He looked at each policy before handing it to Springowski. Eleven policies were written on Florence Bennett's life and each named Casper as the sole beneficiary. Some were as small as $245, while the largest payout was $5,325. The policies totaled $22,002 and all had been purchased more than ten years ago.

"I don't know much about insurance, but I think the payout doubles if somebody dies accidentally," Solomon said.

"That's right," Springowski added. "Whenever there's a suspicious death, those insurance guys are all over me. They're always snooping around, second-guessing my investigation. Take it from me, if an insurance company can avoid paying that double indemnity thing, they do."

"Forget that double indemnity shit. As far as I'm concerned, insurance companies don't pay anything ever," Solomon agreed.

The policemen removed more documents from the strongbox. They found more insurance policies, but these were written on Casper Bennett's life and Florence was the beneficiary. These policies had been taken out at the same time as the others and matched them in payouts.

"I don't know if any of these life insurance policies are going to help us that much," Springowski said. "Casper and Florence are insured for the same amounts and none were taken out recently. Most of them date back to the early 1950s."

"Still," Solomon said, "the guy's got a motive to see his wife dead. There's $22,000 in life insurance, and if you double it for an accident, then that's $44,000."

"I don't know," Springowski replied. "Like I said, these are all small policies and they have the same amount of insurance on each other. Now, if Casper had taken out a big policy on Florence just before she died, well, that would be a completely different story."

"Shit, Charlie, what's the matter with you?" Solomon said. "You want this guy to skate? He hates his wife. He's got a girlfriend. He's got a lot of insurance on his wife. I bet he's got a mountain of unpaid debts. He claims to have found his wife drowned in the bathtub after he's been gone for an hour and a half. We've just established that if she fell into the tub, it was right before he got home. Fat chance. There's blood on the tub. There's a broken bottle on the floor. She's burned all over her body. He's got burn marks on parts of both hands. Do you really believe that crap that he got burned trying to pull her out? Why aren't the tops of his hands burned? Wake up, Charlie."

"The question that gets me is this. If he's going to drown his wife in the bathtub, why use scalding water? Drown her in cold water or warm water, but not scalding-hot water," Springowski said.

"Wait a minute. Wait a minute," Solomon said, hitting his hand against his head. "I can't believe I didn't think about this before. Every Sunday at eight thirty there's this show on Channel Five called *Arrest and Trial.* It's about real cases. I don't know why I watch the stupid show. Anyway, in the last episode, this woman was charged with murdering her architect husband. They claimed she hit him over the head with a walking stick when he was in the bathtub. Then she turned on the hot water full blast. You want to know why? According to this famous medical examiner, it slows down rigor mortis and makes it damn near impossible to figure out the time of death. That TV show was on just five days before Florence Bennett died in scalding water. You wanna bet Casper watched that show?"

Springowski murmured, "I'll be damned." He remained silent as he thought about Solomon's revelation.

"Charlie, it's time to stop thinking Casper is innocent," Solomon said.

"I'll talk to Dr. Kopsch about this," Springowski said, almost in a whisper.

"You damn well better."

****

Back at the station, the two tracked down Kocak and Briggs to find out what they had learned.

Looking at Springowski, Kocak said, "Your friend Casper was at the places he said he was, but not when he said he was."

"He's not my friend," Springowski said. "And don't talk to me in riddles."

Kocak looked over at Solomon and winked. "Okay. Let's start at Don's Sohio. Casper was there yesterday. But get this: he was *not there around* eight o'clock like he claimed. I talked to Ed Warner, who waited on him and pumped his gas. He says Casper was there around six thirty or so. Casper bought about five dollars of gas and then gave him two tiny bottles of whiskey as a Christmas present. Warner's wife was there just after Bennett left, and she was on her way to a funeral home and wanted to be there around seven p.m."

Looking at Springowski, Kocak said, "I guess you know County Auditor Joe Mitock also saw Bennett at the gas station that evening, so I talked to him, too. Mitock said he was driving by the station and waved to Bennett, who he knows very well. Here's the clincher. Mitock was on his way to go bowling and his league started at seven p.m. So our boy is lying when he says he left home around a quarter to eight that night."

Solomon began whistling between his teeth. "Nice work," he said. "Did any of those gas station people notice anything strange about Bennett?"

"No, that's the funny part. Warner says Bennett was in a real playful mood. He was handing Warner a five-dollar bill to pay for the gas and then grabs it back before Warner can get ahold of it. Bennett says something like, 'Now you see it, now you don't.' He does that a couple of times. Warner says Bennett is always pulling stuff like that. I asked Warner if he noticed anything unusual about Bennett's hands and he said no."

Solomon blurted out, "The guy's in a great mood because he's going to knock off his wife in a few minutes. I can't believe it."

"Funny thing is that Mitock said the same thing to me. He spots Bennett talking to the attendant. Mitock volunteered that it seemed that Casper Bennett was in a jovial mood with the attendant. He could see that they were laughing and screwing around." Kocak continued, "I still need to get down to Kingsley's again because the person I talked to wasn't working there on the night of the murder."

"What about Joe Wasilewski?" Springowski asked. "Bennett claims he saw Wasilewski just a few minutes before he drove home. Says he saw Wasilewski driving by and waved to him."

"Yeah, that all checks out," Kocak said. "Wasilewski was on Fifteenth Street between nine ten and nine twenty. He saw Bennett in his car. They know each other and waved. Wasilewski kept going on Fifteenth Street, while Bennett turned right onto Reid Avenue."

Springowski asked, "So let me make sure I got this right. Wasilewski saw Bennett in his car between nine ten and nine twenty p.m., just about a few blocks from Bennett's home on Seventeenth and Long?"

"Yeah, that's right," Kocak said. "We also talked to a neighbor, Mrs. Poletylo. She lives next door to the Bennetts. She was out hanging a wreath on her door. She thinks it was around nine fifteen because she's hurrying to get the wreath up so she can watch *The Price Is Right* at nine thirty. She sees Casper park his car and go into his house. So I think Casper did go home around nine fifteen or so. These two witnesses verify that."

"So part of his story does check out," Springowski said. "He was heading home between nine and nine thirty, parked his car, and went into the house. It's just that he left earlier than he told us yesterday. Maybe he went out, came back, and went out again? Did this neighbor know when he left his house?"

Kocak said, "That's another part of her story. Mrs. Poletylo's quite a character. Once you get her talking, she never stops. Anyway, she says she was hanging another wreath on a north-side window around eight p.m. At first, she says she saw Bennett's car parked there around that time. But as we questioned her more, she then claims that it wasn't there."

"Wait a minute. This woman is hanging a wreath at eight p.m. and then another one around nine fifteen? Why doesn't she do them both at the same time?" Solomon asked, shaking his head.

"All I can gather from Mrs. Poletylo is that Bennett did get home after nine p.m., sometime before she started to watch *The Price Is Right* at nine thirty. If she's hurrying so she can watch her show, it's probably closer to nine thirty," Kocak concluded.

"We know Bennett is lying about the time he left the house," Solomon said. "So what does it mean that he left the house around six thirty instead of seven forty-five like he claims? What's he doing for almost three hours?"

"Nobody could be that far off in estimating when he left," Kocak added. "If he's lying about that, he's lying about almost everything. He's covering something up."

"He's one stupid son of a bitch," concluded Solomon.

CHAPTER 4

Irene Miller
December 27, 1963

Irene Miller sat in the Lorain Police Department lobby, waiting for Sergeant Michael Kocak and Detective Roy Briggs to call her into an interview room. This would be the third time in a week that the police questioned her about Casper, and she had the feeling it would not be the last. Sergeant Springowski had talked to her first, just two days after the incident. Then two days later, on Christmas Eve, Sergeant Solomon took a crack at her. She dreaded being questioned by the police again, but she had no choice. They seemed to believe that Casper had confided in her about his plan to murder Florence, and that she'd either helped him or kept quiet about it. Perhaps they believed that Casper had confessed to the killing when she visited him in jail. She told herself to keep calm.

She realized now that this affair with Casper Bennett was a horrible mistake. She'd met him just after breaking things off with Chester Merves, another bar owner in town. Casper came into the Sons of Italy, where she waited on him. He made a few jokes and she laughed at some of his crazy comments. As he was leaving, he asked if she would go out for dinner with him sometime. She was lonely and saw no ring on his finger. What was the harm in having dinner with this guy? Four years later, she saw things differently. Here she was being questioned about a potential murder and perhaps even suspected as an accomplice—all because she made a bad decision to become romantically involved with Casper Bennett.

Why were all of her relationships with men such disasters? She had been married and divorced twice. At seventeen, she'd eloped with Clifford Hamilton, sneaking off to West Virginia. Their first child was born a few years later. By the time their second child was born, they had moved to Lorain County. Clifford was undependable and stayed out late, and she no longer loved him. She thought more and more about a divorce but knew that conventional morality dictated that a wife was supposed to stick it out, particularly when children were involved. A woman who got a divorce lost the acceptance of mainstream America, led by all those churchgoing, self-righteous prigs who seemed to be everywhere. Irene was twenty-four years old and she was in a lousy marriage with a jerk. She was still young, attractive, and fun to be with, and she had a lot of living to do. In 1935, after seven years of marriage, she divorced Clifford.

She liked the freedom of being single, but she struggled to make ends meet. At forty-four, she married John Miller. She was never sure whether she married him because she loved him or because her looks were beginning to fade and he was her last chance. They moved to Toledo and lived there for three years, until she filed for divorce again because they were fighting all the time and he sometimes hit her. She moved back to Lorain, and for the last five years, she had bumped around, sometimes living in a cheap apartment if she could afford it, or living with her father when she could not. She worked as a barmaid, which did not pay much. If she wanted anything nice, she needed somebody else to pay for it. Sometimes her dad would help out, but more often than not, she convinced a boyfriend to buy her the special things that otherwise would have eluded her.

Irene knew what she was all about. She was a survivor who lived by her own standards—not conventional standards, but standards nonetheless. She was no floozy, and by God, she was no home-wrecker either. She dated only single guys, or if she dated a married guy, he was either separated from his wife or about to leave her. Up until now, Irene couldn't have cared less about what "respectable" women thought of her.

But now, she was mortified at what would happen if Casper's case continued to get media attention. Everyone was talking about it, and that meant that they were talking about her—the fallen woman. When she'd visited Casper at the jail two days ago, he was breezy and self-assured. He told her, "This thing will all blow over." Looking her straight in the eyes, he said that he had nothing to do with Florence's death. He told her to relax—he was the one in jail. The police would bother her for a little while longer and then it would all be over. The charges would eventually be dismissed and he would go free. He scoffed at the idea that the prosecutor would proceed with the case.

Irene was not so sure. What if his case went to trial? She would be called as a witness. Their love affair would be developed to show Casper's motive for killing Florence. Any dodo could see that. Worse yet, the two local newspapers would go wild reporting about their adulterous affair. She could think of nothing more humiliating than total strangers knowing all about her and Casper. No one would know the truth and she would be reviled. She assured herself that once this nightmare was over, she would run out of Lorain County as quickly as her fifty-two-year-old legs could carry her.

Irene had taken care to dress conservatively for the interview. She wore a gray wool skirt, white blouse, and navy jacket. Her red hair was coiffed in a large beehive. She had not spared the makeup and perfume but decided against wearing gloves. Although her face was heavy, with a double chin, she still felt attractive with her penetrating dark eyes and easy smile.

The wooden bench in the lobby was not comfortable. Irene pulled a handkerchief from her purse and began squeezing it with her left hand. Her mind returned to the two previous police interrogations. The first time, Sergeant Springowski had questioned her at her father's house, and he was a gentleman, treating her with a courteous but distant respect. He'd asked if she'd seen Casper on the night Florence died. Irene told him that Casper called her twice, once around 5:10 p.m. and then again around 8:00 p.m. Both times she was at work and she told him that she was busy. Both calls were short. She knew Casper had called from a pay phone the second time because she heard the coins drop. He wanted to know what she was doing after work, and she told him that she was tired and would go home.

Casper promised to call her again that night but never did.

She should have shut up there, but she wanted to set the record straight. Irene told Springowski that she'd broken up with Casper in July. Casper moved back with his wife, and Irene explained that she did not date men when they lived at home. Despite this, Casper kept calling her. What she hadn't told Springowski was that they drove to Massillon with her cousin to visit her relatives on the Sunday before Florence's death. She didn't want Springowski to get the wrong idea because, in her mind, she and Casper were no longer an item.

She would never forget the interrogation two days later. Sergeant Solomon, that loudmouthed lout, grilled her, while Springowski sat next to him, mute as a stone. Irene quickly surmised that, in the interim, the police had talked to her ex-boyfriend Chester Merves. Solomon seemed to be loaded with new information about her relationship with Bennett—things only the jealous Merves would have known or invented and gladly spread. If she ran into that loser again, she would give him a piece of her mind.

That nosy bastard Solomon wanted to know how long she and Casper had "run around and carried on together." She told him four to four and a half years, off and on. Solomon wanted to know if Casper had given her gifts and taken her on vacations. She admitted to birthday and Christmas gifts such as stockings, dresses, a ring, a necklace, and perfume. She didn't consider these things to be out of the ordinary, but Solomon lifted his eyebrows and looked at Springowski as if he were onto something big. No way would she tell Solomon that Casper had helped pay for a mink stole and a refrigerator. That was none of his business and had nothing to do with Florence's death.

As for vacations, it was public knowledge that she and Casper spent time together in Las Vegas. However, she told Solomon that this was not what it looked like. Every year she visited her nephew, who just happened to be a sheriff's deputy living in Las Vegas. She figured Solomon would be impressed by her nephew's law enforcement job, but, if it registered, he didn't seem interested. In August of 1962, she flew out by herself, but then the next day, Casper surprised her by following her there. Her nephew picked Casper up from the airport and helped him find a hotel room while she stayed at her nephew's house. For the next week, Casper took her to fancy restaurants and nightclubs, paying for everything. It was fun, but she wanted Solomon to understand that she didn't know Casper had planned to join her there. She hoped that would end the questions about their vacations together.

Irene also made it clear that all of this happened after Bennett moved out of his house and into in an apartment on Elyria Avenue, a block away from her apartment. She didn't disclose that Casper paid the $90-a-month rent for her. She deserved a decent place where they could meet in private. She had tired of meeting Casper at the flea-bitten Colonial Hotel, where winos gawked at them whenever they walked through the lobby.

She insisted that she and Casper did not live together, but she'd cooked and cleaned for him for more than a year. However, when she saw Bennett's car parked in front of his home on Long Avenue two nights in a row, she ended the relationship. Either Casper was with her or he should stay married to Florence.

Solomon asked if she ever took a vacation to Hawaii with Bennett. She had, but the question caught her off guard and she felt like this was none of Solomon's business. She'd denied the Hawaii trip, which she now realized was stupid. If they asked her again, she would admit to that trip and some other getaways closer to home.

A thin man in a police uniform entered through the lobby door. He called out, "Irene Miller." Irene thought this was strange because she was the only person waiting in the lobby. Irene stood up and the officer seemed to do a double take before introducing himself as Roy Briggs. He led her to an interview room where another officer, perhaps forty years old and in plain clothes, was sitting at a table. He introduced himself as Michael Kocak.

Kocak shuffled through some typed reports before speaking. "Mrs. Miller, thank you for coming down to the station. I know that you've talked to some of my fellow officers before."

Irene stopped him. "You know this is my third time in the last week. If there are questions you want to ask me, I would appreciate it if you would ask them all now and stop bothering me." She had not planned on saying that, but the words just jumped out.

As if puzzled by her outburst, Kocak looked at Briggs for help before he responded. "Mrs. Miller, this is an ongoing investigation, as you know, involving a number of members of the Lorain Police Department. Detective Briggs and I are part of that team and we have not yet had the chance to speak with you. We've also discovered more things since someone from the LPD spoke with you last and want to talk to you about some of those things. I really do hope this is the last time that we talk to you. In fact, we hope to get a written statement from you at the end of our meeting and then we should be done with our questions. Does that sound fair to you?"

"Sure, I understand. I'm just getting a little tired of being questioned all the time," she said.

Kocak began by going over the same background information that she had provided before, but then he asked her, "Have you ever been arrested?"

"Why do you need to know that?" Irene asked.

"It's standard," Kocak replied. "If you don't tell us, we can find it out by going through the records."

"One time," Irene answered. "I sold whiskey to someone on a Sunday."

"That's it? Nothing more?" Kocak asked. Irene shook her head no. Looking down at a report, Kocak asked, "So you've been going with Bennett for four or four and a half years? Right?"

"That's right, but let me make one thing clear. When he went back to his wife, I didn't have anything to do with him."

"Right," Kocak answered. "And you've gone on a trip with him to Las Vegas. Any other longer trips or shorter trips?"

This was Irene's chance to talk about the trip to Hawaii or even their week together at Put-in-Bay, but instead she said, "We've been on some shorter trips to Cleveland several times, even Toledo, Sandusky, and once to Detroit, Michigan. He took me to nice places for dinner dates there."

"Were these expensive places?" Kocak asked.

Of course they were; that's why she enjoyed being Casper's girlfriend.

He treated her like someone special and she didn't have to give much in return, just some female companionship. "These were nice places and nice places cost a lot of money," Irene responded evenly. Anticipating Kocak's next question, Irene added with some pride, "And, of course, Casper paid for it all."

"What about expensive gifts?" Kocak probed.

Kocak was giving her a chance to come clean about the mink stole, but Irene had not mentioned it in her prior conversations with the police. What did the mink stole have to do with the police investigation anyway? What right did the police have to question her about something as private as that? So what if Casper wanted to buy her a mink stole? That was his business. If he wanted to buy his alcoholic wife bottles of scotch, that was up to him too. After a few moments of hesitation, she replied, "No, nothing I would call expensive," she said. "He bought me clothes, like dresses, hose, and sweaters, even this coat I'm wearing. But I wouldn't call it expensive. It only cost $19.95."

"What about a mink stole?" Kocak asked, zeroing in.

Irene's heart began to race. "I bet somebody told you that Casper bought me a mink stole. Not quite. Casper went with me when I picked out the mink stole, but my dad gave me a hundred dollars toward it and I paid the rest," Irene said, looking first at Briggs and then to Kocak.

"You'll swear to that in a written statement?" Kocak continued.

"Of course," Irene responded as she gripped the handkerchief more tightly between her hands below the table. "I still don't see what that has to do with your investigation. I mean, really. Who cares?"

For the first time, Briggs posed a question to her: "Did Casper Bennett ever threaten you in any way?"

Casper had, indeed, slapped her around several times, but so had John Miller, her last husband. If she told the officers this, they would get the wrong idea about Casper. He had been thoughtful and kind to her. Although he'd slapped her before, he'd never threatened to kill her. "No, he didn't," she said.

"You look as if you have more to tell us about that," Kocak continued.

She felt perspiration on her forehead and she pursed her lips. She had to think quickly and give them something. "Casper never threatened me, but he was a jealous guy. I mean, he would call me at all hours to find out where I was. At first I thought it was kind of cute, but then that stuff really gets on your nerves. He would ride around the block where I lived, checking on me—hundreds of times."

Irene stopped herself again. When she broke up with Casper the first time, he continued to show up at her apartment and bother her. Once, he actually broke down her door when she didn't let him in. But he didn't harm her. He just said that he wanted to see her and make sure that she wasn't seeing anybody else. He continued to drive around her house and her workplace. She eventually hired an attorney to write some letters to Casper, telling him to stay away or she would file a restraining order against him. The funny thing is that her attorney was Lon Adams, the same attorney representing Casper now, and Adams eventually filed for the restraining order. That had all blown over when she and Casper resumed their affair a few months later. All the police needed to know was that Casper was a jealous man. They didn't need to know about Casper's obsession with her. He was just a little strange that way but, on the whole, he treated her well and bought her the things she wanted.

Briggs seemed interested. "How often did Casper phone you?"

She had been both upset and flattered that Casper took such an interest in her. "Well, a lot actually. It was fun at first, but then I got tired of it. I put in a private line with a cut-off switch so I wouldn't get his calls all the time." She held up her hands, palms up, as if to emphasize the mystery of a man like Casper. "I even had the phone company put my bill in a plain envelope, just in case Casper might get into my mail and discover my new phone number. But I don't want you to get the wrong idea about Casper; he just wanted to make sure that I wasn't seeing any other guys."

"I'm just wondering if Casper ever proposed marriage to you," Kocak followed up. "It seems to me that he was nuts about you."

Irene thought that she was finally getting through to one of the cops. She locked eyes with Kocak and said, "Yes, he was. When we first started going out together, he talked about marrying me and I told him to forget it. I said, 'If you're going out with me while you're still married to your wife, you'd probably do the same thing to me. You want two women all the time.' He just laughed about that."

Kocak laughed at this too, which pleased Irene. "Smart woman," Kocak said. "Let's go over the last time you saw Casper. I know you've talked to both Springowski and Solomon about this, but I'm thinking that you may have remembered more since then."

Irene took a deep breath to express her irritation at being asked about this again. "The last time I saw him was the Sunday before Florence died. My cousin, her two sons, and I were driving down to Massillon to visit some relatives. My dad was already down there so we just wanted to see everybody too. Casper asked if he could go along, so he drove down with us, but we dropped him off at a restaurant while we visited with my relatives. My dad can't stand the sight of Casper, you know. After the visit, we picked Casper up again and drove back to Lorain. That was it." Irene paused for a moment. "No, he saw me one other time. He called me at work the day before his wife's death and I told him that I went to the beauty shop and the hairdresser put silver highlights in my hair. I told him that it looked really good and then he said that he wanted to see it. So when he finished work on Thursday, he had me come out of the bar to his car where he could check out the highlights. That took about five minutes."

"So you were still seeing him, right?" Briggs asked.

"I don't want you guys to get the wrong idea. Casper drove down with us as a friend. My God, I had my cousin and her kids with me. Like I said, if he was living with his wife, I wouldn't have anything to do with him except to talk to him. We were still friends, you know. Nothing more," Irene replied. She looked first at Briggs and then Kocak, but she wasn't sure that they were buying this part. She thought about explaining more about their relationship but decided against it.

"Well, that takes us up to Friday, December twentieth, the day Florence was—the day Florence died," Kocak said, standing up suddenly from his chair. "So, any contact with Casper Bennett on that day?"

"I've been through this before with you guys," Irene began. "He called me at work around five p.m. and I told him I was busy. Then he called me from a pay phone around eight p.m. and promised to call me later that night. That was it."

"What did he talk to you about that last time? Did his voice sound different? Anything unusual at all about that phone conversation?" Kocak asked, moving closer to her.

Irene paused and thought for a moment. "He said that he was going to stop at my house, you know, my dad's house on Sixth Street, and sweep the snow off the sidewalks. My dad is eighty-four years old so he can't do it. I think Casper said he was going to run a few errands, too."

Both Kocak and Briggs seemed to perk up about the snow. "Well, do you know if he swept your sidewalks?"

"Yeah, he did. They were swept when I came home and they had a dusting of snow before I left," Irene responded, trying to visualize the sidewalks when she returned home from work. "He also left me something by the back door. It was a six-pack of Black Label beer."

"You're sure of this? You didn't mention this in any of the other interviews," Kocak said, scowling.

"Yes. Of course I am," Irene replied. She couldn't understand why Kocak would be so upset by this new information. So what if Casper came by her dad's house and spent about half an hour sweeping away the snow that night? It seemed so unimportant to her. Those were the kind of sweet things Casper did for her all the time. Maybe the police didn't want to know how thoughtful Casper could be.

Kocak's face seemed a bit flushed. "Let's be clear; you and Casper Bennett had sexual relations, right?" Kocak seemed angry.

"What's that to you?" Irene snapped back. "I don't know why that should be any of your business."

Briggs answered for them, "We're sorry to ask you that. It's just something that we have to tie down. Unfortunately, everything Casper Bennett did is potentially important to us. We know the answer to the question, but we still have to get it confirmed."

Irene was unconvinced. "What does that have to do with Florence Bennett's death? What are you guys trying to prove here? Are you saying that Casper is a bad man because he dated me and bad men kill their wives? Believe me, there are lots of guys who run around on their wives, probably some guys here in the police department, but that does not make them murderers."

Kocak folded his hands on the table. "No, we're not saying that, and I'm sorry if you got that impression. Let's just try to get this interview over so we won't have to bother you again. We don't have any more questions now, but we do need to type up our conversation here, have you review it and sign it. If you want to make any changes, just cross something out and put it in your words and then initial the change."

Irene felt more composed now. Her little outburst had succeeded in ending the interview and both officers seemed contrite. She knew when to quit. "Okay, type it up and I'll review it."

CHAPTER 5

John Buddish Jr.
December 28, 1963

His sister was dead. Florentina had been found dead in the bathtub and the police suspected foul play. For the last several years, John Buddish had maintained little contact with his sister. Seven and a half years older than John, Florence had lived a separate life since her marriage to Casper Bennett in 1940 at age nineteen. She had moved out of their parents' house directly into her husband's.

Florence and John were never close, but they were the only two children of John and Mary Buddish, Polish immigrants, both now dead. As a family, their holidays had always been special. They shared the Christmas Eve wafer, the *oplatek*, at the dinner table. At Easter, Florence and his mother would prepare the Święconka basket, the Easter basket filled with foods that the priest would bless during the Saturday mass. Now only he would carry these memories.

During their childhood, Florence and John grew up in a small house on Fourteenth Street in central Lorain, where most of the residents were of Eastern European descent. John Buddish Sr. worked at several jobs, including laborer, meat cutter, and candy maker. As a child, John Jr. was often left to Florence's care. Florence always insisted that he not stray too far from her and he learned to stay within her field of vision. If he did not, Florence became panic-stricken and he would pay the price—a thorough scolding and often a spanking. He could not remember exactly when he realized that Florence was different, more nervous than other people, but that understanding was firmly entrenched by the time he was a teen.

As John Jr. thought about those early years, he wondered if Florence's life would have been different if the family had not, in 1937, moved a few blocks to Long Avenue in the heart of Lorain's Polish neighborhood. Their new residence was near the Bennett family home where the twenty-one-year-old Casper was still living with his parents. It did not take long for Casper to notice the shy and pretty girl who'd moved into the neighborhood.

John Jr. was just twelve when Florence married Casper. Casper made her laugh and she talked of the fancy places he took her. John liked Casper back then. Playing the role of an older brother, Casper would joke with him, bring him candy, and occasionally take him fishing along with his sister.

Early in Florence's marriage, John would overhear his parents talk about her drinking. A friend would tell his mother that Florence had been drunk somewhere and she would relay this to his father. Once, his dad had confronted Casper about the drinking and told him to quit feeding his daughter so much liquor. He said it was destroying his Florentina and they needed to stop. Casper had laughed and told him that they had things under control. In fact, Casper claimed that Florence needed the alcohol to calm her nerves.

Convinced that she would die in childbirth, Florence refused to have children, despite the urging of her mother and Casper. As Florence's drinking got worse, John's mother realized that Florence was not fit to raise children and she dropped the subject.

John initially pitied his sister because of her unfortunate marriage. He tolerated her drinking, rationalizing that her binges were a desperate escape from an unfaithful and abusive husband. But as her reliance on alcohol grew, so did his impatience with her. John repeatedly told her that if Casper was the source of her misery, she needed to leave him. It was that simple. To that end, both he and his aunt Catherine gave her money to pay for a divorce. In 1960, Florence finally hired an attorney and started the divorce action, but then she let Casper back into her life and ended the proceedings. John was both dumbstruck and disgusted by her weakness and inability to follow through. He could not help someone who refused to help herself.

Soon after this, in 1961, he and his wife accepted Florence's invitation to visit and have Christmas dinner with them. Both Casper and Florence had been drinking before they arrived and continued to drink during their visit until they were both quite inebriated. Throughout the visit, Casper embarrassed his sister and criticized her for trivial things. John told Casper to lay off the cruel remarks and Casper stopped for a while, but then he started again. After they left, John and his wife vowed never to socialize with them again.

Then a week ago, a Sergeant Springowski had phoned to inform him about Florence. He explained that Casper allegedly found her dead in the bathtub, but the police were not sure that her death had been an accident. John agreed to talk with him, but postponed the meeting until after Christmas. He wanted his family to have some semblance of a normal holiday.

At first, he felt tremendous guilt for not doing more to help his sister. The guilt quickly turned to anger as he repeatedly asked himself the same questions. Who encouraged Florence to drink to "calm" her nerves? Who willingly supplied her with liquor? Who beat his sister down by ridiculing her at home? Who humiliated her in everyone's eyes by his open unfaithfulness? Casper Bennett was the one who turned his sweet, shy sister into an alcoholic, and he hated him for that.

John would help the police, but they were missing the most important point: Casper Bennett killed his sister years ago by destroying her self-esteem and sending her into the abyss of alcoholism. In his mind, Casper was responsible for his sister's death even if he did not murder her.

The doorbell rang and John greeted a well-dressed man in his late sixties. After introductions, John directed Sergeant Springowski to the living room, where he sat next to an unlit Christmas tree.

Springowski began hesitantly, "We are investigating your sister's death.

It could very well be an accident, a very tragic accident. But, on the other hand, we would not be doing our job if we did not rule out the possibility that she was killed in the bathtub."

John Buddish interrupted, "You mean, you're looking at whether somebody drowned Florence in the bathtub?"

"Yes, that's exactly right. We are investigating whether Florence was drowned by her husband. I've known Casper since he was a teenager, so I know all about his drinking. I also know about his girlfriend, and I know that Florence filed for a divorce a few years ago. So none of this is new to me. I'm just gathering evidence to find out if there's more. We've done an autopsy and we'll know more once we get all the results back from that."

John Buddish said nothing. He now realized that his sister's life would soon be examined in great detail and, if charges were brought, could be made public. It was one thing to have an alcoholic in the family; it was another for the entire city to become aware of it. But he quickly realized that, because he and Florence no longer shared the same last name, few would know that she was his sister.

Sergeant Springowski went on, "I don't know how much contact you've had with your sister recently, but if you know anything that would help us, that's why I'm here. Do you know if Casper ever threatened Florence?"

John Buddish cleared his throat. "Really, I have had virtually no contact with my sister for a couple of years. Yeah, I know Casper mistreated her. I've heard rumors that he hit her from time to time, but she never told me that, if that's what you mean."

"When did you last see your sister?" Springowski asked.

"We were over at their house at Christmas a few years ago. She and Casper had been drinking and he was belittling her for some of the most trivial things. I couldn't stand it. I decided I was not going to take my family over there again," Buddish explained.

Springowski turned his gaze to John Buddish. "You mentioned rumors. Who did you hear them from?"

"It's more than rumors," John said. "Florence still talks with our Aunt Catherine. I mean she used to talk to Aunt Catherine. Florence told her that she and Casper had huge arguments about his girlfriend, about how Casper spent his money. Sometimes he threatened her. That's what she told her."

"Is that Frank Mishak's wife, Casper's business partner?" Springowski asked.

"Yeah, that's the right one," John Buddish responded.

"Has Casper ever threatened to kill Florence?" Springowski asked.

"I don't know about that. Again, you need to talk to my aunt or some of Florence's lady friends in the neighborhood," John responded.

"That's what we're trying to do. I wonder if you can help me with this letter we found in a strongbox in the dining room. Actually, I was hoping that maybe you could tell me who wrote it. Maybe you know whose handwriting it is or maybe it sounds like someone you know." Springowski reached into his coat pocket, pulled out several sheets of paper, and handed them to John Buddish.

Buddish looked at the handwriting, which seemed more like a man's than a woman's, but he could not tell. The letter was undated and unsigned. Whoever wrote the letter had poor penmanship, but by concentrating, Buddish could make out the words. The letter began:

> *Mrs. B.*
>
> *How dumb can you be that you can't see through your husband? Do you know why he wants you back? Well, I'll tell you, he's not in love with you and don't want you. He don't want to give you any money or property so he's trying to keep you buttered up, so you will drop the divorce. He's going to keep you drunk until you sign off or die. He has boasted of this in numerous bars in front of lots of people on one of his drunken sprees.*

Buddish stopped reading. "Where did you get this? Is this some kind of sick joke?"

"I assure you that we found this in a box in your sister's dining room. For some reason, she saved it. It was in with another letter and a newspaper article written by Ann Landers about an unfaithful husband," Springowski told him.

Buddish began reading again:

His ex-girlfriend gave him the gate as she knew what he was doing. She was too smart to let him make a fool of her, but he didn't know that she was doing the same thing to him right along. Where do you think he was when you went to his apartment and didn't find him there? He was with her. He would take you to his place one day and her the next and sometimes he would have you both there the same day.

Buddish looked up at Springowski and said, "What am I supposed to do with this stuff? Who would write this to my sister? This is just cruel." Signaling that he had read enough, Buddish held the letter out for Springowski to grab.

Springowski's right hand slowly motioned for Buddish to stop. "If you can, please keep reading it. Maybe something in it will give you a clue to who wrote this. It is vindictive, but these claims that your brother-in-law boasted about killing your sister need to be checked out."

Buddish's hands were shaking, but he looked down at the letter again. He found where he had left off:

You are kidding yourself if you think you can hold him as he dressed her pretty sharp and bought her a new car. He also bought her a 5-carat diamond ring and intends to marry her after he gets rid of you and gets what he wants. He is so jealous of her, he checks on her every day and has people watching her for him while he works. He keeps her phone busy all the time. You must be stupid to let him drive you by her house and why do you think he's drinking like he does because he loves her and it's killing him, because he don't know what she's doing and he wants her back.

"Look, I don't have any idea who wrote this. You're the detective, not me," Buddish said, looking at the base of the Christmas tree. He almost handed the letter back, but then, he wanted to know what else this sick person had written to his now-dead sister.

He read on:

So why don't you wise up and buy some decent clothes and fix yourself up as you have too much competition. Why don't you do a little checking when he leaves the house and maybe you will see for yourself just how dumb and blind you are. Watch him when he works nights. He closes early and heads for South Broadway.

He never has a good word for you. Calls you all the names he can think of, said he made a drunk of you once and he'll do it again. So here's to you, Toots. I wish you the best of luck because you need it. Why don't you visit a few bars he goes to and listen and you will find out the truth.

A Well Wisher

Buddish held the letter in his lap and did not say anything. Springowski broke the silence. "Are you finished with it?"

"Yeah," Buddish replied.

Again there was a long silence as Springowski waited for Buddish to comment. Finally, Springowski prompted, "Anything? Know anybody that calls her toots?"

"No," Buddish replied. "You had to know this letter would really upset me. I told you straight off that I hadn't had much contact with my sister. Why show me this damn letter? What's the point?"

"I'm sorry. I really am. I thought you might know something more, that's all," Springowski said, not making eye contact with Buddish.

"Just doing your job. Right?" Buddish said.

"It's not easy," Springowski answered.

Buddish could see that Springowski had another letter in his hand.

"What's that?" Buddish asked.

Springowski seemed flustered. "I have another one that we found. I won't ask you to read it, but could you look at the handwriting to see if you recognize it?" Springowski handed another two-page letter to Buddish.

The handwriting was neater and the letters rounder than the last. Buddish read the first sentence: "I see your husband has a new business now. Babysitting with his sweetheart, Irene."

Buddish handed the letter back to Springowski.

"I don't recognize the handwriting at all," Buddish said.

"Who else knew your sister well?" Springowski asked.

"Hell, I don't know. I really don't know. Maybe the woman who did her hair. She went to school with her, Bernice Kulick," Buddish answered, trying to suppress his irritation. Then, in a more civil tone, he added, "If you haven't already, you should talk to my aunt Catherine and uncle Frank Mishak."

"They're being contacted," Springowski replied. "Anything else you can help us with?"

"No," Buddish said stonily. "I'll show you to the door."

CHAPTER 6

John Kozich
January 7, 1964

If Lon Adams was going to force him to prove probable cause at a preliminary hearing, John Kozich was going to have some fun in the process. Of course, the fun would be at Adams's expense. As an assistant city prosecutor, Kozich handled the misdemeanor criminal and traffic cases that usually traveled quickly through the Lorain municipal court system. At thirty-nine, he longed for the day when he could say good-bye to the prosecutor's office and devote himself full-time to his private practice, but he still needed the steady paycheck this part-time position provided.

The son of Hungarian parents, Kozich had graduated from Lorain High School in 1943 and immediately enlisted in the navy to help in the war effort. After the war's end, he went to college on the GI Bill and then continued to law school and returned to Lorain. Kozich was a thin, wiry man known as much for his sarcastic wit as for his chain-smoking. He was well liked by his fellow attorneys, who found him to be competent at work and good company at play.

Kozich was familiar with the case filed against Casper Bennett. On December 27, he had been part of a team that reviewed the investigation to date and then discussed whether to charge Bennett with murder. County Prosecutor Paul Mikus, Assistant County Prosecutor John Otero, Sergeant Springowski, Sergeant Kocak, Sergeant Solomon, and Dr. Kopsch participated in the meeting. All agreed that the case against Casper Bennett was based solely on circumstantial evidence. No one saw him drown his wife and they all agreed that people could accidentally fall into a tub of water, hit their head, and drown. However, some of the pieces just did not fit this scenario.

The group decided to charge Bennett with first-degree, premeditated murder. Dr. Kopsch was convinced that Bennett had drowned his wife. He harped upon the absence of any burns on the victim's lower legs, the blood on the tub, and the broken bottle. If Florence Bennett had fallen into the tub and been found sitting up with her back to the faucets, he insisted that her lower legs would have been burned like the rest of her body. Kocak pointed to the problems with Bennett's alibi. The police knew that he left home a good hour and fifteen minutes earlier than he reported. Although not admissible, the lie detector results indicated that Bennett was lying about some aspect of his wife's death.

During the meeting, County Prosecutor Mikus and Assistant County Prosecutor Otero behaved like excited predators around downed prey. Mikus, in particular, boasted that he would destroy Bennett on the stand, exposing him not only for the lying adulterer that he was, but also as a cold-blooded murderer. His assistant, Otero, nodded vigorously in agreement.

Kozich remained quiet throughout the powwow, largely because he did not expect to have any significant involvement in the case. Bennett's attorney would plead his client not guilty at the arraignment and waive the preliminary hearing, and the case would be transferred to the county court, outside of Kozich's jurisdiction.

However, at the arraignment, Adams asked for a preliminary hearing. The burden would now fall on Kozich to show that there was *probable* cause to suspect that Bennett killed his wife. Unlike an actual criminal trial in front of a jury, the preliminary hearing would be held before a judge, who would decide only if the prosecution had presented enough evidence to justify a belief that the defendant had committed the crime. Kozich knew that the state had gathered more than enough evidence to establish probable cause.

He also knew that criminal defense attorneys asked for a preliminary hearing to go on a "fishing expedition" to discover what evidence the police had gathered against their client. For Kozich, the trick would be to present enough evidence to establish probable cause but not give away all of the incriminating evidence against Bennett. Prosecutor Mikus wanted Kozich to save some of the "good stuff" for the trial, where Mikus would reveal it and watch the surprised defense scramble and stumble.

Kozich knew that Lon Adams was regarded as Lorain County's best criminal defense attorney. He wasn't sure if that honor was earned or if Adams had just inherited the title from his father. Kozich reveled in competition, whether in the courtroom or in athletics, and saw the hearing as an opportunity to deliver a message to Adams, namely that he was someone to be reckoned with.

The Lorain Municipal Court was located in an old brick building that housed the police and many other municipal departments. The building had been constructed before the turn of the century when Lorain was still a town of under ten thousand residents. The city's leading citizens did not anticipate the rise of industry along the Black River and the influx of immigrants that this would bring. On this cold January morning, the small courtroom felt cramped and insubstantial.

Kozich had subpoenaed Patrolman Metelsky, Sergeant Kocak, Sergeant Springowski, and Dr. Kopsch. His surprise witness had not been subpoenaed, in order to keep Adams in the dark. Adams, in turn, had subpoenaed Dr. Chesner, the deputy coroner who performed the autopsy.

Adams and his client, Casper Bennett, were already seated at one table when Kozich walked into the courtroom. Adams was cordial in his quiet way and engaged in some pleasantries, inquiring about Kozich's wife, Harriet, and their children. Kozich was anxious for the hearing to begin and did not feel like exchanging small talk with Adams. To Kozich's consternation, Bennett smiled while Adams talked to him. He could sense that Bennett wanted to interject himself into the conversation and be part of the friendly banter, but neither lawyer gave him an opening.

Judge John Kolena entered the courtroom and asked if the attorneys were ready. Kolena was a former assistant city prosecutor appointed to the bench when the position became vacant in midterm and then elected to it a few months later. After making the easy transition from a prosecutor to a judge, Kolena intended to spend the remainder of his career in the city's municipal court. Kolena identified with a prosecutor's position and establishing probable cause would not be difficult.

Patrolman Metelsky, the first officer to arrive on the scene, was also the state's first witness. He testified that when he arrived, the rescue squad was administering oxygen to Florence Bennett, who was draped over a bed. Her hysterical husband was insistent that he had been out of the house on errands for about an hour and, when he returned, found her unresponsive in the bathtub, her back to the spigots. Metelsky saw a broken bottle on the floor and found blood on both the tub's edge and a nearby windowsill. Touching the water, Metelsky had found it to be scalding hot. The officer could not understand how Bennett's clothing was clean and dry if moments before he had just pulled his wife from the tub. Bennett's left-hand palm was burned, as was the little finger of his right hand.

During cross-examination, Adams established that Bennett's clothes were orderly, the furniture was in place, and he had no cuts or bruises to his face. Metelsky was forced to admit that he saw no signs of a struggle in the house. As for the cleanliness of Bennett's clothes, Adams asked Metelsky if he thought someone other than Bennett placed his wife on the bed. Metelsky replied that he believed Casper Bennett did that.

Kozich debated whether he should ask Metelsky an additional question. Metelsky believed that Bennett took off his original clothes because they showed signs of a struggle. If Kozich elicited this information, he might open himself up to an Adams counterpunch. Adams could ask why, if Bennett had the presence of mind to change his clothes, he didn't also wipe the blood off the tub or sweep the broken bottle from the bathroom floor.

It's only a preliminary hearing, for Christ's sake, Kozich thought. He might as well push it a little bit. "Do you know if Casper Bennett changed his clothes before you arrived at his house?" Kozich asked.

Before Metelsky could answer, Adams objected, "This would be pure speculation on Patrolman Metelsky's part."

Judge Kolena sustained the objection and Kozich excused the witness.

"As its next witness, the state calls Charles Springowski," Kozich said. Dressed in a gray suit, Springowski walked slowly and deliberately to the witness chair. As he sat down, he looked at Judge Kolena and gave the former prosecutor a nod and just the faintest of smiles.

Kozich had Springowski tell the judge what he saw at the Bennett home and what Bennett told him about his evening's activities. Completing his testimony, Springowski brought up Bennett's girlfriend.

"He wanted to call this girl," Springowski said.

"What girl?" Kozich asked.

"Well, he didn't tell me the girl's name, but I know the girl," Springowski replied.

Adams objected and the judge sustained the objection.

Kozich was not finished. "How did you know the girl's name?"

"He's been going out with her for a long time and he told me that he had already talked to her twice that day, but he was supposed to call her a third time," Springowski said, continuing to speak over Adams's objection. "We didn't let him call her. I'll tell you that."

When it was Adams's turn to cross-examine Springowski, Adams stood up and studied his yellow pad for a few moments before beginning.

"Okay, let's see. My client says he went to Don's Sohio. Did you check that out and find out if that was true?" Adams asked.

"Yes, we did and he had," Springowski replied.

Springowski could easily have volunteered that Bennett was not there around eight p.m., as Bennett claimed, but arrived at the gas station around six thirty p.m. according to four other witnesses. Kozich had coached Springowski not to reveal this. At trial, the trap would be sprung and Bennett would look like a liar. After that, the jury would be hard-pressed to believe anything he said.

"What about Kingsley's Cigar Store? Did you check out whether Casper Bennett was there?" Adams went on.

"We haven't verified that yet," Springowski replied.

"You have no evidence that this is untrue, do you?" Adams continued.

"We have no evidence that this is false. Correct," Springowski dutifully replied.

"What about this Joe guy that my client says he saw just before he drove home? Did you talk to him?" Adams asked.

"Yes, we talked to Joe Wasilewski, and yes, Wasilewski did see Casper Bennett driving around Fifteenth and Reid Avenue sometime between nine and nine thirty that evening," Springowski responded.

"So every place my client says he went that night checks out?" Adams concluded.

"Yes, that's right," Springowski said.

It was almost noon when Kozich finished with Sergeant Kocak, whose testimony closely mirrored Springowski's. Rather than break for lunch, Kozich asked the court to allow him to proceed with Dr. Kopsch, who had already spent most of the morning waiting in the hall. Judge Kolena agreed to keep going.

Other than this case, Kozich had never had dealings with the coroner. When Kozich had asked Dr. Kopsch if they could meet in person to prepare for this hearing, the coroner said that he was far too busy. However, Dr. Kopsch suggested that they talk then for a few minutes on the phone. During the call, Kozich found Dr. Kopsch to be brusque and condescending, but Kozich attributed this to the coroner's busy schedule.

Kozich began his examination by reviewing the doctor's medical training and then asked a preliminary question to direct the coroner to the case at hand.

"Bringing your attention to December 20, 1963, did you have the occasion to go to 1733 Long Avenue in Lorain, Ohio?" Kozich began.

"Yes, sir. I did," Dr. Kopsch answered.

"And what did you find when you arrived there?"

"A house," Dr. Kopsch answered, smiling at Judge Kolena. Kozich's face reddened and he struggled not to show his anger with the coroner's inane response. Ignoring Dr. Kopsch's attempt to be clever, Kozich asked, "And who was at the house?"

The assistant prosecutor kept the direct examination short and crisp, revealing as little of the medical evidence as possible. Dr. Kopsch told the judge that he examined Florence Bennett's body at the house around ten p.m. and found second- and third-degree burns on 80 percent of it. He explained that second-degree burns caused blistering, while third-degree burns extended through the full thickness of the skin. The coroner did not find any burns to her lower legs from just above her knees down to her feet and concluded that this part of her body had not been submerged under the scalding bathwater. Dr. Kopsch also found lacerations or scrapes along both ankle bones that he correlated with a streak of dried blood on the bathtub's edge. His deputy coroner, Dr. Chesner, performed an autopsy the following day and concluded that Florence Bennett had drowned. Kozich did not inquire further.

Adams began his cross-examination by showing that Dr. Kopsch was not a pathologist, a surgeon, or even a general practitioner. He was an anesthesiologist. This would set the stage for a later argument that Dr. Kopsch's opinions were beyond his area of expertise. Although Dr. Kopsch was competent to put people to sleep and wake them up, he was over his head when dealing with forensic evidence. Adams pointed out that Dr. Chesner (who performed the autopsy) concluded that the victim's death was due to "probable drowning," which was not the same as Dr. Kopsch's categorical statement that Florence Bennett drowned.

Holding the autopsy report in his right hand, Adams asked Dr. Kopsch about statements in the report that Dr. Kopsch found two bottles of sleeping pills at the Bennett house when he was searching it with the police. Kopsch confirmed that he found bottles of Sleep-eze and Sominex, both with just a few pills left in them. Before Adams could ask any additional questions, Dr. Kopsch pulled the bottles from his briefcase and placed them on the witness railing in front of him.

Adams wanted to show that these pills, when taken in conjunction with alcohol, would make a person unsteady and prone to falls.

"Calling your attention to the Sleep-eze bottle, what is the effect of these tablets when taken?" Adams asked.

"They are supposed to get one sleeping," the coroner responded.

"Do you know if they do?" Adams continued.

"I never took them," Dr. Kopsch answered. Kozich did not appreciate Dr. Kopsch's glibness and he began to feel uneasy about his witness.

"Well, if taken in excessive quantities, do they make a person dopey or dull or stagger or anything like that?" Adams asked.

Kozich expected his witness to concede that the pills could inhibit a person's motor coordination, but Dr. Kopsch surprised him again.

The coroner answered, "Let's see what it says on the label. They don't mention it."

Kozich looked away from his witness and rolled his eyes.

After further questioning by Adams, Dr. Kopsch finally conceded that both of these sleep aids "presumably get folks sleepy." The coroner grudgingly admitted that these pills, if taken in excess, could make a person "dopey and cause them to lose their coordination." The coroner also revealed that the toxicology results showed that Florence Bennett had both salicylamide and methapyrilene in her system, two components found in Sominex. Dr. Kopsch stated that the toxicology results showed that Florence Bennett probably took two or three tablets within four hours of her death.

Despite suggestions from Adams that Mrs. Bennett died from other causes, Dr. Kopsch maintained that Florence Bennett drowned. The autopsy and the toxicology report supported him. As for the time of death, Dr. Kopsch claimed that Mrs. Bennett died anywhere between eight and nine thirty p.m. The coroner denied that the scalding water in any way affected this determination. Because the victim's lower legs were never in the hot water, Dr. Kopsch was able to determine the body temperature from them.

As Kozich listened to this testimony, he wondered if a trained pathologist would have done additional testing to determine Florence Bennett's body temperature and the time of death. Kozich was equally unimpressed when the coroner volunteered that the time of death was "hard to figure for sure."

Adams returned to the toxicology results and focused upon Florence Bennett's blood alcohol level of .19. Dr. Kopsch had to admit that, under Ohio law, a person with a reading in excess of .15 was deemed legally intoxicated and unable to safely operate a car. Adams obviously wanted Dr.

Kopsch to concede that it was at least possible that Florence Bennett lost her balance, hit her head on something, and drowned.

Kozich knew that most doctors will agree that almost anything is possible, but they will then indicate that a doctor has to base an opinion on probabilities (something that is more likely than not) and that the scenario presented by the questioning attorney, although remotely possible, was not probable. Dr. Kopsch, on the other hand, was unwilling to consider any possibility other than homicide. He defended his position by claiming that any person whose body comes into contact with scalding water will react instinctively to get out, regardless of the effects of a depressant such as alcohol. He admitted that an unconscious person would be unable to save himself, but found no evidence that Mrs. Bennett was unconscious since she had no visible head trauma.

Adams plunged along. "Both you and Dr. Chesner found burns on Mrs. Bennett's head that were so severe that parts of her scalp detached along with her hair. Is that correct?"

"Yes, we did," the coroner replied.

"Wouldn't damage that severe hide or destroy signs of head trauma?" Adams asked.

Dr. Kopsch seemed undaunted. "No, not in my opinion."

Kozich expected the coroner to go on and explain his opinion, but he did not. Perhaps he did not have an explanation.

He could see that Adams wanted to keep exploring the possibility of an accidental death and he feared that at some point, Dr. Kopsch would slip and give Adams some ammunition to support the defense's theory.

"So you just don't think that Mrs. Bennett would have been able to stay in the scalding water long enough to drown?" Adams asked.

"She would not. This was not an inert body. You have a living, breathing woman who comes to her death by drowning in extremely hot water."

"That's right," Adams said, urging the coroner to continue.

"You have no evidence of unconsciousness. You do have evidence of a struggle. No, I don't think she got this by falling into the tub," Dr. Kopsch opined.

Kozich sensed that Adams was getting close to something important. "What evidence of a struggle is there, doctor?"

Dr. Kopsch was ready to spar with Adams. "The blood on the window-sill. There is a broken bottle on the floor. This is a very neat house and well kept, and the only broken glass in that place is the broken bottle on the bathroom floor," Dr. Kopsch said.

Kozich could see that Dr. Kopsch had no medical evidence consistent with a struggle. Neither Casper Bennett nor Florence Bennett showed any signs of serious trauma—no broken bones, no deep lacerations, and no indications of choking. As for the broken glass, Mrs. Bennett could have been holding the little bottle when she fell into the tub.

Adams seemed to be winding down. "Isn't it true then, doctor, that the only reason you say it is homicide is because you don't believe that anybody could fall into hot water long enough to be drowned without trying to get out, unless somebody held them in there?"

Kozich rose to object. Adams was boxing his witness into a corner and the prosecution needed Dr. Kopsch to maintain flexibility. He could sense that his overconfident witness was about to blunder, and he stepped in.

"With the court's indulgence, Dr. Kopsch's opinion is based on a number of facts that lead him to conclude that Mrs. Bennett's death was not an accident or a suicide. Mr. Adams is asking him whether his opinion is based on one fact. The doctor has already told us that there are a series of things that have led to his opinion. That is the basis of my objection."

Kozich's "objection" had no legal basis. Adams's question was proper, but, by objecting, Kozich warned his witness to be careful and coached him on the proper reply. Judge Kolena saw that Adams's question seemed to correctly summarize the basis of Dr. Kopsch's opinion. "Overruled. He may answer if he can," the judge said.

However, Kozich's objection was sufficient to alert Dr. Kopsch. "I call it homicide because it is the only way I can put all the pieces together, sir," the coroner replied.

Kozich could hear the frustration in Adams's voice as he asked, "Will you answer my question?"

Dr. Kopsch remained on track. "The answer to your question is no, sir."

Adams tried a few more questions, but when Dr. Kopsch remained evasive, Adams announced that he was through interrogating the witness. Kozich breathed a sigh of relief.

The assistant prosecutor turned to Judge Kolena and said, "As our next witness, the state of Ohio calls Lon Adams." Kozich had been waiting all morning for this moment. Smiling, Kozich stared at Adams, whose cool reserve vanished. Lorain County's leading criminal defense attorney looked completely bewildered.

As if Adams's confusion had been transmitted to Judge Kolena, the judge asked, "Do you mean as a witness?"

"Yes," Kozich replied.

"Well, because Mr. Adams is an officer of the court, I do not believe that he needs to be sworn. Do you agree, Mr. Kozich?" Judge Kolena asked.

"That's fine with me," Kozich answered as Adams slowly lowered himself into the witness chair.

Kozich wasted no time with preliminaries. "Mr. Adams, you at one time represented Mrs. Florence Bennett in a divorce action against your current client, Casper Bennett. Isn't that correct?"

"I object to this line of questioning," Adams shot back. "This information is privileged."

Judge Kolena was equally quick to respond. "The fact that you represented Mrs. Bennett does not involve any privilege. Your representation is a public record. Objection overruled."

Squirming in the witness seat, Adams replied, "Yes, I did represent her." Kozich and Adams locked eyes and each knew where this line of questioning was headed. From Adams's distracted look, Kozich could sense that he was searching for some way to escape.

"You filed the first petition for divorce in 1960, didn't you?" Kozich continued.

"I don't know exactly when. It was a couple of years ago," Adams muttered.

"In your first petition, you alleged that Mr. Bennett displayed aggressive behavior toward Mrs. Bennett?"

"I object, Your Honor. This is improper," Adams said, biting his lower lip and scowling at Kozich.

"It is a public record," Kozich countered.

"Overruled, you can answer," the judge stated.

"If I had known I was going to be questioned on this, I would have reviewed my file before I came. I don't recall," Adams said.

"Didn't the petition also contain statements to the effect that Mr. Bennett threatened her?" Kozich pushed.

"I don't recall," Adams said, looking away from Kozich and exhaling deeply.

"Well, didn't you use words to the effect that he abused her and caused her bodily harm?"

"I don't recall. I have probably filed a couple hundred divorces in my career. We routinely allege extreme cruelty or gross neglect of duty. It's what we have to do in order to demonstrate that our client is entitled to a divorce," Adams explained.

"You mention extreme cruelty and gross neglect of duty. Don't those terms necessarily include either mental or physical punishment of some sort?" Kozich asked.

"You know the answer to that," Adams shot back.

"That divorce petition was dismissed?" Kozich continued.

"Yes, it was."

"You filed a second divorce petition a few years later. Correct?"

"Yes."

"Why did you do that?"

"Probably because Mrs. Bennett came into my office and told me to do that," Adams replied.

"You don't just file a divorce petition because someone asks you to. You have to have had some conversation with her about why she wanted a divorce again."

"Yes. I am sure that we did."

"You filed another divorce petition?"

"Yes."

"The final allegation in this petition was that Mrs. Bennett stated that Casper Bennett had, on several occasions, threatened to take her life?" Kozich asked. Adams's face had blotchy red spots and his forehead was wet from perspiration. Kozich waited for Adams's response, but Adams delayed. "Yes or no. Did the petition make that allegation?"

"I don't recall that," Adams said quietly, but his eyes betrayed a rage that was building within him.

"In the petition, you notarized her signature?" Kozich asked.

"I don't know if I did. Sometimes my office girl notarizes these things," Adams said indignantly.

"I have reviewed the petition and I represent to you that you, Lon B. Adams, notarized it," Kozich said, digging in.

"I will take your word for it."

"You would have believed her to be telling the truth, would you not?"

"Objection," Adams yelled.

"Sustained."

"Did you believe that Mrs. Bennett was telling the truth when she came in to see you?"

"Objection."

"Sustained."

Kozich would not stop. "Doesn't every lawyer have the right to believe that his client is telling the truth?"

"Objection."

"Sustained."

"Let me ask you this question. Would you have notarized this if you had known it to be false?"

Adams was caught. "Of course," he answered, "I wouldn't notarize a false statement if I knew it to be false."

Kozich looked at Judge Kolena. "No further questions, Your Honor. The prosecution rests."

Adams then addressed the court. He explained that his client had always proclaimed his innocence. Adams said that Casper Bennett had been charged with first-degree murder, a charge that required evidence that his client intentionally killed his wife and that the act was deliberate and premeditated. Adams went on to say that the prosecution had not produced one shred of evidence that linked his client to Mrs. Bennett's death by drowning. Everything was based on inferences and guesses, and this did not establish probable cause.

Kozich thought Adams's reasons to request a dismissal were extremely weak. He spoke in generalities and failed to discuss specific evidence. Kozich had expected more of a fight from a defense attorney with such a lofty reputation.

Kozich began, "At this very moment all over this country, there are prisons loaded with persons who have protested their innocence to crimes and do so even after they are behind prison walls. Protestation of innocence does not mean a great deal."

The assistant prosecutor went on to explain that many defendants are convicted on circumstantial evidence similar to the evidence that existed in this case. "Casper Bennett's rendition of the facts is contradicted by the findings of Dr. Kopsch, particularly the location of the burns. This is a preliminary hearing. This is not a trial on the merits and we do not have to prove our case beyond a reasonable doubt. We do not have to put our entire case before you. We only need to indicate that we believe that a crime has been committed and that we have probable cause to believe that Mr. Bennett is the guilty party."

Judge Kolena wasted no time. "The motion to dismiss the charges is denied."

Kozich had begun packing up his papers when Adams said, "I am not through. I have subpoenaed Dr. Chesner and I intend to question him."

The assistant prosecutor rolled his eyes and said, "Whatever you want, Lon, but you know we have established probable cause regardless of what Dr. Chesner says." Kozich knew that Adams hoped that he would get some useful admissions from Dr. Chesner, who perhaps would be more objective than the feisty coroner.

Dr. Chesner had been the pathologist at Lorain's St. Joseph Hospital for the past twenty-five years. As he walked to the stand in his rumpled navy suit, Dr. Chesner did not hide his annoyance at spending the morning waiting in the hall.

Adams quickly elicited Dr. Chesner's medical education and his work experience. Dr. Chesner testified that he dictated the autopsy report and a secretary transcribed it. The report was mainly correct, but he had not proofread it nor made any corrections to it yet.

"Do you recall the location of the burns on Mrs. Bennett's body?" Adams asked.

"Well, the only thing that I can remember is that I approximated that three-quarters of the body was burned and that there were no burns at all below her knees," Dr. Chesner responded.

"Isn't it true that there were some small burns below the knee?" Adams probed.

"There were no burns at all, sir," Dr. Chesner answered.

"Well, wait a minute, doctor, your report says that the lower legs and the bottom of the feet show very little involvement. Wouldn't that imply that there *was some* involvement, some burns to the lower legs?" Adams asked.

Dr. Chesner did not hesitate. "This sentence is vague and it should have been corrected. What I meant was this: the involvement was not with the burns but with a few bruises and abrasions. That was the only involvement of the lower legs."

Kozich smiled at Dr. Chesner. The assistant prosecutor decided it was time to close Adams down and conclude this hearing. Because Adams had called this witness, Dr. Chesner was technically Adams's witness and Adams could only ask him general, wide-open questions, known as direct questions. Adams was asking leading questions, questions that suggested the answer to the witness. Although these questions were proper on cross-examination of an opposing witness, they were not proper with one's own witness.

"Doctor, were there any burns on the right side of her forehead and her right lower face?" Adams asked.

Kozich objected. "Your Honor, before we proceed much further, I would like to remind the court that this is Mr. Adams's witness and these are leading questions. Mr. Adams is reading this report back to his own witness. These are leading questions and this is not a proper examination."

The court sustained this objection and others, blunting Adams's ability to gather additional information from Dr. Chesner. Eventually, Adams gave up questioning him and the hearing concluded.

Throughout the hearing, Kozich had ignored Casper Bennett, but now, with the hearing concluded, Kozich looked over at him. Bennett, who had seemed almost jovial when Kozich first walked into the courtroom, looked dejected. Adams was talking to his client and Kozich could hear bits and pieces of the conversation. He overheard Adams say, "This is about what I expected." He missed the next few comments but then heard Adams tell his client, "Don't worry. Judge Kolena was going to find probable cause no matter what." Adams suddenly looked over at Kozich. "So you had some fun today, John?"

Kozich tried not to look too pleased. "Oh, you know, Lon, I was just doing my job."

"Next time, just don't enjoy yourself so much at my expense."

CHAPTER 7

John Bolcis Otero
February 7, 1964

Taking a break from his work, John Bolcis Otero sat at his desk in the Lorain County prosecutor's office and thought about his life's journey. At times, the forty-two-year-old assistant prosecutor could not believe that he had returned home to Lorain after being separated from his parents as a boy and then serving long stints in the National Guard and army. John was the oldest son of immigrants from Slovakia, John and Sophie Bolcis. After World War I, the family moved from Pennsylvania to Lorain, where his father traded work in the coal mines for employment in the steel mill.

While in Lorain, John's father befriended a Spaniard by the name of Manuel Otero who owned a restaurant near the mill. This friendship would have a profound impact on John's life and shape him in ways that he could not have imagined. As a ten-year-old boy, young John ran errands for Otero. Otero immediately took a liking to the intelligent boy, who worked hard and did whatever was asked of him. When Otero's Lorain restaurant began to falter a few years later, Otero decided to move to Detroit but wanted to take young John with him. Otero explained to John's parents that he had no children of his own and had grown fond of their hardworking son. If given the chance, he would like to raise him and make sure he received a good education.

John's father was struggling to support his wife and their three other children. After some soul searching, John's parents agreed to entrust their son to Otero. John and his new guardian left Lorain for Detroit, where Otero registered John for public school under a new name, John Bolcis Otero. John missed his family but gradually reconciled himself to the separation and developed a resilience that would serve him throughout his life. The pair later moved to New York City, where John continued his schooling. He became fluent in Spanish while he lived and worked with Otero.

After graduating from high school in 1931, John enlisted in the National Guard. Finding that he liked the order and discipline of military life, he reenlisted in 1934. While in the National Guard, John found time to take college courses at NYU, City College, and Columbia. After a brief stint with an investment banking firm, he returned to the military in 1940 and served another nine years in active service. During World War II, he rose to the rank of major and was eventually stationed in Puerto Rico where the bilingual Otero helped to train thousands of Puerto Rican troops. It was there that he met and married Esther Vazquez, the daughter of a judge. After his discharge from active duty in 1949, he obtained a law degree and returned to Lorain in 1951.

In Lorain, Otero reunited with his birth family and took advantage of a unique opportunity. After World War II, Puerto Ricans migrated to Lorain in great numbers to work in its steel mill. Desperate for able-bodied male workers to meet the increased steel demand, the mill recruited Puerto Rican men to work its blast furnaces. Already U.S. citizens, the Puerto Ricans were hard workers. Otero's fluency in Spanish and his Hispanic last name gave him a virtual monopoly on providing legal services to this group. In addition to his law practice, Otero remained active in the Ohio National Guard, where he was now a colonel.

Several years after he returned to Lorain, Otero joined the county prosecutor's staff as an assistant prosecutor. Hardened by his separation from his family and years in military service, Otero soon gained a reputation as a tough, no-nonsense prosecutor. After three years, he rose to the position of chief criminal assistant prosecutor, and lately, Otero had his eye on the top job. Due to its growth, Lorain County would soon add a third common pleas judge. Prosecutor Mikus told him that he planned to run for that new judgeship, which would leave an opening for Otero in the prosecutor's office. If Otero could make a name for himself, he would likely be Mikus's successor.

Otero was doing just that. Last week, he and Mikus had secured a conviction in a high-profile murder case involving John Woodards. The jury concluded that the twenty-six-year-old Woodards had brutally raped and murdered an elderly woman, and they sentenced him to die in the electric chair. Along with the sheriff's department, Otero gathered and organized much of the incriminating evidence that led to the conviction. In trial, Mikus was the chief litigator, questioning key witnesses and delivering the closing argument. However, Otero questioned several of the witnesses and effectively argued many of the important legal issues that arose. He hoped Mikus would give him more responsibilities in the Bennett case, but he also realized that Mikus's ego and desire for the limelight might relegate him to a supporting role.

Mikus assigned him to the Casper Bennett case from the outset. Otero met with the Lorain police the day after the incident and insisted on being present when the police questioned Bennett again on December 22, two days after the incident. Otero had great respect for his fellow national guardsman Dr. Paul Kopsch, and if Dr. Kopsch concluded that Bennett had held his wife's head under the water, Otero readily accepted that verdict.

At the interrogation, Otero immediately disliked the fast-talking Bennett and thought he was anything but truthful. During the questioning, Otero accused Bennett of being a liar several times. If the interrogators were using the "good cop, bad cop" technique, Otero saw himself as the bad cop. Otero and others pressed Bennett to confess, confronting him with his failed lie detector results. Despite this pressure, Bennett maintained his innocence.

Evidence about the Bennett case was now being presented to a grand jury. Yesterday, Otero had called his first witnesses, and more would testify over the next few days. Although the municipal judge had already ruled that the state had probable cause to charge Bennett with first-degree murder, a grand jury also had to issue an indictment against a person who was to be charged with a felony. Although Otero enjoyed all the stages of a criminal case, he particularly relished presenting a case to a grand jury, because he was in control of the hearing. In private and without a judge, a prosecutor presented evidence to nine jurors, who decided whether to issue an indictment against an accused. Unlike a public trial, neither the accused person nor his attorney was usually involved.

Otero liked that he was ordinarily the only person who questioned witnesses during the grand jury session. The rules permitted a grand juror to ask questions of a witness, but Otero believed that if the prosecutor was thorough and organized, jurors never needed to ask questions.

He also had great latitude during the grand jury proceeding. Because the rules of evidence were not strictly followed, even hearsay evidence (testimony given by one witness about what another person said) was permitted. Otero was usually able to present much of a case to the grand jury through the testimony of police officers, who could also tell the jurors what other witnesses told them during their investigation. After all of the evidence was presented, Otero usually advised the grand jury on whether he believed that the prosecutor had enough evidence to secure a conviction.

For Otero, the moment of truth arrived when the grand jury voted on whether to issue a bill of indictment. Seven of the nine jurors had to vote to indict for the case to proceed. If three or more grand jurors did not find probable cause, the accused could no longer be charged with that crime. This finding was known as a "no bill," and Otero could count on one hand the rare occasions when a grand jury had no-billed someone he believed should have been indicted. In each of these cases, the accused person had appeared before the grand jury and testified.

Otero knew that people subject to a criminal investigation usually invoked their Fifth Amendment right to remain silent and refuse to testify before the grand jury when subpoenaed. An accused's testimony to a grand jury was given under oath and transcribed by a court reporter. If, at trial, a defendant strayed from his grand jury testimony in any way, the prosecutor pointed out the changes and "impeached" the defendant. For that reason, defendants almost never testified before the grand jury.

Five days ago, Mikus had told a newspaper reporter that the grand jury would hear testimony about the Bennett case in a few days. After this news was published in the Elyria paper, Lon Adams called Otero and made the unusual request that Bennett be allowed to "tell his story" to the grand jury. Otero and Mikus needed to talk about this, and they would do so today before Otero convened the grand jury for the second day. Otero busied himself and reviewed the Bennett file for about fifteen minutes before Mikus walked into his office and quickly took a seat across from his chief assistant.

"So this asshole wants to tell his story to the grand jury," Mikus began.

"Yes, he does. Adams called me a couple of days ago and made the appeal," Otero replied.

"I see Adams also told several reporters that he'd made that request," Mikus added.

"Yeah, I read that in the *Chronicle* yesterday," Otero answered.

"We both know this guy's guilty as hell. Why should we give Bennett the chance to bullshit his way out of this?" Mikus asked, pounding his right fist into the palm of his left hand.

"In my opinion, he won't convince the grand jury of anything. Look, I know there's an outside chance that the jurors could believe him and not indict, but I really can't see that happening. I listened to him tell the police what he was doing that evening. He goes into lots of detail, so it all sounds plausible, but he doesn't fool anybody," Otero replied.

"Still, we run a risk if we let him go in there. Are the grand jurors going to think that only an innocent man would show up without an attorney and talk to them? Let's face it, this guy can tell a good story. He's glib and he's got an answer for everything. I don't like it." Mikus paused for a moment. "What kind of people do we have on that grand jury?" Before Otero could answer, the politician in Mikus bubbled to the surface. "Christ, I run a risk if I deny his request. The newspapers will eat me alive if I don't allow him to tell his side."

"Paul, leave it to me. I've got a good rapport with these grand jurors. They've already heard from Springowski, Kopsch, Kocak, and Solomon. They know about Bennett's girlfriend. They're not going to believe Bennett. I'm not going to let this grand jury no-bill Bennett. It's just not going to happen," Otero said, exuding the confidence of a career military man.

Mikus studied his chief assistant. "Okay. Okay. You've got this under control, don't you?"

Otero replied, "Yes I do. I've been doing a lot of thinking about Bennett and what questions I'll ask him."

"Like what?"

"I'll tell you what I'm *not* going to allow him to do. He's not going to go in there and just tell the jurors what happened that night and leave. When he goes in there, I am going to tie down his story, piece by piece. He's going to hang himself. I'll get him to confirm that when he saw his wife in the bathtub, her lower legs were submerged in the water. That's impossible according to Kopsch. I'll tie him down about the time he left the house. He'll say he was at the gas station at eight and I'll bring in the gas station people later to show that he was there an hour and a half earlier," Otero said, speaking rapidly and loudly.

"Oh, that's good," Mikus replied.

"That's not all," Otero said. "That grand jury is going to know everything about his relationship with Irene Miller—the gifts, the trips. I'll ask him questions about his affair and he will have to answer. It's not like he can pick and choose what he wants to talk about. I control that."

"Yeah. Also ask him about the restraining order that Miller filed against him. Shows he has violent tendencies," Mikus interjected.

"Don't worry. That's on my list. When I'm done with him, our chances for a conviction will be much improved," Otero answered.

Mikus leaned back in his chair and put his arms behind his head. His eyes danced as he said, "Lon Adams is nuts to let Bennett testify. Who's going to call Adams, you or me?"

"I want to give him the good news personally," Otero said.

"I'd like to phone him myself," Mikus said. "But, you know, it's probably better that you call him back. Adams talked to you before, so you can say that we talked and we want to give Bennett his chance."

"I'll call him right now. You want to listen?" Otero asked.

"Yeah, I do."

Otero reached Adams and got to the point quickly.

"So, Lon, we've talked this over, Paul and me, and we want to be fair to your client. He can testify before the grand jury. We could squeeze him in tomorrow morning if that would work," Otero offered.

"Of course that'll work. Bennett's just sitting in the county jail. I'll make arrangements with the sheriff to get him there whenever you want him," Adams replied.

"Let's say at ten tomorrow morning," Otero said.

"Good, that'll be fine. You know, Casper just wants to tell his story. He doesn't know any more about how his wife died than you guys. He just wants to put an end to this travesty. When he does, I expect the prosecutor to do the right thing," Adams said.

Otero's back muscles tightened and he took a deep breath before answering. "You know I can't make any promises. I think Paul Mikus has an open mind on this case." Otero looked over at Mikus, who was grinning.

"That's what I wanted to hear," Adams replied.

"No promises," Otero said just before the two hung up.

Otero scribbled a few notes on his yellow pad before looking up at Mikus. "Are you going to do the 'right thing,' Paul?" Otero asked Mikus.

"Yeah, no plea bargains, no deals. This guy's guilty, and for what he did to his wife, he deserves to die in the chair. That sounds like the right thing to me," Mikus replied coolly.

✱✱✱✱

The next morning, Otero questioned Bennett before the grand jury. When he returned to his office two hours later, he was elated. Bennett had testified in great detail about the events of December 20, 1963. Bennett insisted that he had left his house around seven forty-five that evening. When he returned sometime around nine twenty, he found Florence unresponsive in the bathtub, her back to the faucets and her lower legs submerged in the scalding water. Bennett also answered dozens of questions about his relationship with Irene Miller. Otero then questioned him about his debts, the life insurance policies, and his stormy relationship with his wife. After Bennett left the room, the grand jurors looked at one another in disbelief. They were ready to indict.

Otero picked up his phone to call Mikus, but before he dialed, he hung up and walked out of his office to find his boss. As he entered the prosecutor's office, Otero said, "I got him. He testified to stuff that we can show is all wrong. There's no way Bennett can wiggle out of this one."

CHAPTER 8

Ray Miraldi
February 28, 1964

Ray Miraldi opened the door to his waiting room and brushed the snow off his overcoat. Janice Cunningham, his secretary, sat at her desk at one end of the room, typing. She looked up when he entered. "While you were out, a Chester Bennett called."

"Oh, he did?" Miraldi said as he hung up his coat.

"Do you know him?"

"He's Casper Bennett's younger brother."

"He wanted an appointment this afternoon, so I set it up for four p.m. Is that okay?"

Miraldi looked over to a framed plaque on the waiting room wall. Abraham Lincoln stared back at him, along with these words: "An attorney's time is his stock in trade."

"If that's not okay, I can call him back."

Miraldi shrugged. "Did he give a reason for the appointment?"

"He said that he just wanted a few minutes with you. He said it was personal. He said he had a few questions. That's all."

"It's all right. I'm sure he just wants to pick my brain about the way Lon Adams is handling his brother's case. He'll find out real fast that I don't second-guess other attorneys," Miraldi replied. "I'll talk to him and get this over with."

Miraldi had represented Casper Bennett several times before, twice when Casper was sued for divorce, once for a liquor law violation, and just last year in a collection matter. He would talk to Chester. He owed a former client that courtesy.

Miraldi was a Lorain native, the son of Italian immigrants, who, at age forty-four, was just beginning to gain some attention as a skilled trial attorney. Miraldi had been encouraged to attend Oberlin College by his grandfather's first cousin Ben Nicola, the first Italian-American judge in Cleveland. After graduating from Lorain High School in 1937, Miraldi was working as a meat cutter at Jacoby's Grocery when Nicola offered to pay his first semester's tuition at nearby Oberlin. With that help, Miraldi enrolled in the fall and then earned enough through campus and summer jobs to pay for the rest.

After graduation, he was working at Lorain's National Tube plant when the Japanese bombed Pearl Harbor. He immediately enlisted in the navy and began its officer training program in February 1942. During the war, he captained a minesweeper in the Atlantic campaign, and then later took the same boat into the Pacific when US forces mobilized to end the war with Japan. Miraldi always credited his wartime experiences for building his self-confidence. After the war, the GI Bill paid for his law school education at the Western Reserve School of Law in Cleveland, Ohio.

After working for a Cleveland law firm for one year, he returned to Lorain in 1949 and, within several months, became an assistant city prosecutor. The next year he was appointed city prosecutor. He found himself in the courtroom constantly, and jurors seemed to like him. There was something about his courtroom manner that appealed to them; he was courteous yet tenacious. His face was expressive and he used it to communicate to the jury. During a trial, he seldom raised his voice, whether he was cross-examining a hostile witness or summarizing the evidence for the jury.

In 1959, he left the comfort of the prosecutor's office to devote himself to his private practice full-time. He avoided criminal defense work because he had no desire to represent the same habitual criminals that he had prosecuted for the last ten years. However, he would make an exception for the "average joe" who had never been in trouble before.

Instead, he focused on civil matters: real estate, probate, divorce, business transactions, and personal injury cases. In 1961, he turned heads when a Lorain County jury awarded his client $500,000 for injuries sustained in a car crash. At the time, it was the largest verdict in the county's history and one of the largest in the state. Unfortunately, the defendant was insured for only $10,000, and because he was without assets, the rest of the award was never paid. Miraldi received almost no fee from the case. The verdict, however, did give him publicity, and he was hopeful that it would lead to future cases.

By early 1964, his caseload had steadily increased, but he was hardly at full capacity. After his large verdict, he had hoped to develop a strong core of personal injury and business clients, but he did not have enough of them yet to sustain his practice.

* * * *

An hour later, Chester Bennett sat in a green leather wing chair across from Miraldi. Chester introduced himself as Casper's brother, as if the two had never met. *Does he think I've forgotten?* Miraldi wondered.

Miraldi's mind traveled back thirty years to the Hawthorne Junior High School playground. Chester and his buddies were taunting a slow learner named Pepper Johnson who occasionally played baseball with Miraldi's friends. Miraldi rushed over and told Chester and his buddies to knock it off. "If you want to pick on somebody, pick on me." Chester's gang walked away and, according to Pepper, never bothered him again. Although he saw Chester about town from time to time, the two always ignored one another.

Chester's discomfort made Miraldi think that he remembered that encounter too. Despite Miraldi's reservations about Chester, he liked his colorful and entertaining older brother Casper.

"Nice office you got here," Chester began. He looked around the room as if admiring the spartan furnishings.

"Thanks. It's not much, but it's all I need right now," Miraldi said. He knew why Chester was there and decided to give him an opening to speed things along. "So, how's Casper holding up?" he asked.

"Well, that's kind of why I came. He'd come here himself but he's still in jail because the bail is so high," Chester said. "He's not doing so well. He's really worried, you know."

He should be, Miraldi wanted to say, but didn't. He was still peeved that Casper had called his home right after his arrest and never called back. He wasn't even sure that he would have wanted Casper's case, but Casper should have called him again. At the very least, he should have asked his advice about who to hire to defend him.

"We're just not getting answers from Adams," Chester continued. "Casper asks him about developments and Adams just blows him off. He tells him he's working on the case, but we don't know what the hell he's doing."

"When's the trial?" Miraldi asked.

"It's about three weeks away," Chester answered.

"Don't worry, you're in good hands. I'm sure Adams is working hard on Casper's case. He's quite experienced and he'll get the job done." Miraldi was never one to steal somebody's client. Someone dissatisfied with his current attorney would eventually become trouble for the new one.

"Yeah, we think Adams is a good attorney and all. It's just that this Woodards case has got us spooked," Chester said.

The Woodards murder trial had concluded about a month earlier. Even Miraldi wondered how Adams could have defended someone as despicable as John Woodards.

"Mikus and Otero won that case. They beat Mr. Adams pretty bad. We're afraid the same thing could happen to Casper," Chester said.

You should have thought of that back in December, Miraldi thought, but again kept quiet. There was no way that he would replace Adams just a few weeks before trial. That would be lunacy. Miraldi began, "I know you're worried, but Woodards is a different case altogether. The defendant practically admitted to the crime. Nobody was going to believe Woodards's story that he killed the woman accidentally. Don't blame Adams for that result."

"It's just that Adams has spent the last few months working on the Woodards case. No way could he be working on Casper's case. How can he be prepared for Casper's case in just a few weeks?"

"Adams has a partner. I'm sure his partner has been preparing for it," Miraldi suggested.

"I don't think so. If he had, I think Adams would have told us. We just don't want Adams to be outnumbered again. It ain't fair to have two lawyers against one," Chester said.

"Sometimes a jury feels sorry for the one attorney. It makes you the underdog, and juries love underdogs," Miraldi said. He'd had a long day and he just wanted to get home. "It'll all work out."

"I'm not sure you get what I'm saying. Casper could die if we don't get him some more help. My brother could die for something he sure as hell didn't do," Chester pleaded.

"So tell me exactly why you're here," Miraldi said. "You can't get a new attorney to replace Adams at this late date. You might as well guarantee a conviction if you do that."

"We don't want to replace Adams. We want you to defend Casper along with Adams. That's what I meant when I said that the prosecution has us outnumbered."

"What am I supposed to do? Close my office and just work on Casper's case for the next three weeks? You know that's what you're asking me to do."

"Look it, Mr. Miraldi—"

"It's Ray," Miraldi interrupted.

"Okay, Ray. Casper says he trusts you. He knows you and he's convinced you can save him. He's got great respect for you. He's not so sure Adams can do it all alone."

So he's going to appeal to my vanity, Miraldi thought before he spoke. "I appreciate the kind words, but at this late—"

Chester interrupted him. "Don't turn us down. Casper didn't do this. Yeah, he ran around on Florence. They fought all the time, but he didn't kill her. I know my brother. He wouldn't hurt anybody. They think just because she died in the bathtub, somebody had to kill her. That's bullshit. The police made up their minds that Casper killed her on the night it happened. Mikus and Otero just want another conviction. They don't give a damn about justice."

Miraldi looked up at the ceiling as he weighed what to do. Frankly, he could not picture Casper drowning his wife in the bathtub. He knew the guy. Twice Casper had come to him to fight the divorce Florence filed. If he wanted Florence out of his life, he could have easily agreed to the divorce. It wasn't as if Florence refused to give him a divorce and he decided to kill her. And then there were the Lorain police. As a former Lorain prosecutor, he knew how shoddy some of their investigations could be.

Chester interrupted his thoughts. "Casper says he wished he'd hired you in the first place. You were always prepared whenever he gave you a case. And I've talked to lots of people. They all say that you're really good with a jury."

Sometimes you have to take risks, Miraldi thought. *This guy needs my help. He's not a bad guy and he may get railroaded if I don't step in. Hell, it's not as if my waiting room is overflowing with clients. I could probably shut my office for a few weeks and just work on his case. The newspaper publicity wouldn't hurt me either.*

Miraldi cleared his throat before he spoke. "Okay. I understand. I'll talk to Lon Adams tomorrow. If he wants me to help him, I will. If he wants to fly solo, I'm not going to force my way into this. Do you understand?"

"Yes, I do. Thanks, Ray," Chester said.

As Chester left, Miraldi squeezed his eyes shut as if to block out what he had just done. A wave of anxiety passed through him and then just as quickly left him. He chuckled to himself. *Well, maybe appealing to my vanity wasn't such a bad tactic.*

CHAPTER 9

Ray Miraldi
March 2, 1964

Miraldi sat in the Lorain County jail's interview room with Casper Bennett and Lon Adams. He had brought a court reporter with him in order to take a detailed statement from Bennett.

Miraldi and Adams had talked the day before. Miraldi liked Adams and he thought Adams reciprocated. He immediately sensed that Adams seemed shaken by the Woodards verdict. They agreed that the key to the Bennett case was proving that Dr. Kopsch was wrong—that his opinions were based on hunches and shoddy medicine. Miraldi learned that Adams had not retained a medical expert to dispute Kopsch's opinions. Although Miraldi kept his thoughts to himself, he was shocked by that news, particularly since the trial was just three weeks away.

The other challenge would be to defuse a jury's bias against Bennett. The men agreed that Prosecutor Mikus would viciously attack Bennett's character. In a case based on circumstantial evidence, the prosecutor would paint Bennett as disreputable, someone the jury could see killing his wife. For many jurors, Bennett's open infidelity would be enough to demonstrate his moral depravity. Most Lorain County jurors attended church regularly and expected marriage vows to be honored. Divorce was still a rarity. What the prosecutor lacked in direct evidence, he would try to overcome by focusing on Bennett's adultery, his alcoholism, and his occupation as a barkeep.

As their meeting concluded, Miraldi sensed Adams's relief that another attorney would shoulder some of the responsibilities. They both understood the consequences if their advocacy fell short. Knowing that Adams welcomed his assistance, Miraldi entered the case.

Dressed in his jail jumpsuit, Bennett looked tired as he entered the room, but when he shook Miraldi's hand, his grip was strong.

"You know I tried to call you the night it happened, but when I called your house, I got some kid and I just hung up," Bennett began.

"You should have called me again," Miraldi replied.

Miraldi explained that he wanted a detailed statement covering Bennett's activities on December 20, his interaction with the police and their investigation, and some background information about his wife, Florence.

During the next forty minutes, Bennett went into great detail about the events of December 20, 1963, surprising Miraldi with his recall. Bennett talked about what he had eaten, his conversations with Florence, his domestic chores, and minute details about his house and what it looked like when he left.

Bennett described his last conversation with his wife.

"So she wanted to go to the toilet, and I walked with her to the toilet because she was a little unsteady on her feet, because once in a while her feet have a little numbness in them, maybe poor circulation, I don't know. Dr. Pastuchiw was treating her for this. So, she went to the toilet and I walked her back, seeing that she wouldn't fall or anything like that."

Bennett paused and watched the court reporter's hand finish the last few strokes on his machine. "So I got her the drink, and she said, 'Would you please give me two Nytols?' Well, we both had taken Nytols before and I don't know if she took any during the day or anything like that. So I told her I would give her two Nytols under one condition, that she lay down in bed, and I would go uptown, and she should not get up until I got back, and I would fix her something to eat, and that would be it."

He continued, "So she agreed. I got her the drink and gave her two Nytols and put the bottle of Nytols and whatever pills were in the cabinet into my spare room cabinet, so she wouldn't get to them."

"Did she say anything to you before you left?" Miraldi asked.

"I told her that I was going uptown to get a few papers, also to get my coat that was being repaired at Richman Brothers since I lost a number of pounds, maybe thirty, since I was in the hospital a few months before that. I got a call that it was ready to be picked up. She agreed not to leave the room after I left. So she kissed me twice and said, 'Please do not stay out too long.' She also said, 'Are you angry at me because I'm drinking?' And I said, 'No.' She also said, 'I'll fix your jacket.' We were shopping the week before and she bought iron-on mending tape. And she also said that she would wash our clothes on Monday because my underclothes were piling up. I told her I would be home as early as possible."

Miraldi found Bennett's narrative believable. Other than his wife's drinking, Bennett described a rather mundane conversation between a husband and wife.

Bennett then said that he left the dishes unwashed and departed from the house around 7:40.

When Miraldi and Adams had talked about the case yesterday, Adams did not think Bennett had described enough events to explain his absence from the house until he returned sometime around 9:15 that night. However, as Bennett talked in great detail about his trip downtown, Miraldi began to see how the errands could have taken an hour and a half.

Bennett described his stop at Don's Sohio sometime around 7:55. From there, Bennett drove down Broadway, intending to stop at Richman Brothers. However, due to the crowds, Bennett could not find a parking spot near the clothing store.

"The traffic was heavy, and the parking spaces were pretty filled up as I went down Broadway trying to spot a place to park. I kept going all the way to the Loop, back of Heilman's, down Reid Avenue, back down Broadway, looking for a parking place. I think I went around about four or five times, and, thinking I would get no parking place, I went for a little ride down West Erie. I drove a couple of miles to the Hoop Restaurant, where I turned around and headed back. Then I realized that since it's on my way to town, I might as well stop at Irene Miller's house. And I always carry a shovel and broom in the car in wintertime, so I stopped the car and got the broom. I don't know if I had the shovel or not, but I cleaned off the walks, which took me about ten or fifteen minutes. From there, I headed back to Richman Brothers. Still there were no parking places around there, so I went two or three times around in a circle. And then I usually get a final *Cleveland Press* and a *Chronicle* just about every day."

Bennett talked about stopping at Kingsley's Cigar Store and then seeing Joe Wasilewski as he neared his home. Just as Adams had done several months before, Miraldi studied Bennett's face and body language, searching for signs of deception. Describing the scene in the bathroom, Bennett's eyes filled with tears. He remembered seeing Florence in the tub with her back to the faucets, the opposite of how she would normally place herself. Her face was slumped in the water, which was almost to the overflow holes.

"So I struggled to get her out, and finally with a hard drag under the arms, I yanked her out of the water. There was no response from her. She didn't say nothing to me or anything. She slipped away from me on the floor, and it seemed to me that I wiped my hands on my pants or maybe a nearby towel around there. I don't know for sure. I was quite panicky, so I grabbed her under the arms and dragged her to the bedroom, talking out loud so she would answer me. I put her head on the bed first on the pillow or near the pillow, and then I grabbed her by the legs and swerved her over, so she would be lying down. I remembered a little bit about artificial respiration and I tried that for a while. I kept hollering to her, 'Speak to me.' I got no response."

He continued, "I got all hysterical and ran downstairs, put the lights on, and called the telephone operator, because I didn't know the fire department rescue squad number. I called 112 and the operator answered, and I says to her, 'Operator, please send the rescue squad at once to 1733 Long Avenue. I just pulled my wife out of the bathtub.'"

Adams looked at Miraldi and Miraldi nodded to him, confirming what both men were thinking. Bennett still seemed genuinely distraught about discovering his wife's drowned and scalded body. If not, he was one hell of an actor.

"A few minutes later the rescue squad arrived. I believe I went with them, or maybe I was upstairs before that, and I was very panicky and shouting. And I asked the firemen if she was all right. I didn't get no replies and I saw some policemen, detectives—I think they chased me out of the bedroom, sent me downstairs to the front room for a few minutes. I don't know for sure, but I wanted to call someone up and tell them what happened. I don't know who I wanted to call, if I wanted to call back to the club, my brother, or who. I don't recall. I was very hysterical."

Bennett took a deep breath before he continued. "So the firemen and policemen tried to quiet me down, and my hand was all burned from hot, boiling water. I somehow went back upstairs again, and the last thing I remember is that they put me on a stretcher and put me in the rescue squad or ambulance or whatever it was and took me to the hospital."

Miraldi posed additional questions to Bennett and was surprised by some of Bennett's responses. Bennett could not remember what his wife was wearing when he discovered her. He also thought that her body was pale and white, when, in fact, it was red and blistery. Knowing that his answers were probably not accurate, Bennett reiterated that he was hysterical and said this explained his memory lapses.

Bennett did not remember giving a statement on the night of his wife's drowning, but he did remember giving a signed statement two days later. One of the men in the room, the assistant county prosecutor, John Otero, kept yelling at him and telling him that he was a liar. Charlie Springowski brought in a typed question-and-answer statement. Bennett reviewed it and thought the information was accurate and signed it. He recalled going to the sheriff's office in Elyria to take the lie detector test.

"Some of the questions were absurd, such as do I drink coffee or something like that, and picking certain kinds of numbers, and did I put my wife in the bathtub, did I return in the meantime since I left the house, and other questions." Bennett seemed genuinely perplexed by the questions that had been posed to him.

"Did they tell you the results of the lie detector test?" Miraldi asked.

"Yeah, they said I flunked it," Bennett replied.

"What did you say to that?" Miraldi asked.

"I told them that I didn't do it. The test was wrong. They looked at each other kind of funny. You know, one of those guys doing the test was Henry Zieba, somebody I've known from the neighborhood since I was a kid. And then they took me back to the jail in Lorain," Bennett stated matter-of-factly. Miraldi was not impressed with the lie detector results. Even when the suspect passed the test, the testers sometimes told the suspect that he failed in order to prompt a confession.

Miraldi questioned Bennett for a few more minutes and then left with Adams and the court reporter.

"Let's talk for a few minutes in private," Miraldi said. "How about in my car?"

The two attorneys got into Miraldi's car.

"You know, Lon, I believe the guy," Miraldi said.

Adams looked at Miraldi. "Yes, he does talk a good game, doesn't he? Of course, he's had a long time to think about things while he's been in jail."

"I thought about that too, but I think I can tell when a guy's lying and when he's telling the truth, and I think Bennett is telling the truth," Miraldi said.

"Well, let's hope so," Adams replied.

Miraldi continued, "I know all the policemen that worked on this investigation. I worked with them for a decade when I was their prosecutor. They don't always get it right and I know that better than anyone. Springowski and Solomon are good guys, but I wouldn't trust their work on a difficult case. They do fine when there's been a confession or someone implicates an accomplice, but they are over their heads in this one."

"So what do you think we have to do next?" Adams asked.

"I've already made some inquiries about pathologists. My feeling is that we need to get someone who is extremely qualified to review this. Tomorrow, I'm going to call Dr. Moritz from Western Reserve's medical school, who is probably one of the top guys in that area. I'm hoping that if I talk to him personally, he'll agree to evaluate this case. The doctor would just need to review the autopsy and the transcript of Kopsch's testimony from the preliminary hearing. Then, if he thinks he can help us, we have to hope that he can clear his schedule to be available for the trial," Miraldi said. "We need an expert. That much I know. Whether we can get one at this late date, I don't know."

"I know," Adams said. "I think Judge Pincura might give us a few more weeks if we ask for a continuance."

"As long as he sees that we aren't asking for a lot of time, I think he would," Miraldi agreed.

The two lawyers then discussed the division of labor on the case. Miraldi would contact some of the witnesses, while Adams would talk to the others. Miraldi was to prepare a brief to exclude the results of the lie detector tests in the unlikely event that the prosecutor would try to sneak that evidence into the case.

"Good meeting," Adams said as he shook hands with Miraldi and exited the car.

CHAPTER 10

Judge John D. Pincura
March 9, 1964

Judge John D. Pincura sat behind his office desk, facing the four men who would soon try the case of *State of Ohio v. Casimir Bernatowicz.* Three of those attorneys had just completed the capital murder case involving John Woodards. Pincura knew all four and what to expect. Without question, Paul Mikus would dictate the atmosphere of the trial. When Mikus tried a case, it resembled something between a barroom brawl and a three-ring circus. Mikus was cagey and aggressive and came at opposing witnesses like a bulldog. During his dozen years on the bench, Pincura had watched many attorneys fold under Mikus's relentless attacks.

Pincura saw his role to be that of a referee, and only that. He would not help either side regardless of his perception of the case's merits. The attorneys had to do their jobs, and that meant objecting quickly to inadmissible testimony and improper arguments.

Pincura knew Lon Adams well but knew his father better. The elder Adams and Pincura used to borrow each other's chewing tobacco. Pincura still kept a spittoon in the courtroom and used it, a throwback to the days when the courtroom could literally become a spitting match. Pincura liked Lon Adams and thought he was competent. Although Adams was controlled in the courtroom, he could also drop his pen or yellow pad on the floor when an opposing attorney was making an important point. He felt Adams was quick on his feet and knew how to find a hole in the prosecution's case and capitalize on it. If Adams had a shortcoming, it was that he relied too much on his mental agility at trial and would take shortcuts in preparation.

The judge had presided over a number of criminal trials with John Otero. Otero, like Mikus, was blunt and did not back down from a fight. Usually affable, Otero could on occasion become emotional and vent his anger at opposing counsel. Pincura had also watched Otero deliver several fiery and moving closing arguments. If the Woodards case was a preview, Otero would question the less important witnesses, while Mikus would prosecute the more critical parts of the case.

Miraldi was the only attorney who had not participated in the Woodards case, but Pincura knew him well. Miraldi had been on his staff when Pincura served as Lorain's law director and worked under him a short time before Pincura was appointed to the bench. He'd seen Miraldi's work ethic, courtroom ability, and consistently good results.

Pincura had also presided in some of Miraldi's civil trials, including several large personal injury verdicts. Recently, Pincura had felt that one of Miraldi's closing arguments was too persuasive, causing the jury to award more money than Pincura thought was reasonable. Pincura ordered a remittitur, which meant that Miraldi could either accept the judge's reduced damage award or try the case again to a different jury.

After Pincura ordered the remittitur, Miraldi stormed out of Pincura's courtroom and still seemed angry a week later when he again appeared before Pincura in another matter. Pincura reminded Miraldi of the judge's forty-eight-hour rule. Judge Pincura told attorneys that they could be mad at him for forty-eight hours, curse him under their breath, and complain to other attorneys about the judge's "unfair" decision. However, after forty-eight hours, the judge expected attorneys to move on and understand that judicial decisions were not personal affronts. The judge and attorneys were colleagues and officers of the court, and they needed to act like it. Although unhappy with the remittitur, Miraldi accepted the judge's reduced damage award rather than incur the expense and uncertainty of another trial.

In 1964, Pincura had been on the bench for fourteen years and was just a year shy of sixty. He was born in Pennsylvania, but his parents had moved to Lorain when he was a toddler. His father was a grocer when Lorain had over a hundred tiny neighborhood groceries. Pincura's parents were from Galicia, an area in Eastern Europe located between Poland, Hungary, and the Ukraine, and they spoke Polish.

Pincura was the oldest of eight children. He excelled at Lorain High School in both academics and athletics. After high school, he went to college and played quarterback for Penn State and then obtained a law degree. By 1940 he was the Lorain city solicitor and also maintained a private practice with Lorain attorney Austin O'Toole.

Pincura was appointed to the bench in 1950 and quickly became adept at his job. He gained the respect of the bar with his command of the law and his ability to keep control of his courtroom. Pincura loved being a judge and he relished presiding over difficult, interesting cases. He was confident and smart and had no doubt that Casper Bennett would receive a fair trial in his courtroom.

Adams had filed a motion for a continuance. In his brief supporting the motion, Adams asked for additional time, citing Miraldi's recent involvement and the need to fully prepare for this capital murder defense. Adams asked for a delay of fourteen days and Pincura was inclined to grant it.

Pincura sat upright in his chair with his gray hair slicked straight back. He knew that he needed to keep a distance from the local attorneys now that he was a judge. As a result, he rarely exhibited his wry sense of humor or engaged in small talk with them. He usually looked stern, and today he appeared out of sorts as he started to address the four attorneys before him.

"I have before me the defense motion to continue this case from March 16, 1964 to March 30, 1964. I have read the brief in support and understand that the defense will not be making another request for a continuance. Is that correct, Mr. Adams?"

"Yes, that is, Your Honor," Adams replied.

"What does the prosecution say?" Pincura asked.

"Your Honor, we are ready to proceed on the date originally set for this trial. This case was set for trial two months ago. The defense has had abundant time to prepare. The prosecution sees no good reason for granting a continuance," Mikus responded.

"I understand the prosecution's position, Mr. Mikus," Pincura answered. "I also know that Mr. Adams has been quite occupied in the defense of a capital murder trial that concluded at the end of January. Since then, he has filed an appeal in that case. I know that the prosecution was also involved in that case; however, this court is well aware that the prosecutor's office has a larger staff than either Mr. Adams or Mr. Miraldi. Furthermore, Mr. Miraldi just recently entered this case. I find the defendant's request for a short continuance reasonable under the circumstances and I will grant it."

"Note my exception," Mikus grumbled.

"Mr. Adams and Mr. Miraldi, I have granted your continuance today, but I want to advise you that I will not grant any additional extensions of time. Do you understand that?"

Both Adams and Miraldi nodded their heads and said, "Yes, Your Honor," almost in unison.

"Very well, counselors," Judge Pincura concluded. "I will see you all back in three weeks ready to try this case."

CHAPTER 11

Paul Mikus
March 26, 1964

Prosecutor Paul Mikus was exultant. This mercurial man, known for his ever-changing moods, had just received some exciting news. On the end of the line was Sergeant Springowski.

"Tell me again what you found in the Bennett house," Mikus bellowed into the receiver.

Two days before, Springowski, Kocak, two sheriff's deputies, Casper Bennett, Miraldi, and Adams had met at the Bennett home. The defense attorneys had requested a view of the house in preparation for the trial that was to begin in less than a week. Springowski and Kocak kept their eyes on the defense team throughout the inspection. Both Adams and Miraldi spent most of their time in the bathroom, familiarizing themselves with the layout and, in particular, the bathtub. As they were leaving, Springowski saw Adams in the living room, opening various drawers in the cabinet of the combination stereo and television set. Adams seemed to be looking for something. Bennett was talking to Adams while Adams opened the drawers. To Springowski, it appeared that Adams and Bennett did not find what they were seeking.

"Well, you know, Kocak and me thought there was something funny going on about the television console when Bennett and his attorneys were checking out the house," Springowski said. "So Solomon and me went back to the house today and we decided that we would check out the drawers on that TV console. There was one that was locked or jammed, so we decided to pry it open. Paul, there was all kinds of papers in this compartment. Like I said, I think we found Mrs. Bennett's diary for the last six months."

"That's fantastic," Mikus replied. He had a yellow pad of paper in front of him and was scribbling notes as Springowski talked.

"It's a spiral calendar where somebody wrote stuff down. It starts in July of 1963 and ends on December 15, 1963. If this is Mrs. Bennett's handwriting, and frankly, I don't think it can be anyone else's, she is writing down the times Casper's coming home at night. She even writes down what she thinks he's been up to. It's like she's making a record so she can use it in a divorce."

"Well, we need to tie down that it's her handwriting. We already have her signature on some of those life insurance papers and mortgage documents. We can get a handwriting expert to tell us if it's the same person. Get somebody on that right away," Mikus said. "Anything else I can use?"

"There are a bunch of astrology books and pamphlets in there, too. I guess them things didn't do her much good in the end. There's also a piece of paper where someone stapled airline and taxicab receipts, phone numbers for hotels and motels. There are two letters from Lon Adams to Casper Bennett dated from 1961 where Adams is warning Bennett to stay away from Irene Miller," Springowski continued.

"Well, well, well. Go on," Mikus said.

"There are two promissory notes where it looks like Casper borrowed money from his wife, a letter from Prudential Insurance responding to Mrs. Bennett's letter about a policy, and a divorce petition dated May 18, 1962. Oh yeah, there's a book called *Solid Gold Dream Book* and it says on the cover something about a thousand and one dreams interpreted and lucky numbers discussed. There's also a paper from a land title company about property that Casper Bennett owns in Florida."

"Tell me more about the diary," Mikus demanded.

"Like I said, whoever wrote this was keeping track of Casper Bennett's comings and goings. She was recording when he was coming home and the excuses he was giving her as to why he was coming in late. I don't think she was buying any of it," Springowski replied.

"You know, Adams was giving me this bullshit that Casper and his wife were getting along like turtledoves just before she died. They were going to start a new life together in Florida just as soon as he could sell his interest in the bar. This is great. Good work, Springer," Mikus said, using Springowski's nickname. "Call me if you turn up anything else in those papers."

"Will do, Paul. Solomon and I are making an inventory right now and will get it over to you later today."

Paul Mikus leaned back in his leather chair and smiled. At age fifty-three, Mikus was of medium height, fifteen to twenty pounds overweight, and slightly paunchy. Hard drinking was taking a toll on him, and his face had grown round, his skin red. Despite this, he always looked like a man ready for a fight or to pounce upon someone's careless words. As a young man, he had been handsome, with dark blond hair, a strong chin, and deep-set eyes. At Lorain High School, he excelled at basketball and debate and was a member of the school's German Club.

His parents came to the United States at the turn of the century from Slovakia, then a state in the Austro-Hungarian Empire. His father worked long hours at Lorain's steel mill while Mikus was growing up in central Lorain. Mikus was the oldest of his siblings and, as is common with first-borns, was driven to excel in sports, academics, and anything else he tackled.

After high school, Mikus worked a short time in the steel mill before going on to college and then getting a law degree. For the past sixteen years, he'd been Lorain County's prosecutor, speaking loudly and carrying a big stick.

Mikus always took his prosecutorial responsibilities seriously and was determined to rid Lorain County of its "scum," as he put it. With his commanding voice, he could take control of a courtroom. He personally tried all of the county's high-profile cases and was looking forward to the upcoming trial of Casper Bennett.

Two months before, Mikus had made sure that John Woodards was on his way to the electric chair. He smiled as he thought back to his rollicking closing argument, when he called Woodards whatever popped into his head. At one point he described him as "a gangrenous leg on a diabetic body." Later he called the defendant "an inflamed, useless appendix that threatened the body." The medical analogies had just rushed into his head, almost like divine inspiration. He told the jury that Woodards had caused a "cruel, unnecessary death and wanted their mercy. Yet, he showed none." Mikus closed by urging the jury to remove Woodards from society like they would a "parasite." The jury wasted no time in finding Woodards guilty of first-degree murder with a recommendation of no leniency. Judge Pincura did his job and sentenced Woodards to death.

The county prosecutor wondered how Lon Adams could defend someone as disgusting as Woodards. Mrs. Van Arsdale, an eighty-five-year-old woman, had rented an upstairs room to Woodards for several months. He eventually moved out, but returned on the night of the murder because he saw a light on at her house around one a.m., or so he claimed. Woodards also told authorities that he consumed seventeen beers that day. He and Mrs. Van Arsdale talked that evening. Woodards maintained that the two engaged in consensual sex on the kitchen table, as he claimed they had done several times before when he used to live there. Unfortunately, the kitchen table collapsed and he fell on top of her, his elbows crashing into her ribs. He panicked and rolled her up in a blanket, tied the blanket with her nightgown and underwear, and left her in the utility room, unsure if she was dead.

The next day two sheriff's deputies came to Woodards's house. He had just returned from a shopping trip with his wife. When questioned about Mrs. Van Arsdale's death, Woodards told his incredible tale. The coroner's autopsy showed that Mrs. Van Arsdale had been brutally beaten, suffering a ruptured spleen, tears in her perineum and vaginal wall, fractured ribs, and bruised arms and legs.

Mikus felt that it was his mission to make sure that scumbags like John Woodards and Casper Bennett never walked free in Lorain County or anywhere else.

The prosecutor thought it was about time that he got some good news on the Bennett case. The blood samples taken from the rim of the tub had been sent to Cleveland to be analyzed. The sample was too small to show that it was Mrs. Bennett's blood. In fact, the report was only able to demonstrate that the sample was human blood.

Two weeks before, while Mikus was talking to Adams about another case, Adams had disclosed that Bennett was wrong about the time he left his house on December 20. Mikus tried to act unconcerned but asked Adams what time he believed Bennett had left his home that evening. Adams told him that Bennett would now probably testify that he left around six thirty p.m. Mikus did not think that his face betrayed any disappointment, but he immediately knew that he had lost something very important. In any case built on circumstantial evidence, it was crucial to destroy the defendant's credibility and, consequently, his alibi. Mikus would have crushed Bennett and his defense team if Bennett had testified about a seven forty-five p.m. departure in front of the jury.

Mikus at first believed that someone within the Lorain police had leaked Bennett's inaccurate departure time to Bennett's lawyers. Miraldi was close to many of the police officers because he'd worked with them during his stint as their city prosecutor. Mikus also knew that Miraldi and Frank Pawlak, Lorain's police chief, were extremely good friends. They'd played baseball together as kids, and as adults they socialized on the weekends with their spouses, and even traveled together each year to take in the Major League Baseball All-Star Game.

Mikus decided to take the no-nonsense approach and phoned Police Chief Pawlak directly. He did not accuse Pawlak of the leak but told him that he thought the chief had a mole in his department. Pawlak seemed genuinely upset by the revelation and promised to look into it. Although he did not believe it to be true, Pawlak said some officers believed Springowski was lax in his investigation, cutting Bennett some slack because of their prior relationship. Pawlak would find out if anyone was feeding information to Bennett's defense team.

A few days later Pawlak called Mikus back. Pawlak had sent Detective Roy Briggs to talk to the witnesses from the gas station. Briggs learned that

Adams had talked to Ed Warner, the gas station attendant who waited on Bennett that night. From that conversation, Adams gleaned that Bennett visited the station much earlier, sometime around six thirty. Pawlak assured Mikus that no leaks were coming from the Lorain Police Department.

Mikus could not wait to surprise Adams and Miraldi with the diary. If the defense was going to claim that the Bennetts' marriage was all sweetness before Florence's death, he had irrefutable evidence to the contrary. Mikus liked to win, but when the opportunity arose, he preferred to crush his opponent.

Florence Bennett circa 1940

Casper Bennett circa 1955

Rear of Bennett Home; Rental Property Leased to Mary Mitchell on Far Left

Bennett Bathroom Showing Bathtub on Night of December 20, 1963

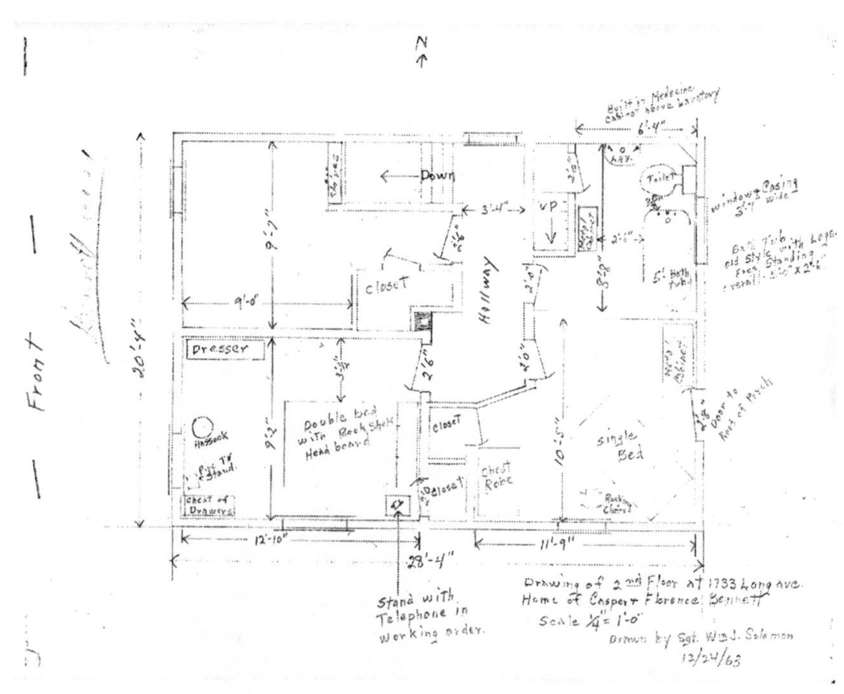

Diagram of Second Floor of Bennett Home Sketched by Sergeant Solomon on December 24, 1963

27 Dec 1963

CATHERINE M. MISCHAK (wf)(50)   58362
1822 Garden Ave.
Florence's mothers sister

Florence told her that Casper that threatened her life and told her also that he is going to 'get rid of me'. She was in fear of her life. One time had $500.00 hidden which he found and wouldn't give to her. Florence had $2,000.00 which she kept as she didn8t know when she would need it. Had it kept in a sweeper but then changed the hiding place as Casper was serching for it. SCARED OF WATER.

Bet y Jean Buddish (wf)(24) 88362
1609 Ohio Ave.   sister in law
at Florences house over Chiistmas holidays in 1961, heard personallw how Casper picked on Florence, berrated her and seemed so vicious on minor things

Sergeant Springowski's Notes Regarding Interviews with Catherine Mischak and Betty Jean Buddish

This writer remembered seeing a program on Television Station WEWS Channel 5 on Sunday 15 December 1963 starting at 8:30 PM. Name of the program is Arrest & Trial, the presentation on this date was titled "Some Weeks Are All Mondays". The program started out with a noted woman playwright being charged with the murder of her architect husband. It was narrated but not shown where the victim had been struck on the head with a walking stick while the victim was in the bath tub and the hot water was then turned on in the tub. This was done so that the hot water would retard Rigor Mortis and make the time of death either hard to place or impossible to place. This was mentioned to Dr.Kopsch the Coroner and he stated that hot water speeds up the action of Rigor Mortis and makes it hard to place the time of death.

Portion of Sergeant Solomon's Report of December 27, 1963

Thursday Ma4 26th 1964 at 1:30 PM Sgt. Solomon & Sgt Springowski drove over to the Bennett's home at 1733 Longe Ave to check the contents of a combination T.V. & Record Player in the living room

The following items found in the lower right hand compartment of the set.

1 Websters New School & Office Dictionary with various notes and clippings
1 Astrology (Your Daily Horoscope) paper back book
1 Pieeeof paper with numerious calling cards of Air lines, motels, hotels, taxi cab, tickets and stubs, receipts
1 letter from the Prudential Insurance dated Aug. 3,1962. Mrs Bennett inquiring re to policy # 11 873 473
2 Letters from Atty Adams to Casper Bennett one dated Mar 22, 1961 and one dated Sept. 19, 1961. Miss Irene Miller requesting thet he Casper Bennett stop bothering her and to leave her completely alone.
2 Notes alleged written by Florence showing where be borrowed money from her.
2 Customers receipts glued to a piece of paper showing I. Miller purchase
2 Your 1963 Horoscope booklets (Scorpio & Pisces) opened to pages 34 & 35
1 Booklet Scorpio 1963 forcast, by Constella
1 Miss Chans Astrological Chart
1 Receipt from the First Federal & Saving & Loan Association # BR 26524 made out to Chester Bennatowicz, Frieldly Tavern, 182 Lear Rd Avon Lake, Ohio State of Ohio Dept. of Liquor Control $1,000.00* $ 1,000.00
2 Cognovit Notes Casper Bennett 1 for $2000.00 1 for $1000.00
1 Divorce Pition # D3063, Florence Bennett plaintiff Vs. Casper Bennett dated May 18th 1962 also Summons in action for divorce # D-3063
1 Lucky Day Chart & Success Numbers indicator
1 Solid Gold Dream Book (1001 dreams interpreted, fortunate numbers)
1 Envelope with writting on the back
1 Spiral note book with various entries starting July 4th & ending Dec. 15th
1 Letter from Lee County Land & Tital Co. Lehigh Acres, Florida to Casper Bennett requesting information regarding his property in Lehigh Acres dated Mar. 1st 1961
1 Letter from U.S.District Court re to Dan Joseph Bennett 1112 5th St Lorain regarding pitition on bankrupt May 8th 1963
Numerious household receipts paid

Inventory of Items Found in Secret Compartment of Bennett Combination Television/Record Player Including Florence Bennett's Diary

Mrs. B. How dumb can you be that you
can't see through your husband? Do you know
why he wants you back? Well I'll tell you, he's
not in love with you and don't want you.
He don't want to give you any money or property
so he's trying to keep you buttered up, so
you will drop the divorce. He is going to
try to keep you drunk until you sign off
or die. He has boasted of this in numerous
bars in front of lots of people on one of his
drunken sprees. His ex girl friend gave him
the gate as she knew what he was doing.
She was too smart to let him make a fool
of her, but he didn't know that she was
doing the same thing right along. Where
do you think he was when you went to
his apartment and didn't find him there?
He was with her. He would take you to
his place one day and her the next and
sometimes he would have you both there
the same day. You are kidding yourself if
you think you can hold him as he
dressed her pretty sharp and bought her
a new car. He also bought her a 5 carat
diamond ring and intends to marry her.
after he gets rid of you and gets what
he wants. He is so jealous of her, he
checks on her every day and has

Page One of Anonymous Letter #1 Saved by Florence Bennett

people watching her for him while he works
He keeps her phone busy all the time.
you must be stupid to let him drive
you by her house and why do you
think he's drinking like he does because
he loves her and it's killing him, because
he don't know what she's doing and
he wants her back. So why don't you
wise up and buy some decent clothes
and fix yourself up as you have
too much competition. Why don't you do
a little checking when he leaves the
house and maybe you will see for
yourself just how dumb and blind
you are. Watch him when he works nights
He closes early and heads for south
Broadway. He never has a good word for you
Calls you all the names he can think of
said he made a bumle of you once and
he'll do it again. So here's to you I hope
Toots
you the best of luck because you
need it. why don't you visit a few bars
he goes to and listen and you will
find out the truth.

A well wisher

Page Two of Anonymous Letter #1 Saved by Florence Bennett

Mrs. Bennett,
I see your husband has a new business now. Baby sitting with his sweetheart, Irene.
Two weeks ago, when your husband was working days, he spent 3 nights over to Richard's house on Post Road baby sitting with Irene, while Richard's wife was sick in bed. And one night, he was there for supper. Neighbors say he has been a frequent visitor there since last summer — especially on Sundays.
Ask him to explain this!!
He will only tell you a bunch of lies, like he has been doing for the past 9 months.
One Sunday he took you to Airport Tavern for dinner. Why? because he wanted to see who Irene was with. He is only making a fool out of you.
Everybody in town knows this but you. Ask yourself this question: Would your husband be baby sitting with Irene if he wasn't carrying on a love affair with her? That's proof enough. Wake up, before it's too late.

A friend

Anonymous Letter #2 Saved By Florence Bennett

Bennett leaving police cruiser near Lorain City Hall before his preliminary hearing.

Casper Bennett Arriving for Preliminary Hearing on January 7, 1964

Sunday Afternoon
382 MIDDLE-AVE
ELYRIA-OHIO

HELLO BOB & Dorothy:

How are you nice folks today. Fine and in good shape I hope. I wish I was around there myself maybe we could have a bottle of nice cold Root Beer or so. I feel kinda blue and lonesome and then that's when you miss nice people like you two. I had contact with my brother Chester and he told me that you two were in contact with him. Thanks for talking to him. How is the gossiping lady south of your house doing since this unfortunate incident. I suppose it's all Bla' Bla' Bla' as usual. I believe I told you in the last letter that when I came home sometime after 9 P.M. that I found Florence in the tub with water running and her face down slumped in it. I tried to get her out four or five times and finally I yanked her out and she slipped on the floor and then I grabbed her under the arms and dragged her to bed.

Page One of Casper Bennett's Letter to Friends While Awaiting Trial in Jail

II

Then I tried breathing into her mouth. I received no answer from her. I rubbed around her heart and opened one of her eyes which were glassy so I got scared out and went downstairs in a hurry put the lights on and called the telephone operator 112 and told her to call the rescue squad cause I just pulled my wife out of the water. They came in about 5 minutes and you know the rest. I am not Guilty. As God is my judge Bob & Dorothy I had nothing to do with the death of my wife Florence - and I know that you believe me. I miss both of you. Hope we can get together soon. Maybe you can drop me a short letter. Only 2 pages allowed. All mail is read by the depart. Coming in and going out.

Thank You Very Much
Your Friend Always - Casper

Page Two of Casper Bennett's Letter to Friends Written While Awaiting Trial in Jail

PART 2: THE TRIAL

CHAPTER 12

March 30, 1964

It was a cold and overcast Monday morning, like so many spring days in northern Ohio. Despite the chill and the early hour, people were already arriving at the Lorain County courthouse in Elyria. The eighty-year-old sandstone building sat alone at the southern end of Ely Square, towering above the churches and bank buildings that surrounded it.

Oliver Johnson, the courthouse custodian, spotted Judge Pincura as he exited his car and headed toward the courthouse's side entrance. Johnson was a short, wiry African-American in his late forties who had worked at the courthouse for more than twenty years. Seeing the judge, Johnson opened the door for him.

"You already got a barn full of people up there, Judge," Johnson said. "They started coming here around seven thirty this morning."

After he unbuttoned his overcoat, Pincura slapped his hands together as if to warm them. "Doesn't surprise me, Ollie. Did you unlock the courtroom for them yet?"

"No sir, Judge. They're all packed into the rotunda and the halls. I was waiting for you to tell me it was okay to let 'em in."

"Well, open the doors in about fifteen minutes, say around eight fifteen."

"Okay, that's kind of what I thought."

"Who's up there? Anyone I should know about?" the judge asked.

"Some of them are the regulars, but then there's a whole bunch of ladies I never seen before. And they're mean looking, the scowling-around types.

You know what I'm saying. And then some of them, you can't understand a word they're sayin'—talkin' like they just got off the boat. But the ones talkin' English, oh, they say that man is guilty."

"Oh, so they think he's guilty already," the judge said, smiling as he took in Johnson's words.

"They don't just think he's guilty, they know he's guilty," Johnson replied. "Drowned her in scalding water and burned his hands while he done it. That's what they're sayin' up there."

"Well, what do you think, Ollie?"

"Don't matter what I think, Judge."

"Humor me," Pincura urged.

"Oh, I don't know. He probably done it."

"So you made up your mind too," Pincura said.

"Now you're putting words into my mouth, Judge. First thing I said is I don't know." Johnson paused for a moment and then looked over his shoulder before he spoke again. "You know, maybe she deserved it."

Pincura raised his eyebrows. "You don't mean that, do you, Oliver?"

"No, I guess not."

"I figured you didn't. Anything else I should know?"

"Well, it stinks up there. Too many bodies and most of them carrying sack lunches. The hall smells like baloney sandwiches and old potato chips, like a high school cafeteria. Why do you let them bring lunches? If you ask me, which you don't, it's a bad idea. Gives us more clean up."

"I don't know which judge first allowed it, but we'd have a riot if we kicked them out at the noon recess. They all want to keep their seats for the entire day."

Avoiding the elevator, Pincura began climbing the stairway to his second-floor courtroom. Each tread slumped toward the middle, the result of thousands of shoes infinitesimally rubbing away some of the surface over the past eighty years. He realized that this sturdy sandstone building would not be here forever. Like its predecessor, it could be destroyed by fire, or perhaps it would just slip into disrepair.

All of this caused Pincura to think about the legions of troubled litigants who had trudged up and down these same stairs. Decade after decade, disputes great and small had been fought here between people now long forgotten. The courthouse was like a cemetery, swallowing up people and their problems and leaving barely a trace behind. The courthouse basement was full of old files that would eventually become illegible from dampness and decay, like gravestones worn smooth by weather. These disputes, so important when they happened, would ultimately be forgotten when the actors and their audience had passed into oblivion.

As he approached the second-floor landing, Pincura could hear the murmuring of the would-be spectators. Their steady, low voices reminded him of crickets in the morning. As angry as these people were right now, this case, too, would eventually be forgotten. At some point, the players would all be dead and the drama would die with them.

When he reached the anteroom to his chambers, he didn't unlock the door. Instead, he walked through the narrow hallway to the building's central rotunda in order to catch a glimpse of the waiting crowd. Just as the custodian had reported, the area outside his courtroom was jammed with people. He, too, could hear words in a foreign tongue, but unlike Oliver Johnson, Pincura could identify it. It was Polish, the language his parents often spoke at home or at his father's store. He quickly turned around, walked back to his chambers, and unlocked the door.

Once at his desk, he looked out the window and stared at the First Congregational Church and YMCA buildings, which dominated the other side of Court Street. Although it was not raining, a grayness pervaded the downtown. Despite the dreariness outside, Pincura felt a nervous excitement, something he always experienced when he was about to start a case involving high stakes like this one.

He opened the Bennett file and looked at the names of the prospective jurors, curious to see if he knew any of them. He did not.

Prospective jurors, called the venire, had been chosen from all over Lorain County, but most came from its two largest cities, Lorain and Elyria. Outside these two cities, the county included several towns, and beyond them, to the south, one of the largest farming areas in the state. Pincura was constantly surprised by the strange mix of city dwellers and farmers that served on his juries.

A lifelong Lorain resident, Pincura was also well aware of the differences between the people of Lorain and Elyria. Elyria, located in the center of the county, had developed more rapidly than Lorain, largely because the first railroad stopped there, bypassing Lorain. Elyria had always been the county seat, wielding whatever power came from small-county politics. When he first ran for judge, Pincura had courted voters in both cities. He had sensed that Elyria's established families felt superior to their Lorain counterparts, viewing them as distant and somewhat backward cousins. Although both cities could be counted upon to vote Democratic, Elyria had more Republicans. After its growth spurt at the turn of the century, Lorain's slightly larger population was now primarily blue-collar and immigrant based, demographics that strongly favored the Democratic Party and Pincura, a Democrat.

Pincura also understood the intense rivalry between the two cities. As a former quarterback at Lorain High School, he had experienced it firsthand. Fans would take an automobile or the interurban streetcar to the other city. Once at the game, their cheers often turned into taunts, and later deteriorated into bloody fights. At other times, it was as if medieval walls surrounded the two cities. Elyria residents rarely frequented Lorain stores and restaurants, and vice versa. It was hard to explain why the residents of these two cities rarely mingled with one another, but they didn't. Sometimes that separation could be important when attorneys selected a jury.

Judge Pincura got up from his chair and walked to the sliding pocket door that opened into his courtroom. He peeked in and could see Prosecutor Mikus noisily unloading papers from his briefcase onto one of the trial tables. Pincura didn't feel like talking to Mikus, who usually rubbed him the wrong way, and he retreated back into his chambers.

Over the last decade Pincura had watched Mikus select a jury many times. Mikus was known for exuding a careless, almost brazen attitude when picking a jury. He sometimes unnerved his opponents by announcing that he would take the first twelve prospective jurors on the list. The message was clear: his case was so strong that anyone, regardless of preexisting biases, would side with him. Pincura knew Mikus couldn't do that in this case. He couldn't ignore a prospective juror's opinion about the death penalty, and he needed "law and order" types since his case was built solely on circumstantial evidence.

Pincura also could not resist thinking about the types of people the defense would try to bump from the jury. They would get rid of as many women as possible because they would identify with the dead wife. The defense would also want to knock off the teetotalers. Those straitlaced people might convict Bennett simply because he made his living by selling booze. And then there was Bennett's adultery. Bennett's lawyers would try to get rid of all the deacons, Sunday school teachers, and inflexible church people too.

Although his decisions on evidentiary questions were important throughout a trial, Pincura understood that his rulings during the jury selection process were critical. How he ruled here could have a profound impact on the jury's composition and perhaps the ultimate outcome of the case.

Prospective jurors could be eliminated in two ways. An unlimited number of prospective jurors could be dismissed "for cause," reasons that were spelled out by statute. In a capital murder case, each side could also exercise up to six "peremptory" challenges, dismissals that required no legal justification.

Pincura would be the first person to question the prospective jurors, and his questions would be designed to identify jurors who should be disqualified for cause. He was not a judge who believed in dominating the jury selection process. He had been a competent attorney before taking the bench, representing the city of Lorain as solicitor and representing insurance companies and banks in his private practice. As an attorney, he'd cringed whenever a judge invaded his turf in jury selection. Many of these other judges had forgotten how mediocre they once were as trial attorneys and saw jury selection as a time to again "strut their stuff." As a judge, Pincura would ask just a few questions, get some basic information, and let the attorneys do their job.

His first questions would be narrow ones: were any of the jurors going to be called as witnesses in the case, did any have a legal action pending against one of the parties, had any served on the grand jury that indicted Bennett, and other questions hewing closely to the established grounds for juror dismissal. However, these clear-cut situations were very rare and Pincura seldom saw them.

Eliminating jurors for cause would also involve his discretion. The statutes allowed a judge to excuse prospective jurors if they demonstrated bias against either the defendant or the prosecution. He would have to decide whether a prospective juror was sufficiently biased to warrant removal. Likewise, Pincura could excuse prospective jurors if they said that their personal beliefs would not allow them to follow the law. Determining this was difficult because prospective jurors usually flip-flopped on that point the longer they were questioned about it. Pincura would have to decide whether a prospective juror had convincingly renounced his or her initial disqualifying statement. He was a good judge of people, but, nevertheless, the call was often damn difficult. As a result, he found this part of the trial to be a virtual minefield.

Once the attorneys started questioning the prospective jurors, Pincura was always on high alert for impermissible questions. Mikus and Miraldi usually pushed things to the limit here, but Pincura doubted that Adams, as lead defense counsel, would allow Miraldi to question the panel—so one-half of his problem was already solved.

He also knew that both sides would try to establish as many cause challenges as they could because there was no limit to them. In this way, each side could preserve its six peremptory challenges. Because peremptory challenges allowed the attorneys to excuse anyone for any reason, Pincura was constantly surprised by the people whom the attorneys chose to dismiss.

In this case, he had ordered seventy-five people to show up for the venire even though only twelve would be sworn as jurors to decide the case. He knew that when the death penalty was involved, many of the prospective jurors would be eliminated after laborious questioning, through either cause or peremptory challenges.

Pincura gathered the file documents and placed them back in the court folder. He hesitated a few more moments before getting out of his chair and walking into the courtroom. He sensed that this trial would last several weeks and would be a contentious affair. He hoped that the lawyers would pick twelve decisive people. He did not want to go through a long trial and end up with a hung jury. He had seen it happen before. The jurors would listen for days to the testimony and then would be unable to reach a unanimous verdict. A defendant was convicted or acquitted only if all twelve jurors agreed.

Pincura stretched his arms, took a deep breath, and exhaled. "Reasonable doubt, that's the boulder they have to push to the finish line," he muttered to himself. "Does the prosecution have enough evidence? I guess I'm going to find out soon enough." Bennett would be guilty if twelve jurors agreed that the state had proved its case beyond a reasonable doubt, and he would be acquitted if all agreed that the state had failed to meet that same standard. It sounded simple, but Pincura knew it wasn't.

While Pincura was thinking about the imminent trial, sheriff's deputies were transporting Casper Bennett from the jail to the courthouse. Around eight forty-five, two uniformed sheriff's deputies escorted Casper Bennett into the courtroom. When he entered, the courtroom spectators suddenly became silent. Many of the female observers knew Bennett, but for the others, it was their first glimpse of a man who had drowned his wife in scalding water. They had been wondering what such a vile man looked like.

Bennett wore a dark blue suit and appeared subdued as he talked with his attorneys. He also seemed distracted, often looking away from his attorneys to see who was seated in the gallery. Women far outnumbered the men in the audience. The women were from his neighborhood, his wife's friends and acquaintances, and they did not avert their eyes when he looked in their direction. Florence's brother, John Buddish, was there, his eyes so concentrated on Bennett's skull that it looked like he was trying to divine Bennett's thoughts. Bennett turned his back on the spectators, took a seat at the trial table, and slumped in his chair.

Miraldi talked animatedly with Adams and other court personnel. He did not look like a man who had slept fitfully the night before. Although he had tried many cases, never before had he been involved in a case where his client could die if he lost. Adams, on the other hand, was more comfortable in this setting; he often found himself fighting for the liberty of his clients, and occasionally for their lives. Belying his own anxiety, Adams appeared relaxed and his warm handshake to Miraldi earlier that morning had reassured his younger co-counsel.

At the other trial table, Mikus and Otero were whispering loudly. They were joined by Inspector Maurice Mumford, a high-ranking member of the Lorain Police Department who directed its detective bureau. Otero, who knew that he would not have much involvement in today's events, looked casual. Betraying his own nervousness, Mikus rubbed his thumb along a sheaf of papers as he talked.

Judge Pincura came into the courtroom a few minutes before nine a.m., took his seat, and pulled some papers out of his file and placed them in front of him. As he surveyed the scene, he saw two different types of trial attorneys in the courtroom. Although all of these lawyers were capable of advocating passionately, two of them, Adams and Otero, never seemed to forget that they were playing a role. Even when they believed that their cause was just, they also understood that their adversary's position had some merit too. For them, the truth was somewhere between the two rival positions.

However, Pincura believed that the other two lawyers fit another mold. Before entering the courtroom, both Mikus and Miraldi had convinced themselves that justice belonged only to their cause. Over the last few weeks, they had systematically purged themselves of any doubts about their case. Although Mikus and Miraldi had completely different personalities in and out of the courtroom, they were both the kind of men who saw no gray areas or reasonable grounds for compromise. If fireworks were going to explode in his courtroom, Pincura knew they would come from these two.

Pincura noted that all of the attorneys, except for Adams, had strikingly similar backgrounds. Mikus, Otero, and Miraldi were all first-generation sons of poor, working-class, and basically uneducated immigrant parents. Each was either the oldest sibling or the oldest male child. Each had shown strong academic promise in the public schools. Each had pursued college and law degrees and returned to his hometown to play a prominent role in its judicial and civic activities. These men were driven, ambitious, and competitive. They were used to navigating their own way and finding success. At the end, the jury would decide which of them won and which lost. On the way to that outcome, this trial would prod their egos, feed their anger, and test their resolve.

"Are we ready to proceed?" Judge Pincura asked. The four attorneys nodded their assent. "Okay then. Bailiff, bring in the prospective jurors."

Several rows of benches were closed off to spectators and reserved for the prospective jurors. They would wait there until called to the jury box. In the back of the courtroom, the prospective jurors slowly filed in, some quiet, others still engaged in conversation with the person in front of or behind them.

Casper Bennett and the attorneys all stood and faced the prospective jurors as they entered. The attorneys alternated between nodding at them, looking over their heads, and occasionally giving them a half smile that looked more like a grimace. Appearing both serious and unhappy, none of the prospective jurors smiled back. Yanked from their homes and jobs into this alien setting, they studied the faces of the men at the tables, trying to identify which one was the defendant, the person who had forced them to be here today.

Then it began.

After asking them all to be seated, Judge Pincura said, "You have been called as prospective jurors in this criminal matter known as *The State of Ohio vs. Casimir Bernatowicz, also known as Casper Bennett.* Jury duty is one of the solemn civic responsibilities that all Americans are asked to perform. Because of our Constitution and the Bill of Rights, Americans are guaranteed the right to have their cases decided by a jury of their peers, people like you. It is one of the bedrock principles upon which our country is founded."

Pincura paused for a moment, adjusted his glasses, and studied the faces of the prospective jurors, gazing at them as if they were slightly out of focus. He rarely read from a prepared script and today was no exception. He had conducted hundreds of trials and his opening remarks followed a familiar format.

The judge then discussed the juror's civic duty, introduced the attorneys, described in general terms the charges against the defendant, and outlined the jury selection process. When he finished, he asked his bailiff to call twelve names and place those people in the jury box.

With that accomplished, Pincura addressed the twelve. "I want you to raise your hand if any of these things apply to you." He read from a list in a perfunctory way, "Were any of you on the grand jury that issued the indictment in this case?" Seeing no hands, he continued, "Are any of you related to the defendant in any way?" Again no hands.

The prospective jurors remained silent as Pincura asked if any of them had been subpoenaed as a witness in this case, were chronic alcoholics, had difficulty understanding the English language, had been convicted of a felony, were involved in litigation against the defendant, or themselves had cases pending that involved any of the attorneys in this case.

Pincura had saved the difficult "cause" questions for last. He would now explore the jurors' potential biases against the parties and any hesitations they might have about following the law.

Clearing his throat, the judge asked, "This case has received considerable coverage in our local papers. Some of you may have already formed strong opinions in this case. Do any of you already feel any enmity, ill will, or bias toward either the defendant or the prosecution in this case?"

Pincura scanned the twelve jurors in the box and those sitting in the courtroom. Five persons raised their hands in the jury box, while another dozen sitting in the back of the courtroom also raised their hands. "I'm only interested in those people in the jury box. The rest of you out there can put your hands down," he said in a slightly irritated tone.

"Okay, let's start with you, Juror Number Three, Mr. Antil. Why did you raise your hand?" the judge asked.

"I'm from Lorain and I've heard a lot of talk about it. We've talked about it at work several times. I know that the defendant's wife drowned in the bathtub and the defendant's hands were burned. They were getting a divorce too. I think I know too much about this case to be fair," the juror responded.

"So you think you are biased against Mr. Bennett, is that right?"

"Yes, Your Honor," Mr. Antil said.

"Well, I am not going to go into the evidence in this case because, frankly, I don't know too much about it at this point. However, I can tell you that, as a juror, you will hear a lot of testimony from both sides about what happened. As a juror, you are to make your decision based solely on what you learn in this courtroom. We all have some ideas about a case before we hear the evidence. If you are chosen as a juror, are you telling me that you cannot make your decision based just on what you learn in this courtroom?"

"I guess if you put it that way, I think I could decide the case on what I learn from the witnesses," the juror answered.

"So you think you could be fair and impartial to both sides in this case?" the judge asked, using the time-worn phrase that usually prodded a hesitant juror back into line.

"I like to think of myself as a fair person. I think I could," Mr. Antil finished.

Addressing the attorneys, Judge Pincura said, "Well, I will let both sides question Mr. Antil further, but right now, I am not going to excuse him for cause."

The judge questioned the four other jurors who had raised their hands and reached the same conclusion about three of them. However, one of them was a friend of Mrs. Bennett's aunt, and they had talked about the case. The judge questioned this prospective juror extensively and she continued to shake her head when asked if she could be fair and impartial.

Eventually Judge Pincura said, "Well, Mrs. Kosalowski, I thank you for your honesty. This court will excuse you for cause. Any objections, counselors?"

Mikus began to stand, but then sat back down. The bailiff called another prospective juror to fill Mrs. Kosalowski's vacant chair.

"There is one other area in which I am going to inquire briefly. As you know, Mr. Bennett has been charged with a capital offense. That means that the state is seeking a conviction that carries with it a sentence of death. Do any of you hold conscientious or religious convictions that under no circumstances allow you to put someone to death for a crime?" the judge asked.

Several of the prospective jurors squirmed in their seats but did not raise their hands. The prospective jurors sitting in the courtroom benches focused on their colleagues in the box.

"All right, by your silence, I take it that none of you do," the judge stated.

As the judge was saying this, a thin, dark-haired woman in her thirties raised her hand. "I don't know exactly if this is based on religious beliefs, but I don't think it is right for the government to kill anyone under any circumstances. I just can't see myself agreeing to do that," she replied.

"Okay, Juror Number Seven, Miss Bernstein, is that correct? You know that we all have strong reservations about sentencing someone to die for a crime. It is something that the law imposes when the defendant is responsible for a horrible crime. If you are picked as a juror, you will be guided by jury instructions on whether a death sentence is appropriate in this case. I am not asking you if it would be hard to impose that sentence, but I am asking you if, no matter what the evidence showed, you would never impose a death sentence under any circumstances," the judge explained.

"I just don't know," Miss Bernstein replied. "I can only tell you that I would be very, very reluctant to do something like that. Maybe I could, but I really doubt it."

The judge stared at her, squinting as if that would help him look into her mind. Before he could say anything, Miss Bernstein said, "I'm just trying to be very honest with everybody. You asked the question and I am answering it as best as I can."

Pincura realized that his penetrating gaze had been interpreted more severely than he had intended. His look softened and he said, "Miss Bernstein, I appreciate your honesty. I have not heard from you that you could never impose a death sentence, is that right?"

"I guess that's right," she replied.

"Based on that, I am not going to excuse you for cause at this point. I will let the attorneys question you further and I will reconsider this decision later. Thank you."

Mikus again was fidgeting in his seat but did not say anything. He knew that in just a moment the judge would be finished and the attorneys could begin questioning the prospective jurors.

As if reading Mikus's mind, Judge Pincura stated, "The prosecution may now inquire."

Mikus rose deliberately from his chair and positioned himself about a foot from the jury box railing, so close that jurors sitting in the front row could see the perspiration beading on his forehead.

"Good morning, ladies and gentlemen. My name, as you have learned, is Paul Mikus. I, along with John Otero, have the responsibility and privilege of representing the State of Ohio in its case against Mr. Casper Bennett, who the State of Ohio has accused of intentionally murdering his wife. This is an immensely important case for the people of this state and of this county. At this stage of the case, I am allowed to ask you questions, not to pry, but to find out how you feel about serving as a juror on this particular case and the issues that will come up during this trial. You may have some things in your background that would make you unsuitable for judging Mr. Bennett. Some of your beliefs may affect your ability to judge the evidence fairly, and I am going to explore that with you. Because this case is so important, I am going to question each of you individually. So this is going to take a lot of time, but both Mr. Adams and I need to do this properly."

Judge Pincura smiled to himself as he listened to Mikus's preamble. This time the prosecutor was not going to accept the first twelve jurors who were called. Mikus obviously realized that he could lose this case in jury selection if he was not careful.

Despite his history of routinely spurning the questioning of jurors, it soon became evident that Mikus would be slow and methodical today. He began by asking questions to the entire panel. Did they understand that they would be the sole deciders of the disputed facts? Did any of them feel that they were not up to the task of deciding whether an accused defendant had committed a crime? Did they understand that a criminal trial was the most important way for a community to keep itself safe? Miraldi could see that Mikus was indoctrinating the jury about the importance of convicting "bad people" and trying to empower them to make their neighborhoods safer. Mikus continued to ask questions that were designed to prod them to take responsible action and to scrutinize any defenses that were far-fetched.

Mikus then asked each juror about their family, job, prior jury service, and experience with the criminal justice system, either as a victim or as a perpetrator. Although he spoke in a loud and forceful voice, Mikus could also be friendly. He smiled and expressed interest in almost anything a juror said to him. He loved the patience of schoolteachers, admired the stamina of steelworkers, and respected the diligence of retail workers. Adams leaned over and whispered to Miraldi, "Charming guy, isn't he?"

Miraldi rolled his eyes, but he was worried. He could see that Mikus was developing a rapport with the prospective jurors. If they liked him, they would probably trust him too. And that would be trouble.

Addressing Juror Number Two, Mikus said, "As the court will tell you, the state must prove its case with evidence that establishes each element of the crime by proof beyond a reasonable doubt. Now, I want to talk to you a little about reasonable doubt and what it means and what it does not mean. For example, do you believe that the state has to prove this crime to you with evidence that leaves not a shadow of a doubt that the defendant is guilty?"

Miraldi and Adams had expected that Mikus would try to minimize the concept of reasonable doubt," and they looked at one another in anticipation of Mikus's next question.

Juror Number Two, a middle-aged factory worker, looked perplexed, unsure if this was a trick question. "I don't know. I know that you have to prove it to us so that we are convinced," the man replied.

"Well, the defense is going to talk about reasonable doubt all the time. You, as a juror, can have doubts, we all have doubts, but reasonable doubt means much more. It means a significant doubt that a reasonable person would have in evaluating something very carefully, do you understand that?"

Realizing that it was time to rein Mikus in, Miraldi jumped out of his chair. "Objection, Your Honor, Mr. Mikus is giving this juror a definition of reasonable doubt that is not accurate. Can we approach?"

Miraldi and Adams reached the judge's bench before the two prosecutors. However, in order to place himself directly in front of Judge Pincura, Mikus leaned hard to his right when he got there. In so doing, his right shoulder bumped against Miraldi's left shoulder, causing Miraldi to move awkwardly to his right. Mikus and Miraldi began whispering at the same time, making it impossible for either the judge or the court reporter to follow their comments. A few of the prospective jurors were also straining to hear what they weren't supposed to hear.

"Mr. Miraldi, you made the objection so you can speak first," the judge whispered.

"Your Honor, our point is simple: If Mr. Mikus is going to ask the jurors about points of law, he absolutely needs to state the law correctly. His explanation of reasonable doubt is not legally correct," Miraldi stated.

"I have not misstated the law. Reasonable doubt is more than just a passing doubt. It is a substantial doubt after a reasonable person has fully, fairly, and carefully considered all of the evidence," Mikus replied.

"There he goes again," Miraldi responded. "What is this 'substantial doubt' stuff? It is a doubt, a reasonable one, not a substantial one."

"Gentlemen, I will let Mr. Mikus's question stand. I will let counsel ask some questions regarding the law if it could reasonably lead to a challenge cause, but not to indoctrinate or mislead the jury. I think the prosecutor's question, although not perfect, is a fairly accurate statement of the law."

Mikus asked the question again and the prospective juror agreed that he would be bound by the concept of reasonable doubt. Mikus asked no further questions about reasonable doubt. He was on notice that the defense was going to object if he tried to misstate the law to favor his position. More importantly, he did not want to be interrupted by the defense or corrected by the judge.

However, Mikus was far from done. “Do you understand that there are two types of evidence, circumstantial and direct evidence?”

Juror Number Two said, “I guess, if you say so.”

“Well, direct evidence is when somebody sees or hears something directly and testifies about it. Circumstantial evidence involves things that you can infer based on the circumstances. For example, if you see horse prints in the snow, you can infer through circumstantial evidence that a horse has passed through. Does that make sense to you?”

The juror nodded in agreement.

“Our case against Mr. Bennett is built on circumstantial evidence only, not direct evidence. Some people think that if they are going to convict a man of first-degree murder, they want direct evidence, not circumstantial evidence. Are you that kind of person?” Mikus asked.

“Well, I want to see strong evidence before I would feel right about finding someone guilty of murder,” the man said.

Again Miraldi and Adams were fidgeting in their seats. Mikus was getting close to the impermissible areas of questioning, but they held back for now.

“I am going to be very blunt with you, Mr.—let me see—Graham. Would you refuse to convict Mr. Bennett on circumstantial evidence even if that evidence established each element of the crime beyond a reasonable doubt?”

“Objection,” Miraldi said. “Can we approach?”

“No, it’s not necessary,” Judge Pincura stated. “I am going to let the question stand. The state has a right to let the jurors know that its case is based solely on circumstantial evidence. The prosecution also needs to know whether any of these jurors are going to require eyewitness testimony to convict the defendant. He has a right to know the answer to this.

It could lead to a cause challenge."

Miraldi, now admonished, sat down. *Pincura is letting Mikus get away with murder*, Miraldi thought. Adams sat dispassionately, doodling on his yellow pad.

Juror Number Two responded to the question, "Well, if it is strong circumstantial evidence, then I guess so."

"You can be assured that we will present very strong circumstantial evidence," Mikus replied.

This time Adams stood up and objected.

"Sustained," Judge Pincura said. "Mr. Mikus, this is not the time to argue your case to the jury. I don't expect to have to remind you of that again."

Without apologizing, Mikus continued. "Mr. Graham, I want to talk to you about the death penalty. Are you a strong enough person to recommend the death penalty if the state proves this crime and the heinous nature of it beyond a reasonable doubt?"

"Objection," Miraldi and Adams yelled in unison.

"Sustained," Judge Pincura responded. "Mr. Mikus, you can inquire about this juror's beliefs about the death penalty, but not with that question."

Mikus had expected the objection and the admonition, but he had made his point. He had connected a person's personal strength with their ability to recommend the death penalty. The obverse was all too obvious: weaklings would shrink at such a decision. Mikus followed up with additional questions about the death penalty. Juror Number Two let Mikus know that he was tough enough to recommend the death penalty if the facts and law warranted it.

As midday approached, Mikus had not completed his examination of the twelve. Judge Pincura recessed at noon and reconvened the trial at one fifteen p.m.

By three o'clock, Mikus indicated that he had completed his questioning of the panel. Through his questioning, he'd established cause challenges to two jurors, including Miss Bernstein and another, who were now adamant that they would not recommend the death penalty based on their belief that this penalty was morally wrong under any circumstance. Without objection from the defense, Judge Pincura granted the cause challenges.

Rising slowly, Lon Adams approached the prospective jurors with his yellow legal pad in hand and came to a stop about three feet from the jury railing. Like Abraham Lincoln, Adams had a slightly stooped posture that evoked humility. He began by introducing himself and his co-counsel again. He talked about the importance of a jury trial and the need to choose jurors who would listen to the evidence with a completely open mind. He asked the jurors if they would wait before drawing any conclusions until both sides had an opportunity to present their case.

Adams had a set pattern of questions that he used in almost all criminal cases and he painstakingly asked them of each juror. Did they understand that just because someone had been arrested, it did not follow that the person had committed a crime or done anything wrong? Did they know that a defendant was presumed to be innocent under our law? Did they understand that the police made mistakes? Did they understand that a defendant was not required to testify or present any evidence? He let them know, however, that Casper Bennett would testify in this case, and the defense would present its own witnesses.

For this case, he also had tailored specific questions that he intended to ask of each individual juror. He wanted to know their attitudes about alcohol, tavern owners, and spouses who were unfaithful. He would inquire about their religious beliefs on these subjects. If prospective jurors indicated that they knew anything about the case, he would question them carefully. He did not want to open a Pandora's box by asking them exactly what they had heard. Instead, his plan was to find out if any had unshakable opinions because of that information. Would the prosecution be starting ahead of the defense in this case?

As the day's proceeding neared four p.m., Adams had only questioned two of the twelve prospective jurors. He asked a question of Juror Number Three, a stout woman in her late forties who indicated that her brother-in-law was a policeman in Cleveland, Ohio. "Mrs. Southworth, because your brother-in-law is a policeman, will that cause you to conclude that a policeman's testimony is more believable than other witnesses?"

"Well, my brother-in-law is a very honest man. He and his fellow officers work hard and risk their lives every day," she replied.

"I know that they do," Adams agreed. "But, because of your relationship with your brother-in-law, would that affect your objectivity when listening to the police officers in this case?"

Mrs. Southworth was quiet for a while as she pondered the question. "I think I would value the police testimony more so than the others," she said.

"What if the judge told you not to automatically value their testimony more just because they are police officers? Could you follow that instruction?" Adams asked.

Mikus quickly rose and objected, "Your Honor, I know of no instruction of law that states that the testimony of a police officer is to be given no greater weight than any other testimony. Mr. Adams is trying to discredit the officers' testimony even before they have testified. This is wrong."

Judge Pincura held up his hand to forestall any further discussion. "I'm thinking about this," he said. After a few moments, he continued, "I am going to sustain that objection. Mrs. Southworth, I will tell you that, at the end of this case, you will be the sole determiner of the credibility of any witness and you will decide how much weight to give anyone's testimony. You will judge the witnesses' demeanor, their ability to observe the things that they are testifying about, and their intelligence. Will you do that for each witness who comes before this court?"

"Yes, I will," she answered.

"Counsel, it is now four p.m. I am going to recess the court for the day and we will resume jury selection tomorrow. For you folks who have been called as prospective jurors, you are not to discuss this case with your fellow jurors or with family members. You are not to read any newspaper articles about this case or listen to any radio reports either. Family members are curious and I guarantee that they will ask you questions. You cannot talk to them about this case. Is that absolutely clear? I want you all back in the jury room tomorrow at eight forty-five and we will start again at nine a.m. sharp," Judge Pincura finished.

After the jury left, the two sheriff's deputies walked up to escort Bennett from the courthouse back to the county jail. As one of the deputies opened the door to the waiting squad car, Bennett quickly ducked in, tilted his fedora over his face, and slumped low into the seat.

Miraldi and Adams watched as the sheriff's black cruiser slowly pulled away from the curb. "He's getting a real education, isn't he?" Adams said.

"Everybody wants a jury trial," Miraldi answered, "until they see the actual jurors who will decide their fate."

"He looks scared," Adams said.

"Who wouldn't be?" Miraldi answered as the two attorneys headed for their cars.

CHAPTER 13

March 31, 1964

The second day of jury selection had proceeded much like the previous day. By four o'clock, the attorneys had eliminated nine jurors for cause. Because of the extensive pretrial publicity, the defense had been able to eliminate jurors who claimed to have fixed opinions about Casper Bennett's guilt. At the other trial table, the prosecution had rid itself of those jurors who were categorically opposed to the death penalty. As soon as one prospective juror had been excused, another would be called to fill that slot and the extensive questioning would begin again.

Lon Adams looked exhausted as he and Miraldi packed up their briefcases.

"I don't think there's anyone left on that panel that either side can excuse for cause. We're going to have to start using our peremptory challenges tomorrow," Miraldi said.

"Things will go a little quicker from that point," Adams replied. "We'll probably get to our opening statements tomorrow."

"I think we'll reach the opening too," Miraldi agreed.

Miraldi was glad that Adams had mentioned the opening statement because he wanted to talk to him about it again, in particular what they should tell the jury in their opening. Several days earlier, the two had discussed this. Adams had been adamant that he, as lead counsel, should deliver the defense's opening statement, a summary of what the defense believed the evidence would show. When Miraldi had pressed him about the themes he would weave into the opening statement, Adams had looked perplexed. Adams had told him that he usually delivered his opening statement extemporaneously because that kept it stronger and fresher. He thought a jury could sense when an opening statement had been rehearsed.

Miraldi had looked quizzical, showing his disagreement. Adams had become defensive and snapped that opening statements weren't that important anyway. He saved his best rhetoric for the closing argument. Miraldi had dropped the subject, but he was troubled by Adams's casual approach.

Miraldi would try again today. Over the last five years, he had attended a number of advanced trial seminars sponsored by civil attorneys who specialized in personal injury cases. At these seminars, the speakers did not just tell "war stories" about successful outcomes; they shared scientific studies that revealed how jurors thought and made decisions. One message was clear: trial attorneys could no longer overlook the importance of an opening statement. It was critical.

Miraldi was impressed by the research. Studies showed that 80 percent of the time, jurors did not change their view of the case after opening statements. These results were explained by two psychological theories, primacy and cognitive dissonance. Miraldi had initially been skeptical about this psychological mumbo jumbo, but as the speakers explained these principles, he became convinced.

Primacy simply meant that people remembered and found more important those things that were presented first. Cognitive dissonance was a little more complex. Once a person held an initial belief, that person often rejected new information that conflicted with that belief. People became psychologically uncomfortable if they had to hold two inconsistent beliefs at the same time. To eliminate that discomfort, or "dissonance," a person rejected new information instead of changing the initial belief. The speakers also explained that jurors retained more information if it was told to them in story form.

Adams was from the old school. Trial attorneys first learned their craft by watching other successful trial attorneys and copying their techniques. Then it was a process of trying many cases and discovering what worked.

Miraldi doubted that Adams would be persuaded by scientific research done by psychologists, but if he handed Adams the finished product, perhaps Adams would use it or take some parts from it. After his conversation with Adams he had written his own opening statement and his secretary had typed it up the following day. Now he would approach Adams with his work.

"I don't want you to think that I'm butting in or overstepping my bounds here, but I want to talk to you about the opening statement," Miraldi began.

Adams was leaning over the trial table, but his head jerked up as soon as he heard the words "opening statement." He was wary. *Does this hotshot want to give the opening statement? He may have won a few civil trials, but he's never been in this position before, trying to save a man from the electric chair.*

Miraldi sensed that Adams was edgy. "You've done a masterful job with the jury selection. I just wanted to tell you that first off," Miraldi started. "I also know how exhausting it has been these first two days. You've been on the front line, while I've had the luxury of just watching you."

"Well, thanks, I appreciate that," Adams replied. His shoulders relaxed and he began to gather his papers again.

"I thought maybe I could be most helpful if I outlined the points we want to make in the opening statement," Miraldi said. He pulled out his draft opening statement and went on, "I thought this might be helpful to you as you prepare tonight."

Adams exhaled loudly but said nothing. "I'll take a look at it when I get home." He folded the pages into thirds and shoved them into his breast coat pocket.

"I hope you get a few ideas from it," Miraldi said. Adams did not reply.

Miraldi left the courtroom first and Adams followed a few minutes later.

CHAPTER 14

April 1, 1964

This can't go on much longer, Pincura thought as he looked at his watch. It was now 11:40 and both sides had exercised four peremptory challenges, resulting in eight new faces in the jury box. Each side still had the option of using two more challenges.

Mikus and Otero were arguing about their next move.

"We need to get rid of Juror Number Nine," Mikus whispered to Otero. "There's just something about that guy I don't like. I can't put my finger on it, but he seems like a smart-ass to me and I don't want any smart-asses on my jury."

"I think he's fine. He says he's in favor of the death penalty. He's married and has a large family. He's not going to like Bennett. We've got a good jury right now; let's stick with what we have and waive our last two challenges," Otero replied.

Neither Mikus nor Otero wanted to exercise their last peremptory challenge unless it was absolutely necessary, and they were getting close to that now. At some point in their careers, each had used a last peremptory challenge only to find the replacement juror less suitable than the one dismissed. With no more peremptory challenges left, they had been stuck with that juror.

The two men talked for a few more minutes. Finally, Mikus rose slowly from his chair. "The prosecution is satisfied with the jury as now constituted."

The jury selection process would be over if the defense waived its next peremptory challenge.

Miraldi leaned his head toward Adams. "Right now we have nine men and only three women," Miraldi whispered to Adams. "Looking at the list, I think the next two people to be called are women. We're not going to do any better than just three women. I'd hold it right here."

"I agree. Mikus really helped us. He kept excusing women who were a little squeamish about the death penalty, although none of them were really against it. We got a break there," Adams said.

"You know Mikus. He thinks he can win his case with any twelve. They can be men, women, or chimps," Miraldi whispered back. "And we only have one juror from Lorain. Who would have thought we could do that?"

The defense team wanted as few Lorain residents on the jury as possible. The greater the number of jurors from Lorain, the greater the chance that someone would actually know Bennett or would have heard rumors about him. Bennett had a lot of baggage, and it looked like this jury would not know any of it, except for what was disclosed during the course of the trial.

Adams and Miraldi were also very concerned about one rumor that, if known by a juror, could convict Bennett by its power alone. For the last four months, the Lorain police had been unsuccessful in finding the source of a rumor that an intoxicated Bennett had boasted in a bar that he would kill his wife. Whether true or not, this rumor, if carried into the jury room, would likely decide the case.

People from Lorain were also much more likely to know something about Bennett's bar, the B & M Grille, and that would only hurt his defense. Women were not welcome there and were often turned away at the door. Bennett and his staff frequently served underage teens ten-cent beers when business was slow. It was also about the only place in Lorain where a young man could walk into the restroom, put coins in a dispenser, and walk away with a condom. Men played pool and card games at the B & M, often gambling on the outcomes. It was all small-time stuff, but none of it would improve Bennett's chances with the jury.

"Right, one Lorain juror. We dodged a bullet there," Adams whispered back to his co-counsel. Adams stood and said, "The defense is also satisfied with the jury as now composed."

The attorneys, however, were not completely done with the selection process. Two alternate jurors had to be questioned and seated, too. Both Mikus and Adams were tired and their questions were perfunctory. They figured that neither of the alternates would ever deliberate on the case and did not bother to fully vet them. After ten minutes, two alternate jurors, both men, were seated with the other twelve.

As it was just past noon, Judge Pincura addressed the jury: "We will now take our noon recess. I want you back by one thirty. Normally, the first thing that we do at this point is listen to opening statements, where both sides tell you what they expect the evidence will show. However, the prosecution has requested that you go to the Bennett home to view the premises and see the bathroom where Mrs. Bennett died. This is called a jury view, and it is done to help you understand the evidence. The jury view will allow you to picture where things happened in the house. Later on, when you listen to testimony and see photographs, it will give you a framework. So with that, we are adjourned until one thirty p.m."

The yellow brick Gothic church stood guard over the Polish neighborhood as the chartered bus slowly made its way down Fifteenth Street. This Polish church, Nativity of the Blessed Virgin Mary, had witnessed Florence Bennett's baptism, first communion, and marriage. Why shouldn't it also glimpse the jurors who would decide if Florence had been murdered in her nearby house?

As the bus came to a stop, one of Bennett's neighbors, the widow Jane Poletylo, looked out from behind the curtain of her house. A subpoena was on her desk, an unpleasant reminder that she was scheduled to testify tomorrow in the Bennett case. The police and attorneys had questioned and confused her so many times now. They were interested in the exact time that she saw Casper Bennett enter his house on December 20, 1963.

She couldn't say for sure, but the persistent police detectives had finally convinced her that it was very close to nine p.m. After that, they finally left her alone.

The attorneys came in two separate cars, with Casper Bennett being allowed to arrive with his attorneys. Except for a brief chaperoned visit here with his attorneys a few weeks earlier, Bennett had not been back to his house since the night of the incident. As the jurors and attorneys entered, they saw Casper's newspapers from December 20 still sitting on a chair, as unruffled as when he had dropped them there that Friday. On the mantel, Florence Bennett peered out at the visitors from two wedding photographs taken almost a quarter century earlier.

The bailiff took the jury upstairs. Because the bathroom was small, only four jurors could fit in it at a time. The prosecution had purposely not cleaned the tub. Some of Florence's hair and skin still clung to the tub's sides, while a few tiny spots of blood, now dried and brown, remained on the tub's far end. Although Casper went upstairs with his attorneys, he did not walk into the bathroom with them. Instead, he stayed in the hallway and looked the other way, almost absently, into the sewing room, where another of Florence's wedding photographs was mounted on the wall.

****

Back in the courtroom, John Otero stood center stage in front of the jury. Mikus, exhausted from two days of jury selection, had surprised Otero that morning by asking him at the last minute to deliver the opening statement. Although Otero thought himself good on his feet, he would have appreciated some advance notice to prepare more thoroughly. Mikus complained that he had an overpowering headache and needed Otero to outline the state's case to the jury. Otero wondered if Mikus's headache was a hangover from the previous evening, but he did not ask. Otero was finally getting his chance to have a meaningful role in a high-profile case, and he did not care how or why the battle sword had been passed his way.

Otero would outline the evidence that showed Bennett to be the murderer. Unlike a closing argument, which could turn into a rhetorical free-for-all, an opening statement was limited to the recitation of facts. Facts, however, could be marshaled in a persuasive way. If he did this well, he would advance the prosecution's case greatly.

Each side had some surprises for the other. Neither wanted to divulge those surprises in their opening statement. The prosecution had two potential shockers: Mrs. Bennett's "diary calendar" and the bathtub's leaky overflow system. On the other side, the defense had several top-notch pathologists waiting in the wings to discredit Dr. Kopsch's conclusions.

John Otero began:

"Ladies and gentlemen, the State of Ohio will prove beyond a reasonable doubt that Casper Bennett murdered his wife, Florence, for one overriding reason: money—to be more exact, for life insurance money. You will learn that Mr. and Mrs. Bennett were married in 1940. Their marriage was unhappy. They argued and they fought and they drank. Mrs. Bennett filed for a divorce in 1960 and again in 1962. For the last couple of years, Mr. Bennett had a girlfriend and was unfaithful to his wife. Mr. Bennett was living beyond his means. He spent lots of money on his girlfriend, paying for vacations to Las Vegas and Hawaii, buying clothes (even a mink stole), and taking her out to dinner at expensive restaurants. To do this, Mr. Bennett needed money and then more money. The life insurance proceeds on his wife's life were just too enticing for him. To get that money, though, he needed to kill Mrs. Bennett, and he had to make it look like an accident. You see, Mr. Bennett had twenty-two thousand dollars of life insurance on Florence's life, but if she died in an accident, the polices would double to forty-four thousand dollars.

"The state will prove that on December 20, 1963, Mr. Bennett plied his wife with alcohol and sleeping pills around suppertime. A few hours later he pushed or knocked her into a tub of scalding water. He then held her head down under the water until she drowned. At nine thirty-four p.m. on that Friday evening, he called the operator and asked her to get the rescue squad to his house. He said that he'd found his wife in the tub and she was unresponsive. Later, when the police got there, Mr. Bennett told them that he had left his home around seven forty-five or eight o' clock to run some errands. He had been to Don's Sohio and picked up newspapers at Kingsley's Cigar Store. According to Bennett, he came home from his errands to discover his wife in the bathtub. A few minutes later, he said he called the operator.

"But you will learn that Mr. Bennett's story does not hold together. The police could see that Mr. Bennett's left palm was badly burned, as was the little finger on his right hand. The tops of his hands were not burned. He claimed that he had received these burns when he was trying to pull his wife out of the steaming-hot bathwater."

Miraldi was waiting for Otero to explain why the absence of burns demonstrated foul play, but Otero did not develop the point. *The jury looks confused here*, he thought.

Otero continued:

"You will see photographs of Mrs. Bennett's burned body and hear testimony from our county coroner, Dr. Kopsch, who examined the body on the night of her death. Over seventy-five percent of her body was burned with horrible burns, burns severe enough to cause her skin to blister and peel off. Even some of the hair on her scalp burned off and floated in the water. We are sorry that we will have to show you these photos. They are difficult to look at, but there is a reason."

Yeah, you want to prejudice the jury, Adams thought.

"Mrs. Bennett's legs were not burned from the knees down, not at all. You will learn from Dr. Kopsch why this is important. This fact was so significant that Dr. Kopsch concluded that Mrs. Bennett was murdered, that she did not die because of an accidental fall into the bathtub."

Otero did not want to get bogged down in forensic details. He wanted to keep things simple and emphasize that Casper Bennett had lied about several key details regarding his whereabouts on the night Florence died. He believed that once the lies were established, the jury would conclude that he lied for one reason: to cover up a murder. Otero continued.

"Mr. Bennett's own statements to the police will show his guilt. As I said, Mr. Bennett told the police that he left his house just before eight p.m. The first place he said he went was Don's Sohio. However, you will hear from others that Mr. Bennett was at the gas station around six thirty p.m. that night. Ed Warner, the gas station attendant, says that Mr. Bennett arrived there around six thirty because Warner's wife got there a few minutes later on her way to a funeral, and Warner's wife needed to be there by seven o'clock. Joe Mitock, our county auditor, saw Bennett there around six thirty. He was on his way to a bowling alley where his league started about then. Mr. Bennett told everyone he was there at eight p.m. That is absolutely contradicted by these witnesses. Mr. Bennett was there an hour and a half earlier than what he claims. No one will verify Mr. Bennett's time frame. No one.

"Mr. Bennett says that he got home a little before nine thirty, just a few minutes before he called for the rescue squad. However, a next-door neighbor, who was hanging a wreath on her door, saw him arrive home around nine p.m., almost half an hour sooner. This would have given Mr. Bennett plenty of time to drown his wife before phoning for help.

"Mr. Bennett's own statements will show that he is guilty. They are filled with inconsistencies and lies. That is really all you have to know. Mr. Bennett had the opportunity and the motive to kill his wife and he did.

"After you have heard all of the evidence, I am convinced that you will find that Casper Bennett was a cold, calculating murderer who killed his wife in order to get forty-four thousand dollars in insurance money. We will prove this to you beyond a reasonable doubt. Thank you."

As Otero walked back toward the trial table, Mikus nodded his head in approval. Bennett had sat stone-faced throughout Otero's remarks. Before he sat down, Otero looked into the gallery, which was filled mostly with women. Like Mikus, several were nodding in agreement with him.

Although his comments were brief, Otero felt that he had made a strong opening. Several jurors' faces registered surprise when he mentioned Casper Bennett's burns and Florence Bennett's unburned lower legs. Another man raised his eyebrows when Otero mentioned Bennett's extramarital affair. Although Otero knew it was only an opening statement, he believed that he had scored strong points for the prosecution.

Lon Adams rose slowly and stood in front of the jury. An attorney who for his entire career had tried cases with note cards, Adams held two typed pages in his hands and placed them on a small lectern. Miraldi was surprised to see that these were the two pages that he had handed to Adams yesterday afternoon.

Adams looked at the first page. He began with introductions and explanations, a good way to establish rapport and sincerity with the jury. Adams began:

"Your Honor, ladies and gentlemen of the jury, it is now the time for the defense to tell you what we believe the evidence will show. As Mr. Otero told you, he and Mr. Mikus are the attorneys representing the prosecution. Mr. Miraldi and I are the attorneys representing Casper Bennett. Mr. Miraldi should perhaps be making this opening statement. He is better acquainted with the facts of Mr. Bennett's life, since he has been Mr. Bennett's personal attorney for a number of years. These opening statements are not evidence. They are merely the claims of each side as to what they believe the evidence, which is to come, will show. The prosecutor charges that Casper Bennett deliberately, purposely, and with premeditation killed Florence Bennett.

"Mr. Bennett has at all times denied this. He denies that he had anything to do with his wife's death. We believe that the evidence will show:

"Florence and Casper Bennett married in 1940.

"After the marriage, both drank too much and too often.

"In 1946, Casper quit drinking and touched nothing until 1960.

"Florence was a periodic drinker—she would go a month or two without it, then go on a binge and drink and drink for days and weeks until she was sick in bed.

"Florence refused to have children because she was afraid of childbirth.

"As the years wore on, her drinking binges came more and more frequently.

"Sometime in 1958 or 1959, Casper got disgusted with everything and started to run around with a woman the prosecutor will doubtless bring in to testify.

"Florence's drinking got worse and worse, and in 1960, Casper started to drink again.

"From 1960 to 1963, Florence was several times hospitalized for extreme alcoholism and because of falls and injuries suffered while drunk.

"In September of 1963, Florence was in the hospital for alcoholism."

Because of the simplicity and brevity of his opening, Adams had the jury's attention. He was telling them a story about Casper and Florence Bennett, and they were drawn to it. Casper Bennett, who had sat impassively through the prosecution's opening statement, began to cry, and his face reddened. Miraldi could see that some of the opening statement was his draft, but Adams had altered it, deleting some things and adding others. Miraldi had to acknowledge that the changes were an improvement and Adams's delivery created a mesmerizing rhythm.

"Right after Florence came home from the hospital, Casper was hospitalized for three weeks because of gallbladder trouble.

"Since this gallbladder attack, Casper has not had a drink.

"Casper quit seeing his girlfriend in July of 1963 and from July to December, Casper and Florence got along better than at any time since their marriage."

With that recitation, Mikus looked at Otero and smiled broadly. He knew Florence's diary told a different story.

"Florence and Casper borrowed eight thousand dollars and used half of that amount to pay bills and planned to use the other four thousand dollars to start fresh again in Florida after Casper sold his interest in his bar.

"In November of 1963, Florence began to drink again.

"On Sunday, December fifteenth, she started on a drinking spree.

"Florence kept drinking all that week.

"On December nineteenth and twentieth, she was too sick to leave her bed."

Mikus again looked at Otero. Mikus would be calling a neighbor who had seen Florence outdoors in her winter coat during the afternoon of December 20.

"On December twentieth, Casper worked all day until five p.m. He came home about five to five thirty, got supper, gave Florence what attention he could, and left the house between six thirty and seven to do some errands. When he left, Florence was alive and in her bed."

Mikus again exchanged glances with Otero. Just as Mikus had suspected, the defense was aware of the time differences between the gas station witnesses and Bennett's previous statements. *Casper may have adjusted his times to fit with the gas station witnesses, but three times he's given a far different timeline. I will still make him look like a liar*, Mikus thought.

"He came home shortly after nine p.m. and found Florence apparently dead in the bathtub.

"He had nothing to do with her death and knows no more about how it happened than you or I.

"He has at all times denied any knowledge of her death, has voluntarily told the police all he knew about it, voluntarily appeared before the grand jury, and has never concealed anything.

"This whole case is based on supposition and guesses on the part of the police, the prosecutor, and the coroner. There is not one bit of real evidence to connect Casper with her death.

"In the end, Casper Bennett is the victim of an incomplete police investigation and is in this courtroom today only because the police felt the need to pin Florence's death on someone.

"Casper is innocent of these charges and will, I am sure, be acquitted when you have heard all of the evidence."

Adams finished, nodded to the jury and the judge, and sat down. Miraldi thought that Adams had told a story that captured the jurors' imagination. The story implied that Casper had married the wrong woman—a woman who drank, would not have children, and drove him into the arms of another woman. It was the old "blame the victim" strategy. Miraldi knew that this theme would resonate more strongly with the men, although women jurors were often harder on another woman than men. If any of the jurors had favored the prosecutor's position, Miraldi believed that they had evened the score. These jurors likely would take a wait-and-see attitude until they heard some evidence.

Mikus saw the swing in momentum and, although it was close to the four o'clock recess, asked to put on one witness, apparently to switch the direction of the tide. However, Judge Pincura was not willing to do that, unsure how long the witness would actually take.

Judge Pincura ended the day by excusing the jury. "Mr. Mikus, I think the jurors have had a long day. You can start with your first witness tomorrow at nine a.m. Jurors, remember the admonitions I gave you earlier. I will see you tomorrow. This court is recessed until then."

CHAPTER 15

April 2, 1964

"When are you going to present the evidence about the television show?" Inspector Mumford asked Mikus and Otero as the trio met in the prosecutor's office about an hour before the trial was to begin its fourth day. The three were reviewing the order of the prosecution's witnesses. Because Mumford was in charge of all the detectives in the Lorain police force, he would sit with the two prosecutors throughout the trial and coordinate the appearance of the investigating officers. He had also been involved in the investigation and eventually he would take the stand, presumably to clear up any gray areas.

Mikus glanced at Otero, who had a blank look on his face. "What exactly do you mean?" Otero asked Mumford.

"The TV show that was on a week before Bennett murdered his wife. You know, the one where the wife knocked her husband out in the bathtub and then turned on the hot water. Solomon and Springowski mentioned it in some of their reports. The medical examiner on that show said the scalding water affected the onset of rigor mortis and the calculations for the time of death," Mumford replied.

"Yeah, we know all about that show. What do you expect us to do with it?" Mikus asked.

"Get it into evidence for Christ's sake," Mumford said, his voice rising. "That's critically important. It's the clincher."

Otero rifled through the two-inch-thick police file and pulled out one of Springowski's reports that mentioned the television show. "Here it is," he said. Otero looked at Mikus, expecting him to tell Mumford why the prosecution would not even try to introduce this. There was an awkward silence.

"Is anybody going to tell me what's happening here?" Mumford asked.

Mikus cleared his throat. "We can't use it, Maurice. We can't prove that Bennett watched the show. If we can't demonstrate that, the information is irrelevant. It's as simple as that."

"What do you mean you have to prove he watched the show? Of course he watched the show. It was on a week before he killed his wife. Nobody's going to believe that was just a coincidence," Mumford said, his face reddening.

Now it was Mikus's turn to get angry. "Okay, Maurice, I want you to picture this. Bennett is on the stand and I'm cross-examining him. I ask him, 'Did you by chance happen to watch a television show on December 15, 1963, where a woman knocked her husband unconscious in the bathtub and then turned on the hot water?' What the hell do you think Bennett is going to say? 'Oh yeah, that's my favorite goddamned show. I never miss it.' You gotta be crazy if you think we can ever lay any type of foundation that will allow us to introduce that evidence."

"You don't have to prove that he watched the show. Just get someone from Channel Five to go over their programs for that evening. Get someone who watched the episode to tell the jury what it was about. Let the defense try to prove that Bennett didn't watch it. Just get it in," Mumford answered.

"There's another little problem here. It's called the hearsay rule of evidence," Otero chimed in. "You want someone who watched the show to tell the jury what the people said during the show. You can't do that. You can't have someone testify to what somebody else said. That's hearsay, plain and simple."

"You got to at least try," Mumford said, but he was no longer sounding insistent.

"Look, we ran this by Dr. Kopsch," Mikus said. "He said scalding water sped up the onset of rigor mortis. In the television show, the medical examiner said it retarded it."

"Pincura could even declare a mistrial if we tried to mention this TV show. We can't prove Bennett watched it, so it's speculative. It's also prejudicial as hell," Otero added. "Hey, we'd love to introduce the results of the lie detector tests too, but we can't. The law says the science is too unreliable to prove that a defendant is lying."

"It seems to me that the jury won't get to hear our best evidence," Mumford said.

Mikus was tired of Mumford's whining. "Hey, if you wanted to give us something good, your detectives should have found somebody that had actually heard Bennett claim that he was going to murder his wife. All we have is this rumor that he was drunk in a bar and claimed that he would kill her. He said that in front of a room full of people. How come your detectives couldn't find just one of them? Is that asking too much?"

"We tracked that rumor down to Chester Merves, Irene Miller's old boyfriend," Mumford shot back. "When we asked him for the details, he said Bennett was supposed to kill her before Christmas of 1962, not 1963. He said he never personally heard Bennett say that and he couldn't remember who told him that. He clammed up on us."

"Hey, we're all on the same side," Otero said, holding up his hands to signal that they needed to stop sniping at one another. "We've got a strong case. Sure, all of this other stuff would have been nice, but we don't have it. Let's focus on what we do have."

"We have a damn strong case," Mikus agreed. "Our coroner is sure that Florence Bennett did not die from an accidental fall. He says all of the facts scream homicide. If it is homicide, there is only one suspect—that bum of a husband whose hands were burned."

"By the time this case is over, we will have caught him in so many lies, nobody will believe anything he says," Otero added. "After Paul destroys Bennett's credibility, the conviction will follow."

"I'm not so sure about Dr. Kopsch," Mumford said. "He's always struck me as a little weird. You're basing your whole case on this guy's opinions. If the defense takes him down, you could lose."

Mikus made a fist with his right hand and pounded it into the palm of his left. "I've had many cases with Dr. Kopsch. He's smart. He's tough. He doesn't back down. He doesn't get rattled. Adams couldn't make any points against any of my doctors in the Woodards trial and he won't touch Kopsch in this case either."

"What makes you so sure that Adams will cross-examine him?" Mumford asked. "Miraldi is the personal injury lawyer. He questions doctors all the time in those cases. I worked with him for ten years when he was the city prosecutor. That guy comes prepared. My bet is that Miraldi will take on the coroner."

"It won't make any difference," Mikus replied.

****

At nine o'clock, the bailiff swore in the first witness, a young woman in her early twenties, short and pretty. This woman looked quickly at the judge, then the jury, and finally down at her feet. Her hands followed a pattern of clasping together, unclasping, rubbing against each other, and then clasping again.

Her name was Bonnie Brawn, and she worked as an operator for the Lorain Telephone Company. She said that at 9:34 p.m. on December 20, 1963, she was working at the switchboard when she received a call from an unidentified man.

"What did he say to you?" Mikus asked.

"He said something about an attempted suicide. He wanted the rescue squad sent to 1733 Long Avenue."

Miraldi looked at Adams in disbelief. Bennett had never claimed that his wife had committed suicide. Miraldi was convinced that this woman was letting her imagination fill in details that she had obviously forgotten.

"Can you describe the tone of his voice?" Mikus directed her.

"That was the strange thing," Miss Brawn stated as she kept her eyes fixed on her hands, now clasped in her lap. "He didn't sound nervous or excited about this at all. He sounded normal, real calm."

"No further questions," Mikus said. He smiled at Otero as he walked back to the prosecution's trial table. Then he looked over at the defense attorneys, hoping that they looked surprised.

If Lon Adams was surprised, he didn't show it. He slowly pulled himself out of his seat, stood, and nodded toward the witness.

"Good morning, Miss Brawn," he said. "How are you this morning?"

"Nervous," she replied. For the first time, she glanced at the jurors, some of whom smiled back at her.

"I'm interested, Miss Brawn, in how long you were on the phone with this unidentified caller."

"Not too long, I guess."

"Did he just say three or four sentences to you?" Adams asked gently.

"Yes. It was a very short conversation," Miss Brawn answered, her eyes darting to Mikus as if to say, *You didn't tell me that the other side was going to question me, too.*

"In fact, it was so short, you couldn't really say whether the caller was nervous or not, isn't that right?" Adams asked.

Miss Brawn looked again at Mikus, this time with a perturbed expression on her face. "No, I guess that's correct. It would be hard to say."

"Thank you, Miss Brawn. No further questions," Adams finished.

"Any redirect?" Judge Pincura asked.

"No, Your Honor. For our next witness, the prosecution calls Lucille Hawk," Mikus replied, his voice betraying a false jauntiness. Mikus refused to look at Miss Brawn as she passed him quickly on her way out of the courtroom.

Mikus elicited from Mrs. Hawk that she lived across the street from the Bennetts. To poke another hole in the defense's case, Mrs. Hawk was called to show that Florence Bennett had not been completely confined to her bed for the last two days of her life as claimed by Casper Bennett.

Mrs. Hawk told the jury that she had lived across the street from the Bennetts for the last four years and she would talk with Florence Bennett from time to time, usually about sewing and knitting. Mrs. Hawk was employed at Popa's Poultry, but she had the flu on December 20, 1963, and stayed home.

"Did you see Mrs. Bennett on December twentieth?" Mikus asked.

"Yes, I did," Mrs. Hawk said, looking directly at Mikus.

"Tell the jury about this," Mikus coaxed.

Mrs. Hawk turned in her seat and looked at the jury for the first time. "Well, I was looking out the window between eleven thirty and noon that morning when I saw Mrs. Bennett in the front of her house. She was wearing a coat but didn't have anything on her head. I opened the front door to call to her, but she was already walking along the side of the house, as if she was going to go in the house from the back."

"Did you talk to her?" Mikus asked.

"No, that was it. I didn't talk to her or see her anymore that day," Mrs. Hawk said.

"Your witness," Mikus said as he sat down.

Neither Miraldi nor Adams had talked to this witness and they looked at each other, trying to decide whether to even question her at all. They both knew that when cross-examining a witness, lawyers should not ask a question to which they did not know the answer. Miraldi shrugged his shoulders and stood up.

"Hello, Mrs. Hawk, how well did you know Mrs. Bennett?" Miraldi asked, believing this was a safe way to begin.

"Not really well, but we were friendly enough when we saw each other," Mrs. Hawk said.

"Did you know Mr. Bennett?" Miraldi followed up.

"Yes, a little bit. I talked to the missus more than I talked to him, but I knew who he was. We said hello to each other every now and then. He seemed friendly enough to me," she said. There was no animosity in her voice.

"Getting back to your seeing Mrs. Bennett, did you know that she had been sick that week? Did you know that?" Miraldi asked.

"No, I was not aware of that," Mrs. Hawk answered.

"Did you know that Mrs. Bennett drank a lot?" Miraldi asked, believing this was a fairly safe question.

"Yeah, it was something that everyone in the neighborhood knew about," Mrs. Hawk said.

"Yes, that is a hard thing to hide from the neighbors, isn't it?" Miraldi confirmed.

"Yes," said Mrs. Hawk. After a short pause, she added, "Drink or no drink, she was still a very pleasant woman to talk to."

"Did it look like Mrs. Bennett was carrying anything, maybe a bag of something under her coat?" Miraldi asked, trying to suggest that perhaps Mrs. Bennett was carrying a bottle of alcohol under her coat.

"I couldn't tell you that one way or another. I just caught a glimpse of her and before I could say hi to her, she was already on her way to the back door. I don't know where she had been," Mrs. Hawk said.

"And you don't know where Mrs. Bennett was coming from?" Miraldi confirmed.

"That's right. I don't know where she had been," the witness answered.

"As far as you know, she may have just walked out the front door, got some fresh air, and walked back into the house through the back door?" Miraldi asked.

"That's possible," she answered.

"Thank you, Mrs. Hawk. No more questions, Your Honor."

John Otero called the prosecution's third witness, Dan McNutt, the fireman who headed the emergency response to the house. McNutt was a handsome, dark-haired man in his late thirties who spoke with a friendly authority.

"Mr. Bennett was waiting for us at the curb when we arrived," McNutt began.

The prosecution wanted the jury to picture the death scene through the eyes of this fireman, who, unlike the police, had no vested interest in the outcome of the trial. He described Mrs. Bennett's partially clad body on the bed, blistered and reddened, with skin caught in her hair and on the bedding. In the bathroom, he saw gray water in the tub with Mrs. Bennett's skin floating on the surface. Later he treated Mr. Bennett for burns to his left palm and right little finger.

On cross-examination, Miraldi simply asked him to describe Bennett's demeanor at the scene. McNutt told the jury that Bennett was hysterical and claimed to have just recently come home.

The prosecution next called Patrolman Dan Turcus, who came to the scene on December 20 to photograph it. He identified the black and white photographs that included shots of the bathroom and bedroom. He had also photographed the deceased Mrs. Bennett. She was naked from the waist up, with her nightgown pulled up to her neck. From the waist down, a bedspread covered her spread legs.

Here they go, Adams thought. *They've got to shock the jury*. Miraldi and Adams knew why the prosecution was so keen on admitting these photographs. The prosecutors wanted to trigger an emotional response that would push the jury to conclude that this unnatural death was due to foul play.

"Your Honor, the prosecution moves that these photographs be admitted into evidence now. They may be graphic, but they are accurate representations of what the police found that evening. The jury needs to see them to understand exactly what happened to the victim," Mikus said.

Adams stood and asked to approach the bench. Out of earshot of the jury, he argued that the photographs were gruesome and that other witnesses would testify about Mrs. Bennett's burned body, including the coroner. He argued that whatever value they had was outweighed by the prejudice and shock that they conveyed. Adams knew that Judge Pincura had admitted grisly photographs in the Woodards murder trial just two months before, so he doubted that Pincura would exclude these photographs. Pincura admitted the photographs and Mikus handed them to the jurors.

The defense lawyers watched as the jurors passed them one at a time to each other. Some jurors flinched when they looked at the photographs. Some jurors studied them carefully, while others barely gave them a glance. By the time all of the photographs had been viewed, Judge Pincura recessed for lunch.

After the noontime recess, Patrolman George Metelsky, the first police officer to arrive at the scene, took the stand. Metelsky had testified at the preliminary hearing and his testimony at trial was no different. He described the same scene that McNutt had outlined earlier. He again noted that Bennett's shirt and pants were dry, something he found odd for someone who had supposedly just pulled his wife from the tub.

Mikus was convinced that Bennett had lied three times to Metelsky that night. The young patrolman told the jury that Bennett claimed that he left the house around eight p.m. and returned a few minutes before nine thirty. Mikus would show through other witnesses that Bennett had left before six thirty and returned home around nine. Metelsky testified that Bennett claimed that when he found his wife in the bathtub, her head was on the faucet side and her torso was slumped forward with her legs submerged in the hot water. Dr. Kopsch would tell the jury that the lower legs were not burned and could not possibly have been submerged.

The prosecution hoped that the next witness, Jane Poletylo, would establish one of Bennett's three lies. Mrs. Poletylo, a fifty-nine-year-old widow, lived next door to the Bennetts, having moved back to her old neighborhood seven years before. She strode into the courtroom wearing a housedress, looking as if she had just recently come from her kitchen. She glanced up at the judge and then she studied the jury, smiling nervously, like a schoolgirl about to recite a poem in front of the class.

Detective Kocak had first talked to Mrs. Poletylo the day after Florence's death. When her memory was the most vivid, Mrs. Poletylo estimated Bennett's return to his house at around nine fifteen p.m.

Different police officers had talked to her periodically since then. When questioning her, these officers did not show Mrs. Poletylo her original statement summary from December 21. By suggesting an earlier time to her, the officers gently guided her to "remember" Bennett returning closer to nine p.m. Although her original statement was consistent with Bennett's alibi, her current story was not. Mrs. Poletylo, an honest and trusting person, had no inkling that her memory had been manipulated by the police investigators. By the time Miraldi had questioned her a week before the trial, she estimated that Bennett returned home at nine p.m., a time that the police first planted, then reinforced, and finally anchored into her mind.

After asking some preliminary questions, Mikus asked, "What was it like living next door to the Bennetts?"

"Oh my, how do I say this? They argued a lot. He would come home late and she would have changed the locks on the doors so that he couldn't get in. She wouldn't give him a key, you know. He would be banging on the doors late at night and begging her to let him in. It happened so much—I hate to say this, but I could almost ignore it."

"Anything else you can remember about the two of them?" Mikus asked.

"Well, she would go on drinking binges where she would stay in the house for several weeks and nobody would see her," Mrs. Poletylo said.

"Okay, but that's not quite what I asked. Do you know how they got along together?" Mikus asked.

"Well, do you mean the divorces that she filed?" Mrs. Poletylo responded with a question.

"Yes, what do you know about that?" Mikus said, his voice impatient.

"She filed in 1960 and then they reconciled. He moved back and then things got bad again and she filed a couple of years later. He moved back this last summer, but she had not dismissed the second divorce action. She told me that she wanted to see how things were working out before she did that."

Mikus looked at the jury to make sure that they were paying attention. "So she kept the divorce action alive because she didn't trust her husband, is that right?"

"Oh, I don't want you to get the wrong idea," Mrs. Poletylo said. "They were getting along pretty good from what I could see. Just a few weeks before she died, Mr. Bennett bought her a new armchair for the house and she brought me over to look at it. She was just tickled pink by it. She was also excited because Mr. Bennett let her pick out the color for their new car."

Mikus pivoted abruptly away from the witness and stared out the window. He folded his arms to his chest before turning back to the witness. "Back to the divorce, why had Mrs. Bennett not dismissed it?"

"Like I said, she was seeing how things went," Mrs. Poletylo said. Mikus's face seemed to relax, but then Mrs. Poletylo added, "And I think things were going pretty good up to the point until, you know, she died." Mrs. Poletylo turned her hands palms up, shrugged her shoulders, and sighed.

"Turning your attention to December 20, 1963, were you home that night?" Mikus asked.

"Yes, I was. I was looking out the window and I said to myself—" Mrs. Poletylo began.

Judge Pincura abruptly interrupted the witness. "Never mind what you said to yourself, just tell the jury what you saw."

"Well, since there was nobody home, I said to myself . . ." Mrs. Poletylo continued, but the rest of her answer was drowned out by tittering and laughter from the courtroom spectators. Trying to conceal a smile, Judge Pincura looked away from the witness.

"Can you repeat your answer, Mrs. Poletylo? I am not sure that the jury heard what you just said," Mikus said. "What were you doing that evening and when?"

"Well, it was around nine p.m. and I wanted to hang my Christmas wreath on the front door before *The Price Is Right* came on the TV at nine thirty. As I'm hanging it, Mr. Bennett drives up and parks the car in the neighbor's driveway, as he always does, and he waves to me," Mrs. Poletylo said.

"I want you to tell the jury what time you saw Mr. Bennett come home that evening. This is important," he said.

"It was right around nine p.m., a few minutes either way," she responded.

"Are you sure of that?"

"Yes."

"No further questions."

Miraldi looked at the jury before approaching Mrs. Poletylo. *There's a carnival lurking within that woman*, he thought. *The jury likes her, but they're not going to set their watches by anything she says.*

"Hello, Mrs. Poletylo, we had a chance to talk with one another last week, isn't that right?" Miraldi asked.

"Yes, we did," she responded.

"So we are not strangers?" Miraldi asked.

"No, we are not," said Mrs. Poletylo.

"My understanding is that you were hurrying to put up your wreath before one of your favorite television shows started at nine thirty, is that correct?"

"Yes," she agreed.

"To put up that wreath, it wouldn't take more than five or ten minutes, is that right?" Miraldi probed.

"That's about right," Mrs. Poletylo answered.

"Thank you, Mrs. Poletylo. Those are all of the questions that I have for you," Miraldi finished.

"No redirect, Your Honor," Mikus told the judge.

The prosecution would now prove the second of Bennett's lies—that he left the house around seven forty-five to eight p.m. Mikus had two reliable witnesses to contradict this.

Joseph Mitock, the Lorain County auditor, took the stand next. A few years earlier, the popular Mitock had easily won the election for county auditor. Despite his expanding waistline, Mitock was still a good athlete, and he testified that he was on his way to the Saxon Club, where he bowled every Friday night.

"So tell us what you saw," Otero said.

"Well, I came over the Henderson Bridge and stopped at the light at Twenty-First and Elyria Avenue. Don's Sohio is just there to my right. I saw Casper Bennett standing in front of his car and he was talking to the attendant. Casper was smiling and seemed to be joking with the attendant. I would have waved to Casper because I know him fairly well, but he did not look in my direction."

"What time was this?" Otero asked.

"It had to be sometime between six thirty and seven because we always start at the Saxon Club at seven. I only go there on Fridays and it's always the same start time."

Miraldi and Adams saw no need to cross-examine Mitock. When Bennett took the stand, he would admit his mistake and testify that he left around six thirty p.m.

Otero called Ed Warner next. Warner worked full-time at the steel mill but also worked part-time at Don's Sohio and waited on Casper Bennett on December 20, sometime between six thirty and seven p.m.

"I am sure it was before seven p.m. because my wife was going to a funeral home and she needed to be there before seven p.m. She stopped at the station after Casper had already come and gone. I gave her one of the miniature bottles of whiskey that Bennett gave me," Warner testified.

Otero sat down and Miraldi began his cross-examination while still seated. "So tell me, how did it come to pass that Casper Bennett gave you two tiny bottles of whiskey?" Miraldi started out.

"You see, I'd heard that Bennett was giving out little bottles of whiskey as Christmas presents to customers at his bar, so I asked him about it. He had some in the backseat and he gave me two of them, one for me and one for my boss, Don Heizerling."

Miraldi rose slowly from his chair and asked, "Did you notice anything strange about Bennett's behavior?"

"No, he was just being a wise guy, you know, being funny like he always does. When he was handing me a five-dollar bill for his gas, he would put it close to my hand and then pull it away. He was saying stuff like, 'Now you see it, now you don't.'"

"Anything more?" Miraldi prodded. He had talked to Warner earlier and was not venturing into uncharted territory.

"Well, I do the same thing to him. We give out S & H Green Stamps at the station, so I start to put them in his hand, and then I pull them away real quick like. I do that a couple of times and we're laughing. You know, that kind of stuff," Warner said.

"Did you notice anything unusual about Casper Bennett's hands?" Miraldi asked.

"No, I didn't," Warner answered.

"Now, Mr. Warner . . ." Miraldi paused and then looked at the jurors and not at the witness. The jurors looked back at Miraldi expectantly. "Did you notice anything, anything at all, that would make you think this man had just murdered his wife or was planning to murder her later that evening?" Miraldi knew that this question would raise an objection, but the question would make his point.

"Objection, speculative and indefinite," Mikus roared.

"Sustained," Pincura responded quickly.

"No further questions," Miraldi said.

Prosecutor Mikus next called the clerk of courts who brought the Bennett divorce files with her, including the two divorce petitions. The first had been dismissed, but the prosecution believed that the second was still pending. However, when the prosecutor opened the file, he saw that Adams, on his own volition, had belatedly filed a dismissal entry on December 27, 1963, one week after Mrs. Bennett's death. Mikus's face turned red and he asked to approach the bench. It was near the afternoon recess and Judge Pincura excused the jury for a short break.

With the jury gone, the lawyers lost any pretense of civility toward one another.

"This dismissal on December 27, 1963," Mikus shouted, "Mr. Adams had absolutely no right to dismiss it."

"Wait a minute, wait a minute," Adams said. "My client was dead. My partner, Ed Connolly, was supposed to have dismissed it several months earlier—before she died—so we just did it then. Are you implying that we did something improper?"

"Improper!" Mikus screamed. "This was highly improper."

Miraldi jumped in. "Your Honor, we object to the introduction of these two petitions. Just because something is alleged in a petition does not make it true. These petitions are filled with legal jargon and they would just confuse the jury. A lot of that stuff has to be included in the petition in order to state a claim. We will stipulate that Mrs. Bennett commenced two divorce proceedings. That is all the jury needs to know. Everything else is highly prejudicial."

Otero entered the argument. "This is a public record and it is admissible. There is a specific exception to the hearsay rule that allows public records to be considered by a jury if they are relevant. These petitions are relevant because they show the ill will between Mr. and Mrs. Bennett. And this second case was still active and pending on the day Mrs. Bennett died."

After more argument, Judge Pincura ruled that he would admit the divorce petitions.

"Anything else, before I call the jury back in?" the judge asked.

"Yes, Your Honor. Our next witness will be Tom Clemento, the court reporter who transcribed Mr. Bennett's grand jury testimony. We will ask him to read the seventy-seven-page transcript to the jury at this time," Mikus said, his voice, loud and authoritative.

"Wait a minute," Adams yelled, his face now flushed. "In all my years of practice, I have never heard of grand jury testimony being read to the jury. The grand jury is a private and secret affair. None of the record is ever to be made public."

Otero then explained that an Ohio statute permitted the defendant's grand jury testimony to be admitted at trial when the defendant voluntarily appeared and waived his constitutional right to remain silent. Otero handed a copy of the statute to the judge. The judge passed the paper to Adams, who read it while Miraldi peered over Adams's shoulder.

"This statute has no application here," Adams told the judge. "Our client will take the stand at this trial. This statute applies only if the defendant is not going to testify at trial. The only way Casper Bennett's grand jury testimony can come into this case is if Bennett strays from it in his trial testimony. If he does, the prosecutor can then impeach Bennett with his prior inconsistent testimony from the grand jury. That's it."

For the next thirty minutes, the two sides wrangled about the admissibility of Bennett's grand jury testimony. Finally, the judge made his ruling. Although he had never before admitted grand jury testimony in a trial, he would do so in this case. Casper Bennett had waived his constitutional right against self-incrimination at the grand jury hearing and the statute allowed the prosecution to present that testimony to the trial jury.

Adams and Miraldi felt outmaneuvered. Although the defense attorneys had decided to let Bennett testify as part of his defense at trial, they still had the option to change their minds at any time. Now the defense had no choice. Bennett would have to take the stand in order to correct the inaccuracies in his grand jury testimony.

At 3:40, Tom Clemento began reading the grand jury transcript, which included John Otero's questions to Bennett and Bennett's responses. Clemento was a short man with a prominent Roman nose that was accentuated by his large, black-rimmed glasses. He spoke in a nasal, staccato voice. Although easy to understand, he did not read with expression, and if the testimony had not been so important, the jurors could easily have tuned him out. However, they did not.

After Otero asked Bennett about his activities, Bennett went on at length. Otero just let him talk. Clemento read:

"'I got home around five thirty p.m. I can't remember if she was upstairs or downstairs when I got home, but I believe upstairs, so I called to her and went up. She looked on the sick side, like she had been drinking and sleeping a little bit, and on previous days, Monday and Tuesday, she had her period and cramps in her stomach. I told her to come downstairs and I would fix her some supper . . .

"'As I came downstairs, I noticed something sticky on the kitchen floor, like she had spilled pop or some drink. I don't know. I had been gone since morning because I worked ten hours that day. She came down and sat with me and pulled out a cigarette. I told her I was going to the basement to get a mop and clean up the floor and was going to heat up some leftovers. I asked her if she wanted some and she said no, she just wanted another drink. So I fixed her a drink and she said she wanted to go back up to the bedroom, so I helped her up the stairs . . .

"'Later I heard her in the bed. You know, she didn't have the radio or a TV on so I went to the stairs and asked her what she wanted. She said she wanted another drink. I told her, "Florence, you just had a drink. Go back to bed." I told her I would bring her another drink after I finished my supper and she said okay. . . .

"'A little later she came back to the stairs and I told her to stay up there. I said to her, "Florence, you know I don't want you coming down the stairs. You have fallen three times already and I have had to take you to the hospital. And you yourself know that you got hurt and when I took you to the hospital the nurses and police asked you how it happened, whether I pushed you or not. And you told them just how it happened, that you had a blackout and fell." So I told her that I would be up just as soon as I put the dishes in the sink to soak . . .

"'I gave her the other drink . . . And after I tucked her in and gave her a Nytol, I told her I would be back soon to give her a bath. I left I think around twenty to eight . . .

"'So I looked at my gas tank and I see I'm almost out of gas, so I go to Don's Sohio, where I buy almost all of my gas. It's around five to eight . . .

"'Ed Warner says to me, "Are you giving out those miniature whiskey bottles to your customers for Christmas?" And I am, you know, it's better than giving away novelty items like pens or combs. So he wants one and I have some in the backseat. It is Malrose Whiskey . . .

"'I stopped by Kingsley's Cigar Store, where I always like to buy the latest editions of the *Chronicle* and the *Cleveland Press*. I had a hard time finding a place to park, but I finally park by the Yellow Cab office and walk over there. This woman waits on me. I don't remember her name, but she is Mr. Fisher's wife. . .

"'After that call to Irene Miller, I headed back up Broadway and turned west onto Fifteenth Street. As I neared Reid Avenue, I recognized the car in front of me. I think its license plate number was three thirty-four or something like that. It was an old friend of mine, Joe Wasilewski, who worked at Runyan's. Recognizing me and me recognizing him at the same time, he waved to me and I waved to him.

"'And what time was this, Mr. Bennett?'"

"'Well, I think it was around nine fifteen or so. I was going to drive by the bar to see how many cars were parked around it before I headed for home . . .

"'As I drive down Eighteenth Street and turn onto Long Avenue, I see a light on in the basement and I'm trying to figure out if Florence is down there, and then I remember that before I left, I put the pans to soak in the basement sink because we have a leak in the kitchen sink . . .'"

Judge Pincura looked at his watch and saw that it was almost four p.m. He looked at the attorneys sitting at the trial tables. Bennett sat at the table with his hands on his face and was crying. The judge interrupted Clemento: "How many more pages do you have to read?" he asked.

"Your Honor, I just finished reading page thirteen," Clemento responded.

"And there are what—seventy-seven pages?" the judge asked.

"That's right."

"Well, it's four o'clock. I am going to recess the trial until nine a.m. tomorrow morning. Jurors, remember the admonitions that I gave you yesterday. Do not talk to anyone about this case. Do not read any newspaper articles about it. Don't listen to the news on the radio. I want you here at eight forty-five and we will start at nine a.m. sharp. See you then."

CHAPTER 16

April 3, 1964

As the court reporter continued to read Casper Bennett's grand jury testimony, Lon Adams sat quietly, staring straight ahead and trying to keep a neutral expression. He was angry, not at the prosecutors, but at himself. In hindsight, he had made a huge blunder by allowing his client to testify in front of the grand jury. He had been deceiving himself when he thought Bennett could convince the grand jury not to indict him. At the close of yesterday's proceedings, Miraldi, who had the benefit of 20/20 hindsight, had implied the same thing. Why had Adams allowed Bennett to testify?

Three months ago, Bennett was eager to tell his story to the grand jury. In Adams's experience, only persons who knew themselves to be innocent were willing to go before the grand jury, alone and without the help of an attorney. Adams found Bennett's story compelling and credible, and he wrongly assumed that the grand jury would draw the same conclusion. *What was I thinking*? Adams kept saying to himself. Because of the coroner's opinions, Adams should have known that the grand jury was going to indict, regardless of what Bennett said. Otero and Mikus were pushing for an indictment and the grand jury was not going to overrule them.

And now Adams was listening to the court reporter, Tom Clemento, drone on and on.

"'I got home sometime around nine twenty to nine thirty. I opened the door and headed for the cellar. I opened the cellar door and I hollered, "Florence, are you there?" Then I realized that the light was on, that I had forgotten to turn it off when I took the mop water down . . . and hearing this water running, I stepped into the bathroom, and I see her sitting down with her head slumped and the water running, and I shouted, "Florence, what did you do?" I got panicky, and I don't know if I shut the water off or not, but my intentions were to get her out of that water. Her head was by the spigots and her legs were submerged, but I'm not sure if her head was under the water . . .

"'It was a pretty hard job and the water was real hot. It took me about eight minutes or so to get her out and then drag her to the bed.'"

The jury was listening to not only his client's rambling monologue about the events of December 20, but much more. Like a gossip columnist, Otero asked Bennett detailed questions about his relationship with Irene Miller and Bennett answered all of the questions, almost as if Bennett believed this was his penance to escape an indictment.

"Otero: 'Did you have a girlfriend by the name of Irene Miller?'"

"Bennett: 'Yes, she was my bar lady friend. We went out together for about four or five years, but we had broken things off in July and I went back to live with Florence.'"

"Otero: 'Well, during the time you were going out with your bar lady friend, did you take her on trips?'"

"Bennett: 'A couple. I took her to Las Vegas, where her nephew lives. He is a deputy sheriff out there. We were out there for about a week, went to shows and out to dinner. And I took her and her nephew out to California and Hawaii.'"

"Otero: 'Did you buy her things?'"

"Bennett: 'Well, yeah. There were things that she wanted and I bought her stuff like dresses, gloves, jewelry. I helped pay for a mink stole . . .'"

Miraldi, like Adams, was in agony as he listened to Tom Clemento read Bennett's testimony. Clemento was one of Miraldi's good friends, and although he had no choice in the matter, Clemento was reading testimony that was damaging Miraldi's defense. As if to buck himself up, Miraldi had a fleeting hope that he was overreacting. It was possible that Bennett's unflinching revelations about his "bar lady friend" showed that he was hiding nothing and, hence, credible. That thought lasted until he heard the next exchange between Otero and Bennett.

"Otero: 'And did you ever get violent with Mrs. Miller?'"

"Bennett: 'I don't know what you mean by that.'"

"Otero: 'Did you break down her door one time when she would not let you into her apartment?'"

"Bennett: 'Yes, but—'"

"Otero: 'Did she file a restraining order against you to keep you away from her?'"

"Bennett: 'Well, yes, but she dropped that. We had a good relationship for most of our time. We had a few bad times, but who doesn't?'"

"Otero: 'People file restraining orders because they fear for their safety. Right?'"

"Bennett: 'Irene never feared for her safety with me. I was just kind of being a nuisance. You can ask her.'"

Miraldi was ready to object. His client was not accused of committing any crimes against Irene Miller, and this part of the grand jury testimony was completely irrelevant and prejudicial. The jury would conclude that Bennett was a man who could use force against a woman, something Bennett could not deny because he had broken down Irene Miller's door.

The prosecution had never given the defense a copy of the transcript. Without a transcript, neither Adams nor Miraldi knew when something damaging was about to be read. They were helpless and unable to object to inadmissible testimony until after it was read. Finally, Clemento finished and the judge recessed the trial for the morning break.

Miraldi and Adams walked out of the courtroom together. "That was bad, wasn't it?" Miraldi said.

"Oh, you didn't enjoy that either?" Adams replied. "Let's face it, damaging testimony at the end of the trial is a hell of a lot worse than bad testimony at the very beginning. If we can keep everything else on track, the jury may forget all about this by the time they deliberate next week."

"I know. Every trial has its highs and lows; we just have to appear unfazed. We can't get too shook up or overconfident."

"I wouldn't worry about the overconfident part," Adams replied.

After the recess, the prosecution's next witness was attorney Joseph Zieba, the administrator of Florence Bennett's estate. As administrator, her life insurance policies were in his possession. A son of Polish immigrants, Zieba had been a sophomore at Ohio University when World War II began. He left school and enlisted in the army, where he was trained as a pilot and flew many missions. After the war, he'd finished college, graduated from law school, and returned to Lorain. He and Miraldi were good friends, and for the last two years, Zieba had been teaching Miraldi how to fly a single-engine airplane.

Zieba was slightly over six feet tall with dark black hair, and his formerly thin, athletic frame was thickening about the waist. He was a handsome man with an engaging smile. As he took the witness stand, Zieba gave Miraldi a quick grin.

Zieba produced eleven insurance policies, totaling $22,002. He confirmed that each policy had a double indemnity provision that would be triggered upon an accidental death. Zieba also had possession of $2,800 in cash that was found in a strongbox at the Bennett home. Otero sat down. The prosecution was methodically presenting the evidence it had promised.

On cross-examination, Zieba admitted that the couple also had nine other policies written on Casper Bennett's life totaling $22,002, in which Florence Bennett was the beneficiary. Zieba readily agreed that whenever the couple purchased life insurance, they purchased it together with almost the same amount for each other. The jury could see that the life insurance purchases were part of a reasonable financial plan and not something sinister. Don Miller, the *Chronicle* reporter, perked up when he heard that testimony. Up until then, he'd believed that the prosecution's case was moving forward without a hitch. In his notebook, he jotted, "The defense scores its first solid blow."

The rest of the morning's witnesses were rather dull. Zigmund Dombrowski, the funeral director, testified that Florence Bennett's lower legs were not burned. On cross-examination, Miraldi established that the body was not intact due to the autopsy. Dombrowski had the last word, however, telling the jury that the rest of the body looked like a "red lobster."

Frank Bailey, the secretary-treasurer of the First Federal Savings and Loan Association, produced two $4,000 loans that the Bennetts took out in 1963. One was to repair and remodel their home, while the other was for personal use. The prosecution hoped to show that Bennett was debt-ridden and needed the life insurance payouts to right his financial ship. Adams understood what the prosecution was doing, but he hoped that the jury would remember that Zieba had just testified that a "financially strapped" Bennett had $2,800 in cash in his strongbox. Would the jurors see the inconsistency?

After Judge Pincura recessed for lunch, Bennett whispered to Adams, "How do you think we're doing?" Like all clients, Bennett wanted to be reassured that his case was going well.

"It's going like we thought it would, Casper," Adams replied. "We've got a long way to go, so what the jury thinks right now is not that important."

"Oh, I know, Mr. Adams," Bennett said, "I just thought that maybe you saw something that I missed."

"This trial will go at least another ten days, so you just have to be patient. We're doing our best and I'm encouraged at this point," Adams said.

Miraldi approached Mikus to find out who was going to testify in the afternoon.

"Depends on who's available this afternoon," Mikus replied, even though he knew that he would have Detectives Kocak and Solomon testify next. He wanted these officers to start putting the pieces together for the jury.

"Come on, Paul, you have to know who you're calling this afternoon," Miraldi persisted.

"You'll find out soon enough," Mikus said as he walked away.

****

Wearing a new brown suit, Detective Michael Kocak sat up straight in the witness chair. Prosecutor Mikus had met with Kocak the evening before and hoped that parts of Kocak's testimony would surprise the defense.

Kocak testified that he was a fifteen-year veteran of the Lorain police force and had joined the LPD a few years after he was honorably discharged from the armed services. He became involved with the Bennett investigation the day after Florence Bennett's death. That weekend, he interviewed witnesses and talked with Bennett several times at the jail. Kocak related Bennett's story about his whereabouts that evening. It was no different than the versions Bennett had told everyone else.

"Did Casper Bennett tell you anything about his wife and water?" Mikus asked.

"Yeah. He said that his wife was afraid of water and normally took sponge baths," Kocak responded.

"Can you elaborate?" Mikus asked.

"Well, according to her husband, Mrs. Bennett would never take a bath in anything more than just a couple inches of water and often just dabbed herself with a washcloth—you know, what they call a sponge bath," Kocak explained.

Miraldi immediately whispered to his client, "Did you say that, Casper, or is he making this up?"

Bennett whispered back, "Yeah, it's true. That's what I told one of the cops. I know I told someone about that, but I don't remember which one."

Miraldi took a deep breath and let it out slowly. "Casper, you should have told us that," Miraldi whispered.

"I didn't think it was important," Bennett whispered back.

By now, Mikus was on to another point.

"Did Mr. Bennett have any explanation why his wife was taking a bath?" Mikus asked.

"He did say that she'd been sick for a couple of days and he was going to help with a bath when he got home. Mr. Bennett thought maybe she'd just decided to do it on her own."

"Let's talk about your search of the Bennett home. When did you last search it?"

"Well, we searched it about a week ago. Mr. Bennett and his two attorneys were there the day before and we could see that Mr. Adams was trying to get into a drawer in the television console, but they couldn't get it open. So Springowski and me went back the next day and jimmied open the drawer and we found private papers in the drawer."

"Did you find anything that helped with your investigation?"

"Yes, we found this diary of sorts. It had notations in it from July through December fifteenth of last year," Kocak responded.

"Tell the jury about the notations, please," Mikus continued.

"Mrs. Bennett was writing down when her husband was going out at night and what time he was coming back," Kocak said.

"Objection," Miraldi shouted. "There has been no evidence that the calendar was Mrs. Bennett's or that these notations are in her handwriting."

"Sustained," Judge Pincura ruled.

"We will set the foundation later," Mikus replied calmly. "When you went back into the house, did you determine how many telephones the Bennetts had in the house?" Mikus asked.

"They had two. One was on the main floor in the hallway and the second one was in the bedroom where the body was taken," Kocak said, looking at Mikus and then at Bennett.

"Did Mr. Bennett tell you which telephone he used to call the operator on December twentieth?" Mikus continued.

"Yes, he said that he called from the phone on the main floor, not the one next to his wife's body."

"Did he give you any explanation why he did that?" Mikus asked.

"No."

"Your witness," Mikus concluded.

Adams had not heard the whispered conversation between Miraldi and Bennett. Miraldi wanted to tell Adams that he would cross-examine Kocak, but Adams shot out of his chair. The usually calm Adams was upset, and as he stood in the center of the courtroom, he was waving his yellow legal pad at the witness.

Adams was sure that Kocak had made up the story about Mrs. Bennett's fear of water and Adams was determined to show the jury that it was a recent invention. Returning Kocak to his testimony at the preliminary hearing, Adams said, "Last January, you testified in court for over fifteen minutes and never once did you mention that Mrs. Bennett had a fear of water or that Mr. Bennett disclosed this to you. Right?"

"Well, I didn't mention it in the preliminary hearing because you never asked me specifically about it," Kocak said.

"The prosecutor asked you about your conversations with Mr. Bennett and you did not mention that," Adams bore in.

"Correct. I didn't think it was that important," Kocak countered.

"But between the preliminary hearing three months ago and your court appearance today, this fact went from being irrelevant to important. Is that what you are telling the jury?" Adams asked as he slammed his yellow legal pad against an open palm.

"I don't know how important it was back then or how important it is right now. I just am telling the jury everything about my dealings with Mr. Bennett and they can determine if that fact is important," Kocak said. There was some hesitation in his voice.

"You typed up a report about your interrogation of Mr. Bennett, right?"

"Yes."

"You never mentioned this in your written report?" Adams asked.

"I can't remember," Kocak said. He fidgeted and then glanced down at his lap where his reports rested on his left knee. "But there is no question in my mind he said that, whether I put it in my report or not."

Although Adams's cross-examination was fiery and his indignation was real, Miraldi knew that the jury would eventually believe Kocak when Bennett took the stand and admitted telling the police about Florence's fear of water. *If only we had been able to talk for a few minutes before this cross-examination, we could have taken a different approach*, Miraldi thought. He had never tried a case with another attorney before and he could see that the team approach could lead to some disjointed moments.

Miraldi believed that Bennett's admission about Florence's bathing habits demonstrated his truthfulness. Florence's fear of water suggested that she would not take a bath by herself and was, thus, inconsistent with what he claimed had happened. A man who had just drowned his wife would not volunteer this incriminating information. However, a man who felt guilty about leaving his sick wife alone would. While Bennett was sweeping the snow from his girlfriend's sidewalks, Florence ventured from her sickbed and fell into the tub. Bennett was telling Kocak just how out of character this was for Florence, and thus trying to excuse his own absence.

When Adams returned to the defense table, Miraldi nodded to Adams and said, "Good job, Lon." Adams's cross-examination might later be blunted by Bennett's own admission, but for now, the jury had just witnessed a testy cross-examination. Adams had been angry, indignant, and confident, and the jury could sense that.

After Mikus declined to ask any questions on redirect, Judge Pincura said, "It is now the time for a midafternoon recess. Mr. Mikus, who is your last witness before we recess for the weekend?"

"Your Honor, we will call Sergeant William Solomon and his testimony should take us to four p.m.," Mikus replied.

"I'll do the cross-examination on Solomon," Adams told Miraldi after the jury had been excused. "I've had pretty good success with him in the past. He likes to exaggerate and I can have some fun with him if I can get him to lose his temper."

"Well, I feel comfortable crossing Solomon. I know him pretty well. I don't think he'll pull any tricks on me," Miraldi said. As a former city prosecutor, Miraldi had worked with Solomon on a number of cases, and, as Adams had just mentioned, Solomon's strong opinions could cause him to overstate his findings and get him into trouble. Despite Solomon's strong personality, Miraldi still liked him and routinely hired him to do plumbing jobs around his house.

"I'd still like to question him," Adams said.

"That's fine," Miraldi responded, deferring to Adams's seniority.

****

Sergeant William Solomon's deep baritone voice was both loud and authoritative as he answered questions posed by Assistant Prosecutor John Otero. Both Miraldi and Adams expected that Solomon's testimony would be a repeat of Sergeant Kocak's and would simply reinforce prosecution points. This was indeed the case as Solomon went over his interrogation of Casper Bennett. Solomon then testified about going to Bennett's home, where he found the insurance policies and other documents in a strongbox.

Otero abruptly moved on to another subject. "Did you examine the bathtub where Mrs. Bennett was found?"

"Yes, I looked at it with Sergeant Springowski the day after Mrs. Bennett's death. That would have been Saturday the twenty-first of December," Solomon replied. "I think it was in the afternoon."

"What did you find?" Otero asked.

"It was an old-fashioned bathtub, you know, the ones with feet. It had a white porcelain handle for cold water and a silver handle for hot. The tub had a rubber plug on a chain that the Bennetts apparently used to close off the drain to fill it with water."

"Anything else?"

"Well, it had a bath mat in it. There was still some dried skin, hair, and other stuff in the tub. You could tell how high the water had been in the tub on the night Mrs. Bennett died because there was what I would call a scum line from its last use," Solomon added.

"Did you and Springowski turn on the water at any point?" Otero asked.

"Yes, we determined that the water must reach eleven inches before it goes into the overflow holes and out the tub," Solomon reported.

Miraldi was watching the jurors to see if they were showing any interest in what appeared to be rather dry and tedious testimony. Adams was doodling on his yellow pad.

"Could you tell if there was a mark where the dirty water reached a maximum height on the tub?" Otero went on.

"Yes, sir. It was seven inches from the bottom," Solomon replied.

Otero looked back at Mikus and smiled. Mikus stared back, his eyebrows raised, showing his impatience.

"Let's talk about the overflow system. Did you run any tests on it?" Otero asked.

Miraldi sprang to his feet. "Objection," he yelled. "Your Honor, can we approach the bench?"

Judge Pincura had been bored by Solomon's testimony, and his chin jerked upward as Miraldi rushed to the bench, followed closely by Adams. Otero and Mikus walked slowly toward the judge. Shaking their heads as they approached the bench, Mikus and Otero were signaling to the jury that Miraldi's interruption was unwarranted and launched only to keep important information from them.

"This is totally improper, Your Honor," Miraldi began. "The prosecution gave the defense absolutely no notice that the police were going to run any tests on this bathtub. They needed to notify us and let us be present. Otherwise, how do we know whether they are telling the jury what they actually found?" Although Miraldi was trying to whisper, his agitation made his voice loud and the jurors could hear every word.

"Keep your voice down, Miraldi," Mikus said as he squeezed his way between Miraldi and Adams and put his hands on the judge's bench. "We can run a hundred tests on this tub and we don't have to let the defense observe any of them. This police officer is testifying under oath and will tell the jury exactly what he found. If the defense has any questions about the tests, the defense should have run its own tests."

"We would have run our own tests if we had known you had done some yourself," Adams jumped in.

"Oh, so you are surprised by what the prosecution has done?' Mikus replied. "Come on, any defense attorney worth his salt would have considered this. You didn't run any tests because you were afraid of what you would've found."

"That's ridiculous, Paul," Adams responded. Miraldi walked briskly back to the defense table, rifled through a folder, and pulled out several pieces of paper.

"Judge, do you remember what happened when we tried to inspect the house a few weeks before trial?" Miraldi asked. "These prosecutors refused to let us enter. They claimed we had no right to 'snoop' around the place. We had to file a motion just to get a look. The prosecution opposed our motion and filed an opposing brief. In that brief, Prosecutor Mikus wrote, and I quote, 'There is no provision in the Ohio Revised Code or any judicial opinion that gives the defendant and/or his attorney the right to examine and inspect the premises,' end of quote," Miraldi said, jabbing his finger at the words on the paper. "So how were we going to run our own tests on the bathtub before trial?"

"As Mr. Miraldi knows, the judge granted the defendant's motion to enter the house to inspect every part of it," Mikus replied. "So nothing stopped my experienced opponents from testing the bathtub then. Mr. Miraldi and Mr. Adams were asleep at the wheel and it's not the court's job to pull them out of the ditch." Otero nodded vigorously as if to add an exclamation point to his boss's last statement.

"Hold on there," Miraldi answered. "If we ran tests at that time, the prosecutor and the police would have been there. Everybody would have had the right to see the results. So whatever is fair for us is fair for you," Miraldi said, looking directly at Mikus and challenging him.

"Would counsel all calm down?" Judge Pincura scolded. His voice was loud and everyone in the courtroom could hear him. "Both sides are making arguments that are without a context for me. I'm going to dismiss the jury for the weekend. I sense that this dispute is going to take a while to sort out and I want to conduct the discussion outside the presence of the jury."

After the jury left, Judge Pincura looked at Mikus. "Okay, tell me what tests were run and how they are relevant to this case. Maybe then I can rule on whether I'm going to let this testimony in."

Mikus told the judge about the tests that the detectives ran. They tested water temperatures, fill times, and the overflow system. He explained that the overflow system was corroded and leaked in two places. When water reached the overflow holes, the water leaked and formed puddles on the floor.

Adams cut Mikus off. "How do we know that the police didn't tamper with the overflow system in some way, either intentionally or accidentally when inspecting it?"

Before Mikus could respond, Miraldi interjected, "If you guys had nothing to hide, then why weren't we invited?"

"You and Adams weren't even Bennett's attorneys when these tests were run," Otero said. "The police looked at the tub the day after Mrs. Bennett died. Bennett hadn't even hired an attorney, so how could we invite you?"

"Then you should have done these tests in Casper Bennett's presence. You just can't trample on people's rights like this," Adams shot back.

"Trample on his rights? What the hell are you talking about?" Mikus said as he leaned his face just a few inches from Adams's.

"Counsel. I am not going to put up with this," the judge said as he struck his gavel on his bench. After everyone was quiet for a few moments, he continued. "Let me see if I understand what the prosecution is trying to establish," Judge Pincura said. "What you're saying is if the water reached the overflow system, there would have been puddles on the floor. And there were no puddles on the floor. Is that correct?"

"Absolutely," Mikus said, glad that the judge immediately grasped the import of the tests. "If Mrs. Bennett had been in the tub for more than ten minutes, there would have been puddles all over the floor, and there weren't."

"These tests are probably all wrong and they will take on tremendous significance with the jury," Miraldi pleaded. He instantly understood how damaging these results were.

"Mr. Miraldi, you will argue about anything. You remind me of the ancient Greeks who argued about how many angels could dance on the tip of a pin," Mikus said, confusing the ancient Greeks with medieval Christian scholars. He pulled out a handkerchief and blew his nose loudly. When he began talking again, he was shouting. "The jury deserves to hear about these critically important tests. If I have to, I will bring the bathtub into this courtroom and run the tests right here in front of everybody—the jury, the judge, and the defense attorneys."

Adams looked at Mikus in astonishment. "You can't be serious, Paul. Are you going to hook the tub up to the courthouse's pipes? That is absolutely crazy."

Judge Pincura squinted at the men below him. "Despite the objections of the defense attorneys, I am inclined to allow this testimony. Here is my reasoning. On cross-examination, the defense can bring out that it was not present when these tests were conducted. You can go into the qualifications and competence of the police officers conducting these tests. Mr. Adams and Mr. Miraldi, you are both experienced trial attorneys, and the law gives you the right to cross-examine this witness and bring out any shortcomings in these tests or how they were conducted."

"This is your ruling, then?" Miraldi asked, sounding like a child who had been denied outdoor playtime after a late dinner.

"This is my provisional ruling," Pincura answered. "The jury has been dismissed for the weekend. If you find any cases that say that the defense must be present when tests like this are conducted, then I will perhaps change my ruling on Monday. It just seems to me that the defense does not have to be present when the police conduct any tests on tangible evidence. You have no right to be present when ballistic tests are run on guns. You have no right to be present when blood samples are tested in the laboratory for identification. So I don't see why the law would say that you had a right to be present when the police inspected and tested the bathtub in this case. However, if you can find some cases that say otherwise, I will leave open my final decision until Monday morning."

Miraldi wanted to continue the argument—ballistic and blood tests were conducted by outside consultants, not by the police themselves—but he sensed that the judge had made up his mind. He would briefly do some legal research, but both he and Adams needed every spare minute this weekend to work on other things. Miraldi had to prepare for a cross-examination of Dr. Kopsch. He and Adams also needed to work with Bennett before he testified. They knew that Mikus's cross-examination of their client would be blistering. As they packed up their papers, both attorneys believed that Solomon would ultimately testify about his tests, regardless of how unscientific the method or tainted the results.

Bennett did not ask either of his attorneys how the trial was going. Outside the presence of the jury, his attorneys had let down their guard and looked dejected. Bennett nodded to his defense team as the deputies escorted him out of the courtroom.

CHAPTER 17

April 4, 1964

Lon Adams slumped in his chair after reading the afternoon's *Elyria Chronicle* newspaper. He knew that Miraldi was at his office preparing for the week ahead and he hated to distract his co-counsel, but today's article by Don Miller was so upsetting that Adams had to call.

Judge Pincura had instructed the jurors not to read any newspaper articles about the trial. However, a juror's family members were not so restricted. Despite the warnings, one of the eight jurors from Elyria could potentially read the *Chronicle* article or have its contents divulged to them by a family member.

Miraldi picked up on the fourth ring.

"I've done some research and I can't find anything that will help us on Pincura's ruling," Miraldi volunteered. Adams could feel the weariness in Miraldi's voice. The prosecutors had beaten them up all week and they needed something positive to bolster their spirits.

"Don't put any more time into it, Ray," Adams responded. "I can handle Solomon on cross-examination. He can say whatever he wants. I should be able to raise a question in the jurors' minds that the tests lack any objectivity. I'm calling because I wondered if you read today's *Chronicle*."

"No, why?" Miraldi asked. "I just get the *Journal* at home."

"Well, how do I put this? Don Miller didn't do us any favors. He wrote two articles. One just covered the events from Friday afternoon's session. That part's okay. He's pretty accurate about what the witnesses said. But the guy wrote a second article. Geez, how do I say this? The second piece could have been written by Mikus or Otero. It is so damn biased. Miller has already convicted our client after three days of testimony."

"How so?" Miraldi asked. His voice no longer sounded tired.

"I'm just going to read parts of it to you and you can go down to Kingsley's and pick up your own copy. Here's the headline: 'Defense Faced with Grim Struggle.' Then Miller begins, 'Not even halfway through their presentation and with no experts called as yet, the prosecution in the Casper Bennett murder trial has woven a strong web around the accused wife slayer. The defense faces a monumental task in its efforts to answer at least six major questions, all of which must be answered satisfactorily if Bennett's innocence is to be established.'"

"I can't believe that," Miraldi replied. "'Monumental task'—he used those words? And then he says we have to answer six questions to prove our client's innocence? How long has this guy been covering the courthouse? He knows damn well that it's up to the prosecutor to prove Casper's guilt beyond a reasonable doubt. We don't have to prove innocence. He's got to know that. He's made up his mind and he's trying to influence the jury."

"I know. So here are the six questions that Miller says we need to answer. One, could Mrs. Bennett's body have been in the position where Bennett claimed to have found it in the bathtub? Two, if his left hand repeatedly slipped into the scalding water as he tried to pull her from the tub, why were the burns only on the palm of the hand and not on the back? Three, how could Bennett leave home at seven forty p.m. and still have been at the service station at six thirty p.m.?" Adams read.

"We're going to deal with those things," Miraldi interrupted. "We know Bennett is all mixed up about the time he left his house. He'll straighten that out when he takes the stand. So we're fine there. As for the burns, Bennett will show how he reached over Florence's chest to seize her under her armpits. The water was at her armpit level. It would not burn the top of his hands. We can handle those things," Miraldi said, trying to reassure himself. "Okay, what else?"

Adams cleared his throat. "Four, how could he arrive home at nine thirty p.m. to discover his wife dead when a neighbor saw him at nine p.m.?"

"Because that neighbor is about as goofy as they get," Miraldi interrupted.

"Five, with a telephone on the nightstand, inches away from his wife's body, why did he go downstairs to telephone for assistance?"

"Because you don't think straight when you find your wife dead in the bathtub," Miraldi shot back.

"Six, in removing his wife from the bathtub, dragging her to the bedroom, and placing her on the bed, how did he avoid getting water or stains on a white shirt he wore? Those are the questions," Adams finished.

"For that last question, well, it had to be thirty minutes or more by the time Metelsky got to the scene. How long does it take for a wet spot to dry on a shirt when you're wearing it? Ten minutes." Adams could hear Miraldi breathing hard on the other end of the line.

"It only gets worse," Adams answered.

"How's that possible?" Miraldi asked.

"He then goes point by point and summarizes the testimony and evidence on each of the six questions. For example, for the first question, he says that Mrs. Bennett's body was not burned below the knees, yet our client said that her legs were submerged in the scalding water. Miller is saying that is impossible."

"Oh, great," Miraldi moaned.

"For the second question, Miller says that Bennett testified that his left hand slipped into the water repeatedly as he tried to remove the body, yet only the palm of his left hand and the little finger of his right hand were burned. Again, he implies that this is impossible," Adams said.

"Bennett said that he kept losing his grip on his wife. He was grabbing her from the front. His hands were not diving under the water. Miller has misstated Bennett's story," Miraldi said. Adams could hear a loud thump on Miraldi's side of the phone.

"What was that?" Adams asked.

"I just slammed my hand down on my desk," Miraldi replied. "You don't have to read any more of it to me. I get the idea."

"Well, I won't read any more about the testimony, but I will read you the end of the article. He writes, 'The verbal picture painted so far adds up to a woman flat on her back in a bathtub of scalding water, a hand holding her down, while her feet flailed about the ledge and the tub rim at its foot.'"

Miraldi let out a loud sigh.

"I'm not finished," Adams said, and quoted the article again. "'Lon B. Adams, Ray Miraldi, and Casper Bennett face the grim task of answering those damaging questions on time, position, and burns. They face the task of repainting that verbal picture created by the prosecution. On how well they do this, depends the life of a man.'"

"You know, he's right about that last part," Miraldi said, his voice quiet and resigned. "The jury will be asking us to answer some of those questions. I just hope that they're still listening and haven't made up their minds like the reporter."

"Me too," Adams replied. "Hey, we have some things to say before this is all over. Ray, you need to take a break from the work. It doesn't do you any good to get exhausted over the weekend. We both need to be fresh on Monday."

"Okay, I'll leave in about an hour. I'm not sure I want to pick up that newspaper though," Miraldi said.

"No need. I gave you the gist of it. Let's just use it to motivate ourselves."

"I will. See you tomorrow at the jail. We'll talk to Casper one last time. Get him ready for his testimony later in the week. Good-bye," Miraldi said.

CHAPTER 18

April 6, 1964

Judge Pincura looked at the defense counsel before he brought the jury into the courtroom. "Anything for me to review?" he asked.

"No, Your Honor. We still believe that Sergeant Solomon should be barred from discussing any testing because neither the defendant nor his attorneys were present when the tests were conducted," Miraldi responded.

"Overruled. Before we start, one of our jurors, Mrs. Virginia Meschke, collapsed at her doctor's office this morning. We have a note from Dr. Hoke that says that she has heart problems and I am going to excuse her. She will be replaced by our first alternate, Walter Corn of Lorain. Any objections to that, counselors?"

No one objected. With one less woman, the jury was now composed of ten men and two women, a breakdown that probably favored Bennett. About 80 percent of the courtroom spectators were women, many of whom had been attending every day wearing stern and unhappy expressions.

Sergeant Solomon quickly stepped back into the witness chair. Otero began, "Sergeant Solomon, before we recessed for the weekend, I asked you to describe tests that you ran on the Bennett bathtub. Will you please describe the first test?"

Solomon told the jury how he and Springowski held a rubber bath mat in the middle of the tub to simulate Florence Bennett's body. With the hot tap fully opened, they ran the water for several minutes until it reached its maximum temperature. After that, they plugged the drain and waited until the water was about seven inches high, a point equal to the scum line. Solomon then measured the temperature of the water with a plumber's thermometer.

"Near the spigot, the water was one hundred and fifty-eight degrees, and at the center of the tub, the water was one hundred and forty degrees," Solomon reported. What Solomon failed to say was that just six inches from the far end of the tub, the point farthest from the spigot, the temperature was only 120 degrees. The defense and the jury would never know that there was a difference of 40 degrees between the two ends.

As part of his investigation, Solomon researched the effect of scalding water upon human skin. He learned little from the manufacturer's instructions and warnings that came with hot water heaters other than the ideal temperature for bathwater was 100 degrees. Because he was still curious, he went to the public library, and with the aid of a reference librarian, he found a magazine article that cited two studies on the subject. From the article, he learned that when water reached 155 degrees, a person received a third-degree burn in one second. At 140 degrees, third-degree burns occurred after five seconds. At 120 degrees, third-degree burns developed after a five-minute exposure. At 110 degrees, burns normally did not occur.

At first, the information made Solomon uneasy because it explained how Mrs. Bennett's lower legs could have been submerged in the water, yet remained unburned. If Florence Bennett had turned on some cold water with the hot, the water coming out of the tub's spigot could have been 140 degrees or less. If so, the water at the far end of the tub would have been 40 degrees cooler, a harmless 100 degrees. Because he was convinced that Bennett was a murderer, he kept this information to himself, not even mentioning it to Springowski.

Otero next launched into the tub's capacity. "Did you test the bathtub to determine how much water was required to reach the scum line and then the overflow system?"

"Well, it would take twenty-five gallons to reach the seven-inch scum line and forty gallons to reach the overflow holes," Solomon replied. Solomon failed to consider that Mrs. Bennett's body would have occupied space in the tub and affected that measurement.

"How long would it take to reach those levels?" Otero asked. Neither defense attorney objected despite the prosecution's failure to establish the flow rate at the time that Florence Bennett died.

"Well, we ran the test two different ways. With just hot water on, it took eighteen minutes to reach the scum line. And if we added cold water to the mix and increased the flow, it only took twelve minutes," Solomon said.

"How much time would it take to reach the overflow system?"

"The overflow system is four inches above that scum line and it takes another fifteen gallons to reach that. We're talking about another four or five minutes," Solomon replied.

"Did you test the overflow system?" Otero asked.

"Yes, we did."

"How did you do this?"

"We simply let the water reach the overflow holes and watched what happened," Solomon replied.

"And what happened?"

"The water spilled out at two places where the tub was corroded. One was in the tub itself, while the second was in the overflow pipe that led to the drain."

"How much water leaked out?"

"In one minute, we saw a puddle of about four inches by the overflow drain," Solomon said, looking at the jury and then glancing at the defense table.

"What was the significance of the leak?" Otero asked.

"On the night Mrs. Bennett died, the bathwater never reached the overflow holes because none of the investigating officers or the coroner saw water on the bathroom floor."

"Well, what does that mean?" Otero continued.

"It means if Mrs. Bennett had turned on the water for her bath and fallen in, she did so just a few minutes before Mr. Bennett came home, because the water never got high enough to empty into the overflow system."

Otero stopped his questions for a moment to allow Solomon's testimony to register with the jury. The courtroom spectators seemed to understand its significance and many whispered to their neighbors, making sure that they realized its import too.

"In your testing, did you put any tool into the corroded areas?" Otero began again.

"Absolutely not," Solomon said, keeping his eyes fixed on Otero and not the jury.

"Have you seen anyone tampering in any way with the corroded part of the overflow system that you just mentioned?" Otero said, looking at Miraldi.

"Yes, I did. When we went to the house for the inspection about a week before trial, I saw Mr. Miraldi squatting and getting real close to the overflow pipe. I'm not saying that Mr. Miraldi tampered with it, but his hands were really close to it."

Miraldi and Adams looked at each other in disbelief, and then they both glared at Solomon. Despite having no question before him, Solomon blurted out, "When I saw Miraldi so close to that pipe, I said, 'Oh no,' to myself, and I started that way to make sure nothing happened."

Attempting to defuse an angry outburst from the defense counsel, Judge Pincura interrupted the witness. "I don't think Mr. Miraldi is on trial here."

Otero finished with the witness and Adams took his place.

"So did you ever see Mr. Miraldi's hands on the overflow pipe?" Adams asked, his finger pointing at Solomon.

"No, I didn't," said Solomon.

"Would you explain to the jury why you thought this was important to bring up now?" Adams asked. Judge Pincura could see that his attempt to bring calm to the proceedings was not successful.

"I was just answering the question," Solomon responded.

"Mr. Miraldi had my lighter in his hand and was looking closely at the pipe, wasn't he?"

"I don't remember any lighter."

"Tell me how Mr. Miraldi's viewing of the pipe last week had any effect on your tests done more than three months ago," Adams said.

"You've made your point, counselor," Judge Pincura interrupted. "Let's move on to another topic."

Adams was not finished.

"So you thought to deflect attention from your own actions in handling the pipe, you should try to implicate my co-counsel as someone who damaged it?" Adams asked.

"I said that was enough on that topic, Mr. Adams," Judge Pincura snapped.

"Yes, Your Honor," Adams said, bowing his head slightly at the judge.

Adams finished his cross-examination by establishing that the defense was not present when these tests were made and that the police did not use a neutral person to conduct the tests.

Sergeant Charles Springowski followed Solomon to the witness stand. The gray-haired sergeant looked distinguished in his navy blue suit, white shirt, and red tie. Springowski was the fourth police officer to testify and he followed the same script as the prior three.

"Bennett said he went out for errands around a quarter to eight and that he got home around nine p.m.," Springowski said.

"Are you sure that Casper Bennett told you that he got home at nine p.m. that evening?" Otero asked.

"See, that's just the thing. The first time I talked to him, Bennett said he got home around nine p.m. I know that he now says it was closer to nine thirty, but he told me nine o'clock when I talked to him that night."

"Is that significant?" Otero asked.

"Bennett's call to the switchboard came around nine thirty-four p.m., so this would mean he was home for about a half hour before he called the rescue squad," Springowski replied. "So the question is, what did he do for a half hour?"

"Objection. We ask that the witness's last comment be stricken," Adams said.

"Overruled. That statement is fair comment," Judge Pincura responded.

"What else did Bennett tell you that evening?"

"Like I said, he kept saying, 'I came home around nine o'clock and I can prove it.' He also kept repeating, 'I didn't do it. I didn't do it. I just got home and this is how I found her.'"

"Thank you, Sergeant Springowski," Otero said and sat down.

"So let me get this straight," Miraldi said as he got up from his chair and approached the witness. "You say Bennett told you he got home around nine o'clock. This is not what you said at the preliminary hearing, is it? This is not what Bennett told the grand jury, is it? He told them he got home closer to nine thirty, didn't he?"

"Is that one question or five?" Springowski countered. "Now, Mr. Miraldi, I think you're trying to confuse me, but I don't think you're going to succeed." Some courtroom spectators chuckled.

"Okay. Let me make it one question then," Miraldi said as he walked over to the defense table and picked up a copy of Casper Bennett's signed statement, prepared on December 22, 1963, at the police station. Holding the statement in his hand for a long moment, he eventually walked over to the witness stand and handed it to Springowski. "Do you know what this is?"

Springowski pulled out his bifocals, positioned them on his nose, and began reading the document as if he had never seen it before.

"Well, have you read it?" Miraldi asked.

"I believe I have," Springowski replied, setting the three-page document far away from him.

"So, what is it?" Miraldi continued.

"It's Bennett's statement that we typed up for him and he signed," Springowski admitted.

"Were you there when Bennett signed this? Strike that. I only want to ask you one question at a time. I don't want you to claim that I am confusing you. Did you help prepare this statement? I mean, my client didn't have a typewriter in his jail cell, did he?" Miraldi asked.

"No. Kocak and I talked to Bennett several times and wrote down his statement on paper and then we got one of the girls to type it up for us," Springowski explained. "We then gave it to Casper, I mean Mr. Bennett, to review it, make any changes if he wanted to, and then he signed it."

"Let's read together what Mr. Bennett said when asked what time he got home, okay?" Not getting a response from the witness, Miraldi pressed, "Would you please pick up the document and turn to the bottom of page one?"

Springowski grabbed the statement and readjusted his glasses. "Okay, I'm ready."

Miraldi read aloud: "Question: 'Did you go home after this?'"

"Answer: 'Yes, I don't know the exact time, but it was probably about ten minutes before the rescue squad came down. I used up time in pulling my wife out of the tub and trying to blow air in her mouth with my mouth.'"

"Have I read that correctly?" Miraldi finished.

"You did a good job, Mr. Miraldi," Springowski said, trying to inject some humor.

"Thank you. On December twenty-second, the date this statement was signed, Casper Bennett did not know exactly what time he got home, but estimated about ten minutes before the rescue squad arrived, is that correct?" Miraldi summarized.

"Yes, I think you have read that correctly," Springowski said.

"So if Casper called for help at nine thirty-four and we use that as an anchor, then Casper got home probably ten or so minutes before then, maybe nine twenty-five, nine twenty, something like that. He is only approximating, right?"

"He told me nine o'clock when I first talked to him that night and he changed the time later," Springowski countered.

"Wait a minute here. Do you have any written or recorded statement where Casper said he got home at nine p.m.?"

"No I don't," Springowski said.

"The only real statement, the only official statement by Casper, is that he got home about ten minutes before the rescue squad arrived, correct?"

"Well, if you put it that way, yes," Springowski conceded.

"Let's move on to another topic. Did Casper Bennett ever refuse to answer any of your questions?" Miraldi asked.

"Let me think. I guess not. I can't remember. You know, he might have refused some," Springowski equivocated.

"If he refused to answer a question, then you would have put that in one of your reports, wouldn't you?"

"I don't know."

"Well, you put important facts in your reports, right?"

"Yes."

"And if a prime suspect refuses to answer a question, then that would be important? It would go in a report?"

"Probably."

"So I ask you again, did Casper Bennett ever refuse to answer any of your questions?"

"I guess not."

"Thank you. How about your fellow officers? Did Casper ever refuse to answer their questions?"

"I can't speak for them."

"Wait a minute. All of the officers write up reports and share them with one another. That's how you stay current in an investigation. You have reviewed all your fellow officers' reports in this case, right?"

"I think so."

"Did any of them mention that Casper failed to answer a question?" Miraldi asked.

"I can't think of any that said that."

"So your answer is no, there are no questions that Casper refused to answer, either to you personally or to another officer? Do you agree with that statement?"

"I agree based on my memory right now," Springowski said.

"Well, that's true of any person on the stand. All witnesses are testifying based on their current memories, aren't they?" Miraldi asked.

"Yes," Springowski answered.

"And Casper Bennett never asked for an attorney while you were questioning him, did he?"

"No, he didn't." Springowski did not hedge here because if Bennett had asked for an attorney and been refused, the police interrogation could be questioned.

"He cooperated with you fully during your investigation, didn't he?" Miraldi asked.

"Let's just say that he gave answers to our questions and leave it at that."

"That's cooperation, isn't it?"

"That depends."

"Now, wait a minute, you have suspects that you bring in for questioning and they refuse to answer any questions—nothing at all, correct?"

"Yes, that happens," Springowski agreed.

"But that never happened with Casper Bennett?"

"No, that never happened."

"And he was questioned by you, by Kocak, by Solomon, by Metelsky, by Inspector Mumford—that's five police officers? Did I leave anyone out?"

"Those are the ones who questioned him. Yes."

"And he answered all of their questions to the best of your information?"

"Yes."

"Throughout these grueling interrogations over several days, Casper Bennett consistently told you and your fellow officers that he had nothing to do with his wife's death, am I right about that?"

"That's not unusual, for a suspect to say he's innocent."

"Please answer my question. Did Casper Bennett always tell the officers that he knew nothing about his wife's death and that he had nothing to do with it?"

"Yes."

"You've known Casper Bennett since he was a boy, haven't you?"

"Yes."

"You knew that he has had serious marital problems in the past?"

"Yes."

"You knew Casper Bennett had a girlfriend, didn't you?"

"Yes."

"You knew Florence Bennett had filed for a divorce from Casper Bennett before you ever arrived at their house on December 20, 1963?"

"Yes, I knew that."

"So, with that background information about Casper and Florence Bennett, you just naturally concluded that Casper and Florence had a stormy relationship, and if she died under unusual circumstances, she died at the hands of her husband?" Miraldi continued.

"I wouldn't say that. We follow the evidence. We don't jump to conclusions without evidence, Mr. Miraldi," Springowski said calmly.

"You arrested Casper Bennett on suspicion of murder several hours after his wife's death. Are you telling this jury that you hadn't already made up your mind that Casper Bennett had murdered his wife as soon as you got to the Bennett home on Long Avenue and saw her dead body?"

"I went into this investigation with an open mind."

"In your 'open-minded investigation,' did you determine that Florence Bennett was an alcoholic? Strike that. Did you know that Mrs. Bennett was an alcoholic before you arrived at the Bennett home on December twentieth?"

"I might have known that about her, but I'm not sure. Now, for Casper, I did know that Mr. Bennett had a big drinking problem."

"Did you smell any alcohol on Mr. Bennett's breath when you got to the Bennett home that night?"

"No."

"Did you notice anything about Casper Bennett that suggested that he was drunk or had been drinking?"

"No, but he was pretty hysterical when I was there."

"Well, you would expect that of someone who had found his wife dead in the bathtub, would you not?"

"Yes."

"But he did not slur his speech or walk unsteadily, right?"

"That is correct."

"Did you learn in your 'open-minded investigation' that Mrs. Bennett had fallen several times in the house? In fact, one time she was hurt so badly from a fall that she was hospitalized for it. Did you know that before you charged Casper Bennett with her murder?"

"I don't remember when we learned of her falls. I'm sure that you'll tell the jury about her medical issues as part of your defense, Mr. Miraldi."

"Let's just stick to answering my questions and not volunteer your thoughts about our defense. Okay?"

"Okay."

"So you don't remember if you were aware of Mrs. Bennett's history of drunken falls before charging her husband with her murder?"

"No, I don't remember."

"And, of course, you investigated this case thoroughly before you charged Casper Bennett with first-degree murder?"

"Yes, we did."

"Even though you hadn't gathered any information about Mrs. Bennett's serious falls or chronic alcoholism? Is that right?"

"I don't remember."

"Thank you. That's enough with this witness, Your Honor." And with that, Miraldi sat down.

After lunch, the prosecution called five witnesses, none of whom were questioned extensively. Detective Roy Briggs testified that he took the calendar/diary along with the Bennetts' mortgage documents to Joseph Tholl, a handwriting expert. Sergeant Joseph Trifiletti reported that, after the autopsy, he delivered Mrs. Bennett's vital organs to Dr. Sunshine, a toxicologist. Both witnesses were providing rather technical but necessary testimony. Evidentiary rules required the prosecutor to show the chain of custody of tangible evidence.

Mary Mitchell, the next witness, rented the home directly behind the Bennetts' house. She and another woman had helped care for Florence Bennett after Florence's fall in the house in September of 1963. The police had questioned her the day after Florence's death, but she had not seen either of the Bennetts that day or heard anything unusual at the Bennett home that evening.

Sergeant Springowski and Inspector Mumford had met with Mrs. Mitchell just the day before to help prepare her for her testimony. During previous meetings, she'd been a reluctant witness who grudgingly provided information. But on this Sunday, Mary Mitchell had been a different person, much more talkative and professing to be Florence Bennett's confidant.

Mary Mitchell's dislike for Casper Bennett had been obvious at yesterday's meeting. As the officers listened, Mitchell dropped a bombshell.

"Florence told me that Casper beat her often," Mary Mitchell said. "Mind you, I never saw him strike her and I never saw her bruised or anything like that, but that's what she told me on several occasions."

Springowski thought this testimony would be one more nail in Bennett's coffin, but Mumford feared it was hearsay and therefore inadmissible. He thought that unless Mitchell actually saw evidence of a beating, she could not testify about what Florence told her. After conferring with the prosecutor, the two learned that Mumford was right.

Mary Mitchell walked slowly to the witness stand. She stared straight ahead at Prosecutor Mikus and would not look at either Casper Bennett or the jury. After establishing who she was, Mikus got to the heart of her testimony.

"Did you ever help to take care of Mrs. Bennett?" Mikus asked.

"Yes, I did," she replied, her voice shaking slightly.

"How so?"

Mary Mitchell took a deep breath. "You know, Florence fell down the stairs in September and went to the hospital. Casper said that she had been drinking, but I don't know. I went over there to keep an eye on her and do a little straightening. Now, Florence was a good and neat housekeeper when she was not drinking. I visited with her often."

Mikus nudged the witness. "Other than help with housework, did you do anything else for Mrs. Bennett?"

Mary Mitchell did not answer immediately as she thought. "Oh yes," she finally said, "I gave Florence Bennett a bath several times after she came home from the hospital."

"Tell the jury about this," Mikus urged.

"She was really afraid of water. I put only three inches in the tub and she came into the bathroom and said, 'Oh, Mary, that's too much.' So I let some water out before she would climb into the tub. She was so scared of water, I couldn't believe it. I let some water out and she eventually got into the tub."

"Did Florence use bubble bath in the water?" Mikus asked.

"No, she didn't use bubble bath, but there was a glass bottle of it near the tub. She told me Casper used it because he liked to smell nice."

Miraldi began to rise to object to the hearsay but stayed seated.

"No further questions," Mikus said.

Mary Mitchell looked confused as Mikus sat down. She had much more to say to the jury, but the prosecutor had not asked her about it. Would she get the opportunity to tell the jury about the beatings?

Miraldi stood up and smiled at Mary Mitchell. "Hello, Mrs. Mitchell. How long have you lived in the rental property?"

"Almost three years."

"You told the prosecutor that you gave Florence Bennett several baths and she did not want to step into the tub when it had three inches of water in it. Did I state your testimony accurately?"

"Yes, that's right."

"But Florence Bennett did take a bath in the bathtub, didn't she?"

"Yes."

"She would actually get into the tub for you, right?"

"Yes."

"And you have no information that Florence Bennett was afraid to turn on the water for the bathtub, do you?"

The witness was silent for a few seconds while she searched her memory. "I never heard her say that," she said quietly.

"You never heard her say that she was afraid to turn on the bathwater, is that what you said?"

"Yes."

"Did Florence Bennett drink alcohol to excess?" Miraldi asked.

"Yes, she had periods where she would go on a drinking binge, but she also had periods when she did not. The same was also true about Casper Bennett. He drank a lot too." Mrs. Miller's voice had some anger in it, but Miraldi missed it.

Miraldi continued, "When she did drink, what happened?"

"Well, I just didn't see her. She didn't come out of the house. She just locked the doors and basically stayed inside."

"You came over to the Bennett house several times after Florence fell, didn't you? I mean, you were aware that Mrs. Bennett fell several times last year, right?"

"Yes, I was aware of several falls."

"These happened after Mrs. Bennett had been drinking?"

"Yes, she had been drinking, but it was her husband who fed her the liquor." For the first time, Mary Mitchell turned toward Casper Bennett and glared. "She was a nice girl, a very nice girl, a good housekeeper. He didn't have to buy her the booze, but he did," Mary Mitchell snapped.

Miraldi had missed the warning signs of a hostile witness. He wanted to end the examination right there, but not while the witness had the upper hand. Ignoring her last comment, Miraldi asked, "And you would be the first one to come over after she had a fall, is that right?"

"Yes. Casper would always call me first after she fell and I would get over there right away. I would drop whatever I was doing and help them. I have never understood why in the world Casper didn't call me immediately after he found Florence in the bathtub. I will never ever understand that." She looked at Bennett again, but this time her look was one of distrust and suspicion.

Miraldi understood that Mitchell was implying that Bennett did not call her because he was busy covering something up. Before posing the next question, Miraldi turned his body away from the witness and faced the jury, making eye contact with several jurors. Only the jurors could see Miraldi's expression, suggesting something conspiratorial between them. Finally, Miraldi spoke. "Oh, so you think that you should have received the first call after Casper found Florence in the scalding water?" To the witness, his tone was even, and without a trace of sarcasm. To the jurors, he raised his eyebrows and gave them a quizzical expression. He was putting them on high alert—this witness was about to go off into the deep end, so listen carefully.

"Well, maybe not the first call," Mary Mitchell replied. "But I do think he should have called me right away."

"When was that? You realize that Mr. Bennett was waiting for the rescue squad, then he was talking to the police, and after that he was taken to the emergency room for his burn injuries?"

Mary Mitchell looked helplessly at Prosecutor Mikus, who looked down at his notepad and began scribbling.

"I don't know. I just think it was strange that he didn't get me over there that night. That's all," Mary Mitchell said.

"No further questions," he concluded.

Mikus looked at Otero and then the two whispered with one another for a few seconds. Mikus looked up at the witness and then at the judge before saying, "No redirect, Your Honor."

The next two witnesses were a mother and son who had worked for the Bennetts. Casper Bennett had also hired Sophie Pribanic and her fifteen-year-old son, Joseph, to take care of Florence and the house after Florence's hospitalization in September. Joe Pribanic cleaned at the house and at Bennett's business. Sergeant Springowski had interviewed Sophie Pribanic on January 11, 1964, at the request of Police Chief Pawlak, who had received a tip that the Pribanics might be helpful. When Springowski met with Sophie, he found her to be loyal to Casper Bennett. She told him that Bennett was always very grateful for her help and treated Joey like a son.

Despite this, Mikus and Otero thought they could guide the Pribanics to disclose only testimony helpful to the prosecution—that Florence Bennett was deathly afraid of water and that Joseph Pribanic had only seen Mrs. Bennett drink alcohol once in the year and a half before her death.

When Mikus announced that Sophie Pribanic would be his next witness, Miraldi turned to Adams and whispered, "Why's he calling her? I'm pretty sure she's on our side. I talked to her and she likes Casper."

Prosecutor Mikus established that Mrs. Pribanic also cared for Florence Bennett after her release from the hospital. Mrs. Pribanic confirmed that Florence was a "good housekeeper" when healthy. Sophie cooked and cleaned for the Bennetts and took over all the chores at the house after Casper Bennett was hospitalized for two weeks for an abdominal disorder.

Like Mary Mitchell, Mrs. Pribanic confirmed that Florence Bennett was deathly afraid of water and would either take sponge baths or only fill the tub with a few inches of water.

On cross-examination, Mrs. Pribanic confirmed that Florence Bennett took sleeping pills in addition to drinking whiskey.

"What happened when Mrs. Bennett took the sleeping tablets?" Miraldi asked.

"I was really concerned about that. The pills would make her dizzy and she would stagger around the house, almost like she was in a trance."

"Did she fall when she was in that condition?" Miraldi asked.

"Yes, many times. I was always surprised that she could even walk when she was in that condition," Mrs. Pribanic said.

"By the way, did Florence Bennett take baths in the upstairs bathroom?"

"Yes, she did."

"And there was water in the tub?"

"Yes, usually a couple of inches, not deep, but there was water in the tub."

Miraldi sat down and looked at his client and Adams. For the first time in several days, Bennett smiled ever so slightly. The prosecution had no additional questions for Mrs. Pribanic and called her son to the stand.

Looking at his feet, Joe Pribanic squirmed and fidgeted in the witness chair. In the one and a half years that he'd worked around the Bennett home, he could only remember seeing Mrs. Bennett take a drink once.

"When was that?" Otero asked.

"It was in the autumn. Both Mr. and Mrs. Bennett would not answer the door when I knocked to do some work. Mr. Bennett eventually saw that it was me outside and he came to the door. I could see inside a little bit when he opened the door. There were bottles all over the place and Mrs. Bennett was lying on the couch with a drink in her hand."

"Other than that, did you ever see Mrs. Bennett take a drink in over a year and a half?"

"No, I did not."

The impact of the young man's testimony was weakened when he admitted on cross-examination that he mainly worked for Mr. Bennett at his business. When the teen worked at the Bennett home, he worked outside the house, either cutting the grass or raking leaves. On those occasions, he rarely saw Mrs. Bennett.

Judge Pincura allowed the day's session to run forty-five minutes longer than was customary. As he was dismissing the jury for the day, the judge asked Mikus when he expected to complete the state's case.

"I think we will rest sometime on Wednesday," Mikus replied.

"Well, let's try to keep things moving, Paul," Judge Pincura chided.

Mikus did not reply. He intended to take as much time as he needed to secure a conviction. Although Mikus believed his case was going well, he knew that he should not take shortcuts. As he gathered up his papers, Mikus said to Otero, "We've got them on the run and we're going to keep it that way. We're going to call everybody we've planned to call."

"I agree," Otero replied as they walked out of the courtroom.

CHAPTER 19

April 7, 1964

Orie Camillo, Judge Pincura's court reporter, smiled as he watched Inspector Maurice Mumford take the stand. At age twenty-two, Camillo had been the court's official reporter for a few months. His wife, Gloria, who had never watched a trial, had asked if she could tag along to observe the Bennett murder trial. Yesterday, they'd driven to the courthouse together and Orie had arranged for her to sit in the front behind the bailiff. At the end of the day, Orie was eager to hear his wife's impressions.

"Well, what did you think?" Orie asked as soon as they got into their car.

"I think the defendant looks as guilty as they come. He looks like the type who would murder his wife over someone else," Gloria responded.

"Why do you say that?"

"Well, he just looks sneaky. Usually a gray suit makes a person look distinguished and honorable, but he just looked like someone from an organized crime gang. He's also always scribbling notes to his attorneys."

"Wait a minute, Gloria. Casper Bennett wasn't wearing a gray suit today. He wears the same suit all the time, a dark blue one, and I've never seen the defendant write out anything for his attorneys."

"Well, he was sitting at one of the tables with two attorneys and they were up in the front of the courtroom," she protested.

"Gloria, the prosecution is allowed to have someone from the police force sit with them throughout the trial. The person wearing the gray suit today was Inspector Maurice Mumford, who heads the detective bureau for the Lorain police. That's the person you thought looked so guilty."

"Oh my," Gloria said as they both laughed.

"Some courtroom observer you are," Camillo told his wife.

Today, Inspector Maurice Mumford would be the prosecution's first witness. Mumford arrived at the courtroom forty-five minutes before the morning session was scheduled to begin. He watched as Sergeant Solomon and three other police officers carried the Bennett bathtub up the courthouse steps and into the courtroom. When Miraldi and Adams arrived a half hour later, the bathtub greeted them.

"What the hell's going on here?" Miraldi asked Mikus.

"Your client's lying about how he found his wife and we are going to have a demonstration with the bathtub right here in front of the jury," Mikus said.

"Don't be too sure about that," Miraldi shot back.

"We're going to mark it as an exhibit, establish the chain of custody, and move to introduce it as tangible evidence in this case—just like anything else," Mikus told both defense attorneys. Adams was flabbergasted.

"So you're planning to keep this bathtub in the courtroom for the rest of the trial, is that your strategy?" Adams asked.

"It is the murder weapon," Mikus said belligerently.

"The hell it is," Miraldi replied. "Someone get Judge Pincura."

Judge Pincura could hear the commotion from his chambers and entered the courtroom to investigate. Tired of the constant squabbling between the attorneys, he raised his eyebrows and frowned. "What's going on here?" he asked.

Mikus was the first to speak. "Your Honor, we brought the actual bathtub into the courtroom today so we can have a demonstration. We're going to have a woman the same size as Mrs. Bennett sit in the tub with her back to the faucet. Then we're going to show that the defendant couldn't possibly have pulled her out of the tub the way he claims." After pausing for effect, he said, "This bathtub will expose the defendant for what he is—one big liar."

"No, it won't," Miraldi snapped back. He'd had enough of Mikus's tricks—the guy would stop at nothing. Turning to the judge, Miraldi said, "Are you going to let the prosecutor turn this trial into a circus? The jury's already viewed the bathtub when they visited the Bennett house. It's obvious that the prosecutor just wants another prop for his dog and pony show. And as for this so-called demonstration, it's a farce. It'll be staged to reach whatever result the prosecution wants. If you allow this, you're inviting reversible error."

Judge Pincura left the bench and walked over to the bathtub. Treating it like a ticking time bomb, he approached it slowly and then gingerly touched the faucet before walking back to the bench.

"Very interesting, Mr. Mikus. I will let the bathtub stay in the courtroom for now, assuming you will provide us with a chain of custody. As for a future demonstration, I don't think so, but I will defer my ruling until later. Let's get the jury in here."

After the jury was seated, Inspector Mumford was sworn as the first witness. Mumford had been born in England and came to the United States with his mother and two brothers in 1927 when he was sixteen. In Lorain, Mumford started as a machinist apprentice, but like many others whose employment became uncertain during the Great Depression, he found steady work with the Lorain Police Department. By 1942, he was promoted to sergeant, and a few years later he rose to lieutenant. Now he was in charge of all the detectives.

Inspector Mumford was a well-spoken witness whose English accent gave his testimony an authoritative air. Because he had sat at the prosecution's table throughout the trial, he knew where other officers had stumbled and his job was to bolster their testimony.

Mumford had been summoned to the station on the evening of December 20, 1963, and was present when Springowski and Trifiletti questioned Bennett. Two days later, Mumford talked to Bennett before the suspect agreed to give a written statement. Mikus asked Mumford to point out all the inconsistencies between Bennett's statements and what the police investigation later found.

Mumford's account of the police investigation mirrored much of the previous testimony. Some of the jurors were bored and were staring at the bathtub twenty feet from the jury box.

Mikus eventually asked Mumford, "At your direction, was the bathtub removed from the Bennett home?"

"Yes, it was. I asked Sergeant Solomon to remove it this morning and he brought it here about an hour ago."

"I would ask that the court reporter mark this as Exhibit Forty-One," Mikus said.

Mikus intended to engage the jury in a game of show-and-tell. He asked Mumford, "Have you discovered any other objects from the Bennett home that are important to this investigation?"

Mumford went on to describe how two of his detectives pried open a secret compartment in the television set. With a grim seriousness, Mumford unfastened his briefcase and pulled out a book of horoscopes, a copy of *Solid Gold Dream Book*, several creditor's notes, a divorce petition involving the Bennetts, and a 1963 calendar with diary-type notations. After Mumford briefly described each one, the court reporter marked them as exhibits. Mikus sat down.

Miraldi stood and smiled at Mumford. "Inspector Mumford, this is indeed strange for me to be cross-examining you. For ten years we worked together when I was a prosecutor for the city."

Mumford did not return Miraldi's smile. "Yes, we had a few cases together, Mr. Miraldi," Mumford grudgingly acknowledged.

"More like forty or fifty, and our joint efforts were fruitful," Miraldi ventured. Adams thought Miraldi sounded a bit boastful and hoped his co-counsel would tone things down.

"Objection," Mikus yelled. "Do we have to listen to Mr. Miraldi's self-glory statements to this witness? This is totally irrelevant."

Miraldi had expected the objection, but he wanted the jurors to see that he was a former prosecutor. Knowing that, the jurors might conclude that he would not stoop to defend a guilty man.

"Sustained. Move on, counselor," Pincura chided.

Miraldi had several goals in this cross-examination. He wanted to show that the police had rushed to judgment in charging Casper Bennett with murder. Miraldi also wanted to demonstrate that none of the items in the "secret" compartment tied Casper Bennett to his wife's death. They were simply prosecutorial distractions, aimed at disparaging the defendant again in front of the jury.

After a number of questions about the police interrogation of Bennett on December 20, Miraldi honed in on Mumford.

"There was nothing friendly about the way the police questioned my client on the night of his wife's death, was there?"

"I don't know what you mean by 'friendly.' We treated him with respect. We do that with all witnesses," Mumford replied.

"In fact, you became quite angry with my client in the police interrogation room, didn't you?" Miraldi asked.

"I don't know if I would say I got angry, but I was pretty disgusted with Mr. Bennett that night. Let's leave it at that," Mumford answered.

"Why was that?"

"His wife is an alcoholic. We can agree on that, can't we? She's sick in bed from who knows what. Maybe she's just hungover, I don't know. She refuses food, so he gives her two shots of whiskey instead."

"She asked for the drinks, didn't she?"

"All I know is that he fed her two drinks, and yes, I got a little upset about this. I jumped all over him for this."

"What did you say to him?"

"I said, 'How could you give liquor to a sick alcoholic?' I told him his behavior was reprehensible."

"Those weren't the words you used. You swore at him, didn't you?" Miraldi said, goading him.

"I might have," Mumford said. "I can't remember."

"Before he left that evening, Casper hid the whiskey bottle from Florence?"

"I don't know."

"The police found a whiskey bottle hidden in the dining room behind a bureau," Miraldi said.

"Are you asking me a question?" Mumford replied, his voice testy.

"The police did find a bottle of whiskey hidden in the dining room, didn't they?"

"Yes, we did."

"So my client wasn't always feeding his wife liquor, as you are trying to imply. Correct?"

"That's what he says," Mumford said, switching his gaze from Miraldi to Bennett.

"Your investigation showed that both Casper and Florence received hospital treatment for alcohol addiction at various points in their lives?"

"Something like that."

"Do you know what it is like to live with an alcoholic, Inspector Mumford?" Miraldi pushed.

"Objection."

"Sustained."

"You and Springowski were convinced that Casper Bennett killed his wife because he was having an affair with another woman. Correct?" Miraldi asked.

"We were convinced that we should charge Mr. Bennett because the coroner told us that this was a homicide and not an accident," Mumford rebutted.

"And who was it that told the coroner that Casper Bennett and Florence Bennett had a stormy marriage, that a divorce action was pending, and that Casper Bennett had a girlfriend?"

"I don't know what you are implying," Mumford answered.

"Springowski knew all about the Bennetts' problems. He told the coroner about them when the coroner was in the house trying to determine what happened. Right?"

"You would have to ask Springowski. I was not there."

"It was a tainted investigation from the very start, wasn't it?"

"Objection. Argumentative."

"Sustained."

The jury was no longer preoccupied by the bathtub. Their gaze went back and forth between Miraldi and Mumford as the two former friends and colleagues slugged it out in front of them.

"When you interrogated Mr. Bennett, you asked him question after question about his girlfriend, Irene Miller, didn't you?"

"Of course, I asked him about her. That would be a motive for killing his wife."

"If he wanted to marry Irene Miller, Mr. Bennett could have divorced his wife. He didn't need to kill her. People can get a divorce, can't they?"

"Husbands who get mad at their wives have been known to kill them in fits of anger. I am sure you are aware of that, Mr. Miraldi. It was something that we had to consider."

"Did you ask Mr. Bennett who he'd phoned on the night Florence died?"

"Yes, I did."

"Did Mr. Bennett tell you who it was?"

"No, he refused at first. He said he didn't want to get her involved."

"He told you that he would tell you everything about his whereabouts that evening, but that he did not want to give you the name of his girlfriend, isn't that right?"

"That's right."

"Why was that?"

"He said, 'My lady friend has got nothing to do with this. I did not kill my wife. That's what you're interested in, isn't it?'"

"Whether it was right or wrong, Mr. Bennett wanted to protect his girlfriend from this investigation?"

"Yes."

"In fact, when Casper Bennett agreed to give you a written statement two days later, he stipulated that he would do so only if the statement deleted any reference to Irene Miller and his relations with her?"

"Yes, that's right."

"But Sergeant Springowski knew the identity of Casper's girlfriend?"

"Yes."

"And the police have questioned her many times already about this?"

"Yes. She is part of his alibi. He eventually admitted that he called her twice that evening."

"Your department keeps pretty close tabs on her now, doesn't it?"

"No, sir, we don't."

Miraldi then went through each of the items found in the secret compartment. Mumford eventually conceded that none of the papers connected Bennett to his wife's death or revealed a motive for murder. When he got to the calendar, Miraldi asked, "This calendar with notations on it. It doesn't have an entry after December fifteenth, does it?"

"That's correct."

"So no entries during the time Mrs. Bennett was sick in bed that week?"

"No."

"No entry on the day she died?"

"No, sir."

Miraldi sat down and Adams nodded to him, communicating his approval. Miraldi glanced at Bennett and was surprised to see how tired and drawn his client looked. Except for two occasions when he'd cried briefly, Bennett's face had remained expressionless during the first week of the trial. As the trial dragged into its second week, he wore a constant frown. Miraldi and Adams were so focused on their cross-examinations that they had ignored their client. Miraldi would rectify this at the next recess by talking to Bennett and being upbeat.

As his next witness, Mikus called Mary Cowan, the chief medical technologist for the Cuyahoga County coroner's office. Miss Cowan's testimony merely established that the sample scraping of blood from the side of the bathtub was of human origin, although its type or source (menstrual period or otherwise) could not be determined. After her brief testimony, Judge Pincura recessed the jury for lunch while the attorneys stayed to argue about the proposed bathtub demonstration. Eventually, Pincura ruled that he would not allow it.

After lunch, the prosecution called some minor witnesses. Sergeant Solomon was recalled to establish that he disconnected the bathtub and supervised its transport to the courtroom. Joseph Tholl, a handwriting expert, opined that the handwriting on the calendar/diary matched that of Florence Bennett's notarized signature on mortgage documents. Joseph Rose, an insurance agent for Western and Southern Life Insurance Company, authenticated the policies that insured Florence Bennett. Again, the prosecution established that, with the double indemnity provisions, Casper Bennett stood to gain $44,000 in life insurance proceeds if his wife's death was deemed accidental.

The day's proceedings closed with the testimony of Andrew Bobinsky, the assistant manager of the Metropolitan Life Insurance Company's office in Lorain. Dressed in a brown polyester suit, Mr. Bobinsky was a heavy-set man in his late forties. When he sat down, his right hand nervously brushed his slicked-down hair across the top of his head. As Bobinsky testified, he quickly glanced at Bennett and then lost his train of thought.

"What was I saying? Mr. Bennett called me sometime in 1962 and told me that he and his wife wanted to take the cash surrender value on a $5,000 policy on her life. So I figured it out for them and told them that they would receive $3,042 as its value."

"So who was the one who was calling and instigating this?" Otero asked.

"All my dealings were with Mr. Bennett, not Mrs. Bennett. He actually delivered the policy to me with the signed paperwork and it had Mrs. Bennett's signature on it, so I thought it all looked legitimate."

"Was it?"

"Well, the check was sent to my office. Just a few days later, Mrs. Bennett called me and said she did not want the policy surrendered. She said that she and Mr. Bennett were separated."

"So what did you do?"

"Well, of course, I sent the check back to the home office in New York."

"Thank you, Mr. Bobinsky."

Bennett whispered something to Miraldi before Miraldi stood up to cross-examine the witness.

"Hello, Mr. Bobinsky, just a couple of questions for you," Miraldi began. "This check for around $3,000, did you ever deliver it to the Bennetts?"

"Yes. I'm glad you asked that. As I told Mr. Otero and Mr. Mikus, some months after sending the check back, I got a phone call from Mrs. Bennett. She said that she and her husband had reconciled and she wanted the check."

"So what did you do?"

"I wrote to the home office and the home office sent the check to my office again. Both Mr. and Mrs. Bennett came into the office, signed for it, and I closed out the policy."

"Do people cash in their policies from time to time?"

"Yes. We don't recommend it, of course, but if policyholders need money, it is a good source of extra funds."

"Was there anything unusual about the Bennetts asking for the check, changing their minds, and then changing their minds again?"

"No, not really. People's circumstances change. That's why life insurance is such a darn good investment," Bobinsky said, smiling at the jury.

"Thank you, Mr. Bobinsky."

The day was over. The pawns had been played. Tomorrow, the prosecution would bring in its king piece, Paul Kopsch, the county coroner, who would finally tell the jury why Florence Bennett's death was no accident.

Lorain County Court House, Elyria, Ohio

Judge John D. Pincura

Attorney Ray L. Miraldi circa 1960

Paul J. Mikus and Ray L. Miraldi -
1963 Lorain County Bar Association Composite

John Otero circa 1964
(Photograph courtesy of the Morning Journal in Lorain)

Lon B. Adams circa 1964
(Photograph courtesy of the Morning Journal in Lorain)

7 April 1964

Contacted Ruth Carr (wf)(37) 2040 W.29th St., Lorain, O. (Phone 22452) and she stated that she was the clerk on duty on 20 Dec 1963 at the Neighborhood Store, 912 Ninth St. when Casper Bennett came into the store. She said that Casper purchased a six-pack of Black Label Beer and another item she xx can not recall what it was.

She said that the time as far as she could ascertain was between 7:30p.m. and 8:30p.m. and that Casper appeared normal. Mrs. Carr states that she has known Casper for many years and is sure it was him. She did add that Casper comes into the store on rare occasions,and that is to purchase a Sunday newspaper.

Contacted Irene Miller and she stated that she is sure that it was Casper who cleaned the snow off her walks on 20 Dec 1963 and he left a six-pack of beer on the back porch. She wasn't sure, but said that it could have been either Black Label or Blatz beer that was left on that same date. IRENE MILLER couldn't recall xhatxxitxx if anything else besides the beer was left, but she feels xxxx it was just the beer that was left there, as she didn't find anything else.

mak ms

I heard a clerk at the Neiborhood Store at 912-9 Street tell a customer that Casper Bennett bought wine in that store about eight or nine the night his wife was found in the bathtub.

The clerk is a sister-in-law of Al Molnar the owner of the store.

Michael Kocak's Summary of Undisclosed Interview with Ruth Carr that supported Casper Bennett's Alibi

Foreman and Other Jurors Return With Verdict
(Photograph courtesy of the Morning Journal in Lorain)

CHAPTER 20

April 8, 1964 (Morning)

The nurses at St. Joseph Hospital's surgical ward surrounded Shirley Ann Demyan. The twenty-one-year-old registered nurse seemed embarrassed, but she grudgingly smiled at the attention.

"Well, how did it go yesterday?" one of them asked.

"It didn't go," Shirley said. "It turned out to be a waste of time. I got worried and upset for nothing."

"Well, you scored some points with Dr. Kopsch, at least," another interjected. "He owes you one."

"Who knows? He's a nice man, but I doubt he thinks he owes me anything," Shirley responded.

"So what happened? You couldn't fit into the bathtub?" a large, big-boned nurse said as she patted Shirley a bit too hard on her buttocks.

"Very funny. Very funny. That wasn't it at all," Shirley protested, failing to see the humor. "You know I practiced in the courtroom when only that big-shot prosecutor and a police detective were there. I sat right in the tub with my back to the faucet just like he told me to, but that's as far as we got. I don't know if someone was supposed to pull me out, you know, put their grubby hands on me in some embarrassing place—right in front of everybody."

"You were nuts to agree to that," interrupted a nurse about Shirley's age.

Shirley ignored her. "Before Mr. Big Shot could tell me what I had to do next, his assistant walks in. That stupid prosecutor starts talking to his assistant and ignores me for about ten minutes. I get so mad. I get out of the tub and start walking toward the door. He sees me leaving and says, 'Hey, what do you think you're doing?' and I say, 'Let me know when you want to finish, I'm going to wait out in the hall.' He says, 'Good idea,' and then I wait out in the hall the entire morning."

Several days before, Dr. Kopsch had recruited Shirley Demyan to double as the victim, Florence Bennett. Dr. Kopsch told her that she was roughly the same height and weight as Florence Bennett and that they looked alike with their dark brown hair. From reading the reports in the newspaper, Shirley knew that Mrs. Bennett was a middle-aged alcoholic, and she was insulted by the suggestion that she looked like the victim. She didn't let on that she was offended, but she initially told Dr. Kopsch that she wouldn't do it.

Then Dr. Kopsch tried to make her feel guilty. He explained how the victim's husband would probably get away with murder unless they had a model sit in the tub and, through a live demonstration, show just how impossible the husband's story really was. All she had to do was sit in the tub, look pretty, and follow instructions. "You can do that, can't you?" Dr. Kopsch asked. Shirley knew Dr. Kopsch was an important doctor at the hospital, so she relented after he confirmed that she would be fully clothed during the demonstration.

Nobody talked to her the entire morning while she waited in the hall. She was just about ready to go home when the prosecutor's assistant rushed out and told her to come into the courtroom. Shirley could see that the jury was gone. For the next hour, the judge, the prosecutors, and the defense attorneys argued over whether a live demonstration would go forward. Everyone stared at her at some point—the judge, the attorneys, and the court personnel. She felt like a cow ready to be auctioned, with potential buyers critically appraising her physical dimensions.

"So why didn't you get to do it?" the large nurse asked. "Don't clam up on us." The large nurse punched Shirley on the forearm, jolting her out of her reverie.

"He said he'd never heard of a live demonstration like this being done in front of a jury before. He thought it was too risky for the jury to watch it. I guess he didn't trust the prosecutor to do it right," Shirley replied.

"So what did the prosecutor say to you after that?" the large nurse asked.

"That prosecutor was really angry. He just rushed out of the courtroom and didn't even talk to me. It was his assistant who told me I could leave."

"I hope they're going to pay you something for wasting your entire morning," one of the nurses suggested.

"Are you kidding? Neither one of those prosecutors even bothered to thank me," Shirley replied. "You know, at first I didn't care because I was so relieved that I didn't have to do this thing. Then when I got home, I started thinking more about the way I was treated and I kept getting madder and madder. I mean, I hadn't slept a wink for the last two nights worrying about this stupid thing. And then they treat me like I'm a nobody."

"But, Shirley, what if this wife murderer gets off?" one of the nurses said. "What if he gets off because there was no demonstration? Wow. Think of that."

"Can we change the subject? I just want to get back to work and my normal routine. Okay?"

****

Paul Mikus finished his second cup of coffee before entering the courtroom. The night before, he and Dr. Kopsch had worked until midnight, first reviewing the autopsy report and the preliminary hearing transcript, and then discussing in detail the coroner's answers to the questions Mikus would pose to him the next day. That was the easy part. Mikus then tried to predict the major points upon which the defense would cross-examine his key witness. Mikus soon learned that Dr. Kopsch had a natural ability to anticipate vulnerabilities in his position and effectively blunt them. After the session, Mikus was ebullient.

Mikus was still upset with the assistant coroner, Dr. Chesner, who performed the autopsy. Mikus had met with him several weeks ago and concluded that Dr. Chesner was not a strong witness or a team player.

Although Dr. Chesner believed that Mrs. Bennett had drowned, he was reluctant to say that the facts pointed strictly to a homicide. According to Dr. Chesner, both homicide and accident were possible explanations, and, if asked, he would concede that Mrs. Bennett's death could have been caused by an accidental fall or an alcohol-induced blackout. Mikus could not take that kind of chance with Chesner.

For that reason, Mikus would entrust the medical proof of homicide to one individual, Dr. Paul Kopsch. Everything in Mikus's gut told him that Casper Bennett had murdered Florence Bennett, and he was relieved to have an ally like Dr. Kopsch marching in lockstep with him.

The courtroom was unexpectedly quiet as Judge Pincura entered. The female spectators still outnumbered the men, but there were more local attorneys and court personnel in the courtroom today. The word was out that today's testimony would be pivotal. As the jurors filed in, Prosecutor Mikus scribbled another question onto his yellow pad. Miraldi's eyes, bloodshot from a sleepless night, followed the jurors as they found their seats and sat down.

"Your first witness, Mr. Mikus," Judge Pincura said, his voice finally breaking the silence.

Mikus's voice boomed out, "The State of Ohio will call Dr. Paul Kopsch."

A few seconds later, the county coroner followed the bailiff into the courtroom. Dressed in a gray business suit and carrying a large briefcase, Dr. Kopsch walked at a slow, deliberate pace to the witness chair. He took a deep breath as he sat down. Looking about the courtroom, he exhaled audibly through his nose, clasped his hands together in his lap, and focused his gaze on Mikus. The coroner then nodded to Mikus as if to tell him that he could start.

Mikus had worked hard to craft his direct examination. He wanted his questions to be crisp, precise, and flow seamlessly from one to the next. Because Dr. Kopsch had no background in pathology or forensic medicine, Mikus began his questions by focusing on Dr. Kopsch's leadership in the Ohio State Coroners Association. He also elicited testimony about the forensic seminars that Dr. Kopsch had attended since becoming the coroner five years ago.

Dr. Kopsch explained the important duties of a county coroner. One of the coroner's chief duties was to investigate unexplained deaths in the county and to determine their cause. The county coroner was on call to respond immediately to death scenes twenty-four hours a day, every day of the week. He gathered evidence and published his findings in an official governmental report.

Dr. Kopsch was assisted in his official duties by three deputy coroners, to whom he delegated the responsibility of performing autopsies and running laboratory tests. His deputy coroners were all licensed pathologists, and when an autopsy was necessary, Dr. Kopsch assigned the task to one of them.

Dr. Kopsch paused and looked at the jury for the first time. "After a careful investigation, the coroner issues an unbiased, accurate, and thorough report about the cause and manner of these unexplained deaths."

"Do you work for any law enforcement agency?" Mikus inquired, asking one of the questions that the two had rehearsed the evening before.

"Absolutely not," Dr. Kopsch answered on cue. There was something icy in his voice, as if he resented the question. "The coroner's office is an independent governmental entity. Our job is to search for the truth. No one influences us. No one controls us."

Mikus then quickly turned to Dr. Kopsch's investigation into the death of Florence Bennett on December 20, 1963. Dr. Kopsch explained that the Lorain police had called him shortly after nine thirty that night, and that he arrived at the Bennett home by ten p.m. Once there, he examined the body, noting the extensive burns and the skin that had peeled away, which he called "desquamation." Although her body was 75 to 80 percent burned, Dr. Kopsch noticed that Mrs. Bennett's lower legs were not burned. He also found small lacerations on the outsides of her lower legs about the ankles.

Dr. Kopsch told the jury that after spending five to ten minutes examining the body, he went into the bathroom to investigate. The gray bathwater was still hot to his touch and he saw peeled skin floating on its surface.

"Along the edge of the bathtub, I could see a film of dried blood," Dr.

Kopsch said.

"Tell the jury more about this, please," Mikus prodded.

"Even though the blood was dry, I could tell that it was of recent origin," the coroner said in a resolute tone.

"How could you tell?" Mikus asked.

"It really is a matter of experience. A trained eye can tell the difference between blood that has recently dried and blood that has been dried for many hours. I just know the difference and this was recent blood," Dr. Kopsch offered.

Miraldi nudged Adams and scowled. The pathologists hired by the defense had told Miraldi that there was no way that a film of dried blood could be classified as recent or old.

Dr. Kopsch told the jury that there was also recent blood on the bathroom's windowsill. He also found some broken pieces of glass on the floor.

"What else did you do in the house?" Mikus asked.

"Next I made arrangements for Mrs. Bennett's body to be safely and properly taken to the morgue. Then I walked about the house with Sergeant Springowski to look for additional evidence that could assist in determining the cause of death," Dr. Kopsch related.

"Tell us what you found, if anything," Mikus urged the witness.

"We found two bottles of sleeping aids, Sleep-eze and Sominex. I took the bottles and then did some research. Based on the number of Sominex tablets that are customarily sold in a full bottle of that size, sixteen or so were missing."

Dr. Kopsch told the jury that his deputy performed an autopsy the next day. Mikus carefully went over the autopsy findings and asked Dr. Kopsch to explain many of them, even those that were normal. Dr. Kopsch told the jury that his deputy coroner, Dr. Chesner, concluded that Mrs. Bennett had drowned. The coroner's office sent organs and blood to be tested for various drugs and chemicals.

"This testing for drugs and chemicals—did it reveal anything significant?" Mikus asked.

"This testing is called a toxicology screen. What is most significant is that the toxicology report showed that the body had absorbed both salicylamide and methapyrilene, two of the components in Sominex. It also showed that Mrs. Bennett's body had twelve milligrams of salicylates in her body at the time of her death."

"You referred to two drugs that sound alike, salicylamide and salicylates. Can you explain?"

"Yes, salicylamide is a specific drug while salicylate is a classification of drugs. Salicylamide is a type of salicylate."

Several jurors looked lost, while the rest were hoping that Dr. Kopsch could simplify this for them.

"So what did this demonstrate, if anything?" Mikus asked.

"To reach twelve milligrams of salicylates, and assuming all of the salicylates came from the salicylamide in the Sominex, then Mrs. Bennett had anywhere from fifteen to twenty Sominex pills in her system at the time she died," Dr. Kopsch postulated.

"So what does that mean?" Mikus asked.

"Before I talk about the salicylates, let me discuss the alcohol content in her system. The tests showed that she had 0.19 percent concentration of alcohol in her blood system and 0.22 percent in her stomach. The reason that the two numbers are different is because not all of the alcohol in her stomach had entered her bloodstream at the time of her death. Her last drink had not yet begun to take effect—so to speak. To reach the 0.19 percent concentration, Mrs. Bennett consumed about nine shots of hard liquor.

"As you know, it is against the law in Ohio for anyone to operate a motor vehicle if that person has a blood alcohol level of 0.15 percent or higher. Under the law, Mrs. Bennett would be presumed to be intoxicated. The point I am getting at is that, when she had a blood alcohol level of 0.19 percent and also fifteen to twenty Sominex tablets in her blood, she was either comatose or ataxic."

Mikus looked at the jury and could see that these terms meant nothing to them. "Dr. Kopsch, can you explain that in layman's terms, please?"

"Certainly," Dr. Kopsch said, turning to face and then instruct the jury.

The jurors' eyes were fixed on Dr. Kopsch as he proceeded. "'Comatose' means 'unconscious' and 'ataxic' means 'completely or almost completely lacking in coordination.'" Dr. Kopsch focused on several of the jurors closest to him and said, "What I am saying is that this woman could not walk on her own power. Maybe she could crawl to the bathroom in stages, but she could not walk there by herself and she could not walk down the stairs or anything like that. She was out like a light, or almost out like a light."

Miraldi and Adams exchanged shocked glances. This was a radical departure from Dr. Kopsch's testimony at the preliminary hearing. Three months ago, the coroner had been skeptical that Sominex could even make a person sleepy. Back then, Dr. Kopsch had claimed that Florence Bennett had taken only three tablets within four hours of her death. Here he was today, glib as ever, claiming that these sleeping pills, combined with the alcohol, were enough to make Mrs. Bennett comatose. Miraldi felt as disoriented and double-crossed as someone who was promised a ride home, but was then driven into the country and shoved out of the car.

Miraldi understood instantly why the coroner had switched his theory. If Florence could not walk on her own to the bathroom, then the implication was clear: only her fiendish husband could have dragged her there. Miraldi had more than twenty pages of notes and questions to test Dr. Kopsch's opinions on cross-examination, but he had prepared nothing to dispute this new opinion. His heart raced and its strong beat echoed in his ears, making it hard for him to think clearly.

Miraldi forced himself to focus again on the coroner's answers. He heard Dr. Kopsch say, "From the toxicology screen and the amount of salicylates in her bloodstream, I estimated that Mrs. Bennett had fifteen to twenty Sominex pills in her system when she died. It is no coincidence then that sixteen tablets were gone. It fits perfectly."

Mikus turned to the effects of scalding water upon an either unconscious or very sedated person. Dr. Kopsch testified, "This was a living, breathing person. If someone in Mrs. Bennett's condition fell into scalding-hot water, it would be enough to revive her and she would pull herself out. Unless someone kept her from getting out, she would be able to save herself in this situation."

Miraldi knew that this, too, was wrong. In preparation for trial, he'd talked to three pathologists, two of whom would testify later in the week for the defense. If Mrs. Bennett had struck her head and been knocked out before she entered the water, she would have felt no pain. Likewise, if she was conscious when she fell into the scalding water, its extreme heat could have sent her into shock and unconsciousness, and she again would have felt no pain. Miraldi shook his head in disagreement, hoping that this gesture might cause some jurors to question the coroner's answers. Instead, one of the women jurors looked at him and scowled.

"What about the burns on Mr. Bennett's hands?" Mikus said, moving methodically along. He looked at the jury and saw that some were staring at Casper Bennett, whose hands were hidden below the table in his lap.

"If Mr. Bennett's left hand slipped into the water, there is no logical explanation for the lack of burns on the top of it. We know that the skin on the palm of the hand is thicker than the skin on the top of it and is more resistant to burning. It would make more sense if the top of Mr. Bennett's left hand had been burned and not the palm. But with only the thick skin on the palm burned, one would have to conclude that only the palm of his left hand came in contact with the scalding water, and the top of his hand was above the water's surface." The coroner held out his left hand and patted the underside of it with several fingers from his right hand, simulating water striking it.

"Based on the autopsy, the toxicology results, the burn pattern to Mrs. Bennett, the burns to Mr. Bennett's hands, and your observations at the Bennett home, do you have an opinion, based on a reasonable degree of medical certainty, as to the cause of death?" Mikus asked, putting in the legally required language to elicit an opinion.

"Yes, I have an opinion," Dr. Kopsch responded.

"What is that opinion?"

"My opinion is that Mrs. Bennett died by drowning. It is my further opinion that her death was the result of homicide and was not accidental."

"Did you determine a time of death?"

"Yes. After a thorough review of all of the evidence, I concluded that eight thirty p.m. was the most likely time of death."

At the preliminary hearing, Dr. Kopsch had been indefinite about the time of death. Admitting that it was difficult to pinpoint the time of death, Dr. Kopsch opined that Mrs. Bennett had died sometime between eight p.m. and ten p.m. Miraldi looked at the preliminary hearing transcript and jotted down the page numbers for this testimony.

"Thank you, Dr. Kopsch," Mikus said as he sat down. "Your witness."

Judge Pincura interjected, "It's ten fifteen and it makes sense that we take our morning recess. I am assuming that the cross-examination may take some time, so let's take our break now. We will come back in fifteen minutes."

Adams drew his chair closer to Miraldi and whispered, "You know this is not how Kopsch testified at the preliminary hearing. He didn't say anything about fifteen to twenty Sominex tablets."

"Yes, I know. I've got the page number. You know he's going to claim that he received the toxicology report just before the preliminary hearing and didn't have time to accurately do his calculations," Miraldi responded. "I'm still going to show the jury that he has changed those numbers quite dramatically."

"Okay, I'll leave it to you, Ray," Adams whispered. "I'll leave you alone and let you gather your thoughts."

Miraldi knew that one of Dr. Kopsch's points was absolutely damning. The coroner had told the jury that there was chemical evidence that Mrs. Bennett had fifteen to twenty Sominex tablets in her system and that with the alcohol, she was comatose or practically so. If the entire jury could view the toxicology report while he questioned Dr. Kopsch, they would see that was not true. The courtroom's only visual aid was a movable blackboard on rollers. Miraldi went over to the board and with chalk wrote in large capital letters these words: "SALICYLATES—FOUND IN MANY THINGS AND MEASURED," "SALICYLAMIDE—FOUND IN SOMINEX AND NOT MEASURED," and "METHAPYRILENE—FOUND IN SOMINEX AND NOT MEASURED."

For Miraldi, the recess was over almost as soon as it started, but he was ready. He would have to deal with the Sominex issue early in his cross-examination.

Miraldi rose from his chair and placed a manila folder with his notes on the courtroom lectern. As he did so, Inspector Mumford nudged Mikus as if to say, *I told you Miraldi would cross-examine Kopsch.* In response, Mikus shrugged his shoulders in feigned indifference.

Miraldi decided to keep things simple at the start and then feel his way. He began by establishing that Dr. Kopsch was an anesthesiologist and not trained in pathology or forensic medicine. The coroner conceded that he had never performed an autopsy. With that under his belt, Miraldi was ready to make some quick points that Kopsch would have to concede. In his direct testimony with Mikus, Dr. Kopsch claimed that he had supervised the Florence Bennett autopsy.

"Dr. Kopsch, were you present at the autopsy?" Miraldi said, staring at the jury while the coroner readied his response.

"I was not," Dr. Kopsch admitted, "but I discussed what I had found at the Bennett home with Dr. Chesner before he did the autopsy. He knew what I wanted him to do."

"Just so the jury is clear, Dr. Kopsch, you were not physically in the same room with Dr. Chesner when he performed the autopsy. You did not give him any guidance or suggestions when he did the autopsy. You obviously did not see or examine any of the vital organs."

Dr. Kopsch was silent.

"That was a question, doctor. Is that correct?" Miraldi prodded.

"Yes, I was not present and could not see or examine any of the vital organs."

"Yet, you told this jury that you supervised the autopsy?" Miraldi drove home the point.

"I directed that an autopsy be done. In that sense, I supervised it," Kopsch replied.

"I see," Miraldi said, again looking at the jury and ignoring the witness. Miraldi could feel himself relax. He walked to the lectern and took the toxicology report from his folder. He decided to create an awkward pause before asking his next question. He glanced at Dr. Kopsch, then at the report, and then at Mikus. Miraldi looked at Dr. Kopsch again.

Dr. Kopsch was drumming his fingers on the witness railing, a bemused expression on his face. Moments before, Dr. Kopsch had drawn a verbal picture of Casper Bennett dragging his comatose wife to the bathtub, holding her head under the water, and drowning her. Now Miraldi had to erase that picture.

"Did I hear you correctly when you said that Mrs. Bennett likely had fifteen to twenty Sominex tablets in her system at the time that she died?" Miraldi asked.

"Yes, most likely sixteen, the number missing from the bottle, but it could be fifteen or twenty, based on my calculations," Dr. Kopsch replied. The coroner seemed relieved to finally have a question directed to him.

"Dr. Kopsch, did you testify at a preliminary hearing on January 7, 1964, in regard to your findings regarding Mrs. Bennett?"

"Yes, sir, I did."

"You were under oath at that hearing, were you not?"

"Of course I was."

"Have you reviewed your testimony from three months ago?"

"Yes I have. In fact, I have a copy of it right here in my briefcase." The coroner's tone was almost chipper.

"Would you please pull out the transcript, because I want to read to you part of your sworn testimony," Miraldi said, opening the transcript to the proper page. "At that hearing, Mr. Adams, the man sitting at that table, asked you what quantity of sleeping pills were in Mrs. Bennett's system at the time of her death. You had the toxicology report at that time?"

"Yes. I remember Mr. Adams's question. I had just received the toxicology report either that day or the day before, but I had not had the time to do adequate calculations," Dr. Kopsch interjected.

"Doctor, please just answer my question. I believe your answer is that you remember the question, and yes, you had a copy of the toxicology report. Is that correct?"

"Yes," Dr. Kopsch said. For just a moment, Dr. Kopsch scowled, but he caught himself and quickly projected an expression of inscrutable neutrality.

"On January 7, 1964, did you make the following statement under oath: 'The quantity present would have gone along with two or three of these tablets within the preceding four hours'?"

"As I said, I had not had enough time to do my calculation and that is an error," Dr. Kopsch responded.

"Dr. Kopsch, please just answer the question. The only thing that I asked you was whether you made that statement. Did you make that statement?"

"Of course I made that statement. I just explained that I hadn't had an adequate time to figure this out. I stand by my estimate today that Mrs. Bennett had taken fifteen to twenty tablets. I was wrong on January 7, 1964."

Miraldi tried to hide his frustration. Dr. Kopsch had anticipated this question and had a ready response that perhaps the jurors would accept. Miraldi was about to proceed to another topic when a new thought came to him.

"So you didn't have enough time before the preliminary hearing to carefully determine the number of sleeping tablets in Mrs. Bennett's body, is that what you are telling the jury?" Miraldi asked.

Dr. Kopsch nodded to the jury and then to Miraldi. "Yes, that is exactly what happened."

"Well then, even though you did not have enough time to accurately determine the number of sleeping pills in Mrs. Bennett's system, that didn't stop you from guessing at a number during the preliminary hearing, did it?" Miraldi shot back, glancing at the jury and then looking behind him to see the expressions on the faces of Mikus and Otero.

"It was not a guess. I don't make wild guesses, Mr. Miraldi. I just didn't consider some factors," Dr. Kopsch defended himself.

"If you didn't have enough time to do the calculation accurately, why didn't you just testify that *you did not know*? Wouldn't that have been the right thing to do?" Miraldi pressed on.

"I thought I knew. I just failed to consider one factor," Dr. Kopsch said calmly. Dr. Kopsch continued to make eye contact with several jurors and his body betrayed no sense of unease.

"So there are times when you are wrong?"

"Of course, we all make mistakes, Mr. Miraldi. I venture to say that you have made some yourself. The important thing is to recognize a mistake and correct it, which is exactly what I did," Dr. Kopsch said, looking at the jury for a sign of approval.

"You also told this jury today that Mrs. Bennett would have been unconscious or unable to walk on her own power on the night that she died?"

"I did."

"Since you have the preliminary hearing transcript in front of you, please let's look at the last few lines of the page we were on previously. When asked about the effect of the sleeping aids with the alcohol at the preliminary hearing, your response was, and I quote you, 'They would tend to have an additive action in that she would be unsteady, but probably not unconscious.' Mr. Adams then asked you, 'Then these drugs plus alcohol would produce unsteadiness but not an unconsciousness, is that correct?' Your answer was, 'Right, sir.' Were those the questions and answers that you gave under oath on January seventh?"

"Yes, that is what I said," Dr. Kopsch said. Again his voice showed no strain and he looked evenly at Miraldi.

"That's not what you told the jury today, is it?" Miraldi asked.

"As I previously explained, I made an error in regard to the amount of sleeping pills in Mrs. Bennett's body. I now say that she was either comatose or so unsteady that she would require assistance to walk," Dr. Kopsch answered, shrugging his shoulders.

"So your testimony on that point is different today than what it was three months ago?" Miraldi bore on.

"Mr. Miraldi, I can appreciate what you are trying to convey, but the differences in my testimony are very slight."

"Dr. Kopsch, nowhere in your preliminary hearing testimony did you say that Mrs. Bennett could not walk on her own power. Nowhere did you say that she could only have reached the bathroom by crawling in stages.

Nowhere did you say that she was 'out like a light, or almost out like a light.' You only said that she would be unsteady. Isn't that what you said three months ago?"

"Objection," Mikus shouted. "Mr. Miraldi is being argumentative. Dr. Kopsch has answered his question. Mr. Miraldi just doesn't like the doctor's response so he is asking the question again in hopes of getting a better answer."

"Your Honor, this is a completely different question and Mr. Mikus knows that," Miraldi responded.

"Overruled," Judge Pincura said.

By objecting, Mikus intended to give his witness additional time to think before answering, although Dr. Kopsch did not need any help. "I said in the preliminary hearing, Mr. Miraldi, that Mrs. Bennett could have been unsteady and maybe even unconscious, probably not unconscious, but I did not completely rule that out. A person who is unsteady does need help to walk."

Miraldi did not want to belabor the point. The jury could draw its own conclusions.

Miraldi then rolled the chalkboard from against the wall to the center of the courtroom so that both Dr. Kopsch and the jury could read it. Miraldi knew it was critical for the jury to understand that Dr. Kopsch had taken liberties with the toxicology report in calculating the number of Sominex tablets in Mrs. Bennett's system.

"Let's start with the components of Sominex," Miraldi began. He walked over to the chalkboard and pointed first to the word "salicylamide." "Salicylamide is found in Sominex, is that correct?"

"Yes, it is," the coroner agreed.

"The toxicology report found that salicylamide was present in Mrs. Bennett's liver, brain, kidneys, and blood. Is that correct?"

"Yes, it did."

Pointing to the words "not measured," Miraldi went on, "The toxicology screening did not measure the amount of salicylamide in Mrs. Bennett's organs or blood."

"Yes, that is correct. The toxicology screen was qualitative and not quantitative."

"I don't want you to confuse me with these words, 'qualitative' and 'quantitative,'" Miraldi said. He had learned long ago never to tell a witness that his answers were too technical for the jury because that would insult some of them. However, if the lawyer pretended to be confused, the witness could be asked to simplify without running the risk of alienating any of the jurors.

"'Qualitative' means that it is there. 'Quantitative' means it has been measured."

"Just so I do not get mixed up, can we agree that the report simply found salicylamide was present, but did not measure it?"

"Yes."

Pointing to the word "methapyrilene" on the board, Miraldi followed the same pattern and established that this component of Sominex was also detected by the toxicology screen but not measured.

"So, Dr. Kopsch, both of these chemicals found in Sominex were not measured, and so the report does not tell us how much of these two chemicals were actually in Mrs. Bennett's bloodstream, does it?"

"That is correct, but—"

"You've answered my question. I will get to the salicylates, don't worry, doctor."

"Okay, thank you," the coroner replied. "Because that is critically important."

"Yes, it is," Miraldi agreed. "Let's get to salicylates." Miraldi pointed to that word and to the words "found in many things and measured." "'Salicylates' is actually a classification or group that includes many chemicals, not just salicylamide."

"Yes, that is correct," Dr. Kopsch agreed.

"Let's talk for a moment about the things that contain salicylates. Aspirin contains salicylates, right?"

"Yes, it does."

"So if someone took several aspirin pills before they died and the coroner ran a toxicology screen, the toxicology screen would find and measure the salicylates from the aspirin, right?"

"Yes, it would."

"Salicylates are found in many foods, aren't they?"

"Yes, they are."

"Strawberries, apples, blueberries, grapefruit, prunes, to name a few fruits?" Miraldi asked.

"I don't know, but they are found in fruits."

"Cauliflower, cucumbers, mushrooms, spinach, hot pepper, and other vegetables?"

"I just know that they are found in some vegetables, yes."

"Candies like peppermint and licorice. Also in breath mints, nuts, peanuts, coffee, wine, beer, orange juice, rum, sherry, cheese—"

Mikus could feel his witness getting trapped. "Objection. That is a compound question and Mr. Miraldi is testifying in the guise of a question."

Miraldi resented the interruption. "I am just asking this witness if salicylates are found in these things. He can say yes or no. I could ask him about these things individually, but I don't want to waste the time."

Judge Pincura said, "I will allow it, but let's get to the point. It is near the lunch hour and it does not help us, Mr. Miraldi, when you name all these foods." The judge had not intended to make a joke, but a few jurors laughed.

"I don't know if salicylates are found in all those things," Dr. Kopsch responded.

"What about Alka-Seltzer, muscle pain creams, mouthwash, shampoos?"

"Again, I don't know."

"Regardless, doctor, we can agree that salicylates are found in many foods, drinks, aspirin, and other things around the house?"

"Yes."

"The only thing that the toxicology screen actually measured was this broad classification called salicylates?"

"Yes."

"How do you know that the concentration of salicylates found in Mrs. Bennett's blood didn't come from some of these other things, like aspirin or Alka-Seltzer or one of these foods?" Miraldi asked.

"There is no evidence that she took any aspirin or Alka-Seltzer. We do know that she did not eat supper that night, so she didn't get it from food. Although you listed many things, Mr. Miraldi, I am sure that Mrs. Bennett didn't eat strawberries or cauliflower for dinner." Dr. Kopsch paused and chuckled, but perspiration was beading on his forehead. "The only possible source of the salicylates would have been the salicylamide in the Sominex."

"How do you know that she didn't take a few aspirin that evening?"

"Her husband never mentioned that. The only thing we know for sure is that sixteen capsules of Sominex were missing," Dr. Kopsch said.

"How do you know that Mrs. Bennett didn't take some aspirin after Mr. Bennett left that evening?"

"As a doctor, I have to base opinions on things that we do know. We do know that her husband gave her some Sominex, and Sominex was in the house."

"She was an alcoholic, Dr. Kopsch. Salicylates are found in rum and sherry. How do you know that she didn't get the salicylates from those alcoholic drinks?"

"Her husband fixed her two drinks of whiskey when he got home. He didn't give her rum or sherry."

"You testified that Mrs. Bennett had consumed at least nine shots of liquor at the time she died because she had a blood alcohol level of 0.19. You have accounted for two shots, but not the other seven, have you?"

"Objection."

"Overruled."

Dr. Kopsch responded, "You are right that I do not know what other liquor Mrs. Bennett consumed that evening, but neither do you. I am not going to speculate on this and neither should this jury." Dr. Kopsch spoke rapidly and for the first time, his voice was testy.

"But it's okay for you to speculate that all of the salicylates came from the salicylamide in the Sominex? That's what you did. You are speculating, aren't you?" Miraldi snapped.

"I am not speculating. The Sominex bottle was missing sixteen tablets. I calculated based on the salicylates that Mrs. Bennett would have had sixteen to twenty Sominex pills in her system. Those two facts fit and make sense."

"How do you know that all of those sixteen Sominex tablets were taken at one time as opposed to over a period of weeks?" Miraldi countered.

"Objection. Asked and answered. Mr. Miraldi is badgering the witness and is being argumentative," Mikus yelled.

"That's a new question and the prosecutor knows it," Miraldi snapped back.

"Stop your bickering," Judge Pincura interrupted.

"Your ruling, Your Honor?" asked Mikus.

"The objection is overruled," replied the judge. "Dr. Kopsch, you can answer that question."

"Obviously, no one knows for sure when those pills were taken," Dr. Kopsch said, "but my trained mind tells me that it is no coincidence that sixteen of those pills were gone and Mrs. Bennett had a concentration of salicylates of 0.12 milligrams in her blood," Kopsch answered.

"That's just a long way of saying *you do not know* when those sixteen pills were ingested, isn't it? As far as anyone knows, Mr. Bennett may have taken some of those pills himself, right?"

"Objection. Repetitive and asked and answered."

"Sustained."

"Dr. Kopsch, you are not a chemist, are you?" Miraldi asked.

"All doctors have taken a number of chemistry courses in college, so I am well versed in chemistry."

"You do not make your living in the laboratory, working and experimenting with chemicals or measuring them?"

"Mr. Miraldi, you know that I am a physician."

"And you admit to making a mistake when you first calculated the number of sleeping capsules ingested by Mrs. Bennett?"

"Yes, Mr. Miraldi. We have been over that point ad nauseum. I did," Dr.

Kopsch responded, his voice calmer now.

Miraldi paused for a moment. He knew that a crisp, short cross-examination that limits the inquiry to a handful of points is usually the most effective. Most jurors can stay focused for a half hour, while some will pay attention for an hour, provided the testimony is lively or filled with tension and conflict. These thoughts filled Miraldi's head, but he also believed that, in some cases, a long, meticulous questioning can do the most damage. Miraldi still had dozens of prepared questions that he had not yet asked. After making some good inroads, he now had a decision to make. Should he sprint to the finish line by making a few more solid points or should he turn the cross-examination into a grueling marathon? He wanted more time to think about this.

"Your Honor, I have more questions for this witness, but this is probably a good stopping point," Miraldi suggested, sensing that the jurors were hungry and getting restless.

"Thank you. We will take our noontime recess. It is now twelve twenty. I will see everyone back at one thirty p.m.," the judge said.

After the jury filed out, Miraldi pulled a battered cheese sandwich from his briefcase and began nibbling on it. He again reviewed his pages of cross-examination topics. Should he quit while he was ahead or pound away with everything in his arsenal? His client's life was at stake. Forget the sprint; he and Dr. Kopsch were going to run a marathon.

CHAPTER 21

April 8, 1964 (Afternoon)

Miraldi realized that he would lose the attention of some of the jurors this afternoon, but he also understood that individual jurors would maintain their concentration at different times. Even though a particular juror would not remember the entire cross-examination, he hoped that the collective twelve would remember most of the critical points.

Even though he intended to slug it out with the coroner for what would probably be the entire afternoon, Miraldi did not want the examination to turn into a rambling series of disjointed questions that would lose the jury. He had some definite goals.

He wanted the jury (and Dr. Kopsch) to quickly see that he, too, understood the medicine and could intelligently challenge Dr. Kopsch's pseudo-scientific opinions. Once he had some credibility regarding the medicine, he hoped to show that Dr. Kopsch had rushed to judgment and ignored other reasonable, competing explanations for Florence's death. He would also challenge Dr. Kopsch's bald claim that Mrs. Bennett would have instantly revived when immersed in the scalding water and could have saved herself. He also intended to show that Dr. Kopsch's trial testimony regarding time of death was at odds with his preliminary hearing. Miraldi knew that a strong finish was essential. Dr. Kopsch had made material changes to Dr. Chesner's initial autopsy report, presumably to bolster the prosecution's case. Miraldi would confront him with this, confident that Dr. Kopsch could not wiggle his way out.

When Dr. Kopsch again took the witness stand, Miraldi began by delving into the anatomy of the skin, the definition of various types of burns, the body changes after death, the findings in the autopsy, shock and the body's reaction to it, pulmonary edema, and hyperthermia. Instead of asking questions on these medical topics, Miraldi made a statement of medical fact and asked Dr. Kopsch if he agreed with that statement. This approach eventually drew the objection of Mikus, who saw that this process made Miraldi look as knowledgeable about the medicine as Dr. Kopsch. Judge Pincura sustained the objection, forcing Miraldi to ask questions rather than make statements.

With the medicine out of the way, Miraldi wanted the jury to see just how quickly Dr. Kopsch had decided that Casper was a murderer.

"You knew nothing about the Bennetts before you arrived at their house?" Miraldi asked.

"That's right, although I later learned that I was the anesthesiologist for Mr. Bennett when he had an abdominal surgery."

Ignoring that answer, Miraldi asked, "Sergeant Springowski told you about the Bennetts when you were alone with him in the house?"

"He gave me some basic background."

"He told you that they had a very rocky marriage?"

"Yes."

"That Mrs. Bennett had brought divorce proceedings against her husband?"

"I think so, but I am not sure when I learned that exactly."

"They were alcoholics?"

"Yes."

"That Mr. Bennett had a girlfriend?"

"I can't remember if I learned that then or later." Dr. Kopsch remained composed and polite in his responses.

"That they had verbal altercations?"

"Maybe. I don't know."

"Well, Dr. Kopsch, he let you know that this was not a happy marriage, right?"

"I knew that they were both alcoholics and they had a history of marital problems."

Miraldi could see that several jurors were yawning and struggling to maintain their concentration. He put an edge into his voice and asked the next question in an accusatory manner. "Let me get to it point blank. Did Sergeant Springowski suggest to you that the Bennetts likely had a violent and deadly confrontation on the night that she died?"

"No, sir. He did not." Dr. Kopsch was either indignant or feigning it.

"Did Sergeant Springowski tell you that he was suspicious that Casper Bennett had killed his wife?"

"He did not say that to me."

"Not in so many words, but he implied it?" Miraldi pressed.

"No, he did not. Even if he had, I would have ignored him. That is the way I am trained."

"Yet, that night, before an autopsy was done and before you had the results of a toxicology screen, you concluded that Casper Bennett drowned his wife, did you not?"

"I most certainly did not. I did not reach that conclusion that night, Mr. Miraldi."

"Oh, you didn't?"

"That's right, sir. I did not."

Miraldi walked to the lectern and pulled out an exhibit identified as "Report of Investigation." It was signed by Dr. Kopsch and dated December 20, 1963. He handed it to Dr. Kopsch.

"This document has your signature and the seal of the coroner on it?"

"Yes."

"It is dated December 20, 1963, the night Florence Bennett died, right?"

"Yes."

"Doesn't this report state that Mrs. Bennett's death was due to homicide?"

Dr. Kopsch's eyes fluttered for a second and he momentarily looked up at the ceiling. Miraldi immediately saw the coroner's reaction and wondered if any of the jurors did too. Dr. Kopsch quickly regained his composure. "It does, but I prepared that report a few days after her death," Dr. Kopsch said, his voice edgy with protest.

"Doctor, you never believed that Mrs. Bennett's death was an accident, did you?"

"I was open to that possibility."

"You never believed that her intoxication that evening or her use of sleeping pills made her susceptible to an accident, did you?"

"I took that into consideration, Mr. Miraldi."

"That's not what you said at the preliminary hearing, is it?"

"I don't know what you mean. You will have to show me in the transcript," Dr. Kopsch said as his left hand wiped against the left side of his face.

Miraldi was bluffing; Dr. Kopsch had not directly said this at the preliminary hearing. "You said that you considered three possibilities—accident, suicide, and homicide."

"Yes, that is correct. I remember that."

"An intoxicated person is more likely to fall than a sober person?"

"Yes."

"Mrs. Bennett was clearly intoxicated and had taken some sleeping pills that night?"

"Yes. We have been over that point several times now," Dr. Kopsch replied.

"Doesn't that make her more susceptible to falls and accidents?"

"Looking at all of the facts, these facts only fit as a homicide, Mr. Miraldi." Dr. Kopsch had given that same vague response at the preliminary hearing and he would rely on it again.

"Particularly if you ignore her intoxication and her history of prior falls."

"Objection," Mikus said as he got to his feet.

"I made my point and I will withdraw my question," Miraldi said.

"Objection to Mr. Miraldi's gratuitous comment," Mikus said, his face reddening.

"The jury will disregard Mr. Miraldi's last comment," Judge Pincura said.

Throughout the examination, Miraldi watched the jurors. Although he had lost some of them during the discussion of the medicine, they were alert during this last exchange. He pressed on to discuss other possibilities that he believed Dr. Kopsch had failed to consider before arriving at his conclusion, particularly hyperthermia and Mrs. Bennett's chronic alcoholism.

Over the last several weeks, Miraldi had read many medical articles about hyperthermia in preparation for the trial. He knew that hyperthermia occurs when the body's temperature rises above its normal temperature, and that heat exhaustion was probably the most common example of a condition caused by hyperthermia. Miraldi also learned that if a person's body temperature reached 110 to 114 degrees Fahrenheit, the blood cells became damaged and could not carry oxygen, and death resulted in a matter of minutes. With the bathwater at 150 to 160 degrees, Florence Bennett's body temperature could have reached the 110-degree mark very rapidly.

After asking Dr. Kopsch to define "hyperthermia," Miraldi asked him if he considered hyperthermia as the cause of Mrs. Bennett's death.

"Mrs. Bennett drowned. Dr. Chesner's autopsy confirmed this," Dr. Kopsch replied again, briefly showing a bit of irritation in his voice.

"Let's talk about the autopsy's confirmation of drowning. The chloride test was negative, wasn't it?" Miraldi asked.

"Yes, it was."

"Tell me if I have this correct. If a person drowns, the pathologist doing the autopsy should find a difference in the chloride levels between the right and left chambers of the heart, isn't that right?"

"Not exactly. You only have a difference in the chloride levels if there has been prolonged drowning."

"Oh, I see, only in prolonged drowning." Miraldi paused for effect. "Wait a minute, Dr. Kopsch." Now Miraldi put on a face of disbelief and showed that to the jury. "A person either drowns or they don't drown. Dr. Chesner did the chloride test and it was negative."

"Mr. Miraldi, you understand a little bit of the medicine, but unfortunately for you and the jury, not enough. The chloride test is positive only if there has been prolonged drowning."

"Well, Dr. Kopsch, we will see if any other doctor agrees with you on that point later in the trial."

"Objection!" Mikus screamed. "That's not a question."

"Sustained. Mr. Miraldi, stick to questioning the witness," the judge chided.

"As long as we are on the subject of drowning, shouldn't the autopsy show that there was foam in the esophagus to confirm drowning?"

"Mr. Miraldi, your understanding of the medicine is unfortunately incomplete. There is foam only when a person struggles above the surface of the water for a long period of time."

"Oh, once again, this test was negative because there was no prolonged drowning, is that what you are saying?" Miraldi asked.

"Not exactly. Foam develops when a person struggles for a long time in a body of water and then drowns." Dr. Kopsch realized that Miraldi was mocking him, but he refused to get angry.

"I keep waiting for you to explain to the jury how the autopsy showed that Mrs. Bennett drowned. So far, all you have told us is that she was found in water."

"Her esophagus was burned, Mr. Miraldi, and she had pulmonary edema in the lungs."

"A lot of things can cause pulmonary edema, can't they?"

"Drowning is certainly one of them," Dr. Kopsch shot back.

Miraldi knew that neither pulmonary edema nor a burned esophagus was indicative of drowning, but he knew that arguing with the coroner would get him nowhere. Dr. Kopsch was committed to his opinion and he was not going to back down or be objective. Miraldi would have to wait for his own experts to make those points. But before he switched subjects, he would take another jab at Dr. Kopsch's last few statements.

"Oh, by the way, is Dr. Chesner, the physician who actually performed the autopsy, going to testify before the jury and confirm all these points that you just made?"

Miraldi could see several jurors lean forward toward the witness.

"I don't think that has been decided at this point. That is up to Mr. Mikus and Mr. Otero, not me."

Miraldi stood and faced the jury. "Oh, I see. The prosecutors have never discussed that with you, is that right?" he said, raising his eyebrows to show his skepticism.

"Objection."

"Sustained."

"Can we also agree that Mrs. Bennett was a chronic alcoholic?" Miraldi asked.

"That is the history I was given."

"Thank you, Dr. Kopsch. Isn't it a well-established medical fact that chronic alcoholics die for unexpected reasons?"

"I don't know about that, sir."

"Is that perhaps something you could ask Dr. Chesner?"

"Objection!" Mikus shouted.

"I will withdraw the question," Miraldi responded. "In any event, you did not consider that Mrs. Bennett died as a result of her chronic alcoholism?"

"Mr. Miraldi, I considered everything. There was no evidence in the autopsy that she died of anything related to alcoholism."

"There were fatty deposits found in the liver, were there not?" Miraldi asked.

"Let me check." Dr. Kopsch looked at the autopsy findings before answering, "Yes."

"Those fatty deposits in the liver are routinely found in chronic alcoholics?"

"Yes."

"With chronic alcoholics, aren't those fatty deposits sometimes unexpectedly released into the bloodstream, causing blockages in blood vessels and even death?"

"Dr. Chesner found no evidence of that."

"Did he test for that?"

"He is a competent pathologist and I am sure that he did."

"But you are not sure whether Dr. Chesner is going to testify in this case?"

"Objection."

Before Miraldi could withdraw the question, Judge Pincura said, "Sustained." The judge gave Miraldi a disapproving stare.

Miraldi next attacked Dr. Kopsch's recent opinion that Mrs. Bennett died around eight thirty p.m. This opinion was much more precise than his estimate at the preliminary hearing. Miraldi simply had to contrast the two opinions.

"Doctor, at the preliminary hearing, didn't you state under oath that it was hard to determine the time of death for sure?"

"Yes, sir. I said words to that effect."

"Didn't you testify previously that Mrs. Bennett had been dead for up to two hours when you examined her at ten p.m. on December twentieth?"

"Yes. That was my testimony."

"Your preliminary hearing testimony allows for the possibility that Mrs. Bennett had been dead for only a few minutes when Mr. Bennett found her sometime around nine thirty p.m. Am I correct?"

"That conclusion is consistent with my prior statement," Dr. Kopsch said, continuing to be calm and confident.

"Is that still consistent with your opinion today?"

"That is still an outside possibility, but I think it is much more probable that she died around eight thirty p.m. because she had some apparent rigor mortis when I examined her at ten p.m."

"Doctor, are you telling the jury that there is rigor mortis and then something different—something called apparent rigor mortis?"

"No, Mr. Miraldi, I am not. The extreme hot water increased the onset of rigor mortis so that when I saw the body at ten p.m., it had the beginning signs of rigor mortis."

"But you were able to move Mrs. Bennett's lower legs when you examined the body that night. Correct?"

"Yes, I could move her arms and legs. However, I could tell that the muscles were just beginning to get stiff. It is something that the trained eye can detect."

"I don't see where that finding of rigor mortis was incorporated into the autopsy report as part of the history. Why is that?"

"I am sure that I told Dr. Chesner that information when we talked before he did the autopsy. I can't speak for him on why that is not included."

"Can we agree, however, Dr. Kopsch, that at the preliminary hearing, you did not have a precise time of death, but merely a window of two hours when that death could have occurred?"

"That is true, but my testimony today is totally consistent with my earlier statements."

Dr. Kopsch's last answers frustrated Miraldi. Try as he might to read the jurors' mind, Miraldi could not tell whether they were beginning to doubt the coroner's knowledge or credibility. The coroner remained aloof, confident, and quite capable of extricating himself from seemingly conflicting statements.

Miraldi moved on to another of Dr. Kopsch's damaging opinions. "Dr. Kopsch, is it your opinion that Mrs. Bennett, regardless of her state, would have revived if her body had fallen into a bathtub of scalding water and she could have taken steps to save herself?"

"It is."

"Someone would have to physically hold her in the water to keep her from getting out of scalding water, correct?"

"Yes. As I said, she was a living, breathing woman. A normal instinctive response is to get out of scalding water."

"Would this happen to a person who loses her balance, falls and hits her head, and then topples into the water in an unconscious state?"

"There is no evidence that Mrs. Bennett sustained any injury to her head."

"Please answer my question. Does an unconscious person feel pain when immersed in scalding water?"

"It depends on the degree of unconsciousness."

"Wait a minute, Dr. Kopsch. You are an anesthesiologist. You put people to sleep every day—into an unconscious state—before they have a surgery. Isn't that to keep the person from feeling pain?"

"Yes, properly sedated, a patient under a general anesthesia does not feel pain."

"Thank you." Miraldi paused and looked at the jurors. One of the male jurors slowly nodded back to him. "Wouldn't a person that has at least fifty percent of her body suddenly immersed in scalding water go into shock?"

"I am not aware of any tests that prove that."

"Doctor, neurogenic shock occurs when the skin or interior of the body receives a stimulus and it triggers the cessation of the heart?"

"I believe that is a correct definition, counselor."

"People who are in shock do not feel pain, do they?"

"That is correct."

"Isn't it possible that Mrs. Bennett went into a state of shock the moment her body fell into a bathtub full of scalding water?"

"I am not aware of any specific medical literature that either supports or denies such a scenario."

"But you do agree that people who are in a state of shock do not feel pain?"

"I agree with that, but I do not believe that there is any evidence whatsoever that Mrs. Bennett sustained neurogenic shock or any other type of shock."

"Doctor, are you aware of the case of the college coed who became intoxicated and fainted while taking a shower and scalded to death?"

For most of the morning session, Mikus had felt confident as his expert fended off Miraldi's questions. However, for the last hour, Mikus had sensed that the momentum was beginning to shift away from the prosecution. He saw Miraldi not as a skilled cross-examiner, but as a clever twister of the truth. He knew that the defense team only had to establish reasonable doubt, and Miraldi had caught a rhythm, sowing the seeds of doubt about the objectivity and knowledge of his key witness. Mikus rose to his feet. "Objection. This is highly improper. What evidence is there of this coed case? Mr. Miraldi has probably invented this story for the jury."

Miraldi was tired of Mikus's constant interruptions, guised in the form of objections. He was convinced that whenever he was making headway against the coroner, Mikus interposed a frivolous or technical objection. Miraldi turned slowly to Mikus and in an icily polite tone said, "What are you afraid of, Paul?"

Mikus stood in silence for several seconds while his face reddened. He then pointed his finger at Miraldi and yelled, "I am not afraid of anything, Mr. Miraldi, least of all this case. You are the one that should be afraid." He paused for a few seconds, drew several feet closer to Miraldi, stopped, and then began again. "In my long career, I have never heard any attorney make any statement as improper and prejudicial as the one just uttered by Mr. Miraldi. I want the court to admonish Mr. Miraldi and declare a mistrial."

The jurors looked at one another both quizzically and expectantly. Judge Pincura had been squirting some tobacco into a spittoon when Mikus's outburst first began. Ignoring Mikus's request for a mistrial, Judge Pincura said dryly, "The jury is to disregard the comments of the defense counsel. Proceed, Mr. Miraldi, with your next *question*."

Miraldi had forgotten his last question. He flipped to another page on his legal pad and asked, "Dr. Kopsch, although you concluded that Mrs. Bennett drowned, the skin about her eyes was not burned. Can you explain that?"

"Certainly. This would indicate that her head was tilted a bit backward in the water and the water was up to the air passages."

Miraldi wondered if the jury was as tired of Dr. Kopsch's know-it-all attitude as he was. He turned away from the witness and stared at the jury again as he asked his next question. "Do you mean to tell me that it is possible for you to tell us what position Mrs. Bennett's body was in before her husband found her?" Miraldi asked.

"Yes," the coroner answered.

"You surmise, don't you?" Miraldi prodded, still focusing on the jurors.

"No, I do not surmise."

"Then you are clairvoyant?" Miraldi suggested. He could see two of the jurors in the back row look at each other and suppress a laugh.

Unlike the prosecutor, Dr. Kopsch did not take the bait. "No," he said evenly. "I am just observant."

Miraldi sensed that it was time to make his final point. He walked over to the court reporter and marked the original autopsy report as an exhibit. He then picked up the official autopsy report that had been marked and identified during the coroner's direct testimony.

"We have two autopsy reports, don't we, Dr. Kopsch?"

"We have the initial report that Dr. Chesner did not proofread and then we have the official autopsy report that Dr. Chesner signed after he edited the first report. So yes, we have two reports."

"Let's make sure the jury knows how this report is prepared. And you tell me if I am wrong. As Dr. Chesner is doing the autopsy, he has a dictation machine and he speaks into it as he makes his findings. Or he may dictate into the machine at various times during and after the autopsy. Do I have that right?"

"Yes, that is the way it is done. Dr. Chesner may dictate more after the autopsy is completed, but that is essentially correct."

"A stenographer listens to the dictation tape and transcribes the report with a typewriter. Do I have that right?"

"Yes."

"Then later, Dr. Chesner may make corrections where the stenographer perhaps did not hear him correctly, or he may amend his statements because he does not like the way his findings are formulated."

"Yes, that is the process essentially."

"Now, in the final report, the only history provided is 'This forty-four-year-old white female was found dead in her home.' Is that correct?"

"Yes."

"But in the original report, Dr. Chesner gave a very detailed history. Let me read it to you. 'We are dealing with a rather peculiar history. This is all hearsay. She was found dead in the bathtub full of scalding water. She is said to be an alcoholic. There were empty bottles of sleeping pills. There was a broken liquor bottle in the bathroom and there were said to be five empty bottles of liquor in the bathroom. She was seen by the coroner, who made his examination last night, and she was sent into the hospital for autopsy.' Did I read that correctly?"

"Yes."

"Did you give that history to Dr. Chesner?"

"Not in those words, no, but I told him some of the background information."

"Were there empty bottles of sleeping pills as stated in this history?"

"No."

"Was there a broken liquor bottle in the bathroom?"

"No. There was a broken bottle of what was later determined to be bubble bath."

"Were there five liquor bottles in the bathroom?"

"No, but there were empty bottles under the kitchen sink."

"The stenographer didn't just make up those words and slip them into the report, did she?"

"Probably not."

"Did you ask Dr. Chesner to revise that part of the history?"

"I told him that he was wrong on those facts and he thought it was just easier to omit the entire thing."

"I see," Miraldi said as he again looked to the jury to see if they were buying this explanation. "Let's examine another topic. When describing the area of burns, Dr. Chesner wrote: 'The lower legs, both anteriorly and posteriorly, and the dorsum of the feet show very little involvement.' Did I read that correctly? Very little involvement of the lower legs and feet?"

"Yes."

"In the final report, that was changed. It now reads: 'The lower legs, both anteriorly and posteriorly, and the dorsum and solar aspect of the feet show *no involvement* by the burn process.' Again, did I read that correctly? The new report says absolutely no involvement in the lower legs of any burn process. The first report says very little involvement. Am I correct?"

"Yes, you read that correctly, but can I explain why the change was made?"

"You can explain when Mr. Mikus asks you additional questions. You have answered my question that there has been a change. I have another question for you. You claim that Mrs. Bennett's legs were on the ledge of the tub while Mr. Bennett held her head underwater. Do I have that right?"

"Yes. That is my opinion."

"So your opinion is stronger if there are no burns on the lower legs as opposed to some burns on the lower legs. Is that correct?"

"You are taking things out of context, Mr. Miraldi. Dr. Chesner never reported burns on Mrs. Bennett's lower legs at any time. In his original report, he was referring to the cuts on her lower legs—that's what he meant by 'little involvement.' He was not referring to burns at all."

"Oh, I see, but you asked him to change that, didn't you?"

"I did not ask him to change anything. I talked to him about how confusing that was and it was his decision completely to amend the report there."

"And again, we don't know if Dr. Chesner is going to testify at this trial, do we?"

"Objection!" Mikus screamed. "How many times do I have to object to the same improper question by Mr. Miraldi?"

"Sustained. Mr. Miraldi, I am losing my patience with you," Judge Pincura said in an exasperated tone. "You know that is not a proper question. If you ask it again, there will be consequences."

"Let's go to Dr. Chesner's conclusions on the two reports. In the first report, he determined that Mrs. Bennett's death was due to *probable drowning*. Again, did I report this correctly? Drowning was not certain, but probable."

"I disagree with your final comment that drowning was not a certainty."

"He wrote 'probable.' Doesn't 'probable drowning' mean that it is not the only possibility? That's what it means to me, lawyers, and just about everybody else in the world."

"Objection."

"Sustained. Rephrase your question."

"Doesn't 'probable drowning' mean that there are other possibilities, but that drowning is the most likely?"

"I don't know. It could mean that, and then again, it could just have been the way Dr. Chesner phrased it."

"Anyway, in the final report, the word 'probable' has been stricken. It just says 'drowning.' Am I correct about this?"

"Yes. Dr. Chesner didn't believe—"

"You have answered my question. You are not to testify about what Dr. Chesner believed—that's hearsay unless Dr. Chesner actually testifies." He turned to the judge. "That statement's not going to get me into trouble, is it?"

Judge Pincura and Mikus ignored the comment and Miraldi sat down.

Miraldi's questioning had taken almost the entire afternoon. Prosecutor Mikus knew that he needed to ask additional follow-up questions to switch the momentum back in his favor. He established that Dr. Kopsch had examined the body and found no burns at all on her lower legs and feet. The coroner also confirmed that the blood spots were quite fresh when he got to the scene. Finally, Mikus asked Dr. Kopsch if a person in a drunken or drugged stupor can be roused by painful stimuli.

"Absolutely, they can," Dr. Kopsch said.

"Was Mrs. Bennett in a stupor based on her drug and alcoholic intake?"

"Yes, she was."

"But scalding water would still have roused her completely?"

"Yes, it would. Absolutely."

"Your Honor, pending the admission of our exhibits, the prosecution rests," Mikus announced to the court.

"Very well, I will dismiss the jury and entertain motions for introduction of the exhibits as well as any other motions by either side," Judge Pincura stated. After the judge excused the jury for the day, he admitted the prosecution's exhibits in their entirety. Adams made a motion for acquittal, claiming that the prosecution's case was wholly inadequate to establish first-degree murder. His argument was half-hearted and Judge Pincura quickly denied it, not even asking the prosecution to respond to it.

When the court day ended, Miraldi was exhausted, while Mikus continued to seethe. Miraldi believed that he had destroyed the coroner's theory about the cause of death. Adams told him that he had crushed Dr. Kopsch. Several local attorneys who had witnessed the day's events were equally complimentary. However, Miraldi had a nagging fear. The jury may have already concluded that Bennett was guilty before Dr. Kopsch testified. If so, his cross-examination was an exercise in futility.

Miraldi also had a newfound respect for Dr. Kopsch. Except for a few brief moments, the coroner had never lost his composure. Although Miraldi was convinced that Dr. Kopsch's conclusions were completely wrongheaded, he realized that the coroner was sincere and fiercely believed his own opinions. Sometimes jurors base their opinions not on what the witness says, but on a witness's body language and confidence. If this jury focused only on outward appearances, they could believe that Dr. Kopsch won the day, a thought that depressed Miraldi as he trudged to his car.

Tomorrow would be another grueling day for the defense. Casper Bennett would take the stand, as would his girlfriend, Irene Miller. Miraldi and Adams knew that Mikus could potentially destroy Casper Bennett with an effective cross-examination. If so, the case would be over. Miraldi's cross-examination of Dr. Kopsch would be a small footnote in the story of Bennett's conviction. However, if Bennett held up on the stand, the defense would have a chance. Tomorrow, Adams would handle Bennett's direct examination, thrusting Adams into the spotlight and giving Miraldi a brief respite.

CHAPTER 22

April 9, 1964 (Morning)

Ever since the trial began, Paul Mikus had been waiting for this day. Mikus believed that Casper Bennett had been given great latitude both at the police station and during his grand jury testimony. The authorities allowed Bennett to tell his story uninterrupted and unchallenged. Despite this, both the Lorain police and the grand jurors rejected Bennett's vivid and emotional claims of innocence. No one had believed Bennett's story then, and Mikus would make certain that no one believed that pathological liar today.

Mikus flipped open his briefcase and pulled out his notes for the Bennett cross-examination. Suddenly, he tossed the legal pad on the trial table without looking at it. "I know what I'm going to do," he said to himself.

Feeling both nervous and hopeful, Lon Adams walked up the sandstone steps into the courthouse. He would meet Bennett at the sheriff's civil office, located on the courthouse's first floor. As they had throughout the trial, the deputies would bring Bennett to this office before taking him into the courtroom. When Adams walked in, Bennett was talking to the two deputies assigned to guard him. All three were chuckling about something Bennett had just said. Caught off guard by Adams's appearance, the deputies quickly stiffened and moved out of his way.

After Adams closed the door, he asked Bennett, "What was that all about?"

"Oh, you know. I just was talking about the breakfast I got at jail this morning," Bennett replied. Bennett's eyes closed involuntarily and he audibly exhaled. Realizing what was ahead of him today, Bennett seemed to shrink in front of Adams. "I guess this is it, huh?"

"Yes. Today, you get to tell the jury what happened. And this time, it is not rigged against you," Adams said, patting Bennett on his left forearm.

"For once," Bennett replied, his eyes finding the clock on the wall to his left. "I'm not worried about the questions from you; it's Mikus that I'm worried about."

"We've been over this before, Casper. He's going to try and shake you up as much as he can. He will yell. He will scream. No matter what he does, you are to stay polite and stay firm, okay?" Adams said, looking at Bennett's eyes and trying to make sure that his admonition had registered.

"Yeah, I know," Bennett said, almost in a whisper.

"Anything you want to talk to me about before we go into the courtroom?"

"No." Then, after a brief pause, Bennett said, "I never thought it would come down to this."

"Yeah, I know. Just remember, when you tell the jury about that night, you made a mistake about the time you left the house. It was closer to six thirty. Since you gave those statements, you've had more time to think about it. You were panicked right when it happened. Okay?"

"I know. I know. I was trying to protect Irene, too. I didn't want to tell them about sweeping her walk. Like I told you and Ray, I wasn't wearing a wristwatch that night either."

"Well, Irene will testify before you and she will establish part of your whereabouts on December twentieth. You'll hear her testimony before you go on the stand. You'll want to keep your testimony as consistent with hers as possible."

"Yeah, okay. I got it."

"Good. Then let's get to the courtroom. It's almost nine o' clock."

"Mr. Adams, how do you think things are going?" Bennett asked, his voice tense. Adams glanced over at his client, whose shoulders were slumped as he walked down the hall.

"Good, Casper. Actually, I think things are going very well. We are going to see this thing through."

****

John Otero sat at the prosecution table, doodling on his yellow legal pad as Irene Miller began her testimony. For the last few days, he'd felt shut out from any meaningful participation in the trial, and he was quite unhappy about it. Although he'd expected that Mikus would cross-examine Casper Bennett, Otero was dismayed when Mikus said he was going to cross-examine Miller, too. Otero had questioned her effectively at the grand jury proceeding and he saw no reason to be excluded from some of today's limelight.

Otero watched as Miraldi questioned this strange-looking woman. Irene Miller looked older than her stated age of fifty-two. Her gray hair was dyed a dark red and was worn in a bouffant, beehive style. She was wearing a black suit with a white blouse, and her eyes were hidden behind dark sunglasses. She completed the ensemble with matching black gloves, high-heeled shoes, and a purse.

She trembled as she answered the first few questions, but then her voice lost its nervousness and she began responding with a clear, prompt tone. She told the jury that she lived with her eighty-four-year-old father and worked as a barmaid at the Sons of Italy club. She had two adult sons and three grandchildren, and, indeed, she looked like a grandmother, particularly with her prominent double chin.

Otero thought, *What man would kill his wife so he could marry her?* Her very appearance made this scenario seem preposterous. *Let Mikus question her*, he thought.

"How do you know Casper Bennett?" Miraldi asked.

"He and I have been dating off and on for the last five years or so," Mrs.

Miller responded, stealing a glance at the jury to see how they reacted. For days they had listened to testimony about this relationship. If anything, they were taken aback by her matronly appearance.

Wanting to show that Mrs. Miller was not a tramp, Miraldi asked, "Have you dated other men during those five years?"

"No. Not really. I have had a few dates with other men, but for the most part, I just go out with Casper."

"How much had you seen of him over the last six months before Mrs. Bennett's death?"

"Well, I only dated him when he was separated from his wife. When he moved back with his wife in July, I stopped seeing him. Then I saw him on two Sundays in December when I was off work. We went shopping one time for a few hours and then on the fifteenth, he drove down with me, my cousin, and her two children to visit my relatives in Massillon."

"When was the last time you saw Mr. Bennett before Mrs. Bennett's death?"

"That December fifteenth, when my cousin drove us all down to Massillon." She decided not to mention the five-minute meeting she had with him on the nineteenth when she ran out to his car to show him her new hair coloring.

"I want to turn your attention to December twentieth, that Friday night when Mrs. Bennett died," Miraldi began.

"Yes."

"Did you have any contact with Casper Bennett on the twentieth?"

Mrs. Miller looked straight at Miraldi, ignoring the jury. "I had two phone conversations with him that night. Do you want me to go into those?"

"Yes, please tell us about them, when he called and what you talked about," Miraldi urged.

"The first one was around five p.m. I could tell he was calling from a pay phone because I could hear the coins going in. He asked me how I was doing and I told him that I was busy and that I couldn't talk very long, and we didn't."

"Then what?"

"Well, he called me again at work. This time it was around eight p.m. or eight thirty. Again, I told him that I was very busy. He said that he'd brushed the snow off the sidewalk and driveway at my dad's house. There was like a little dusting of snow then. Not much. I can't remember if he told me that he'd left me some beer or not."

"Did you notice anything unusual about his voice?"

"No, not at all. It was normal."

"Could you tell where he was calling from?"

"Again, I heard the coins jingling into the pay phone, so I knew he wasn't calling from home."

"Did he say anything else?"

"Like I told him, we were very busy at the club and I couldn't talk much. He promised to call me back later that evening."

"And did he?" Miraldi asked as he looked at the jury.

"No, he never did."

Miraldi kept his gaze on the jury and looked at them quizzically. Would a man who was about to murder his wife casually tell anyone that he would give them a call in a few hours? If the jurors were putting the facts together, they would also remember that Bennett displayed that same carefree attitude when playfully withdrawing a five-dollar bill from the reach of the gas station attendant earlier that evening.

"Did you go home after work?"

"Objection. Leading question," Mikus's voice boomed out.

Before the judge could rule, Miraldi asked, "What did you do after work?"

"I went home. The walk and driveway were swept off and there was a six-pack of Black Label beer by the back door, so I assumed Casper had been there and left it."

"Objection. Speculation. I ask that her answer be stricken," Mikus protested.

"Mrs. Miller, you can't guess as to who cleaned off your driveway or left the beer. If you saw someone do it, then you can tell us what you saw, but no guesses," Judge Pincura ruled.

"Is your eighty-four-year-old father able to remove snow?"

"No."

"Does anyone else ever clean the snow from your dad's walks and driveway, a neighbor or someone that you hire to do it?"

"Either I do it or Casper does it."

"Thank you. No further questions." Miraldi sat down.

Mikus jumped out of his seat and stood with his arms akimbo about eight feet from the witness. Mrs. Miller folded her arms in front of her chest and looked expectantly at Mikus.

In a loud staccato delivery, Mikus asked several leading questions, each of which Mrs. Miller quietly agreed to. In a few moments, Mikus established that Mrs. Miller was divorced twice, worked as a barmaid, dated Casper Bennett for the last five years, and did so knowing Bennett was a married man.

Mrs. Miller looked over at the jury. "I did not date Casper when he was living with his wife, only when he was separated from her."

"Oh, I see," Mikus cut in. "You just testified that in December of 1963, you went out with Mr. Bennett on two successive Sundays—and he was living with his wife then, wasn't he?"

Mrs. Miller pursed her lips and then scowled at Mikus. She glanced at Bennett and tugged on one of the black gloves that covered her hands. "Well, you see, I thought Casper was no longer living with his wife at that time."

"Oh, so tell the jury how you had that impression, please?"

Mrs. Miller realized that she was trapped. She could protect either her own honor or Bennett's credibility, but not both, and she would have to choose. "That's what Casper told me," she said, looking down at her now-folded hands.

"So, he told you that he was no longer living at home, is that right?"

"Yes, something like that," Mrs. Miller said contritely.

Mikus was off and running. He then established that Bennett paid for their trips to Las Vegas and Hawaii and spent Christmas with her in 1961 and 1962 at her home. She admitted that Bennett gave her small, inexpensive gifts. Mikus looked at the jury, coaxing them to remember Bennett's grand jury testimony where he admitted spending thousands of dollars on her.

Mikus grinned as he asked the next question. "There were times when Mr. Bennett became insanely jealous about you, weren't there?"

Mrs. Miller pretended to be embarrassed by the question, but once she began speaking, her voice betrayed pride. "There were times when I would go on dates with other men and Casper would somehow find out about it, show up at the restaurant, and embarrass me. So yes, he was jealous."

"He also became violent with you when you refused to see him?"

"Objection, Your Honor. May we approach the bench?" Miraldi said. Although the judge would likely allow this line of questioning, Miraldi had to find out whether Judge Pincura would place some limits on what would be damaging testimony. All four attorneys walked slowly toward the judge.

Once they had assembled, Miraldi whispered, "The defense has been very patient with the prosecutor throughout his questioning of this witness. The defense called Mrs. Miller merely to establish parts of our client's alibi. The only proper line of inquiry is to test Mrs. Miller's testimony insofar as it relates to Mr. Bennett's alibi. The charges against our client are murder, not adultery, which is not a crime in this jurisdiction the last time I checked. Mr. Mikus's titillating inquiries about Mrs. Miller's relationship with the defendant are not relevant to any issue in this case and are prejudicial."

Judge Pincura raised his eyebrows and said to Mikus, "And what do you say?"

Mikus pressed his chest against the outer lip of the judge's bench. "The defendant's motive for killing his wife was because he was involved with another woman. He didn't want to divorce her and pay alimony. Bennett wanted his wife out of the way so that he could marry Mrs. Miller. We have every right to explore this. We also have every right to inquire about Mr. Bennett's violent behavior toward women, including his lover, Mrs. Miller."

"Your Honor," Miraldi said, "I sat through Mr. Otero's opening statement and he said that the state would prove that the defendant killed his wife in order to get the proceeds from life insurance. The state made no claim that the defendant's motive had anything to do with this relationship."

"As Mr. Miraldi well knows, people can have multiple motives for doing something," Mikus said, his voice expressing a feigned patience. "The prosecution can certainly maintain that the defendant wanted to murder his wife for multiple reasons. I am sure that when Mr. Miraldi was a prosecutor, he had cases where he argued multiple motives for a crime. Also, Mr. Bennett was spending lavishly to entertain Mrs. Miller. He needed the insurance money to pay off his debts and continue to spend big dollars on his very special *lady*."

"I am going to allow this question and others that develop the relationship between the defendant and this woman. The defense put her on the stand and the defense can't limit her testimony to just those topics that help its case." Looking at Miraldi, the judge said, "You put her up there and now you are stuck with her."

"Thank you, Your Honor," Mikus said as he quickly turned away from the bench, his head held high and his body almost pulsing with vindication. Except for Mikus, the men quickly took their seats again.

"So, Mrs. Miller, did the defendant ever get violent with you?"

"I wouldn't use the word 'violent,'" she replied. "That's too strong a word for it."

"Didn't Mr. Bennett break down your apartment door when you refused to see him?"

"That may have been an accident," she replied, looking nervously at the defense table.

"If it was an accident, why did you hire Mr. Adams, the attorney sitting next to Mr. Bennett, to get a peace bond, or restraining order, against him?" Mikus's eyes gleamed. He couldn't help but think that this cross-examination was a helpful warm-up to the one he would inflict on Bennett in a short while.

"Not because of the door incident," she replied, her voice cracking. "He just wouldn't leave me alone after I broke up with him. He was always calling me on the phone, driving around the block, like he was spying on me. He was just being a nuisance," she maintained.

"And you weren't afraid of a man who did these weird things to you?"

"No, I wasn't," Miller assured him.

"You just wanted a restraining order against him to stop him from phoning you and driving around the block where you lived?"

"That's about right."

"Despite this, you got back together with Mr. Bennett?" Mikus asked.

"Yes, Casper can be a lot of fun. He took me to many fine restaurants and he provided good companionship," she said, glancing again at the jury and then back to Mikus.

"Mr. Bennett discussed marriage with you, didn't he?"

"I had no intention of marrying Casper Bennett," she said, her voice crisp and firm but not angry.

"He mentioned it to you though, didn't he?"

"It's not like what you're trying to portray. Casper mentioned something about getting married when we first started seeing each other—like in 1959. I am talking years ago. I told him that . . ." Mrs. Miller paused. She'd told Bennett that she didn't want to marry a man who cheated on his wife because he would probably do the same thing to her. She'd told the police that, too, and she concluded that Mikus had read her statements in the reports. Nevertheless, she decided not to complete her sentence. "So we never discussed it after that."

"Any reason you didn't discuss it anymore?" Mikus wheedled.

"No, no reason. He knew I didn't want to marry him and we were happy just seeing each other."

"Trips to Hawaii, fancy restaurants. Sounds to me like you two were really living it up. These are expensive things, aren't they?"

"Yes. Casper treated me quite well."

"So what did you contribute toward these good times with Mr. Bennett?"

"Objection," Miraldi said, making another futile attempt to save his witness.

"Overruled."

"Casper had my company and my companionship, just like any man who takes a woman out on a date."

"Is it true that you offered your body to him for sexual relations?" Mikus said, his words stilted and unnatural, almost as if they had sprung directly from the Ohio Revised Code's criminal statutes regarding prostitution.

"Objection."

"Overruled."

Mrs. Miller looked down at her gloved hands and quietly said, "Yes."

"Many times?"

Miraldi looked at Adams and the two exchanged glances of resignation.

"Yes." Mrs. Miller's voice was weak and barely audible.

Knowing that he had completely humiliated the witness, Mikus sat down. The defense asked no further questions of Mrs. Miller and she quickly exited the courtroom. She looked straight ahead, her eyes focused on a point on the wall above the spectators' heads.

****

As Casper Bennett took the stand and swore to tell the truth, the jury knew what he was going to say. They had heard it now six times. His grand jury testimony had been read to them in its entirety. Five police officers had summarized Bennett's story to them—first Metelsky, then Springowski, followed by Solomon, Kocak, and Mumford. The jurors would be on the alert for changes in his story, but it was his demeanor that they would scrutinize. They would study his facial expressions, his eyes in particular; his body language; and the way he said things. They had to decide for themselves whether this man was lying or telling the truth.

Adams and Miraldi had prepared an outline of questions for Bennett's direct exam. They wanted the jury to know who Casper Bennett was—his life before he met Florence, his marriage to Florence, and their struggles with alcohol. Once those things were covered, the defense would ask Bennett to talk about Florence's last week and then about the day that she died.

For the entire trial, Bennett had worn a navy blue suit, and he was wearing it again today. He had lost more weight while in jail and the suit no longer fit him. It now hung on him loosely and was wrinkled from almost constant wear. His face looked haggard and there were dark circles under his eyes. However, as he began his testimony, his voice was calm and clear.

He told the jurors that he was the oldest of four children born to Ksaiver and Antoinette Bernatowicz, Polish immigrants who'd settled in Lorain. He'd dropped out of high school after his junior year and had worked ever since, eventually as the owner of a pool hall and later a tavern. He and Florence were married in 1940. Casper expected that they would have children, but Florence refused because she was afraid that she would die in childbirth. Early in the marriage, they both drank and would go on binges. In 1946, Casper claimed that he stopped drinking and stayed sober until 1960, joining Alcoholics Anonymous.

Although Florence went into the hospital several times for alcohol rehabilitation, Casper claimed that she never stayed sober for very long. She might abstain for a week or even a month, but then she would start again and drink constantly until she became so ill that she was bedridden. Casper started drinking again in 1960 when he was at a birthday party. He claimed that Florence was drinking heavily and he just got "disgusted with things" and started drinking too. He drank until the early fall of 1963, when he was hospitalized for abdominal issues.

Bennett admitted that he began dating Irene Miller in 1959. He told the jury that Florence was drunk most of the time and he just wanted to "associate with someone for companionship," particularly since he was not drinking then. Casper claimed that it was "no secret" that he took Irene Miller on trips and had even disclosed the trips to Florence because they were living apart at the time he vacationed with Mrs. Miller.

As Bennett testified, Mikus listened with a deep scowl on his face. From time to time, he wrote notes on his legal pad, savagely digging the pen into the paper and then ripping the paper clear from the pad. He objected a few times, claiming that Adams was leading the witness. In response, Adams looked perturbed and then simply rephrased the question in a more general way. Bennett remained composed throughout, and the jurors continued to scrutinize his words and gestures.

The defense decided to start the defendant's detailed story in September of 1963. Casper explained that Florence, while intoxicated, fell so badly in the house that she was hospitalized for a few days. Soon after Florence came home, he, too, was hospitalized for severe abdominal pains and stayed in the hospital for several weeks. Before he entered the hospital, Casper made arrangements with Sophie Pribanic, a former neighbor, to stay with Florence and do housework. After Casper came home from the hospital, Mrs. Pribanic continued to care for Florence because Florence was weak and unsteady on her feet. By the end of October, Florence was better, and Casper no longer had Mrs. Pribanic come to the house.

Mikus began fidgeting in his chair, while Otero stared at the jury, trying to read their minds about the impact of Bennett's testimony. As Miraldi listened to his client, he was hopeful that the jury was beginning to see the defendant in a different light. Although Bennett was a flawed human being, he had not abandoned his wife, and, to his credit, had made sure that someone always cared for her.

Bennett also maintained that he always provided Florence with enough cash for her personal use. They did have an unusual number of bills in 1963, and, as a result, took out a loan. After paying the bills, they had about $2,000 left, and they put that cash in a dresser drawer (which the police found when they searched the house the day following Florence's death).

Adams gently led Bennett to talk about Florence's drinking in the days immediately before her death. Bennett told the jury that Florence started on another of her binges on Sunday, December 15. By Wednesday and Thursday, she was so sick that she spent most of the day in bed. Bennett told the jury the familiar story about his going to work on Friday the twentieth and coming home around five thirty, fixing supper for himself and also offering to warm up leftovers for Florence, doing some chores about the house, fixing two drinks for Florence per her request, giving her two over-the-counter sleeping pills, helping her to the bathroom, putting her back to bed, and kissing her good-bye before leaving to run some errands.

In the course of this testimony, Bennett brought out some new and important facts. He claimed to have seen some aspirin, vitamin A, and vitamin B tablets near the sink. In the sink, he found an unrinsed glass that had deposits of Alka-Seltzer in it. Bennett had told Miraldi about the Alka-Seltzer and aspirin when they first met on March second, so Miraldi knew that this was not a recent invention designed to undermine Dr. Kopsch's calculations. This testimony explained why the toxicology reports showed high levels of salicylates in her bloodstream. Both Alka-Seltzer and aspirin contain salicylates, as Miraldi had pointed out in his cross-examination of Dr. Kopsch.

Adams was now ready for Bennett to describe his activities after he left home. "When did you leave home that evening?"

"I left sometime around six thirty," Bennett replied, looking first at Adams and then turning to the jury.

"You told the police and the grand jury that you left home around twenty to eight, didn't you?"

"Yes, I did. But I have been doing a lot of thinking about this since it happened and I now know that my original estimate was wrong. Thinking things through, I must've left around six thirty that evening."

"Is there any other reason why your original estimate about this was wrong?"

"I very seldom wear a wristwatch and I was not wearing one that day."

"Why is that?"

"I wash glasses all day at the bar and I'm always plunging my hands into soapy water. I also tape the tips of my fingers, because if I don't, my fingers start to dry out and crack from all the time they spend in the water. You know, it's just easier not to wear a watch rather than always taking it on and off."

"Were the tips of your fingers taped on December twentieth?"

"Yes. Springowski even asked me about this. I think he mentioned that in his testimony."

"Do you own a wristwatch?"

"Yes."

"Did you put it on when you got home?"

"No, I didn't. I was still cleaning things up, dishes and stuff, and I also mopped the kitchen floor. I forgot to put it on before I went out."

Mikus snorted to register his disbelief with the jury. Judge Pincura stared at Mikus for several seconds, silently admonishing him to save his skepticism for his cross-examination. The judge then looked at his own wristwatch, noted that it was ten thirty, and announced the regular midmorning recess.

After the brief recess, Adams asked Bennett to detail his whereabouts after he left the house. Once again, the jury heard about his visit to Don's Sohio. He stopped at a pay phone at Twentieth and Broadway and called his bar to check on business that evening. Adams thought it best to let Bennett tell his story in one long narrative and not interrupt him, despite Bennett's habit of going into great detail about minor points.

Bennett looked to the jury and spoke directly to them.

"I lost about thirty pounds since I stopped drinking in September, so I had one of my jackets altered at Richman Brothers. I was supposed to pick it up that night, but the traffic was so heavy, I couldn't find a place to park. I kept going all the way to West Erie Avenue, back of Heilman's, back down Broadway, looking for a parking place. I think I went around four or five times."

The courtroom was silent except for Mikus, who was noisily flipping through the pages of the police investigation. He apparently found what he was looking for and looked back at the witness.

"I figured I'd wait a few minutes before looking for a parking spot again. I decided to take a little ride down West Erie as far as the Hoop Restaurant. Now, when I turned to go back toward downtown, I realized that I was pretty close to Irene Miller's house at Sixth and Brownell and I might as well clean off the walks and such. As I was heading out that way, I thought it would be kind of nice to leave her a six-pack of beer, so I went to that little delicatessen at Tenth and Washington and bought a six-pack of something, Rolling Rock or Black Label. I can't remember which now."

Until Irene Miller had testified about finding a six-pack of beer at her back door that evening, Bennett had forgotten about buying her beer at that little neighborhood store. He easily incorporated that into his alibi.

"So now I go back to Richman Brothers, looking for a parking place, and I still can't find a spot. I must have done that loop about three times. There was a space right in front of Jax, the clothing store across the street from Richman's, but the car in front of me pulled into that spot. So I gave up on that for now. I usually get a final *Cleveland Press* and a *Chronicle* just about every day. So I figured I would stop in the back of Heilman's or Fisher Foods Grocery Store, and park my car and walk to Kingsley's Cigar Store and buy the papers. I did this, and there was some heavy-set fellow standing near the papers and he had a little mustache. He kind of looked Spanish or Italian, something like that."

"Objection. Your Honor, Mr. Adams has not asked a question in over five minutes. This long monologue is totally improper. It gives me no opportunity to know whether the witness is going to say something that would otherwise be inadmissible."

"Overruled. He is answering the question. He was asked what errands he ran and he is telling the jury." Judge Pincura then paused for a moment, chewed on his tobacco, and added, "In great detail, I might add. Go ahead, Mr. Bennett."

"So I got in my car again and headed down Broadway, thinking I might find me a lucky parking place close to the store. I did this loop again for two or three times and got disgusted, so I said to myself that I'd pick up my coat tomorrow, which was Saturday. I took a ride down Broadway again and I stopped at Ninth Street in front of the phone company to use one of the public phones. I called the club again and then I called Irene Miller. She was busy and couldn't talk much but I told her that I swept her walks. I told her that I would call her back later."

Miraldi continued to look at the jury. They remained focused on Bennett.

"I drove along Broadway again and was going to go home when I hit Twentieth Street, but then I decided I would drive by the club and see how many cars were parked there. I doubled back and turned left onto Fifteenth

Street, and when I got to the intersection of Fifteenth and Reid Avenue, I see Joe Wasilewski, a guy I know who used to work at Runyan's and sometimes does odd jobs for me. He was driving either in front of me or behind me. I can't remember which. Anyway, we recognized each other about the same time and we beeped our horns and waved our hands to say hi."

For the first time in a long while, Adams decided to interrupt the witness. "Casper, about what time was it when you saw this Joe Wasilewski?" After he asked the question, Adams momentarily froze. What if Bennett told the jury that he looked at his wristwatch?

"I know it was after nine o' clock because a lot of the stores were closed and people were getting into their cars. But as for an exact time, I don't know."

Adams breathed a sigh of relief and asked Bennett to continue.

"Then I headed toward our bar at Fourteenth Street, and I passed it and saw that there were a lot of cars parked around it. I turned south on Lexington and headed for home."

Mikus scrawled a note on his legal pad that read, "If Bennett so concerned about wife, why so many delays in getting home?" He underlined the words "concerned" and "delays." He also wrote, "How long did he drive around the downtown looking for a parking spot—ridiculous." He would work those things into his cross-examination.

Adams then directed Bennett to describe what he found when he got home. Bennett told the jury that he opened the cellar door and called down to see if Florence was in the basement because the light was on. Then he remembered that he had turned the light on before he left. He dropped the newspapers in the living room and as he walked up the stairs, he could hear the water running in the bathroom.

"When I looked into the bathroom, there she was. Her head was by the spigot and was drooped down." For the first time in his testimony, Bennett's voice cracked. As he tried to regain his composure, he began to sob loudly and tears rolled down his cheeks. "So I said, 'Florence, what have you done to yourself?'" Again Bennett stopped to regain his composure. "I could see that the water was running hot and I don't know if the cold tap was on a little bit or not. I turned off the water. I tried to pull her out, but my hands kept slipping. Finally, with my hands under her armpits, I gave her a strong pull and she came out of the bathtub." For the third time, Bennett began to cry. Finally, after he stopped sobbing, he said, "That is the truth, so help me God."

Adams continued to question Bennett about his efforts to revive his wife, his call to the operator, and his cooperation with the police. Adams reinforced that his client never refused to talk to the police and had voluntarily appeared before the grand jury even though he was not required to do so. Bennett maintained that he went before the grand jury because he knew he hadn't done anything wrong and thought that if he told the truth, he would not be charged.

Finally, Adams completed his direct exam. "Casper, do you know how your wife died?"

"I do not. All I know is that she was in the bathtub when I got home."

Although it was not yet noon, Judge Pincura decided to break for lunch. He knew that Mikus would have a lengthy cross-examination. It made sense to begin the prosecutor's questioning after the noon recess.

"I'll see everyone back in the courtroom at one fifteen p.m.," the judge announced.

Bennett's hands were trembling as he stepped down from the witness chair.

CHAPTER 23

April 9, 1964 (Afternoon)

Judge Pincura took the bench at precisely one fifteen. Again his courtroom was packed, with spectators filling every bench and many standing along the walls. For him, this case was a constant challenge to maintain order between attorneys whose incivility toward each other had deteriorated into open hostility as the trial wore on. He'd expected Mikus to try to run roughshod over him and his opponents, but Miraldi, usually the picture of decorum in the courtroom, had actually taunted Mikus about being afraid of a witness and his testimony. He could still see the anger in Mikus's eyes; for a brief moment, he had feared that the enraged prosecutor would charge Miraldi like an angry bull.

"Are you ready to proceed, Mr. Mikus?" the judge asked.

"I am. I do have one preliminary matter with the court before the jury enters."

"Very well, what is it?"

"Your Honor, we believe that the defendant's story about how he found his wife is totally fabricated. A body simply cannot fit into that bathtub the way Mr. Bennett describes it. I plan on asking Mr. Bennett to sit in the bathtub in just the same way that he says he found his wife. I know that the defense will object to this, and I would like your ruling on this now so that we don't have to dismiss the jury later to discuss this."

Before either of the defense attorneys could reply, Judge Pincura blurted out, "No, Mr. Mikus, no. That is my ruling. You can ask the defendant how he found his wife, but I will not allow you to put him in a bathtub in my courtroom."

"That ruling is erroneous and quite prejudicial to the State of Ohio," Mikus protested.

"I can only imagine what the Ninth District Court of Appeals would say if I allowed a man charged with murder to be questioned while he sat in a bathtub," the judge snapped.

"Your Honor, you have the wrong idea. I won't ask any questions of the defendant while he is in the bathtub. I only want him to sit in it."

Judge Pincura's shock and agitation were beginning to subside. "Thank you for that clarification, Mr. Mikus, but my ruling still stands." The judge's mind returned to Mikus's first attempt to authorize a bathtub demonstration. He could still see the pretty nurse, wearing a tight sweater and stretch pants, sitting nervously in the front of the courtroom. The judge continued, "I will not allow this demonstration for the same reasons I did not allow a demonstration with that nurse several days ago. Bailiff, please bring in the jury."

As the judge watched the jurors file in, he continued to think of Mikus's request. If a man's life weren't at stake, the scene that had just played out would have been comical. He would continue to maintain order and do his best to rule accurately. He wanted the defendant to get a fair trial, but he also did not want to make a mistake, be reversed, and be forced to try this damn case one more time.

Mikus dispensed with any preliminary questions and started on a part of the defendant's alibi that he wanted to destroy.

"So after you kissed your wife good-bye," Mikus began, his voice dripping with sarcasm, "what time did you leave your house that evening?"

"It was around six thirty p.m.," Bennett replied.

"That's not what you said under oath in front of the grand jury, is it?"

"No, it wasn't."

"That's not what you told the investigating police officers when they asked you about your activities that night?"

"That's correct."

"You signed a written statement where you said that you left at twenty to eight that evening, right?"

"Yes."

"And now all of a sudden, it's six thirty p.m.?"

"I've been thinking about this for a long time, and I figured out that I left closer to six thirty p.m."

"So when did you start reconsidering this … this departure time?"

"Since I've been arrested—I don't know for sure. I keep going over the events of that evening all the time. And, you know, some of that night's just a big blur."

"Well, it's not a big blur when you got home from work. You told us about heating up food, what food you ate, what pills were by the sink, how you mopped up the floor, how you carefully tended to your wife, kissed her good-bye, and promised to be home early—all those things you've remembered in great detail, right?"

"Yes."

"No trouble remembering that at all, right?"

"Yeah, but that was before I came home and found Florence in the tub. I got all panicky after that."

"Right, you got all panicky after that. But you weren't panicky when you went to the gas station, when you drove around Lorain, when you drove to the Hoop Restaurant, when you cleaned the snow off your girlfriend's sidewalks, when you waved to Joe Wasa—Joe Wasasomething—all those things happened before you got home, right?"

"It's Joe Wasilewski, Mr. Mikus."

Mikus scowled. Bennett then answered the question: "I wasn't panicky when those things happened, but I didn't think none of that would be important later on."

"But none of that is a blur to you, right?" Mikus demanded.

"No, I remember those things."

"So you weren't panicky when you did all these things after you left your house. But you say it's a big blur when you left your house?"

"Well, like I said, I wasn't wearing a watch."

Feigning disbelief, Mikus looked at the jury. "You've changed the time you left the house for one reason, Mr. Bennett, because that time does not *fit* with the testimony of the people who saw you." Mikus's voice rose to a shout. "It does not fit, does it?" He picked up the police investigation and slammed it down on the prosecution table.

"No, it doesn't fit with what Ed Warner and Joe Mitock said. I know that. That's what got me to thinking that I was wrong on the time I left. But I didn't change the time because it didn't fit. What they were saying caused me to think about this real hard. I'm real bad at estimating time and I figured I made a mistake."

"You told Inspector Mumford that you looked at a clock before you left your house, didn't you?"

"I don't think I told him that, sir."

"Is he making that up, then? Is that man sitting at that table with Mr. Otero a liar?"

The jurors all switched their gazes from Bennett to Mumford. Orie Camillo, the court reporter, chuckled to himself. If his wife were on the stand, she would answer that question with a yes.

"I don't know what clock he thinks I looked at in the house. I know I didn't have that in that statement that I signed at the police station."

"So Mr. Mumford is a liar?"

"He could be mistaken, you know. Just like I was mistaken about the time I left."

Sensing that he was losing this battle, Mikus's face reddened. He had to return to a point that Bennett could not dispute.

"But, Mr. Bennett, when your alibi did not match with what Ed Warner and Joe Mitock said, you changed it, right?"

"I changed the time that I saw them. But other than that, everything I said about what happened at the gas station that night is just what they say."

"Except you were there at six thirty instead of eight p.m., right?"

"Yes."

"And to you, that's just a tiny difference."

"I guess so."

"Thank you. Now, Mr. Bennett, when did you get home after running the errands?" Mikus asked.

"Sometime between nine and nine thirty, probably somewhere in between. Again, I'm not sure."

"Right. You've told us that you weren't wearing a watch and you are incapable of judging time. So if you left at six thirty, you have to account for about three hours of time away from home. Is that right?"

"I guess so."

"Now, when you said that you left at seven forty, you had to account for about an hour and a half of time away from home?"

"Yeah. Something like that." Sensing that he was about to be trapped, Bennett squirmed in his chair.

"So first story, you are gone an hour and a half. Second story, you are gone almost three hours. Do I have that right?"

"I guess that's right. I didn't do the math on that."

"So when you changed your time, you had to account for more things that you did, right?"

"I wouldn't say that."

"Well, okay. Let's look at your alibi in more detail. I notice in your story that you checked on your bar, the B & M Grille, what was it, three times?"

"I don't know. I never really counted it."

"Well, you called from a pay phone at Broadway and Twentieth right after leaving the gas station. You called again from a pay phone near the Lorain Telephone office right before you called Irene Miller, and you drove by your bar just before you came home. Is that three times?"

"Yes."

"In three hours, you checked on your bar three times. Was something important happening there that evening?"

"No. I just was curious as to what was going on."

"And you trust your partner? He was there. He knows how to run the bar, doesn't he?"

"Yes."

"Now let's talk about your failed attempt to find a parking spot. You kept looking for a parking place so that you could go into Richman Brothers to pick up your coat?"

"Yes, I did."

"And I think you made three separate attempts to find a parking spot, each with multiple loops around several blocks?"

"I never really stopped to figure it out."

"Well, I jotted down what you said to Mr. Adams, and let's look at all the times you drove around Richman Brothers, okay?"

"Sure."

"Okay, the first time was after leaving Don's Sohio and making a call from a pay phone at Twentieth and Broadway. You went around several blocks four or five times. Right?"

"Yes. That's what I estimated."

"Then you buy beer and clean off your girlfriend's sidewalks and come back and do another three loops. Still no parking spots anywhere in sight. Right?"

"Yes."

"Then you bought the two newspapers and you said that you looked for—I think you said a lucky parking spot again, and drove around and made two or three loops before you gave up. Do I have that right?"

"Yes."

It was now Adams's turn to squirm in his seat. This part of Bennett's story had always seemed fishy to him. He believed Bennett had been out all of this time, but he'd concluded that Bennett had found some gambler friends at Runyan's Bookstore, or worse yet, stopped at Tilly's to have a fling with one of her girls. Both places were within a couple of blocks of Richman Brothers. Either way, it would explain what Bennett had been doing for most of the three hours and why he didn't want to implicate those people in his alibi.

"So three separate times you tried to find a parking spot near Richman Brothers. And you made eight to eleven loops in total. In all of that time, not one parking spot opened up near Richman's?"

"That's right."

"Well, tell the jury, how close to Richman's did this 'lucky' parking spot have to be?"

"I was aiming for about one block or so."

"Do you have any problems with your legs, anything that keeps you from walking more than a block?"

"No, but it was cold that night and there was snow on the ground."

"I see. You had no problem parking behind Heilman's and walking to Kingsley's Cigar Store to buy your newspapers."

"That wasn't too far."

"That's more than a block, isn't it?"

"Maybe. I'm not sure."

"And no parking spots opened up for you?"

"No. All the stores were open late for shoppers and it was very busy."

"All right then. You also decided to kill time by driving over to the Hoop Restaurant at West Erie and Leavitt Road, about a mile or so away from Richman Brothers?"

"Yes."

"I have a teenage son and I know that he and his friends drive around the Hoop Restaurant in their souped-up cars all night long. Did you drive around the restaurant?"

Judge Pincura lived on West Erie Avenue, a few blocks from the Hoop, and he knew exactly what Mikus was referring to. Pincura had to smile as he pictured Bennett joining the parade of high schoolers accelerating and braking their cars in their herky-jerky conga line around this restaurant.

So focused was Bennett on not getting trapped that he was oblivious to Mikus's attempt to make him look ridiculous. "No. I just drove there and turned around," Bennett responded.

"Mr. Bennett, were you in a hurry to get home to your sick wife that evening?"

"I told her I wouldn't be out late and I was planning to be home between nine and nine thirty."

"You didn't answer my question. Were you in a hurry to get back home that night?"

Bennett knew he had no good explanation for his tardiness getting home. "I didn't figure that she really needed my help, you know, right then and there, and I could just drive around a little bit and unwind. I like to do that after working all day."

"Yes, I think you do." An hour earlier, while he was eating his lunch, Mikus had planned his next line. "Since the time of Moses and the Israelites, I can't think of anyone who wanders around so aimlessly as you."

"Objection. That's not a question," Adams interjected.

"Sustained. Mr. Mikus's last statement will be disregarded."

Mikus looked over at the jury to see if any of them appreciated this verbal slap. He knew that Bible references were usually well received by the more religious jurors. One of the women jurors gave him a smile.

"Now let's talk about what you did when you got home, okay?"

Bennett nodded.

"It's between nine and nine thirty, and again you wander around the house for a while, and then when you are walking upstairs, you hear the water running in the upstairs bathroom?"

"Yes, I figured Florence was starting to take a bath."

"And Florence was afraid of water, wasn't she?"

"Yes. I told the police that when they first questioned me."

"It was very strange that she would be taking a bath, right?"

"No, it wasn't strange at all. She took baths all the time, but she just didn't put much water into the tub." Bennett looked irritated. He obviously did not like the implication that his deceased wife lacked proper hygiene.

"Mr. Bennett, will you please come over to the bathtub and point to where you found your wife?" Mikus glanced at the judge to see if he would be stopped. When Judge Pincura nodded his approval, Mikus looked at Bennett again and pointed him toward the bathtub—his gesture an unambiguous command.

Bennett did not hesitate. He stood up and walked to the bathtub, turned to face the jury, pointed his left arm at the spigots, and said, "Her head was here. It was slumped and I'm not sure if her face was under the water."

"And what about her legs?" Mikus's voice boomed.

Bennett pointed to the other end of the bathtub. "They were at this end."

"We know that," Mikus said impatiently. "Were they under the water or not?"

"I think they were. But like I said, a lot of this is just a big blur."

"A big blur," Mikus sneered. "You didn't tell the police this part of your story was a big blur, did you?"

"They could see I was pretty upset when they questioned me."

"You signed a statement of your own free will two days after your wife died. In that statement, you said her lower legs were in the water. You did not claim that your memory was blurred or foggy about this, did you?"

Bennett hesitated and did not answer for a few moments.

Mikus goaded Bennett "Do you want me to show you your written statement from December 22, 1963?"

"No, that's okay. I know what the statement says and I agree that I didn't say that my memory was foggy about that." Bennett stopped and it appeared that he had completed his answer, but then he blurted out, "But I am not the one who came up with the words or typed the thing up. The police did that."

Mikus ignored the last part of Bennett's answer. "When you went before the grand jury, you didn't say that this part of your memory was foggy, did you?"

"No, I guess not."

"Your memory suddenly becomes foggy after you hear Dr. Kopsch say that your wife's unburned lower legs had to be out of the water as a reaction to you holding her head under the water. Isn't that right?"

"No, that's not right," Bennett shot back. "A lot of what happened after I got home is not clear in my mind and never has been." Bennett glanced away from Mikus and stared at the bathtub.

"You forgot to say 'so help me God,'" Mikus cut in.

"Objection."

"Sustained. Don't try that again, Mr. Mikus," Judge Pincura warned, his gravelly voice now loud and forceful.

"Show the jury, Mr. Bennett, how you got your wife out of the bathtub."

Bennett bent over the bathtub, put his hands into its interior, and pulled his hands out, his palms facing toward the bottom of the tub and the backs of his hands away from the spigots. Finished with this maneuver, Bennett faced the jury. He looked bewildered, like a magician facing his audience after a failed trick.

Bennett's discomfort was palpable and Mikus seized on it. "And how did your hands get burned?"

Again Bennett plunged his hands into the tub and as his hands emerged in plain view of everyone, his left hand slipped out of sight, back into the tub. "Sort of like that," he said.

"That's not blurry to you, Mr. Bennett?"

"It's all a blur, but I think that's what happened."

"Mr. Bennett," Mikus paused for a dramatic effect, "now show the jurors your hands, both the tops and the palms."

Adams and Miraldi looked on, unsure what to do. They knew that an objection would be futile and would only make the jury think that they were trying to hide something important from them. They attempted to look unconcerned, but both felt helpless. They did not see their client staring at them, his eyes asking if he had to do this.

Judge Pincura took control. "Mr. Bennett, please just come over to the jury and walk by the jury box, turning your hands so that the jurors can see both sides of your hands," he said.

The jurors were seated in two rows. Those in the back stood up and moved forward to get a better view. Before the judge or defense attorneys could react, Mikus grabbed both of Bennett's hands and held them high in the air, first showing the back of the hands to the jury and then violently twisting them to reveal his palms. When he was finished, Mikus thrust both of Bennett's hands downward as he released his grip. Mikus's utter contempt for Bennett could not have been clearer. In the process, Mikus dared the jury and the defense to explain why Bennett's left palm was burned and the tender skin on top was unscathed. Bennett returned to his seat, staring at the red scar on his left palm, still about the size of a half dollar.

Judge Pincura was seething. This was his courtroom. He did not care how long Mikus had been the county prosecutor. Mikus's long tenure did not give him the right to grab a defendant and manhandle him in front of the jury. Hiding his anger, Judge Pincura said, "I think this is a good time for our midafternoon recess. We will break for about fifteen minutes and come back at two fifteen."

After the jurors filed out, Mikus, still standing, began to shuffle through papers at his table. Sensing Judge Pincura's anger, he turned quickly to leave the courtroom.

"Don't go anywhere, Mr. Mikus," Judge Pincura said. "I have something to say to you and all counsel."

Mikus stopped in midstride and returned to the prosecutor's table. Miraldi and Adams, who had been conferring about Mikus's antics, became quiet and looked at the judge.

"I don't have to remind any of you how important it is that this case be tried fairly and according to the rule of law. I have perhaps been too lenient with some of you and your behavior. I have done so because I realize that all of you are under great pressure. However, my patience is at an end.

"Mr. Mikus, you had no right to touch the defendant in any fashion. I should hold you in contempt of court. I told you that you could not put Mr. Bennett in the bathtub for a demonstration and then you do something far worse. I instructed Mr. Bennett to walk in front of the jury and show them his hands. That is what I allowed. I did not authorize you to touch him in any way or to grab his arms. Mr. Mikus, this is your last warning. Do you understand that?"

At first Mikus was silent. He had actually not planned to grab the defendant's hands, but when Bennett had walked in front of the jury, Mikus had suddenly been seized by an overwhelming impulse to grab what he considered to be murderous hands. Judge Pincura looked at Mikus intently and Mikus realized that the judge expected an apology.

Mikus said quietly, "I will not do that again."

Judge Pincura got up quickly and walked briskly to his chambers. He was confident his message had registered with the attorneys. Little did he know that the next day he would have to admonish Miraldi and then, in a separate incident, threaten to expel all of the spectators to maintain order.

After the break, Mikus stayed aggressive. He asked Bennett to recount in detail how he managed to drag his wife from the bathroom and place her on the bed. This time Mikus pretended that he was Bennett and walked backward in the courtroom, dragging an invisible body. When Mikus reached the envisioned bedroom and bed, Bennett told the prosecutor how he had placed the body on the bed. Bennett described a maneuver that would have required him to move the body in a three-hundred-degree arc. As Mikus followed Bennett's instructions, the jurors looked at each other in surprise. They realized that it would have been much easier for Bennett to simply lift his wife's legs onto the bed and avoid that rotation. Mikus repeated the sequence two more times and Bennett agreed that this was how he had moved his wife.

Miraldi and Adams doubted that Mikus's current theatrics were creating any damage to Bennett's story. Bennett obviously was the person who dragged his wife from the bathroom to the bedroom. Whether the traumatized husband remembered exactly how he moved his wife into the bedroom seemed inconsequential.

Mikus next attacked Bennett because he could not remember any difference in the color of Florence's skin or that any of it had peeled away. Miraldi believed that Bennett's failure to note these things showed only his shock and nothing more. Both defense attorneys hoped that Mikus's hammering style would wear thin with the jurors. They might begin to sympathize with their client, seeing Mikus as the bully and Bennett the victim.

"How long did it take you to drag your wife from the bathroom to the bedroom?" Mikus asked.

"Probably seven or eight minutes, something like that," Bennett responded.

"Well it's only eight feet from the bathroom door to the bedroom door, isn't it?"

"Maybe five to eight minutes then."

Adams could see that his client was tired and wearing down. Although Adams's face displayed composure, his stomach was a bundle of knots. In his head, Adams answered Mikus's questions, hoping that Bennett could somehow read his thoughts.

"Are you telling this jury that it took you five minutes to drag your wife about ten feet and lift her onto the bed?" Mikus said, challenging him.

"All I know is that it seemed like a lifetime. Maybe it was just two or three minutes," Bennett said. "I don't know."

"Well, now you have told us three different times in the span of one minute. Which is it?"

"Like I said, it seemed like a lifetime," Bennett said, repeating an answer that he hoped would keep him afloat.

Looking disgusted, Mikus turned away from the witness and looked first at Otero and then at the jury.

Switching to another subject, Mikus established that Bennett called the operator for help from a downstairs telephone, instead of using a phone just a few feet away in the bedroom. Mikus looked incredulous and bellowed, "Are you going to tell the jury that you were panicked and not thinking clearly?"

"I don't know why I didn't use the phone in the bedroom. I was pretty hysterical right then," Bennett answered.

"No reason then, right?"

Bennett nodded in agreement.

Mikus now decided to change topics completely. "Mr. Bennett, do I understand that the last few months with your wife were some of the best since the two of you were married? That the two of you had turned over a new leaf?"

"Yes, that's right."

"You were going to sell your business and the two of you were to start over in Florida?"

"Yes. I moved back to the house in July and we were getting along pretty well."

"Tell us about that."

"Well, we were talking about Florida all the time. We were doing things together. Florence and I picked out a new chair at T. N. Molas and she was tickled when it was delivered. When I was ordering the new car, I had her choose the color. You know, those kinds of things."

Mikus then went to the small table holding the trial exhibits. He picked up the calendar that had been discovered in the Bennetts' television/stereo console. Opening it up to the month of December, Mikus handed it to Bennett.

"Is that Florence's handwriting?"

"Yes."

"Look at that entry on December fifth. It says, 'Casper got in at three a.m. Wouldn't tell me where he'd been.' Did I read that correctly?"

"Yes."

"Let's look at December ninth. 'Casper did not come home until morning. Claims he was not with Miller.' Is that what Florence wrote?"

"Apparently."

"What do you mean 'apparently'? You didn't write that, did you? Nobody else wrote that, right?"

"I just don't have much faith in that diary. If I came home at five p.m. and she wrote eight p.m., what good would it be?" Bennett explained.

"These entries that say that you were staying out until three or four o'clock in the morning—none of them are true?" Mikus said, challenging Bennett.

"There were times that I stayed out late. Sometimes I worked late. Most of the time when I came home, Florence was already in bed asleep. So I wouldn't believe any of those entries too much."

Mikus then proceeded to read five more entries and have Bennett confirm that he had read them accurately.

"You're saying that Florence was happy with you when she claims you are staying out late and you are not providing her with any explanations?" Mikus pushed.

"I think so. She seemed happy with a lot of things that were going on between us."

"When did Florence change the locks on the doors and not give you a key?"

"I don't know. A couple of weeks before she died. Something like that."

"And everything between the two of you was just great. Your wife locks you out of the house and things have never been better between the two of you. Is that what you want this jury to believe?"

"Florence was a complicated person," Bennett said. "When Florence drank, she did some strange things. I can't explain it any better than that."

"So she changed the locks just as a practical joke?"

"She was complicated. Our life together had its ups and downs, but in the end, we wanted to stay together."

Adams thought his client was doing the best he could with difficult questions. Whether the jury believed Bennett would remain a mystery until deliberations began in several days.

Miraldi noticed that some jurors were now yawning. Mikus began to question Bennett about Irene Miller, his long relationship with her, their vacations, his lavish gifts to her, and eventually the restraining order Mrs. Miller sought against him. *These jurors have made up their mind about Casper Bennett*, Miraldi thought. *As long as Casper doesn't self-destruct, Mikus has done all the damage he's going to do.*

Mikus completed his questions just minutes after four p.m. Adams asked some perfunctory questions on redirect but, observing that the jury was tired, finished his follow-up questions in less than ten minutes.

Judge Pincura looked over at Mikus as if to ask if he was done with this witness. "I have about a half an hour of recross, Your Honor," Mikus volunteered.

"Then we are going to recess for the day," Judge Pincura said. "We will reconvene at our regular time tomorrow, nine a.m."

After Mikus and Otero left the courtroom, Bennett asked his attorneys, "Did I do okay?"

"You hung in there, Casper," Miraldi said. "Mikus had some tough questions and you answered them about as well as we could ask. I'm sorry that he isn't through with you yet."

"Well, I'm hoping the worst is over," Bennett said.

"We think it is," Adams interjected. "Try to get a good night's sleep. I don't think Mikus can ask you anything that we haven't already talked about. I agree with Ray. You did a good job. You never lost your composure. You never got angry. That's important. Just do the same thing tomorrow. Okay?"

Bennett nodded. The sheriff's deputies appeared and escorted him out of the building.

"How do you think he really did?" Adams asked Miraldi, looking worried.

"He did all right. There are some things I wish he had said differently, but, all in all, it could have been much worse." Miraldi paused and looked at the witness stand. "Mikus really hit him hard on his alibi. You really have to question what Bennett was doing for those two and a half to three hours."

"I know. That bothered me, too. Always has."

"If Mikus had just limited his cross-exam to that, it would have had more impact. I think he went into a lot of stuff that was just pure junk. I hope he lost some of the jurors by doing that."

"Me too."

CHAPTER 24

April 10, 1964

The day's session on April 10, the tenth day of the trial, would be remembered because of two witnesses. One was shy, self-conscious, and scared, while the other was brash, wild, and uncontrollable. One would testify for less than ten minutes, while the other would command most of the afternoon. One's testimony would become the linchpin for Bennett's alibi. The other's antics would create so much chaos that the value of his testimony would be debated. Both men had drifted from job to job during their time in Lorain, but that was the extent of their similarities.

Dressed in clean work clothes and heavy boots, Joe Wasilewski looked bewildered as he walked into the clerk of court's office, showed his subpoena to the deputy clerk, and asked where he was supposed to go. Wasilewski saw the spectators peeking through the doors of one courtroom and feared he would be sent there. Seeing his obvious discomfort, the deputy clerk walked Wasilewski to a bench outside that courtroom and told him to sit there. She then went into the courtroom, where Casper Bennett had resumed his testimony, and beckoned Miraldi, the attorney who had subpoenaed this witness.

Miraldi slipped out with the deputy, spotted Wasilewski, and shook his hand warmly. "Joe, just wait here for a few minutes. We'll call you as soon as Casper finishes his testimony. Okay?" Wasilewski nodded and Miraldi returned to the courtroom.

Miraldi had subpoenaed Wasilewski because Wasilewski had observed

Bennett driving his car at Fifteenth Street and Reid Avenue around nine fifteen on December 20, 1963. Wasilewski saw Bennett first and waved to him. He was the sole person who corroborated any of the critical time elements of Bennett's alibi.

Like Bennett, Joe Wasilewski was the son of Polish immigrants. His father, Stanley, immigrated to the United States in 1903 and settled first in Pennsylvania before coming to Lorain around 1930 with his wife and three children to work as a laborer at National Tube. Joe Wasilewski was the youngest of the children and attended Lorain schools until he dropped out in the eighth grade.

Bennett and Joe Wasilewski were acquainted. Wasilewski lived in his deceased parents' former home at 334 Fifteenth Street, just a block from Bennett's B & M Grille. Now forty-six years old, Wasilewski had worked as a laborer at the steel mill, worked at Runyan's Bookstore, and done odd repair jobs. Joe and his brother, Steve, had even made some toilet repairs at Bennett's home within the last year. However, Bennett and Wasilewski were not close friends. Their paths crossed from time to time and that was about it.

Although there were windows in the courtroom's outer doors, Wasilewski could not see what was going on inside. Spectators filled the benches and standing areas to capacity, while outside onlookers peered through the doors' windows and waited for a spot to open up inside. However, Wasilewski had no difficulty hearing Mikus's loud voice. Wasilewski could not understand anything that Bennett said in reply, but he could hear Mikus say things like, "Can't you be definite about anything?" or "What do you mean 'it seemed like a lifetime'?"

Finally, the judge's bailiff came out of the courtroom and called his name. Wasilewski stood up and followed her into the crammed courtroom, which was already warm and humid from the bodies packed inside. His eyes immediately focused on the back of Bennett's head; he was slumped at one of the two tables in the front. To Wasilewski's right, a group of thirteen jurors stared at him as he walked slowly toward the witness stand. The bailiff opened a gate for him and pointed to the witness chair. To his right, the judge peered down at him for a few seconds and then looked away, squirting some tobacco juice into a nearby spittoon.

Miraldi stood up, smiled at him, and asked him his name, address, age, and current job.

"How do you know Casper Bennett?" Miraldi asked.

"I've seen him around town. I go to his bar sometimes. I just know him like that."

"Is he a close friend of yours?"

"No, I wouldn't say that. I know him, that's about all." Wasilewski's voice was quiet and he stared down at his boots.

Miraldi knew that Mikus would inquire further about Wasilewski's ties to Bennett, so Miraldi thought it best to provide the jury with a full disclosure. "Have you ever worked for Mr. Bennett?"

"Never worked for him full-time, but me and my brother, we done one job at his house where we fixed the toilet. You know, that's it."

"Would you tell the jury what you observed on December twentieth, that Friday evening?" Miraldi was careful not to lead the witness. He wanted the witness to tell the story without direction or prodding.

"You mean when I seen him that night?" Wasilewski responded.

"Yes."

"Okay. I was goin' south on Broadway and I turned right onto Fifteenth Street. I was goin' home to my house at Three Thirty-Four Fifteenth Street. I look into the rearview mirror and I see that Casper Bennett is in the car right behind me. I stop for the stop sign at Reid Avenue and I wave to him."

"How did you do that?"

"Well, I turn around and look out the rearview window and I just wave to him. He waves back to me and honks his horn."

"Anything else?"

"I go straight through on Fifteenth and I look again in the rearview mirror and Bennett makes a right-hand turn behind me. See, I don't know where he's going. I know his bar is nearby but I don't know if that's where he's going or not."

"What time did this happen, Mr. Wasilewski?"

"Sometime after nine o'clock."

"Can you be more specific?"

"Somewhere between nine ten and nine twenty."

"How did you know it was Casper Bennett behind you?"

"I know what he looks like and I know his car. I seen his new car before parked outside his bar."

"Any doubt in your mind that you saw Casper Bennett that evening on Fifteenth Street?"

"No, that was him."

"Did you ever talk to the police about what you saw?"

"Yeah, I talked to Charlie Springowski the next day after Mrs. Bennett died."

"Did you tell Sergeant Springowski anything different than what you just told the jury today?"

"Nope. He asked me the same questions as you and I told him the same stuff that I just told you."

"Thank you, Mr. Wasilewski."

Wasilewski thought he was through and began to stand up. Judge Pincura quickly stopped him. "Mr. Wasilewski, you've got to sit there until the prosecutor has asked you some questions, too."

Wasilewski grunted his understanding.

Mikus had read Sergeant Springowski's summary of his meeting with this witness. Wasilewski had said on the stand exactly what he disclosed to Springowski the day after the event. Mikus would make one effort to shake Wasilewski, and if that failed, he would leave the witness alone. Mikus knew that further questioning would only reinforce this witness's testimony with the jury.

"So, Mr. Wasilewski, how long have you known the defendant?" Mikus boomed.

"I don't know. Probably since I was a teenager, something like that."

"And you know Mr. Bennett socially?"

"I guess I don't know what you mean."

"Oh, really?" Mikus feigned disbelief. "I mean you've been his pal and done things together for many years—since you two were teenagers?"

"I said I've known him since I was a teenager, but I don't hang out with him or nothing," Wasilewski said, staring at his fingers, which were now clasped and jumping about on his lap. Wasilewski paused and then added suddenly, "I also known him from my working at Runyan's. I would see him there, you know, talking with the regulars."

"So you did socialize with him?" Mikus attempted to capitalize on this admission.

"Not me. He just talked to the regular guys who always hang out there. Not me. I was working. You know, guys like Carter Smith, Peachy Bill, Burnt Onions, and Slowman. You know, those are the guys he talked to."

If Wasilewski had not been staring at his hands, he would have seen smiles appearing on many faces, jurors and spectators alike. To keep a grin off of his own face, Judge Pincura squirted more tobacco juice into the spittoon. Mikus could see that he was getting nowhere with this line of inquiry.

Puffing out his chest, Mikus tried to hit hard. "Mr. Wasilewski, we cannot have guesses in this courtroom. You do not know when you saw Mr. Bennett. It could have been *before* nine p.m. or it could have been after. This is very important, so you are not to speculate. Do you understand?"

Wasilewski looked away from Mikus, whose withering gaze made him nervous. "I know how important this is. You're warning me the same way Springer warned me when he talked to me right after it happened. I'd looked at my watch before I saw Casper Bennett. I don't know how much time had gone by since I looked at it, but my watch said nine o' clock and then it was at least ten minutes or even twenty minutes after that that I seen Casper."

Mikus knew when to stop. "So you don't know for sure. You're just estimating the time?"

"Yes, sir. But I know it was after nine o'clock, just like I said."

Mikus quickly sat down and Miraldi sprang up to take his place.

"Mr. Wasilewski, you said 'Springer' had warned you not to guess. Who is this Springer person?"

Wasilewski looked embarrassed. "Oh, that's what we call Charlie Springowski, you know, Sergeant Springowski. Most of us Polacks just call him Springer."

Now it was Miraldi's turn to smile. "No more questions. Thank you, Mr. Wasilewski."

Don Miller, the *Chronicle* reporter, jotted down his impressions of Wasilewski as the witness walked out of the courtroom. *One of the briefest appearances of any witness*, he scribbled on his notepad, *but Bennett's life may well hang on that bit of testimony*.

After Wasilewski's testimony, the defense called a series of witnesses whose purpose was to establish that Florence Bennett was a drunk. Mary Ksenich, the medical librarian at St. Joseph Hospital, appeared and produced the medical records for Mrs. Bennett's hospitalization following her alcohol-induced fall in September of 1963. She was followed by Dr. Paul Pastuchiw, the Bennetts' family doctor.

Dr. Pastuchiw brought his medical charts for both Florence and Casper Bennett. When questioned by Miraldi, Pastuchiw confirmed that Mrs. Bennett had been treated since 1961 for alcoholism and for various injuries sustained in home falls. Besides the hospitalization in September of 1963, Dr. Pastuchiw revealed that Mrs. Bennett was hospitalized in January of 1963 for a week for contusions and delirium tremens.

Dr. Pastuchiw explained that delirium tremens, or the DTs, was a severe form of alcohol withdrawal. According to Dr. Pastuchiw, people who have regularly drunk large amounts of alcohol for at least several months will exhibit symptoms of body tremors, confusion, agitation, and even seizures when they have not had any alcohol for twelve to forty-eight hours. He told the jury that delirium tremens is a medical emergency that requires hospitalization to stabilize the patient with liquids, sedatives, and counseling.

Mikus attempted to sidestep Dr. Pastuchiw's testimony by ignoring the doctor's treatment of Florence Bennett and instead focusing upon Casper Bennett's hospital chart and Dr. Pastuchiw's treatment for him. Dr. Pastuchiw told the jury that he treated Casper Bennett for general nervousness, tremors, insomnia, and dipsomania. He explained that "dipsomania" simply meant "the urge to drink alcoholic beverages."

Miraldi's final morning witness was Edward R. Andy, the owner of Andy's Hardware Store, located on Ninth and Oberlin Avenue, about a block from Miraldi's home. Mr. Andy also claimed to be a home decorator and had painted and installed wallpaper in the Bennetts' home a few years before Florence's death. Miraldi did not know that Andy also made money by illegally selling fireworks to anyone willing to pay his high prices. The neighborhood children, including Miraldi's own two boys, were enthusiastic buyers.

"When you decorated the Bennett home, did you have any contact with Mrs. Bennett?" Miraldi asked.

Mr. Andy had a speech impediment that turned an "s" into an "sh" sound. "Yesh, I did," he answered.

"What did you observe?"

"She was often intoxicated and shtumbling around," Andy replied.

Mikus quickly jumped to his feet. "Objection. Mr. Miraldi has failed to establish the time when Mr. Andy observed these things."

"Sustained."

"Mr. Andy, when did you perform these services at the Bennett home?"

"That was Sheptember of 1962," Mr. Andy recalled.

"I renew my objection," Mikus said.

The judge pursed his lips and tilted his head upward as he thought. After about a minute, he said, "I am going to sustain the objection. Mrs. Bennett's lack of sobriety fifteen months before this incident is too remote in time. I will not allow evidence of her condition unless it is closer in time to her death."

Stunned, Miraldi looked at Adams. "Your Honor, I would like to proffer Mr. Andy's testimony into the record."

"I will excuse the jury for lunch. Mr. Miraldi, you can make your proffer to the court reporter out of their presence."

Miraldi believed that Pincura's ruling was arbitrary and lacked any legal basis. However, in order for the court of appeals to evaluate that claimed error, Miraldi needed to read into the record what Andy's testimony would have been if he had been allowed to give it.

After the judge left the courtroom, Miraldi made his proffer to Orie Camillo, the court reporter.

"Mr. Andy would have testified that he was working in the Bennett home for two weeks during September of 1962. On many occasions during that time, Mrs. Bennett was quite drunk. On one occasion, he saw her fall down in the kitchen. On two occasions, he escorted her back upstairs to her room because he was afraid that she was going to fall. He observed her drinking hard liquor throughout the day. That ends my proffer."

Although the jury would hear no more of Andy's testimony, in reality, they would not be able to disregard it. Despite the judge's instruction for the jury to ignore his testimony, Andy had told them that she was drunk when he was there, and they would remember that.

After lunch, the defense called Ray Miller, an employee of Richman Brothers. Mr. Miller testified that Bennett dropped his coat off at Richman Brothers on December seventeenth for alterations and that he was supposed to pick it up on the twentieth but never showed up for it. Mikus had a short cross-examination in which the witness conceded that he did not know if Bennett was actually coming on the twentieth, but only that the jacket was ready on that day.

As he sat down at the prosecution table, Mikus whispered to Otero, "The reason he didn't pick up that damn coat is because he was murdering his wife. My gut tells me that Bennett went home after buying gas at Don's Sohio and then left the house again after he killed his wife."

Otero nodded in agreement. Both men knew that they had no way to prove that.

With Ray Miller's testimony completed, Adams told the court that their next witness would be George Abraham, a Lorain taxi driver. As Abraham strolled into the courtroom, he looked around quickly at the spectators on the main floor and then gazed upward to survey the people in the balcony. Abraham was the son of Syrian immigrants and his dark, darting eyes were wide with anticipation. He sat down quickly in the witness chair and leaned back, trying to make himself comfortable in his new surroundings.

George Abraham's name had come to the attention of the Lorain police early in the investigation. On December 24, 1963, Irene Miller had told the police that Abraham talked to her just before she arrived at the police station to be interviewed. Abraham claimed that an intoxicated Florence Bennett, along with a dark-haired woman, entered his taxicab and offered to pay Abraham to tail Casper Bennett and report back to Florence. Abraham declined the offer. The police never followed up on Miller's tip.

Miller also provided this information to Casper Bennett's attorney, Lon Adams, who did talk to Abraham. Miraldi's young associate Richard Colella also spoke to Abraham a few weeks before the trial and concluded that Abraham would make a great witness. "The jury's going to love him," Colella gushed to his boss. The gist of Abraham's story was that in the two months prior to her death, he'd picked Florence up approximately fifteen times to either visit bars or purchase liquor. She was drunk every time.

Abraham's eagerness to be a critical witness should have set off some alarms for the defense. Miraldi's opportunity to vet this overly enthusiastic witness was literally right at his doorstep. His parents lived next door to Abraham and rented a house to him. If he had been asked, the elder Miraldi, now eighty-three years old but still mentally sharp, would have told his son that Abraham "never shut up" and was "cuckoolini," a word Miraldi's father had cobbled together from English and Italian. However, that conversation did not occur until after the trial.

When the prosecutor discovered that Abraham had been subpoenaed by the defense, he ran a criminal check on the witness. The Lorain police records showed that George Aloysius Abraham, age forty-four, had been investigated by a grand jury for embezzlement in 1948 but had not been indicted. In 1952 he had been convicted of disorderly conduct and later of assault and battery, for which he spent two short stints in the Lorain city jail. From that time on, Abraham had stayed out of trouble except for several traffic violations.

Abraham was a colorful character, full of nonstop stories that could make short taxi trips with him quite entertaining. However, passengers who spent a longer amount of time with the garrulous driver usually had their hands on a door handle, anxious to exit as soon as the taxi came to a stop.

After establishing the witness's name, background, and occupation, Adams asked Abraham if he knew Florence Bennett. Abraham told the jury that he'd picked her up many times and driven her to bars and liquor stores. Mikus quickly objected, arguing that Adams needed to first establish when the rides occurred. When the witness claimed that he drove Mrs. Bennett fifteen times in November and December of 1963, Mikus objected again. This time Judge Pincura overruled the objection.

"Tell us about what you remember from these rides," Adams said.

"Objection. The defense needs to establish when a particular ride took place before the witness can testify about the specifics."

"Sustained."

"If you can, Mr. Abraham, tell us first when a particular ride took place and then what happened."

Abraham was not used to being interrupted. He also sensed that he might be deprived of an opportunity to deliver critical testimony.

"The first one I remember was a week before President Kennedy was shot," Abraham exclaimed as he looked directly at Mikus and smirked.

"What happened?"

"She gets in the taxi and she is smashed and—"

"Objection. The witness is drawing an improper conclusion that Mrs. Bennett was intoxicated. He can tell us what he noticed about her, but he cannot give an opinion regarding her sobriety."

"Sustained. Mr. Abraham, just tell us what you observed about Mrs. Bennett," the judge directed.

"I observed that she was drunk. I can't say it any better than that."

"Objection."

"Sustained."

"What did you notice about Mrs. Bennett that you thought was different?" Adams asked.

Abraham shifted in the witness chair and looked exasperated.

"The woman was slurring her words and talking real loud. All she wants to do is go and buy some hard stuff. She asks me to take her to someplace close. She don't know where—just that I'm supposed to find the store. I says to her, 'Lady, you got to tell me where you want to go.' She says, 'You're a cabbie. Don't you know your way around Lorain?' Stuff like that."

"When was the next time?"

"Am I supposed to have dates and times? I picked her up all the time." Abraham looked at the judge.

"Just do your best," Adams said, trying to encourage the witness.

"About three or four days later—"

Mikus jumped to his feet and objected again.

Miraldi was fed up with Mikus's never-ending objections. In a stage whisper audible to all, Miraldi leaned toward the prosecution's table and again taunted the prosecutor, "What are you afraid of, Paul?"

Mikus's reaction was immediate. "This is the second time you have said that," he yelled. "I'm not afraid of anything, least of all this case." Mikus glared at Miraldi, daring him to say something more.

Miraldi was not intimidated and stared back at Mikus but remained silent. After the two men glowered at one another for a few seconds, Mikus turned to face the judge.

"I request that the jury be told to disregard that statement, and that this court reprimand Mr. Miraldi," Mikus demanded.

Mikus's tactics were wearing thin with Judge Pincura, too, but the judge, nonetheless, scowled at Miraldi. "Your comment, Mr. Miraldi, was uncalled for."

Mikus watched with his mouth open, waiting for the judge to say more, but Judge Pincura was finished. Miraldi stood up quickly and angled his body so that his back was to Mikus. "I will apologize to the court," he said.

Abraham watched this exchange intently. He could not believe that the prosecutor could thwart his testimony and that the attorneys who had asked him to testify were backing down without a fight. Elsewhere in the courtroom, a hundred pairs of eyes were focused on him, waiting for him to deliver testimony that would save the defendant.

"When is the next time that you had any contact with Mrs. Bennett?" Adams asked, returning to the prior question.

"She was drunk in my cab fifteen times in two months. I can't give you exact dates unless I check the company records," Abraham responded.

"I ask that the court strike Mr. Abraham's last comment unless he can provide us with dates and times and locations."

"Sustained."

"You can't shut me up so easy," Abraham yelled at Mikus.

Judge Pincura struck his gavel. "I will not tolerate any outbursts like this, Mr. Abraham. Do you understand?"

"He don't give me a chance," Abraham shot back at the judge.

Adams wanted to keep trying with this witness. "Mr. Abraham, you will need to search your memory as to dates and times that you picked up Mrs. Bennett and dropped her off at various locations. Can you do that, even if they are approximations?"

"Sure."

"Please tell us the date of another encounter," Adams coaxed.

"About two weeks before she died, I remember pickin' her up at her house and she wanted to go to a bar, but I can't remember the name of the bar—"

"Objection," yelled Mikus. "He has to be able to give us dates, locations, and times."

"No, he doesn't," interjected Adams. "Any witness can testify about general events by memory. This is allowable. It goes to the weight of the witness's testimony, not its admissibility."

"Do you know the location of the bar?" Judge Pincura asked the witness.

"That was four months ago. All I know is I picked her up at her house and took her to some bar downtown near Broadway and West Erie."

"The objection is sustained," Judge Pincura ruled.

"Is he going to let me talk or not?" Abraham asked Adams.

"You have to be more specific about where you took Mrs. Bennett," Adams explained to the witness.

Abraham then shook his finger at Mikus. "I know what I know, no matter what you do to try and stop me."

Judge Pincura looked at Abraham. "Stop your chattering. If you can't answer the question, just say so. I am running out of patience with you, Mr. Abraham."

"Is there any way you can be more specific about the times and places that you took Mrs. Bennett?" Adams said, his voice unable to hide his frustration and disappointment.

"I've got records of all of this," Abraham claimed. "But I don't have them with me. They're back at the office."

"Your Honor, I demand that these records be produced now," Mikus interjected.

"You stay out of this," Abraham yelled at Mikus.

Before Abraham could say anything more, Judge Pincura interrupted him. "You may leave right now and get the cab company records."

"The records are at the office," Abraham responded. "You can check 'em."

"I command you to go to your taxi office and return with those records. That is a court order. Can you do that?"

"How much time do I have?" Abraham asked as he stood up from the witness chair.

"It's one forty-five. I'll give you an hour," the judge said sternly.

"Okay," Abraham said as he walked quickly out of the courtroom.

After Abraham left, the defense called the defendant's brother, Chester Bennett, to show that Casper was just a regular guy, not much different from the people who would be deciding his fate. Chester's health was failing and he had difficulty walking to the witness stand. In temperament, Chester was quieter and more reserved, traits the defense team hoped would make a favorable impression on the jurors. However, a few jurors looked surprised when Chester said that he currently resided at the Grandview Hotel in Lorain.

Chester told the jurors of the brothers' ordinary home life growing up in central Lorain, children of Polish immigrants, including a father who worked long hours as a mechanic. He quickly summarized their early life, attending public school and worshipping at Nativity of the Blessed Virgin, and described how Casper married Florence in 1940 and alcohol soon dominated much of their life. Chester said he visited their home sporadically but confirmed that Florence was a heavy drinker and was often very drunk when he stopped by to see them. When asked whether he ever saw his brother become violent, Chester told the jury that his brother "wouldn't hurt a fly."

Mikus asked a few questions, reasoning that the jury would expect a brother to come to the aid of another brother.

"Although your brother wouldn't hurt a fly, as you say, would you be surprised if there were allegations that your brother slapped and pushed Florence around throughout their marriage?" Mikus asked.

"I was around them quite a bit and I never saw none of that. I never saw a mark on her, never."

After Chester Bennett was excused, Adams left the courtroom to see if the volatile Abraham had returned. Adams came back and shook his head as he sat down again next to Miraldi. "I got a feeling he's not coming back," Adams told Miraldi.

"I hope he doesn't," rejoined Miraldi.

Frank Mishak, Bennett's business partner and the uncle of Florence Bennett, took the stand next. He confirmed that for several months before Florence Bennett's death, Casper tried to sell his interest in the bar so that the Bennetts could start over in Florida. Mishak reported that a month before the trial, he'd bought Bennett's one-half share of the business. Mikus chose not to cross-examine Mishak, and Judge Pincura excused the jury for the midafternoon recess. It was now two thirty p.m.

Miraldi and Adams had run out of witnesses for the day. Their two medical experts were scheduled to testify on Monday. Seeking the court's indulgence, the defense team asked the judge to recess the trial until Monday, assuming Abraham was not going to reappear. Before Judge Pincura could rule on the request, Abraham burst through the doors and bounded over to Adams.

"I got to talk to you, quick," Abraham told Adams.

Taking Abraham by the elbow, Adams walked the excited witness outside the courtroom and into the hall. Mikus and Otero could see that

Abraham carried no records with him and they smiled at one other. Miraldi quickly followed the pair out of the courtroom. Judge Pincura got up from his chair and told the prosecutors, "I think this might take a while." The judge walked back toward his office, telling his bailiff, "Let me know when the defense attorneys are back."

Out in the hall, Abraham was agitated. "They get rid of my daily logs at the end of each month. There ain't no records for them months showing my rides. We're screwed."

Adams was calm. "What records does the company have?"

Abraham looked at Adams, his dark eyes flashing. "Didn't you hear what I just said? There ain't no records."

Now it was Adams's turn to be irritated. "I know that," he snapped. "But don't they keep any records from those daily logs?"

"They just show what I earned each week. That's it."

Adams looked at Miraldi. Although neither said anything, both were trying to figure out the next step. Finally, Adams said, "We're just going to tell the judge that those records were destroyed and we cannot produce them. Because we can't back up Mr. Abraham's testimony with cab records, we'll withdraw him as our witness."

"What do you mean you're withdrawing me? What's that supposed to mean?" Abraham asked.

"Look, Mr. Abraham. You claimed that you had records that would show that Mrs. Bennett rode with you fifteen times, and these records would have details about where you took her. You made that claim, not us. Now you tell the judge that those records don't exist. We all look bad if we keep parading you in front of the jury. It's that simple," Adams replied.

"But—" Abraham stopped his sentence in midstream because Miraldi and Adams were already reentering the courtroom, abandoning him in the halls.

When the judge was back on the bench, Adams explained that the defense intended to withdraw Abraham as a witness because he could not produce records that unfortunately had been destroyed. Judge Pincura looked over to Mikus. "What is your position on this?"

Mikus was beaming. He knew that this witness was a fraud and now the jury would know it, too. "I will agree to the withdrawal of this witness on the condition that all of Abraham's testimony be stricken from the record."

Judge Pincura pinched his chin with his left thumb and forefinger. "Gentlemen, I don't think the law permits me to do that. I allowed some of this witness's testimony to come in. It's there, and the fact that Mr. Abraham can't corroborate his testimony with written records does not cause his earlier testimony to become invalid. Even though the attorneys agree, I do not. Mr. Mikus, you can cross-examine the witness and if you bring out something that changes my mind, I will then allow the defense to withdraw him as a witness and strike his testimony from the trial record."

Mikus looked at Otero and shrugged his shoulders. He wouldn't mind cross-examining Abraham. Adams and Miraldi did not move at first, incredulous that the judge would not allow them to withdraw the witness.

"Bailiff, bring Mr. Abraham back to the witness stand," Judge Pincura said. "And bring back the jury."

This time Abraham did not seem anxious to sit in the witness chair. He walked through the courtroom slowly and patted the seat of his chair before sitting. He looked around the gallery and could see that some of the spectators were pointing at him as they talked to their neighbors. Among the general undercurrent, Abraham could hear some laughter, too.

"So you're back," Mikus began.

Abraham said nothing.

"Did you bring those records with you?" Mikus asked.

"You know the answer to that," Abraham said.

"No. I don't know. Did you bring them?"

"What do you think?"

"Your Honor, instruct the witness to answer the question."

"Mr. Abraham, the prosecutor has asked you a question and you are required to answer it," the judge replied.

"No, I don't have no records with me, but I can explain," Abraham replied.

"I don't want your explanations," Mikus said, but Abraham was still talking.

"Because they throw them away at the end of the month—" Abraham said.

Mikus interrupted him. "You've answered my question." His voice grew louder as he tried to drown out the witness. Abraham said something about daily logs. He was ignoring Mikus and taking his case directly to the jurors, talking quickly and gesturing wildly. Judge Pincura struck his gavel and the witness stopped talking.

"That will be enough, Mr. Abraham. You must stop your chattering; do you understand me? You only respond to questions, otherwise you must be quiet. This is my courtroom, not your taxicab," the judge said.

"But he don't give me a chance," Abraham protested. "I thought a guy was supposed to get a fair shake in the courtroom."

The judge ignored the comment. However, Mikus knew a pathological liar when he saw one and his blood was up. He wanted to take on this witness. "Just answer my questions. That's all you are supposed to do. It's not hard," Mikus yelled.

"Why don't you ask me a fair question?" Abraham yelled back. Some of the spectators began to titter, but most sat quietly entranced.

"You just answer my questions. You don't ask me questions. Do you got that?" Mikus screamed at the witness.

"No, I don't got that and I don't have to do that," Abraham shot back. Ignoring Mikus, Abraham looked at the jurors and again tried to talk to them directly. "One time I took her to the liquor store. She was so drunk she dropped both bottles onto the sidewalk."

"Mr. Abraham," the judge said, again striking his gavel, "that will be enough. If you do that again, I will hold you in contempt of court and you will spend the night in jail. Do you understand that?"

Abraham did not reply, but his silence convinced the judge that he understood the warning. Judge Pincura looked at Mikus. He hoped that the prosecutor would end the questioning. The jury had made up its mind on this witness. "Do you have any more questions for this witness, Mr. Mikus?"

Mikus was still angry. "Just answer my next question either yes or no. Can you give this jury one exact date when Mrs. Bennett got into your cab?"

"I told you one week before Kennedy was shot. That's an exact date, isn't it?"

"But you can't tell us where you took her, can you?"

"Do you know where you drove three months ago?" Abraham asked the prosecutor.

"Just answer the question, yes or no?"

"Let me think. One time I took her to the Old Timer's Café."

"When was this?"

"I don't know the date. The records are gone. I told you that already."

"Well, isn't that just great? You tell us that you have the records to back up what you're saying. Then we tell you to go and get them and now they're destroyed. There never were any records, were there?" Mikus said, challenging him.

"I know what I know, which is a heck of a lot more than you," the witness said. The witness's bravado startled some of the spectators, who began to laugh.

Judge Pincura had had enough. "I will not have laughter in my courtroom when a man is on trial for first-degree murder. If I hear laughter again, I will clear every spectator out of this courtroom." Then, turning his attention to Mikus, the judge said, "Mr. Mikus, please finish with this witness."

This time Mikus got the judge's message. "No further questions."

The day was over. The judge recessed the trial at three fifteen p.m. The defense again explained that it had two additional witnesses but they would not be available until Monday morning because of their busy schedules. For the first time, the prosecutor learned that pathologists, Dr. Alan Moritz and Dr. Robert Kelly, would testify on behalf of Casper Bennett. In a trial in which the prosecutor had initiated many surprises, the defense hoped to even the score with these witnesses.

As Miraldi and Adams left the courtroom, they talked quietly about the day's events and the performance of their last witness—something they viewed as a debacle. Waiting for them outside the courtroom was veteran attorney Dan Cook. Cook had watched the afternoon session of the trial and could tell that the defense team was discouraged by its final witness.

Cook was a well-respected lawyer whose bank and insurance company clients were the envy of Miraldi and most Lorain County attorneys. A graduate of the University of Michigan Law School, Cook was a savvy and experienced trial lawyer.

"I sat through the afternoon of the trial," Cook began.

Miraldi shook his head and looked dejected, unable to engage in small talk. Adams took in a deep breath and said, "Yes, and what did you think?"

"I know you think that taxicab driver was a disaster. Why else would you move to withdraw his testimony? But I don't think he was bad at all," Cook insisted.

Now Miraldi looked up. He was anxious to grab any life preserver tossed his way. "How so?" he asked.

"From the balcony, I was watching the jury pretty carefully. I think they actually liked the witness. In fact, I think they liked him very much. They were smiling at what he said and I think they really liked the way he fought back when Mikus tried to bully him," Cook said.

"Even when he couldn't produce the records?" Adams asked.

"Hey, I wouldn't expect daily logs to be kept that long. I doubt the jury would expect that either."

"I appreciate you saying that to us," Miraldi said.

Cook was not finished. "Pincura didn't give you two any breaks today either. He shouldn't have required the witness to know the exact dates and locations of the rides. That was ridiculous. I doubt my dad would have required that," he said. His father was a former Lorain County judge.

Both defense attorneys thanked Cook for his insight and encouragement, and headed for their cars.

****

Paul Mikus walked back to the prosecutor's office to check the messages on his desk. Mikus knew that he should be tired after a second week in trial, but he felt energized. Bennett's defense was in shambles. In a couple more days, he would get Bennett convicted of first-degree murder.

He was smiling to himself as he thought of his encounter with George Abraham. Mikus had been so angry during the exchange that he was unable to remember what he had actually said to that belligerent nut. As a result, Mikus had asked the court reporter to transcribe his cross-examination just so he would know.

When Mikus sat down at his desk, he saw a message that Dr. Kopsch had called and wanted a status on the trial. The coroner had left his home number. Mikus tried that number and reached Dr. Kopsch immediately. After Mikus summarized the day's events, he told the coroner about the two expert witnesses that the defense would call.

"Who are they?" Dr. Kopsch asked.

"One has an Irish name. Here is my note. It is Robert Kelly. The other is Dr. Alan Moritz," Mikus replied. He waited for the coroner to reply, but there was silence on the other end. "Are you still there?" Mikus asked.

"Yes, I am," Dr. Kopsch replied.

"Is something the matter?" Mikus asked.

Again, there was a long pause. "I don't know anything about Dr. Robert Kelly, but anyone who is a pathologist in this country knows who Alan Moritz is."

Now it was Mikus's turn to be silent.

Dr. Kopsch continued, "I have Moritz's textbook in my office. The book is called *Handbook of Legal Medicine*. It is one of the bibles for pathologists and coroners. I've heard the doctor speak at conferences. Somehow, they got one of the world's top experts."

"Son of a bitch," Mikus said.

"What did you say?" Kopsch asked.

"That Miraldi is a sneaky son of a bitch. That's what I said," Mikus shouted into the receiver.

Ignoring that comment, Dr. Kopsch said, "I'll be glad to help you over the weekend. I'll bring over Moritz's textbook and we can get a good idea about what he'll say."

"Thanks," Mikus replied, finally regaining some composure. "I'll do everything I can to keep Moritz from giving any opinions in this case, especially about the cause of death. I'll object to everything but his name."

Dr. Kopsch was a bit unnerved by Mikus's outburst but did not want to upset him further. "I'll leave that to you. I'll help in any way possible this weekend. Just call me when you want to meet."

"Thanks. I will."

CHAPTER 25

April 13, 1964

On the very day that Miraldi was retained by Casper Bennett, Miraldi had phoned several local physicians to recommend a pathologist to review this case. Several suggested Alan Moritz, MD, the chairman of the Department of Pathology at University Hospitals in Cleveland.

Miraldi phoned Dr. Moritz that afternoon, and they agreed to meet the following day to discuss the case. On March 3, 1964, Miraldi met with Dr. Moritz, who, after reviewing the final autopsy report and the photographs, disagreed with Dr. Kopsch's conclusion that Florence Bennett drowned. The doctor checked his schedule and found that he was available to testify in early April.

Five weeks after that initial conference, Dr. Moritz was on the witness stand to tell a Lorain County jury what he believed caused Florence Bennett's death. Dressed in a dark gray suit and a maroon bow tie, the sixty-four-year-old medical school professor peered out calmly at the packed courtroom. His posture was erect as he recited his name in response to the first question.

Miraldi's first job was to ask Dr. Moritz questions about his medical training and background in order to demonstrate that the doctor had the expertise to aid the jury in resolving difficult questions beyond their common knowledge. This process, known as qualifying the expert, would allow Dr. Moritz to give his opinion on Florence Bennett's death and other medical issues. Witnesses are ordinarily limited to testifying about facts and are forbidden to render opinions unless they have specialized training or experience in a field in which the jurors have little or no understanding. Miraldi had "qualified" many physicians when trying personal injury cases and it was a straightforward process.

Miraldi had just begun the qualifying process when Mikus stood up and said, "We will admit to the qualifications of Dr. Moritz." When confronted with an expert with impressive credentials, an opposing attorney can stipulate that the witness has the necessary qualifications to give opinions. The offer is made under the pretense that it will save time and allow the other attorney to move directly to the meat of the expert's testimony. In actuality, the offer is made so that the jury will never know the full extent of the expert's background and expertise. However, when jurors must choose between opposing experts and opinions, they need to know which of the experts is more knowledgeable. Mikus's tactic was an old ploy and would have duped only the most inexperienced attorney.

"Your Honor, we decline the prosecutor's generous offer, and we would like the jury to know Dr. Moritz's qualifications," Miraldi replied.

Dr. Moritz did have extraordinary credentials. Born in Hastings, Nebraska, in 1899, the doctor had completed his undergraduate degree at age twenty, master's degree at age twenty-one, and medical degree two years later. He received five years of postgraduate training in pathology at Western Reserve University and at the University of Vienna in Austria. After his training, he served as a pathologist at Lakeside Hospital in Cleveland for eight years before being appointed a professor of legal medicine at Harvard University in 1937. Before the outbreak of World War II, he was a Rockefeller Fellow and lectured in pathology at universities throughout Europe.

Dr. Moritz returned to Harvard Medical School in 1939 and also served as the pathologist to the Massachusetts Department of Public Safety and Department of Mental Health. He continued to practice pathology at several prestigious hospitals in Boston. In 1949, Dr. Moritz returned to Cleveland's University Hospitals as the director of the Department of Pathology, where he currently served.

He told the jury that he had authored or coauthored more than one hundred scientific articles and was the author of four books on forensic medicine and pathology. Some of his articles dealt with drowning and other forms of asphyxia. He was the past president of the American Association of Pathologists and Bacteriologists, past president of the American Academy of Forensic Medicines, and a governor of the College of American Pathologists. He had performed over ten thousand autopsies, approximately forty of which required him to determine if the victim had drowned.

To qualify as an expert under Ohio law, an expert witness need not be the best witness on the subject but merely have sufficient knowledge to aid the jury in the "search for the truth." Based on his vast background and experience, Dr. Moritz was unquestionably qualified, and Mikus knew that it would be impossible to thwart the doctor's testimony on that basis.

Most attorneys in Mikus's position devise a careful cross-examination that forces the expert witness to concede certain points, but Mikus wanted to keep Dr. Moritz from giving any opinions while Miraldi questioned him. His plan was to defeat the witness during Miraldi's direct examination.

To do this, Mikus would use the rules of evidence to contest the propriety of Miraldi's questions, particularly those that asked Dr. Moritz to give an important opinion. The prosecutor planned to object to those questions and claim that Miraldi had not formulated them according to the technical requirements of the law. If the judge agreed, Miraldi's witness would be stopped before he gave an opinion. Even if the judge ruled against him, Mikus would disrupt the examination, and the jurors would be distracted while the attorneys argued about his objections. Mikus was convinced that Bennett was a murderer and he would use every legally-permissible tactic to thwart the defense.

Mikus lay in wait as Dr. Moritz explained that a pathologist is a physician who studies disease by "using the relatively precise method of the laboratory."

"Doctor, can you very briefly tell the jury what an autopsy is, its purpose and general procedure?" Miraldi asked.

Dr. Moritz had been asked this question many times and he had a pat answer. "An autopsy is a dissection of the body that seeks to establish the cause of death. In addition, we use the autopsy to secure whatever information is available about other diseases or injuries that may be present."

After establishing that Dr. Moritz had reviewed the two autopsy reports, the toxicology report, and photographs of the corpse, Miraldi asked Dr. Moritz if he had an opinion about the cause of death. Mikus sprung out of his chair, objected, and asked for a bench conference outside the hearing of the jury. This was the first of sixty-five objections that Mikus would raise in opposition to Miraldi's final seventy-five questions to Dr. Moritz. If Miraldi was going to get Dr. Moritz's opinions before the jury, he would have to claw his way past these objections.

"That question is the ultimate question for the jury to decide and invades the province of the jury," Mikus claimed. "Only the jury can answer that question, not this expert."

"This is not the ultimate issue in this case," Miraldi interjected. "The ultimate issue is whether my client murdered his wife, not the cause of death."

"I don't think I need to remind the court about this rule of evidence. Perhaps Mr. Miraldi needs an education. The jury always decides the ultimate issue in the case. If this witness gives an opinion on the cause of death, he would be telling the jury how they should decide that issue and, ultimately, the case."

"What do you mean this witness can't give an opinion on the cause of death? What do you think Dr. Kopsch testified to?" Miraldi shot back.

"He didn't," Mikus said.

"That's ridiculous."

"He supervised the autopsy."

"That doesn't make any difference."

"He is the official coroner."

The judge weighed in. "Of course, Dr. Kopsch testified that in his opinion the cause of death was by drowning."

"Right," Miraldi said, encouraged that the judge could see through Mikus's argument.

Mikus was not through. "Well, further than that, this expert can only give an opinion on the basis of a hypothetical question and not on the basis of the coroner's report alone."

Before Miraldi could respond, Judge Pincura said, "I would think so." Turning to Miraldi, the judge said, "I think probably, Mr. Miraldi, you will have to put your question into the form of a hypothetical question that embraces the entire autopsy report."

"You mean, you want me to read the entire autopsy report as a preface to my question?" Miraldi asked. He knew that if he had to do that, it would take fifteen minutes, maybe even a half hour to pose that one question. By the time he finished the question, the jury would either be hopelessly confused or no longer focused on the witness.

The judge nodded to show that this was what he thought was required. Mikus beamed in delight.

"Maybe you also need a refresher course on hypothetical questions?" Mikus needled.

"I know all about them. I just have to ask the doctor to assume that the most important facts are true and ask him his opinion. No one has ever been required to incorporate every medical fact into the beginning of a question in order to elicit an expert's opinion. That's ridiculous," Miraldi replied.

"You are going to have to get in all of the evidence that we have in this case, about where she was found, how she was found, how much she drank, and all of that," Mikus said.

"No, we don't," Miraldi snapped.

"All that stuff's got to be the basis of your hypothetical question or it is not valid," Mikus argued.

"That's all in the autopsy report. The toxicology report shows the amount of alcohol. I don't have to put that in my question."

"Yes, you do. Those reports don't show that," Mikus insisted.

Judge Pincura sided with Mikus. "I'm afraid you will have to."

Miraldi was faced with every trial attorney's worst nightmare. The judge was making a ruling that would prevent him from getting the most important testimony into evidence. Without Moritz's opinion, the case could be lost. Miraldi was convinced that he had phrased the question correctly and that all of the relevant facts regarding the cause of death were contained in the autopsy report, the toxicology report, and the photographs. He believed that he did not need to reference a mountain of other evidence in his question.

"Why do I have to read it over again?" Miraldi asked, referring to the autopsy report.

Mikus said, "Because you don't have all the factors and you need everything."

"Just a minute," Judge Pincura said. He did not like Mikus butting in as if he were the judge.

Miraldi could see Mikus's strategy. Mikus planned to object to any hypothetical question that Miraldi posed, claiming that Miraldi had left out a particular essential fact. Worse yet, he could see the judge sustaining the objection.

Adams had a sinking feeling in his gut as he watched Miraldi struggle with Mikus and Judge Pincura. He, too, could not understand why the judge was buying Mikus's argument that the defense would have to preface all of the autopsy findings into one huge, unwieldly question.

Miraldi tried a different approach. "Judge, the standard jury charge on hypothetical questions instructs the jury that they can consider an expert's opinion even if a fact is omitted from the hypothetical. You don't keep the expert from answering the question. You tell the jury that any omitted fact just affects the weight of the expert's opinion. You don't throw out the baby with the bath water," Miraldi said.

Before Judge Pincura could consider Miraldi's point, Mikus interjected and diverted the judge. "Dr. Kopsch did not have to give his opinion based on a hypothetical question because he was at the scene, examined the body, and had personal knowledge of all the important facts."

"We're not talking about Dr. Kopsch," Miraldi snapped back. However, Mikus's statement had distracted the judge from Miraldi's last point which had been an accurate statement of the law.

In a tone that was almost apologetic, Judge Pincura said, "I am afraid you're required to read the entire autopsy report into your question and reference all that other material too."

Miraldi decided to gamble and just pay lip service to the judge's ruling. He handed the two autopsy reports to Dr. Moritz and asked him to read the reports silently to himself in front of the judge and jury. After Dr. Moritz did this, Miraldi asked:

"Now, doctor, I'm going to ask you a hypothetical question. Assuming the facts as stated and put forth in the two autopsy reports introduced by the State of Ohio, Exhibits B and C, assuming all those facts to be true, and from your examination of the photographs of the decedent, Florence Bennett, taken shortly after her death, do you have an opinion, based on reasonable medical probabilities, as to the cause of death of Florence Bennett?"

Mikus quickly objected. The judge paused for what seemed like an eternity to Miraldi. Judge Pincura eventually said, "Well, the court will overrule the objection. Dr. Moritz, do you have an opinion? Just answer yes or no."

Before his expert could answer, Miraldi said, "Thank you, Your Honor." His relief was palpable.

Dr. Moritz told the court that he did have an opinion. Miraldi then asked him, "What is your opinion, doctor?"

Mikus objected again, claiming that no photographs had been shown to Dr. Moritz.

Perturbed, Miraldi replied, "He has been looking at them for ten minutes, Paul."

Judge Pincura asked the witness, "Have you seen the photographs, doctor?"

"I have."

Addressing his witness, Miraldi said, "Well, go ahead and look at them in the presence of the jury, doctor. I want to satisfy the prosecutor." After Dr. Moritz looked at the photographs one last time, Miraldi asked, "Doctor, what is your opinion, sir?"

Mikus objected again and the court quickly overruled him.

Mikus's objections and attempts to block the opinion only heightened the jurors' overwhelming curiosity, and they were staring at the witness, impatient for his response. Dr. Moritz paused for a moment and then said, "That Florence Bennett died of extensive subcutaneous burning and hyperthermic shock." The courtroom was silent as the spectators and jury took in the significance of his short, concise answer. Dr. Moritz, a pathologist with a national reputation, did not believe that Florence Bennett had drowned.

"Doctor, can you explain briefly what you mean by 'hyperthermia' and 'hyperthermic shock'?" Miraldi asked. For once, Mikus did not object. He too was trying to determine how this opinion affected his case. He assumed it was not good.

"It appears that roughly three-fourths of this person's skin has been burned. It appears that some of this burning occurred while she was alive. Under these circumstances, with the skin in contact with hot water, the body temperature would ordinarily increase very rapidly. That accounts for the term 'hyperthermia'—'hyper' being 'an excess of' and 'thermia' meaning 'heat.'

"When the body temperature is raised to a sufficient level, the circulation will fail abruptly, and this would constitute shock. So hyperthermic shock is an acute circulatory failure caused by an excessively high body temperature."

Miraldi then asked the doctor if there were any other possible causes of death. Again Mikus objected and the judge overruled the objection. Dr. Moritz told the jury that drowning had to be considered because Florence Bennett had been found in a tub of water. The other possibility was alcoholism, because the toxicology report revealed alcohol in the blood and cellular changes in the liver that were consistent with chronic alcoholism.

Over Mikus's objections, Dr. Moritz testified that it was possible that Mrs. Bennett died from a combination of all three conditions: hyperthermia, drowning, and alcoholism. Miraldi wanted the doctor to explain that drowning was the least likely of the possibilities, but Mikus objected and the judge sustained the objection.

Turning to the findings of the autopsy, Miraldi asked Dr. Moritz about the fluid in the lungs known as pulmonary edema. Dr. Moritz explained that excess fluid could accumulate in the lungs from either drowning or hyperthermia. In cases of hyperthermia, the rapidly failing circulatory system leads to pulmonary edema.

Next, Miraldi asked Dr. Moritz to explain how autopsy findings can establish death by drowning. Dr. Moritz told the jury that one would look for fluid that has gone through the air passages into the lungs. One would also test the water from the lungs to determine if the water came from outside the body by looking for contaminants in the water. Finally, a pathologist would likely find foam in the air passages caused by the drowning victim breathing in water mixed with air.

Over objection, Miraldi asked, "From the photographs of the decedent, do you see any foamy mass in either the nostrils or the mouth?"

"I do not."

Again over objection, Miraldi asked, "Did the autopsy or the chemical report show any evidence of foreign matter that came into the lungs from any outside source?"

Dr. Moritz quickly answered, "No. Neither the autopsy nor the chemical report shows that the water in the lungs came from outside the body."

"Doctor, from the study of the autopsy report, the toxicological report, and the pictures, what are the positive reasons that one might suspect death by drowning in this case?"

Mikus objected and the judge overruled him. Mikus looked at Otero in disbelief. Five minutes earlier, Judge Pincura had sided with Mikus and ruled that Miraldi could not question Dr. Moritz about the likelihood of death by drowning. Since then, Dr. Moritz had gone through the autopsy report point by point and told the jury that customary findings that establish death by drowning had not been found.

"The only positive reason to suspect drowning is that this woman was said to have been found dead in a tub containing water," Dr. Moritz said dryly.

"Aside from that, are there any medical facts to substantiate death by drowning?"

Mikus objected and was overruled again.

"I am not aware of them," Dr. Moritz concluded.

Miraldi returned to the topic of hyperthermia and hyperthermic shock. Again over constant objection, Dr. Moritz explained that shock simply means "a rapidly deteriorating situation where circulation collapses and fails." When circulation fails, the brain and heart do not receive enough oxygen. If the shock is not reversed, these vital organs fail and the person dies because either the heart cannot continue to pump blood or the brain fails to "transmit impulses to the muscles that regulate breathing."

"What happens to the blood in cases of hyperthermia, doctor?"

"It gets hot," Dr. Moritz answered, and then smiled for the first time during his testimony.

"Is there a blood temperature where bodily functions cease?"

Mikus objected and the judge overruled him. By now, the judge was summarily overruling Mikus's constant objections. For most of the trial, the judge had watched a defense team that looked confused and on the verge of defeat. As a former college quarterback, Judge Pincura thrilled at competition and relished watching an underdog come from behind. As this preeminent expert continued to methodically destroy the prosecution's medical case, the judge was enjoying the unexpected reversal.

"It varies in different individuals. Somewhere between one hundred ten and one hundred fourteen degrees Fahrenheit."

"What happens to the chemistry of the blood when the blood reaches this temperature?"

"Objection, Your Honor."

"Overruled."

"The first thing that happens is that potassium leaks out of the red blood cells, and this damages the muscles of the heart. The second thing that happens is that the red blood cells go to pieces and lose, entirely, their capacity to carry oxygen.

"The final thing is not chemical. The very warm red blood cells raise the temperature of the contracting heart muscles, and the heart fails because these muscles are too warm to work effectively."

"All right. Doctor, in your opinion, how long can a person survive in water of one hundred fifty to one hundred sixty degrees Fahrenheit if seventy-five to eighty percent of the body is in contact with the water?"

"Objection."

"Overruled."

"It is the ultimate question," Mikus complained.

"No, it isn't," Miraldi responded.

"Overruled. He may answer."

Dr. Moritz looked up at the judge. "I need to qualify my answer, Your Honor."

"You may," Judge Pincura told him.

"So far as I know, there are no available, reliable experiments involving humans who have been immersed in scalding-hot water and kept there. However, experiments on animals, large animals which are physiologically like people in most respects, show that five or six minutes in water of this temperature will kill the animal because of fatal hyperthermic shock. And this occurs when fifty to fifty-five percent of an animal's body is submerged in this extremely hot water."

Miraldi knew that the judge might stop his next line of inquiry; however, he needed testimony that would contradict Dr. Kopsch's claim that any person immersed in scalding water would become alert and get out of the water.

"Doctor, assuming that a person would not deliberately immerse herself in hot water and remain there until she died of heat shock, are there any medical findings in the autopsy report, the toxicological report, and this woman's medical background that would explain how this may have happened in this case?"

"Objection. There is no basis for this opinion and this again is the ultimate question for the jury to decide."

"I think the court will overrule the objection. You may answer," Judge Pincura said.

"There are two things that I see. The first is that the alcohol level of this woman's blood shows she was intoxicated. An intoxicated person might inadvertently enter or fall into water, whereas a person not intoxicated would be less likely to do so.

"As for remaining in the water, there are two medical grounds that explain this."

Mikus again objected and asked to approach the bench. He again argued that the expert was invading the province of the jury by answering the ultimate question. His arguments soon deteriorated into a rant.

"He is speculating. He is setting aside everything that has been factually presented by sworn testimony by every witness in this case. The State of Ohio is prejudiced by his answers." Mikus did not explain how Dr. Moritz was contradicting all of the sworn testimony in the case. Like a prizefighter swinging wildly at his opponent, he continued, "He is giving us a lecture on these books and so forth and so on. We are not interested in that."

Both Judge Pincura and Miraldi could see that Mikus had come undone. Miraldi said, "You will get a chance to cross-examine him."

Sneering, Mikus replied, "That's what you say. But I think that this is prejudicial to the State of Ohio to have this witness keep on answering these questions the way he has been answering them."

Mikus's final comment was the most revealing. Unable to think of a legal reason to exclude this testimony, he had blurted out the real basis for his opposition. He wanted Dr. Moritz to stop testifying because he was destroying the prosecution's theory of the case. It was that simple.

"Overruled."

Just when Miraldi thought he was home free, his expert slipped.

"I have reviewed a prepared summary of the facts involving this incident involving Mrs. Bennett and—"

"Objection. This witness cannot give an opinion based on facts that were provided to him, presumably by Mr. Miraldi."

"On that basis, I will sustain the objection."

Miraldi tried to regroup. "Doctor, based on the medical findings from the autopsy report, the toxicological findings, and the history of alcoholism as given to you previously, will you give your opinion as to why or how or for what reason Mrs. Bennett would remain in the tub?"

"Objection. There has been no history of alcoholism."

"That will be sustained. There is no history of it."

Miraldi knew that the record was replete with references to Florence Bennett's alcoholism. Dr. Pastuchiw hospitalized her for delirium tremens in early 1963 and then again in September of 1963 after she fell at her house while intoxicated. The autopsy report revealed fatty deposits and other changes in her liver that were consistent with chronic alcoholism. Miraldi did not argue with the judge. Instead, he asked the court reporter to reread the original question that he had asked and that the judge had initially permitted. Mikus objected again, and Judge Pincura overruled him. But again, Dr. Moritz's choice of words got him into trouble, and he was stopped.

At this point, Adams spoke up. "Your Honor, I object to the prosecutor's procedures here. He is just making it impossible to examine this doctor."

Judge Pincura answered, "The court will sustain the objection. I must remind you, Mr. Adams, that only one attorney can conduct the examination of a witness and raise objections."

"I am sorry, Your Honor," Adams replied as he slipped back into his chair.

Scrambling to get the examination on track, Miraldi asked a leading question: "Well, doctor, in your opinion, could this woman have fallen into the tub, hit her head, and become unconscious without showing a bruise on the skull?"

"Objection, Your Honor," Mikus said.

"Overruled."

Miraldi knew that his question was wholly improper. A question is leading if, in its form, it suggests the answer. Miraldi's question suggested more than an answer; it telegraphed a detailed theory to his witness. Mikus glared at the judge, but Judge Pincura was tired of Mikus's constant objections. The judge, like everyone else in the courtroom, was so caught up in the doctor's testimony that he wanted to hear the answer.

Dr. Moritz was ready. "Yes, in my opinion that would be possible."

"Doctor, does a person who is either unconscious or in deep shock feel pain?"

Again, Judge Pincura overruled Mikus's objection.

"Well, if they are in deep shock, they do not feel pain. And whether or not they feel pain while unconscious depends on the depth of the unconsciousness."

After a short pause, Dr. Moritz said, "And I would like to add one more thing. I may have said it already, but I am not sure. There is another factor, I believe, that is relevant to answer this question, and that is the state of this woman's liver, described as being a markedly fatty liver. When one combines this with a history of protracted alcoholism, it puts this person in a precarious state of health and into a class of persons who react abnormally to various injurious experiences.

"This is a complicated way of saying that the chronic alcoholic with a fatty liver, in middle age, is a person given to unexplained collapse and death. This is a person who is predisposed to having disastrous reactions to experiences that would not necessarily be damaging to a normal individual."

Miraldi looked over at the jury and nodded his head in approval. He'd achieved his most important goal with this witness. Dr. Moritz had provided the jury with a reasonable medical explanation for Florence Bennett's death that did not involve murder. An intoxicated Florence Bennett could have accidentally fallen into the tub, hit her head, been rendered unconscious, been unable to feel pain, and died within five or six minutes from hyperthermic shock. The defense team did not have to prove that this was how Florence Bennett actually died. They simply needed the jury to consider this as a plausible medical explanation that created reasonable doubt. If so, the jury would have no alternative but to acquit Bennett of murder.

One minor issue still remained. Miraldi asked, "Doctor, can one tell the age of blood spots, particularly thin, dried films of blood found on a tub?"

Dr. Moritz asked for a clarification: "You are speaking of dried blood spots?"

"Yes."

Mikus objected, claiming that the question was leading. The judge disagreed. "Well, I think the doctor can answer that either yes or no. Overruled."

"Well, I would be unable to ascertain the time," Dr. Moritz responded. If this preeminent pathologist did not have the skill to determine the age of dried blood spots, then the jury would have to question how Dr. Kopsch, an anesthesiologist, could make that claim.

Miraldi sought opinions on three more subjects, but Judge Pincura sustained Mikus's objections. Rather than try to rephrase the questions, Miraldi simply proffered the answers, knowing that this would leave grounds for an appeal if the jury convicted Bennett.

Miraldi sat down. In an attempt to show his eagerness to discredit the witness, Mikus bounded out of his chair.

In a booming voice, Mikus began, "Dr. Moritz, isn't it a fact that all of the opinions and testimony that you have given were based on the hypothetical?"

"Objection. Hypothetical what, Your Honor?" Miraldi asked. "Facts?"

"Overruled. If the doctor can answer, he may do so."

Dr. Moritz had been cross-examined many times during his career, and he remained poised. "I don't believe that I can answer that. Hypothetical what?"

His voice showing impatience, Mikus said, "Hypothetical *matters* that were presented to you, assumed to be true."

"No, I don't believe that is entirely true. Because I can't regard the autopsy report and the pictures and the toxicology report as hypothetical, can I?"

Mikus was scrambling to formulate his next thought, and his next question was convoluted and scattered. "Well, actually then, Dr. Moritz, the only positive thing that you do have here in this case so far as was presented to you by Mr. Miraldi, either a month ago or today, is the history that this deceased woman, Florence Bennett, was found in the bathtub? Isn't that so?"

"I have that fact, together with other information, I believe, that was contained in the various documents and exhibits," Dr. Moritz answered patiently.

Mikus was struggling to make a point, and again his question was vague and awkward. "But taking this case here, you are here to testify as an expert, and it was given to you that there is a deceased person who was found dead in a bathtub. That is positive, isn't it?"

"Yes."

"She is not here, she is dead."

"I assume so, yes," Dr. Moritz deadpanned.

"Now, you are a pathologist?" Mikus asked. Miraldi and Adams shook their heads in disbelief. "You are not a toxicologist?"

"No."

"Now, doctor, if the autopsy report is incomplete in that there are slides available of tissues, would you like the opportunity to review those slides under a microscope?"

Miraldi objected, "These slides were never made available to us, nor are they in evidence."

Judge Pincura said, "The question is whether your witness would like to review them. Overruled. You may answer."

"Yes, that might be useful," Dr. Moritz replied without hesitation. Dr. Moritz's willingness to review the slides showed that he wanted as much information as possible before formulating his opinions, something that was not lost on the jurors.

"At this time, we would request that this witness be afforded the opportunity to look at the slides that were prepared as part of the autopsy. We have the slides here in the courtroom along with a microscope," Mikus said.

"Any objection to that, Mr. Miraldi?" the judge asked.

Miraldi suspected a trap. Mikus obviously believed that the slides showed something that would demonstrate death by drowning. As the evidence now stood, Dr. Moritz had provided a medical explanation that pointed to an accidental death due to hyperthermic shock. All of this could be lost if the slides did not support that opinion. In addition, the jury had heard his expert express an interest in reviewing the slides. Miraldi had no decision to make because the decision had already been made for him.

"If the doctor wishes to look at them, Your Honor, I have no objection," Miraldi said, trying to keep any nervousness or reluctance out of his voice. Miraldi just happened to glance in the back of the courtroom, where he saw Dr. Kopsch standing.

The court had ordered a separation of witnesses at the beginning of the trial. If a witness, other than a party, has not yet testified, that witness cannot be in the courtroom to listen to the testimony of other witnesses.

"Your Honor, I just spotted Dr. Kopsch in the back of the courtroom," Miraldi reported. "If he is going to testify on rebuttal, then he should be asked to leave."

"Mr. Mikus, do you plan to call Dr. Kopsch as a rebuttal witness?" the judge asked.

"Yes, we do, Your Honor."

"Dr. Kopsch, would you kindly leave the courtroom until such time as you are called to give testimony again?" Judge Pincura said, projecting his voice so that Dr. Kopsch could hear him clearly. His head bowed, the coroner quickly exited the courtroom. The judge's attention returned to Dr. Moritz, who was holding a box of pathology slides.

"How many slides are there?" Dr. Moritz asked.

"There are thirty," Mikus replied.

"This is going to take at least thirty minutes and perhaps longer," Dr. Moritz explained.

The judge intervened. "Under these circumstances, doctor, we are going to have you continue your examination here, in private, while the jury takes a recess for their lunch. They can come back about one o'clock. Do you think that would be—"

The doctor interrupted, "I expect to be able to examine the slides and have some lunch myself by then." There was something chipper in his voice.

"Can we make it a little later?" Miraldi asked. He wanted sufficient time to meet with his expert if the slides undermined his doctor's opinions.

"One fifteen then," the judge said.

****

Looking as unruffled as he had before the noon break, Dr. Moritz reclaimed his seat in the witness chair.

"Dr. Moritz, you have previously testified on direct examination that you have formed an opinion as to the cause of death in this case, have you not?" Mikus began.

"I have."

"Your opinion at that time indicated that the deceased, Florence Bernatowicz, died of cutaneous burns and hyperthermic shock?"

"Yes."

"Now, Dr. Moritz, upon the basis of your examination of Exhibits Sixty-Two and Sixty-Three, slides of the deceased, do you have a diagnosis now as to the cause of death?"

"I have an opinion."

"Yes, and what is that opinion?"

"My opinion has not changed as a result of examining the slides."

If Mikus was surprised by the answer, he did not show it. "You have found nothing in the slides to indicate that the cause of death was by drowning?"

"I am unable to make a diagnosis of drowning from the slides," Dr. Moritz answered. His tone was deliberate and precise.

"But others viewing these same slides might interpret them and give an opinion contrary to your own?" Mikus wanted to leave the door open for the coroner or perhaps even Dr. Chesner to testify to a different conclusion.

"Well, it is always possible to have differences of opinion."

Moving to his next point, Mikus wanted to show that Dr. Moritz, in reaching his opinions, did not consider that Mrs. Bennett had a high level of salicylamide and methapyrilene in her system, something Dr. Kopsch calculated from the toxicology report. Dr. Moritz agreed that these chemicals would have acted in tandem with the alcohol to depress Mrs. Bennett's nervous system.

"And if there should be any testimony of a substantial amount of these drugs in her system, would that affect your opinion?"

"Well, it would depend on the *credibility* of the evidence," Dr. Moritz answered. If given a chance, Dr. Moritz would tell the jury that Dr. Kopsch's calculations were not credible.

"Have you reviewed the toxicology report in relation to those drugs?"

"I have. Besides alcohol, the only chemical measured in the report is salicylates. The report absolutely does not tell us how much methapyrilene or salicylamide was in her system."

Mikus abandoned this line of questioning and moved to contest Dr. Moritz's statements that the autopsy did not demonstrate a death by drowning. First, Mikus neutralized Moritz's point that the water in the decedent's lungs had no contaminants. Moritz conceded that one would not expect contaminants in city water. As for the foam, Mikus was prepared to challenge Dr. Moritz from the doctor's own book.

"Now, I read from your respected book, on page one sixty-nine, 'If the drowned person struggles on the surface, water is likely to enter the air passages, where it is mixed with air to form foam.' Doctor, was there any fact presented to you, in the hypothetical question, that this woman struggled on the surface of the bathtub water or underneath?"

"No, there was not."

Mikus should have stopped his questioning at this point, but he wanted to hammer his point home.

"Now, of course, this book was written in 1942 and I do not want to be accused of taking unfair advantage of you. Is the principle that you first enunciated in 1942 still valid today in 1964?"

This was the opening that Dr. Moritz needed to explain his answer. "Yes, I have no reason to think that it's incorrect. However, this part of my book emphasizes the importance of foam where there is a surface struggle, but it in no way implies that foam is not formed with total submersion, because there is still air in the lungs."

Dr. Moritz had escaped from the prosecutor's trap.

"No further cross-examination," Mikus told the court and sat down.

The cross-examination had done nothing to undermine Dr. Moritz's opinions. Miraldi did not need to ask his expert any questions on redirect, but he decided to make some additional points. Miraldi's first question was designed to show that the coroner was not an independent witness but an integral part of the prosecution team. Miraldi surmised that Dr. Kopsch had met with Mikus and provided him with Moritz's textbook.

"Doctor, I believe that the book that Mr. Mikus showed you, you now have a second edition, do you not, which was published in 1954, and that is called *The Pathology of Trauma*?"

"That's correct."

Looking at Mikus, Miraldi needled him, "I assume you got that book from Dr. Kopsch, is that correct? Dr. Kopsch doesn't have the latest edition."

"Your assumption, I think, is irrelevant to this case," Mikus replied, his voice dripping with resentment.

Miraldi wanted Dr. Moritz to explain what he found while reviewing the slides. Mikus had hinted that he might call another witness to claim that the slides supported death by drowning. Miraldi wanted Dr. Moritz to counter that potential testimony right now.

"Were there any slides of the lungs?"

"There were four."

"Did any of them support a finding of drowning?"

"No, they did not. I could recognize no evidence of water inhaled into the lungs. These slides were perfectly consistent with a finding of edema based on a failing circulation, or, as we have discussed, because of shock, and in this case hyperthermic shock."

Dr. Moritz went on to describe microscopic findings for the esophagus and the gullet, none of which pointed toward death by drowning. Dr. Moritz concluded his redirect testimony by confirming that his original opinions had not changed because of the slides.

As Miraldi watched Dr. Moritz leave the courtroom, he felt like a tightrope walker who had lost his balance, stumbled, somehow regained his footing, and reached the opposite platform.

Miraldi had one more expert witness to call, Robert Kelly, a pathologist at Lakewood Hospital. Addressing the court, Miraldi said, "Your Honor, I have a Dr. Kelly, with whom I haven't had any chance to talk, and I would like to have five minutes to do so."

Judge Pincura granted a ten-minute recess.

Robert Hines Kelly was understandably nervous as he sat in the witness chair. This would be the first time that this young doctor testified in a court of law. A graduate of the Western Reserve School of Medicine in 1959, Kelly had finished his residency in pathology in April of 1963, served as a deputy coroner for Cuyahoga County, and become an associate pathologist for Lakewood Hospital about six weeks before the trial. The previous summer he'd written an article on death by drowning that was published by the Ohio State Coroners Association.

Miraldi included the same hypothetical facts in his question to Dr. Kelly that he had propounded to Dr. Moritz. After reciting the assumed facts, Miraldi asked, "Do you have an opinion based upon reasonable medical certainty as to the cause of death of Florence Bennett on or about December 20, 1963?"

Mikus objected. Judge Pincura said, "Overruled," then addressed Dr. Kelly: "Yes or no. Do you have an opinion?"

"I have no opinion," Dr. Kelly replied, stunning Miraldi and everyone else in the courtroom.

"Well, will you explain your answer?" Miraldi asked.

Mikus objected, "The answer speaks for itself." Judge Pincura agreed.

Miraldi realized that his witness was confused. He surmised that Dr. Kelly believed that he had to provide an opinion upon which he was absolutely certain. The phrase "reasonable medical certainty" actually means "reasonable probability" or "what is more likely than not." It does not require a standard of actual certainty. Scrambling to save this witness, Miraldi told the court that his witness was confused.

"He says he has no opinion, Mr. Miraldi, based on the hypothetical question," Judge Pincura stated.

Dr. Kelly looked bewildered. He volunteered, "I understood that I had to answer either yes or no. I also understood that I had to have an opinion based on reasonable medical certainty."

Miraldi said, "Well, do you have an opinion, period, without the phrase 'reasonable medical certainty'?"

"I do."

"All right. What is your opinion?"

"In view of the reports that I have read and seeing these photographs, it is my opinion that this woman probably met her death as a result of burns sustained in a tub of scalding water where she was found"

When questioning Dr. Moritz, Miraldi had asked him to explain what other possible causes of death should also be considered. Judge Pincura had allowed this line of questioning. However, when Miraldi followed with this same question, Mikus objected and Judge Pincura sustained the objection. Miraldi appealed to the judge: "I am trying to determine whether there are any other probable causes of death. That's all."

"I object," said Mikus.

"Based on the same medical information and findings in the autopsy report," Miraldi responded.

"I object. This goes to the ultimate question."

"Sustained."

Miraldi was exhausted and he did not feel like fighting another battle against Mikus and Judge Pincura to expand upon Dr. Kelly's opinions. After Dr. Moritz's solid performance, Dr. Kelly was superfluous.

"All right. Well, in that case, I'll just leave it right there. He said that she died from burning. No further questions. Mr. Prosecutor, it's all yours," Miraldi said as he tossed his yellow legal pad onto the defense table.

Judge Pincura looked at Mikus. "You may cross-examine."

Mikus was both tired and unwilling to give Dr. Kelly the opportunity to expand upon his opinion. "No questions," Mikus replied.

"Does the defense have any additional witnesses?" Judge Pincura asked.

Adams rose. "No, Your Honor, we do not. We move that our exhibits be admitted into evidence."

"Do I understand that the defense rests subject to the admission of your exhibits?"

"That is correct."

"Will the prosecution have any rebuttal witnesses?"

"Yes, we do. We have three and they are out in the hall," Mikus replied.

It was three p.m. "Let's try to get these witnesses out of the way today and start with closing arguments tomorrow morning," Judge Pincura said. "I don't need to remind the prosecution that I will limit your rebuttal witnesses to topics that directly contradict evidence produced by the defendant. I won't allow you to rehash points in your case."

"Of course, Your Honor," Mikus responded.

The judge also hoped that all of the attorneys were tired and because of that, the prosecution's rebuttal would be short and uninspiring.

The prosecutor called Frank Bailey of the First Federal Savings and Loan, who testified that the Bennetts refinanced their home several months before Mrs. Bennett's death. The bank provided a cash loan to Mr. Bennett out of the equity. Bennett had claimed that both he and Florence had arrived together to receive the loan. The bank officer testified that only Mr. Bennett showed up to receive the money.

Miraldi and Adams shook their heads in mock disgust. If this insignificant inconsistency was the best the prosecution could deliver, they wanted to silently convey that to the jury.

John Buddish, Mrs. Bennett's brother, told the jury that his sister was afraid of water. Again, the defense attorneys rolled their eyes at one another. This point was not in dispute. Their client had admitted this during his testimony. The defense attorneys knew that the real reason Mikus had called Buddish was to create sympathy for the deceased. The prosecution hoped that Buddish would cry when speaking about his sister and connect with the jury on a purely emotional level. John Buddish, however, remained composed during his brief testimony.

Dr. Kopsch was the prosecution's final rebuttal witness. The battered coroner was asked again about the blood spots on the bathtub.

"When I arrived at the house, the blood was red, damp, and partially dry."

"Could you tell how long the blood had been on the edge of the tub?"

Mikus asked.

"I can tell the difference between old blood and fresh blood. That blood was quite fresh—certainly not more than six hours old, and based on the circumstances, perhaps an hour old."

Just that morning, Mikus had frequently objected to Dr. Moritz's opinions, claiming that those opinions answered the ultimate issue for the jury and usurped the jury's role. Nevertheless, he asked Dr. Kopsch, "What, if any, were the factors that led you, as the duly elected coroner for Lorain County, to determine that Mrs. Bennett's death was a homicide?"

"Objection."

"Overruled."

Again, Miraldi and Adams looked at each other in disbelief. Mikus had asked the ultimate question and Judge Pincura had allowed it. Neither defense attorney had the energy to mount an objection. Furthermore, after Dr. Moritz's testimony, they doubted the jury would believe Kopsch's answer in any event.

"Very simple. The position of the body and the location of the burns on Mr. Bennett's hands."

Before the prosecutor could ask another question, Judge Pincura, himself exhausted from a long day of trial, caught his own error and reversed himself. "I am going to strike the coroner's last statement and instruct the jury to disregard it."

"Your Honor, your ruling is very prejudicial to the State of Ohio," Mikus protested.

"Mr. Mikus, you are asking this witness to give an opinion on what is the ultimate question for the jury. I am not going to allow it. Furthermore, Dr. Kopsch is not providing this jury with anything new. You can't rehash the same evidence that you developed in your case in chief and disguise it as rebuttal testimony."

"If that is the court's ruling, then we have no further questions for this witness."

The defense chose not to cross-examine Dr. Kopsch and the prosecution rested. It was now four p.m.

The judge said, "Very well, then. It is late. We will go straight into closing arguments tomorrow morning. Because of the magnitude of this case, I will allow both prosecutors and both defense attorneys to give a closing argument. We are recessed until nine o'clock tomorrow."

After the jury filed out, Miraldi looked over at his client. Bennett said, "Thank you, Ray. You did a good job."

"I hope so," Miraldi answered.

The trial was finally coming to a close. Tomorrow afternoon, the jury would begin deliberations, and Casper Bennett would soon learn his fate.

CHAPTER 26

April 14 and 15, 1964

The forgotten man, John Otero, stood in front of the jury to give the first of the prosecutor's closing arguments. Otero had been very unhappy to see his role diminish as the case progressed, but that was behind him now. Today, he was eager to sum up for the prosecution. Shaped by his military mind-set, Otero saw this case as a battle between the good guys and the enemy. His closing statement would be an emotional appeal to action, one that would make the jurors angry and eager to do their duty.

Holding the first of the prosecution's exhibits, Otero began, "This case started from a piece of paper—this phone record of Casper Bennett's call to the operator and the rescue squad. From that point on, Casper Bennett has spun a web of lies, trying desperately to cover up a grisly murder."

Otero's closing would employ the same logic that he used in his opening statement. If Bennett was wrong in any detail of his story, then Bennett was both a liar and a murderer. "The ultimate question for you, the jury, to decide is whether Mr. Bennett explained to your satisfaction how he moved the body from the bathtub and onto the bed in the bedroom." Otero was convinced that Bennett had lied when he explained how he placed his wife on the bed after dragging her from the bathroom, and that the jurors shared that conclusion.

Adams and Miraldi were surprised by Otero's decision to highlight this testimony. Bennett's explanation that he swung his wife's body in a three-hundred-degree arc onto the bed was probably inaccurate. However, neither defense attorney believed that Bennett was lying, only that he was so traumatized by the night's events that it affected his memory. If Otero wanted to make this the ultimate issue for the jury, they would let him.

Miraldi thought that the prosecution would eventually focus on the burns to Bennett's hands and make that the critical issue. Had the defense satisfactorily explained why Bennett's left palm was burned but the tops of his hands were not? In defending Bennett, Miraldi and Adams had glossed over this incriminating evidence. Neither Dr. Moritz nor Dr. Kelly, their key experts, had said anything to explain this. The defense had relied solely on Bennett's own self-serving testimony that his left hand had briefly slipped into the scalding water when he was trying to save his wife. Miraldi wondered whether that would be enough, but for now, the prosecution was not focusing on this.

Otero continued, "To the police and the grand jury, the defendant claimed that he left his house around seven forty-five in the evening, yet two witnesses saw him at the gas station at six thirty p.m. After he hired lawyers, the clock seemed to change. Don't be fooled. This man lied to the authorities and the grand jury about the time he left his house. On that, there can be no dispute. Why did he lie? Why would anyone lie in this situation? Only a person trying to cover up a murder would spin a story that fell apart as soon as the police started to check it out.

"The bathroom became the chamber of horrors," Otero claimed, his voice loud and penetrating. He hoped that the phrase, chamber of horrors, would conjure macabre images that would fuel the jurors' imagination and anger. Miraldi saw this as a cheap trick and hoped it would backfire.

Pointing to the bathtub, Otero said, "This is where the murder took place. The executioner in this chamber of horrors is her husband, Casper Bennett, who is holding her head below the water. She is thrashing in the water. Her legs are kicking. She is struggling to bring her head above the water. By the time the executioner finishes, the bathwater is filthy. It has skin floating in it. Her hair has come out in patches and it creates a scum at the surface."

Otero did not talk about the alcohol and drugs in Florence Bennett's system. Listening to Otero's closing argument, Judge Pincura immediately thought that these last statements were at odds with Dr. Kopsch's revised reconstruction of the murder. Hadn't Dr. Kopsch testified that Florence Bennett was so drugged that she was practically comatose and unable to resist her murderer?

Ignoring Dr. Moritz's testimony, Otero attempted to debunk the defendant's theory of the case. "The defense wants you to believe that Florence Bennett was the victim of blackouts." Glaring at the defense table, Otero said, "These blackouts are the creation of these three people." Like Mikus, Otero was blunt, accusing Bennett and his two accomplices, Miraldi and Adams, of inventing this preposterous defense. Miraldi looked at Adams and rolled his eyes. If the jury liked or trusted either of them, the jury would resent Otero's attempt to link them to the crime or its cover-up.

Walking briskly over to the exhibit table, Otero picked up the diary. His next statement was another of the superlatives that laced his closing argument. "This is one of the most important things you will find. Mr. Bennett told you that the last six months before his wife's death were the happiest of the couple's twenty-three years of married life. I direct you to the month of December 1963. You will see in Florence Bennett's own handwriting that her husband stayed out all night for seven of the first eleven days of December. There are no more entries after December fifteenth. The reason is simple. On December fifteenth, Casper Bennett went on yet another one of his little escapades with Irene Miller. Florence Bennett reacted by going on a drinking spree of her own. And those, ladies and gentlemen, are some of the happiest days this man had with his wife since 1940."

By now Miraldi and Adams were painfully aware that they should never have claimed that Casper and Florence had been happily married at the time of her death. After the recent discovery of her diary, this claim was a blunder, exposing Bennett's lack of credibility and penchant for embellishing. *I better address this in my own closing*, Miraldi thought. *We should never have tried to prove more than what we needed to win our case.* The defense had, indeed, broken one of the cardinal rules of trial strategy. Whether Casper and Florence Bennett were living in harmony just before her death was absolutely unnecessary to establish reasonable doubt and Miraldi knew it.

Otero turned next to motive. "Casper Bennett killed his wife because he wanted to collect $22,002 in insurance proceeds. If her death was deemed accidental, he would get double that amount—$44,004. Casper Bennett was spending a lot of money to entertain his bar lady friend, Irene Miller. He had already mortgaged their house to the hilt. If he wanted to keep living like a king, he needed more money."

Returning to Bennett's adultery, Otero said, "Did he ever take Florence to Honolulu? No, but he did find enough time and money to take Irene." Otero paused and looked at Bennett who did not react and continued to stare straight ahead.

"What happened in this chamber of horrors was no accident. It was no suicide either. There was an executioner in this horrible room. The death certificate does not name him, but the arrow of guilt points directly to Casper Bennett. The prosecution has proved to you beyond a reasonable doubt that Casper Bennett killed Florence Bennett. The act was planned and premeditated. Now it will become your duty to review the evidence and deliberate. We are confident that you will return a verdict of guilty for murder in the first degree. Thank you."

Miraldi and Adams had decided that Miraldi would present the first of the defense's closing arguments. He began by thanking the jury for their attention and the judge for his patience. He acknowledged that the prosecutors were part of the process and that they did "what they were supposed to do."

"Our client is charged with a capital crime. The Sixth Amendment to the United States Constitution guarantees that the accused shall enjoy the right of a speedy and public trial, by an *impartial* jury, and have the assistance of counsel for his defense. When I think of what these words mean in a free democratic society and when I think of the blood that has been shed by our ancestors to secure this constitutional right, I stand in awe of you, the ladies and gentlemen of this jury. You have a solemn duty to perform. You must separate the trivial from the meaningful."

From the moment that he'd agreed to defend Bennett, Miraldi knew that a jury would likely be prejudiced against the defendant because of his occupation as a tavern owner and his flagrant infidelity to his wife. Now he had to defuse this.

"This is not Russia or a country where people are condemned because of what they are or the ideas they hold. In the American courts of justice, we lay aside all of our prejudices and try a man on the basis of the evidence alone. If any suggestion is made to implant prejudice because of the defendant's background, occupation, associations, or any other factor, this is un-American and should be rejected completely." Adams nodded in agreement. He liked the way his co-counsel had begun his closing. During the height of the Cold War, Miraldi was evoking images of a totalitarian show trial and telling the jurors that they alone protected American citizens from that kind of gross injustice. At the prosecution's table, Mikus bristled at this comparison.

"I appeal to your intelligence in determining this issue. Sympathy cannot bring back the life of Florence Bennett. Neither will prejudice. Please do not make that mistake.

"The presumption of innocence is no light, unmeaning maxim of law. It embodies a principle that is enduring and fundamental. A person is presumed innocent until that presumption is overcome by overwhelming evidence that the defendant is guilty."

Miraldi continued, "Proof beyond a reasonable doubt is the bedrock principle of our criminal justice system. Each and every one of you must be convinced that the defendant is guilty. Each of you must be able to say, 'I am morally certain that the defendant committed this crime.'"

Miraldi knew that his next statement would likely cause the prosecution to object and interrupt his closing, but he decided to take the risk anyway. In an even tone, he said, "The proof of guilt must be so convincing that, upon this evidence, you would condemn a member of your immediate family." Miraldi was telling the jurors that they were required to judge Bennett as if he were a beloved brother, father, or son.

Pincura looked over at the prosecutors, waiting for an objection that did not come. The law required that a juror be "morally certain" from the evidence that the defendant was guilty. Miraldi had introduced a much higher standard. *How'd he get away with that one*? Pincura mused.

Completing his thoughts on reasonable doubt, Miraldi said, "The prosecution answers to you and only you. Mr. Mikus and Mr. Otero must satisfy you beyond a reasonable doubt on every issue in this case. Do you realize the greatness of your power and the reason you were given that power?"

Mikus squirmed in his seat. He did not like Miraldi's suggestion that this jury could only be powerful if it ruled against the prosecution.

Miraldi continued, "Your decision must be based on the evidence. We are in an American court of justice where we don't try cases by mobs, newspapers, police, or coroners—only by evidence. As one of the attorneys for the defendant, I can argue what I consider the facts to be. However, if you disagree with my memory in any way, you must judge the facts for yourself as you remember them."

Miraldi began by giving the jury a simple way to understand the evidence. "There is no question that Florence Bennett died on December 20, 1963, and was found in the bathtub. She may have burned to death due to hyperthermia, drowned, or even died from alcohol. The fact is that the prosecution hasn't proved to you what caused her death. If the state hasn't proved to you how she died, how can they claim that the defendant killed her? Just because there was a body in the bathtub does not automatically mean that there was a victim."

Miraldi looked over at his client, whose face showed the strain and exhaustion of the two-week trial. The jury now looked at Bennett too. Miraldi continued, "On December 20, 1963, the police and the prosecutor arrested Casper Bennett for the murder of his wife. This was before they had the results of the autopsy and toxicology screen, before they reviewed Mrs. Bennett's medical records, and before they talked to any witnesses other than her husband. They convicted him that night. Sergeant Springowski knew Casper Bennett. He knew Casper was having an affair with Irene Miller. He knew that Mrs. Bennett had filed for divorce and there was marital discord. Dr. Kopsch saw that there were no burns on Mrs. Bennett's lower legs and there were burns on Casper's left palm and right little finger. Springowski and Dr. Kopsch talked it over, and they concluded that it was an open-and-shut case.

"Dr. Kopsch is like the football player who picks up the loose ball and runs the wrong way with it. At the preliminary hearing, he says that Mrs. Bennett died from drowning—period. The alcohol, the pills, and the scalding water had nothing to do with it. We learned at that hearing that Dr. Kopsch, our Sherlock Holmes of the coroner's office, changed the autopsy report because Dr. Chesner's findings were not strong enough. By the way, where is Dr. Chesner? Why didn't he testify in this case?"

Miraldi paused for a moment before answering his own question. "Dr. Chesner is too honorable a man to be involved in this shabby affair."

"Objection," Mikus shouted.

"Sustained. The jury will disregard Mr. Miraldi's last statement about Dr. Chesner."

Miraldi glanced over at Adams who shrugged back at him. Adams himself had often told juries that if the prosecution failed to produce an important witness, they could conclude that the testimony was probably unfavorable to the prosecutor. Miraldi had gone farther than that and had been called on it. It doesn't matter though. *The jury has heard the insinuation and they won't forget it*, Adams thought.

"Then Dr. Kopsch wants to juice up his theory about the murder and he changes his opinions. Remember—at the preliminary hearing, Dr. Kopsch testified about a huge struggle between Casper and Florence, where Casper holds her head under the scalding water while her legs and arms kick. But in front of you, the story is completely different. Now Mrs. Bennett is comatose or almost comatose. He tells you that she has fifteen to twenty sleeping pills in her system. Isn't it amazing that the chemists who did the toxicology screen couldn't tell you that, but he can? He must think that you left your brains in the parking lot."

Picking up a photograph of Mrs. Bennett, Miraldi said, "I'll bet that Florence Bennett's body hasn't been without a cut or bruise in the last five years. You heard from Mrs. Pribanic that Mrs. Bennett was always falling down."

Looking at Mikus and Otero, Miraldi said, "They brought in everything but the kitchen sink, but no evidence. They gave you lots of speculation, lots of trivia, lots of props, but no evidence. Where is the evidence of a killing, malice, purpose, or premeditation—the essential elements of first-degree murder?"

Miraldi walked over to Casper Bennett and stood behind him. Bennett's hands were folded together on top of the table and he was looking down at them. "Let's talk about Casper Bennett." Miraldi paused until he was sure each of the jurors was looking at his client. "Ever since Casper left high school, he has worked hard, often putting in long, twelve-hour days. No matter what the prosecution suggests to you, the truth is—Casper has been a law-abiding citizen his entire life. The prosecution told you about a peace bond, but there is no evidence that he was ever vicious or belligerent. Yes, he broke down a door, but he did not lay a finger on Irene Miller after he entered her apartment. Casper Bennett has always been an average guy who never hurt anyone."

Turning to Bennett's marriage, Miraldi said, "Casper and Florence were married in 1940. They both drank. Casper quit for fourteen years. Casper wanted children. Florence feared childbirth and resisted. He was faithful for twenty years. Those were twenty years of emptiness, loneliness, rejection, and no chance to fill the role of husband and father."

Seated in the balcony, John Buddish clenched his teeth and fought the urge to openly challenge Miraldi's last statements. *Casper made her life a living hell, not the other way around*, he thought. He shook his head as he looked down at the jury, hoping one of them would look his way. None did. Several of the ten male jurors seemed to be nodding in agreement. *Jesus, why aren't there more women on that jury*?

Miraldi continued, "Does anyone really know what it is like to live with an alcoholic? Casper could have divorced Florence long ago if he had no feelings for her."

John Buddish had heard enough and rose to leave. An older woman grabbed his left arm and pulled him back down onto the bench where he and several of Florence's friends were seated.

Otero had mocked the defense's contention that Florence and Casper were living in harmony at the time of her death. Miraldi now tried to defend that beleaguered position. "Casper came back to Florence in July. He stopped seeing Irene Miller. We know Florence was hospitalized in September, and Casper made sure that she was well cared for when she returned from the hospital. Casper was hospitalized in October for several weeks, and Casper again made arrangements for Mrs. Pribanic to tend to Florence. When Casper was discharged from the hospital, the Bennetts got a loan and bought a new car that Florence picked out. Then, in late November, Florence began to drink again. You heard about that from young Joey Pribanic. Then things got worse in December. Florence continued to drink and Casper saw Irene Miller twice. These were social outings between two friends and nothing more. They went Christmas shopping and Casper drove with her family down to Massillon. Florence began a severe drinking spree four days before her death. That's what happened the last few months of their marriage.

"Why did he go out with Irene Miller? I don't think I have to tell you. Are you going to convict a man for his association with another woman? We cannot condone that, but it doesn't make him guilty of murder—only adultery."

Miraldi moved on to Bennett's alibi. "A person can be wrong about the time. Casper Bennett was under incredible stress when the police questioned him and he was mixed up about the time he left his house. You heard Casper tell you that he had taken his wristwatch off earlier in the day while he washed the dishes at his bar. Are you going to convict a man because he wasn't wearing a wristwatch? That's exactly what the prosecution wants you to do."

Miraldi then estimated the time involved for each of Bennett's activities from the moment he left his house until he returned. Miraldi's estimates were generous, but when he finished adding up the time for each activity, he had accounted for about three and one quarter hours of time.

"Both Mrs. Poletylo and Joe Wasilewski agreed that Casper returned home after nine p.m. Joe Wasilewski was more definite. He said between nine ten and nine twenty. So, let us conclude that the defendant got home somewhere around nine fifteen to nine twenty that evening.

"It would take Casper about two minutes to enter the house and go upstairs. Then it would take about five to six minutes to get Florence out of the tub. He tried to revive her for seven to eight minutes and then ran downstairs to call for the rescue squad. This is a total of fourteen to sixteen minutes. The operator received a call at nine thirty-four that evening. Everything Casper told you fits within this time frame.

"Let's look at what Dr. Kopsch and the police say happened and see if it makes sense. Sergeant Solomon said that it takes twenty minutes for the bathtub to fill to the scum line. That was conservative. He also said it could be twenty-six minutes, but let's use the twenty-minute figure to be fair to the prosecution." Otero nudged Mikus who snorted in disgust.

"Let's do some analysis. If Florence was comatose in bed, then it would take Casper at least four to five minutes to drag her from the bed and put her into the tub. It would take five to ten minutes to drown her and then another five to seven minutes to drag her lifeless body back onto the bed. Then add another four to five minutes to make the phone call. All of these activities would take anywhere from forty to forty-five minutes. It would have been ten p.m. before Casper had time to call the operator. And if he had changed his clothes, add another five to ten minutes, and the call would have been made closer to ten after ten. How could Casper Bennett have done all of those things and called the operator at nine thirty-four? It's impossible. These facts lead to one inescapable conclusion—Casper Bennett is innocent.

"The prosecution has not proved Casper Bennett guilty of anything. The courtroom is where important issues and decisions are to be made and entrusted. Go home tonight—thank God for the right of a trial by jury. I will, and so will Casper Bennett."

Miraldi sat down and was replaced by his co-counsel. With Miraldi's foundation, Adams was free to attack the prosecution's case in a series of quick hits. In his years as a criminal defense attorney, Adams had developed some stock arguments, which he now used.

Adams began, "I have never seen a prosecution so successful at keeping secret what the defendant was supposed to have done. Did he kill his wife for insurance money or is it because he wanted to marry Irene Miller? The prosecution can't seem to make up its mind. Another person who can't make up his mind is Dr. Kopsch. Was the alleged victim struggling with all her might or was she a comatose body in the water? Please tell us. I never saw a witness who contradicted himself as much as our coroner. He was guessing all over the place."

Mikus shifted in his chair and studied the jury. He now regretted that he had been in favor of allowing all four attorneys to make a closing argument. It would have been far better if just one defense attorney had been permitted to speak. The jury was being bombarded by defense arguments and Otero's closing statement seemed distant and forgotten.

His tall frame slightly bent, Adams paused and looked at one of his three-by-five cards. "The prosecutor is telling you that there are three villains in this case—Mr. Bennett, Ray Miraldi, and me. Don't get the impression that the prosecutor is some knight in shining armor. He is just a lawyer, the same as I am. And as you saw throughout this trial, he was just grasping, grasping, and grasping."

After discussing the prosecution's fixation on Bennett and Irene Miller, Adams told the jury, "All of that was just window dressing. It had absolutely nothing to do with the case. They presented that evidence just so that you would dislike Casper Bennett."

Now it was time for Adams to take some shots at the prosecution's case. He wanted to take the state's most incriminating evidence and make it exculpatory. "If someone is planning to murder his wife, he would tie up the loose ends. Would Casper Bennett have placed his wife in the bathtub with her back to the spigots? That doesn't make sense.

"If someone is going to murder his wife, then he would create an iron-clad alibi. He would know exactly when he left the house. He would plan to be with people who could vouch for his whereabouts. A cold, calculated murderer would not drive around downtown Lorain and stay away from people. The premeditated murderer tries to be seen by as many people as possible to support his alibi.

"He wouldn't leave blood spots on the bathtub. He would wipe them up. He wouldn't ask the police for permission to phone his girlfriend.

"A murderer does not talk to the police, give them statements, and cooperate with their investigation. I could go on and on, but a cold, calculating murderer does not do the things Casper Bennett did that evening."

Adams paused and scanned the jurors, establishing eye contact with each of them. He now spoke almost in a whisper. "Once you speak the words 'you die' to Casper Bennett, those words can never be unspoken." His eyes again swept the jurors' faces and he then sat down.

It was almost noon when Prosecutor Paul Mikus strode up to the lectern for the final opportunity to persuade the jury. "Ladies and gentlemen of the jury, it is my great privilege to address you in this, the state's final closing argument." His voice was clear and loud, but his manner had changed. After Dr. Moritz delivered his damaging testimony, Mikus had lost much of his swagger. He was tired. He'd handled more and more of the trial as it progressed, and it had taken its toll on him.

For its final closing argument, the prosecution was limited to rebuttal arguments. Mikus could not rehash what Otero had raised in the first closing argument; he could only dispute those points raised by the defense during its closing arguments. The first point Mikus attempted to refute was Miraldi's claim that Florence Bennett's alcoholism led to her husband's unfaithfulness. Miraldi had raised this on the questionable belief that it would create some sympathy for his client, but, instead, it gave Mikus an opening to rebut it.

Mikus still saw Bennett's adultery as a key to winning a conviction. He reasoned that adulterers and murderers shared a common trait—moral depravity. And someone like Bennett could take the leap from adultery to murder if it suited his fancy.

"You have heard that Mrs. Bennett was an alcoholic and drove her husband to seek the companionship of Irene Miller. Nothing could be farther from the truth. Mrs. Bennett turned to alcohol and sleeping pills as an escape when Casper Bennett violated his marriage vows. We need to set the record straight. Did Mrs. Bennett ever do that to him? No. Mrs. Bennett never violated her wedding vows. Never."

Many of the women in the gallery nodded their heads in agreement as did John Buddish. *Tell the jurors about how he ridiculed her, how he threatened her. That's what they need to know*, Buddish thought.

Mikus continued, "Florence Bennett never left her husband because she hoped that one day Casper would come home from those tramps and bimbos and fulfill his marriage vows. Can you imagine what it would be like for a wife to spend Christmas alone while her husband is at the home of one of those women? Casper Bennett spent Christmas in 1961 and 1962 with Mrs. Miller."

Although Mikus was scoring points with the women spectators and John Buddish, Miraldi and Adams hoped that Mikus's focus on adultery was backfiring with this jury of ten men and two women. The jurors' expressions remained impassive and unreadable. *They have to know that a prosecutor with a strong case would stick to proving a murder, not infidelity*, Adams thought.

"Mr. Miraldi tells you that Florence Bennett got to pick out the color of their new car, so that proves how happy they were together. What did she care about the color of the car? She would ride in it a lot less than Irene Miller."

Mikus paused for a moment. "Let's talk about what happened or didn't happen on December twentieth. The defense wants you to believe that Mrs. Bennett blacked out or drunkenly fell into the bathtub. Even if she did, I ask you, who put the hot water into the tub? Who filled it up? Not Florence Bennett; she was afraid of water that deep."

Mikus knew he was entering hot water himself here. By giving some credence to the defense's claim of an accidental fall, he was weakening his own case. However, he was willing to take the risk. He wanted the jury to believe that whatever happened in the bathroom, the defendant orchestrated it. "She had nine ounces of alcohol and probably fifteen sleeping pills in her body. Casper Bennett is responsible for that. First, he dropped her down with alcohol, then he depressed her with drugs so that she could not help herself once she was in the bathtub." Mikus did not explain how Mrs. Bennett ended up in the bathtub, and the jury was left to speculate.

Mikus claimed that Bennett's attempt at resuscitation was a physical impossibility. "The coroner's report shows that rigor mortis had already set in an hour or maybe an hour and a half before Casper Bennett came home at nine thirty." As soon as Mikus said this, Miraldi and Adams shook their heads vigorously, signaling to the jury that Mikus was misstating the evidence. Dr. Kopsch had testified that he was able to move Florence's head, arms, and legs. Undaunted by the record, Mikus plowed ahead. "How can a man give mouth-to-mouth resuscitation when rigor mortis has already set in?"

Mikus's statement about rigor mortis hit Adams like a thunderbolt. If Florence's body was rigid when Bennett allegedly attempted to resuscitate her at nine thirty, when had Bennett killed her? At eight p.m.? At seven thirty? The prosecution was not telling the jury when Bennett had killed his wife.

Adams wished that he had the opportunity to address the jury again because he would have focused on the alibi evidence. The gas station attendant saw Bennett between six thirty and seven p.m. By the time Bennett called Irene Miller at eight that night, he had already cleared off the snow from her driveway and bought her a six-pack of beer from a neighborhood grocery store. Jane Poletylo, the next-door neighbor, and Joe Wasilewski saw Bennett between nine and nine thirty. All of this could be established by other people. When the hell had Bennett been home to commit the murder? Adams had a sinking feeling in his gut. Why had neither he nor Miraldi hammered home this point? They'd let that one slip away and it was a big one.

Mikus was winding down to his final point. "Casper Bennett wanted to see his wife dead. He had everything to gain by staging an accidental death. He would get money. He would not have to pay alimony to Florence. He would be free to marry Irene Miller."

Mikus then turned to face Casper Bennett, who sat expressionless at the defense table. "Nobody else could have done it but Casper Bennett. It is that simple. Thank you."

The closing arguments were over. The judge excused the jurors for their noontime lunch and told them that court would reconvene at one fifteen.

****

Judge Pincura started to read the instructions of law to the jury at one thirty p.m. The judge told them that they would have to consider four possible felony crimes in their deliberations: first-degree murder that included the death penalty, first-degree murder with a recommendation for mercy (life imprisonment), second-degree murder, and manslaughter. Miraldi was livid when the judge told the attorneys that he would instruct on second-degree murder and manslaughter. Bennett was charged with first-degree murder. Miraldi believed that the judge should have instructed on that one charge, and the jury would have been limited to finding the defendant either guilty or not guilty on first-degree murder. By including the lesser offenses, the judge was giving the jury a middle course.

Second-degree murder was an intentional killing that did not involve premeditation, while manslaughter involved an intentional act that occurred in the heat of passion—usually an argument or fight that suddenly turned violent and deadly. The prosecution had not introduced any evidence of a precipitating argument in the Bennett case.

Miraldi and Adams feared that these additional instructions would lead to a conviction. The jurors might conclude that Bennett probably killed his wife, but not beyond a reasonable doubt. In that case, they might work out a compromise—acquit him of first-degree murder but convict him of second-degree murder or manslaughter. If so, the jury would be circumventing the criminal burden of proof. Bennett would be convicted of a lesser charge, even though the jury was not convinced beyond a reasonable doubt that he had purposely killed his wife or otherwise acted intentionally to injure or kill her.

The jury filed out of the courtroom at 2:02 p.m. Bennett shook Miraldi's hand. "For the first time in a long time, I am confident that I will be a free man soon," Bennett told him. He seemed almost manic. His eyes were intense and he bristled with a suppressed energy. Miraldi was unnerved by his client's strange behavior. Bennett again pumped Miraldi's hand. "I can see the crowds carrying us out of the courtroom on their shoulders when this is over."

Miraldi replied quietly. "Casper, a simple acquittal will do."

The two sheriff's deputies assigned to Bennett came over and escorted him to their cruiser. Bennett would wait for the jury's verdict in his cell at the county jail.

For a few fleeting moments, the four attorneys felt some relief, knowing that they had completed their work and they could no longer do anything to change the course of events. Soon that feeling was replaced by a gnawing anxiety. Miraldi and Adams passed the time talking to one another and with several other lawyers who had listened to the closing arguments and stayed on.

Miraldi and Adams usually chatted with opposing counsel while they awaited a jury's verdict, but they had no desire to exchange small talk with either Mikus or Otero. The feeling was mutual. The two defense attorneys soon tired of hearing the voices of the prosecutors and moved into the hallway.

In this courthouse, the jury room shared an adjoining wall with the women's restroom. If any of the jurors began shouting or talking loudly, their comments could often be heard in this restroom. Around three thirty, Miraldi asked one of the women deputy clerks to go into the restroom and see if she could hear anything. After five minutes, she came out and shook her head.

At four p.m., the jury rang the bell to summon Judge Pincura's bailiff. Their hearts racing, the defense attorneys returned to the courtroom. The bailiff reported that the jury wanted to look at an exhibit that had been left in the courtroom. At four thirty, the bell rang again. This time the jury requested coffee, two root beers, and a vanilla milkshake. At six p.m., the judge sent them to a local restaurant, where they ate; they returned to the jury room around seven thirty p.m.

At eight thirty, the bell rang again, but there was still no verdict. The jury wanted to see another exhibit. At ten p.m., they requested coffee.

At eleven p.m., Judge Pincura gathered the attorneys. "I have made arrangements at a hotel to sequester the jury for the night. If they do not reach a verdict by midnight, I will adjourn until tomorrow morning," the judge reported.

All of the attorneys were extremely anxious. The jury's long deliberation meant that the jurors were struggling to reach a unanimous verdict. No one knew whether they were close to an acquittal or a conviction or hopelessly divided.

At eleven forty-five, the jury rang the bell for the fifth time. When the bailiff reported back to the judge and attorneys, she told them that the jury had reached a verdict. The bailiff called the sheriff's deputies, and the deputies drove Casper Bennett back to the courthouse to hear the jury's verdict.

The sheriff's deputies escorted Bennett back into the courtroom at 12:08 a.m. His blue suit disheveled and wrinkled, Bennett sat down at the defense trial table. His breathing was rapid and perspiration showed on his forehead. With his hands folded tightly against his chest, Bennett watched each of the jurors as they filed in and took their seat. None of them met his eye.

The attorneys intently studied the jurors' faces. The jurors did not smile, nor did they seem agitated. The judge spoke first: "Has the jury reached a verdict?"

The jury's foreman, a tall man in a sports coat, stood up and handed a verdict form to the bailiff, who in turn handed it to the judge. The judge studied it for a minute and then read:

"We, the jury, being duly impaneled, have reached a verdict in favor of Casimir Bernatowicz and find him not guilty of first-degree murder, second-degree murder, or manslaughter."

Otero and Mikus sat and absorbed the jury verdict without any emotion. Miraldi let out an audible sigh when the words "not guilty" were read and momentarily buried his head into his right hand. Adams sat quietly through the reading. Bennett began to cry in deep sobs.

Judge Pincura then polled each of the twelve jurors. To each one he asked, "Is this your verdict?" Each juror assented.

At 12:18 a.m., Judge Pincura released Bennett from custody. Bennett stood and embraced his attorneys. The sheriff's deputies who had been Bennett's escorts throughout the trial shook his hand and congratulated him.

The *Elyria Chronicle* and *Lorain Journal* reporters approached Miraldi and Adams for their comments. Adams responded, "The prosecution's case was built on Dr. Kopsch's opinions. Dr. Moritz, our expert, was truly outstanding. He was very knowledgeable and showed the jury just how wrong our coroner was. That was the turning point in the trial." Miraldi nodded in agreement.

The reporters went over to the prosecutor's table where Mikus and Otero were gathering their papers. When asked to explain the jury's verdict, Mikus said, "I don't know. You were there, so you tell me. I wasn't in the jury room. Why don't you ask one of them?"

Mikus pointed to the empty jury box. All of the jurors were gone. None had apparently wanted to talk to reporters or lawyers, and had left the courtroom immediately after the judge had dismissed them.

"So you don't have any explanation?"

"No."

"Are you going to appeal the verdict?"

Sounding more composed, Mikus answered, "You guys have been around long enough to know the answer to that. Unless the judge has made an extraordinary error in the case, either in ruling on evidence or in the jury charges, the prosecution has no basis for a successful appeal. I do not believe that Judge Pincura committed any serious errors during this trial. The jury has spoken and, as far as I am concerned, the case is over. I am very disappointed with the jury's decision, but I will have to live with it. I'm very tired. Good night."

The case of *State v. Casimir Bernatowicz* was closed. Casper Bennett was a free man.

CHAPTER 27

April 16, 1964

The next day Miraldi stayed home. The day after that, he was back in his office. During the morning, he received several phone calls from Lorain attorneys who congratulated him on the result of the Bennett murder trial. Several asked if he would now focus his practice on criminal defense. Miraldi had lost ten pounds during the Bennett trial and had many fitful nights of broken sleep. He never wanted to put himself through such an ordeal again. He did not know how Lon Adams was able to constantly handle that type of pressure. Miraldi knew he could not.

When the mail arrived that morning, his secretary brought in a letter from Dr. Kelly, whose testimony in the Bennett matter had been disappointing. Dr. Kelly submitted a bill for $425, representing the time he spent reviewing the case and attending the trial.

The letter read:

I enclose a copy of the article in the Cleveland Plain Dealer from this morning and hand you my bill in the matter of State v. Bennett. You would do well to charge me tuition for what was a most valuable piece of education for me.

We are pleased at the verdict, although I have caught a small amount of hostility and flak for having involved myself in this case. This is interesting, but not germane. To the extent that the law profession has failed to educate people about the merits of adversary proce-

dure in a courtroom, our profession has failed equally in communicating what carefully seasoned judgment from a medical point of view may offer in your realm of endeavor.

This case bothered me far less from my personal interest than from the fact that arbitrary semi-scientific nonsense, coupled with an unrestrained imagination, can be used to indict and convict in capital crimes. It is equally bothersome that the average defendant does not have recourse locally, often as not, to rebut unfounded medical allegations. This is an area in which the physicians' characteristics of avoiding criticism of colleagues might be safely left at home.

This case, I suppose, and as the prosecutor suggested, involved some fairly sophisticated medical gymnastics. How one can reasonably expect a jury to safely grasp this escapes me as an outsider. I feel safe in offering to buy you a large dinner when Ohio significantly alters its whole fabric of criminal procedure.

With congratulations and very best wishes to you and yours, I am
Very truly yours,

Robert Hine Kelly, MD

Miraldi smiled as he put down the letter. At the beginning, Dr. Kelly had been an enthusiastic expert, but Miraldi knew that the doctor's less-than-stellar court appearance would temper Kelly's eagerness to get involved in future cases.

For most of the afternoon, Miraldi worked on cases and matters that he had neglected for almost six weeks. He had a civil trial coming up in two weeks, and all of his other matters seemed wonderfully ordinary after the grueling murder trial.

Around four p.m., he walked a block to Runyan's Bookstore to pick up the *Lorain Journal*. He wondered if the paper had any follow-up now that the trial was over. Again, Miraldi smiled. Someone at the paper apparently liked Prosecutor Mikus. The article's headline was "Circumstantial Evidence Hard for Prosecutors." The article began, "While yesterday's acquittal of Casper Bennett was a major victory for defense attorneys Lon B. Adams and Ray Miraldi, it should not be considered a major defeat for Paul J. Mikus and John B. Otero, according to local attorneys last night."

Miraldi wondered who the unnamed local attorneys were. Perhaps they were members of Mikus's prosecutorial staff. The article noted that the case was based on circumstantial evidence "from beginning to end" and that Mikus and Otero had to prove the case beyond a reasonable doubt. The next line caused Miraldi to chuckle: "Mikus had no choice in trying the case once the grand jury indicted Bennett." The reporter obviously was not aware that both Otero and Mikus had met with the Lorain police on December 22, 1963, and pushed to charge Bennett with first-degree murder. They could not pretend that their hands were tied by the grand jury.

The article quoted an unnamed observer as saying, "The case consisted of a bunch of loose ends which just couldn't be tied together."

"Amen," Miraldi said aloud as he dropped the newspaper into the trash can.

CHAPTER 28

September 1965

The insurance claims adjuster walked up the stairs to Ray Miraldi's office over Nielsen Jewelers in downtown Lorain. The stairwell had an overwhelming smell of rubber from the surface of the steps, an odor that lingered years after its installation. The man climbing the steps worked for the Prudential Life Insurance Company, and he needed to talk to Miraldi. The claims adjuster had called about an hour earlier and asked Miraldi's secretary if Miraldi was in, and if he could have just fifteen minutes of his time. He said that the matter was personal.

Miraldi's waiting room was small, and his secretary sat at a wooden desk at the far end. It had been eighteen months since Miraldi temporarily closed his office to defend Casper Bennett. The man introduced himself, gave the secretary his card, and sat down. Miraldi came out a few minutes later and showed the man into his office, closing the door after them.

Miraldi was both irritated and concerned. He had listened to more than enough salesmen make their pitch for life insurance, and he wondered if this was about to happen again. If so, he would show the man the door.

The claims adjuster was in his late thirties, handsome and tall. He sat down in a chair across from Miraldi, who sat in a leather chair behind his desk. The adjuster placed his briefcase on his lap and flipped it open as if to steady himself before launching into a long monologue.

The claims adjuster began, "Thank you so much for seeing me on such short notice, Mr. Miraldi. I'll get right to the point. Two weeks ago, Casper

Bennett filed a claim for payment on a life insurance policy taken out on his wife, Florence. The policy was purchased and issued about four months before she died. The policy is for $100,000. Fortunately for the company, there is no double indemnity provision in case of accidental death. It is, obviously, very unusual for a beneficiary to take so long to try and collect under a life insurance policy. It did not take us much research to figure out why he delayed."

Miraldi's face turned white, and his feet and hands began to tremble slightly. He stared at the adjuster but did not interrupt.

"We know that you represented Mr. Bennett in the murder charges that were brought against him. Is that right?"

Miraldi nodded.

"Do you know if the police were ever aware of this insurance policy?" the adjuster asked.

Miraldi tried to compose himself before speaking. He had encountered demoralizing situations in the past, but this one was different. His mind tried to reject this new information, while his gut ached from disappointment and dismay.

"I am sure that they were not," he said.

"Why is that?" the adjuster asked.

"If they had been, the prosecution would have admitted the policy into evidence along with the other insurance policies," Miraldi answered.

"There were others?" the adjuster asked.

"There were eleven or twelve very small polices that totaled around $22,000, but with the double indemnity provisions, they grew to around $44,000," Miraldi recited.

"And the jury was aware of those other policies?"

"Yes."

"And he was still acquitted?"

"Yes."

"I'm surprised," the adjuster said.

"The prosecution did claim that Mr. Bennett's motive for killing his wife was to get the insurance money," Miraldi explained. "However, all of those policies were taken out many years before Mrs. Bennett died, and Mrs. Bennett was the beneficiary on about the same number of policies on Mr. Bennett's life. Also, $44,000 did not seem like a lot of money."

"What do you think the jurors would have done if they'd known about this policy and when it was purchased?" the adjuster asked.

While he thought, Miraldi took a deep breath and held it. He wanted to say that it wouldn't have made any difference, but he could not. If he had known about this insurance policy, he would have refused to represent Bennett in the first place. Miraldi looked down at the blotter on his desk. He brought his hands together and placed them there. He sighed.

"He probably would have been convicted," Miraldi admitted.

"That's what I think, too. And that's also what the claims committee thinks about this claim. Can we reopen the criminal case?" the man asked.

Miraldi sighed again. "No. The case is closed," he responded.

"What do you mean? This is new evidence. This guy shouldn't be able to get away with murder, should he?" the man asked as he twisted in his chair, causing his briefcase to fall to the floor.

"Have you ever heard of double jeopardy? It is an important principle in our criminal law. It means that a person can only be tried once for the same crime. It's up to the prosecutor to put the best case forward, because he doesn't get a second chance," Miraldi explained.

"Are you sure about that? I think there should be an exception when there is new evidence," the man pleaded.

"I understand your point, but think about it. The government could always claim new evidence and keep trying a defendant until it got a conviction or forced him to plead to the offense. The prosecutors had one chance and they lost. That is the end of the story."

"I still find that hard to believe," the man continued.

"You can ask other attorneys, and I would suggest that you do that. However, Mr. Bennett was acquitted of the charges of first-degree murder, second-degree murder, and manslaughter."

"What does that mean in regard to his insurance claim?" the man asked.

"I can't tell you what to do with this insurance claim. I can only tell you that Mr. Bennett's criminal case cannot be reopened. What you do with this policy, whether you pay it or not, that's up to you," Miraldi answered.

"Thank you, Mr. Miraldi. I will get another opinion on this, but I wanted to hear from you first," the man said.

"You're welcome," Miraldi said as he rose to show the man out of his office.

"Well, maybe we'll see you again if we refuse to pay on the policy," the man said.

"No, you won't see me again. I don't represent Mr. Bennett anymore, and I don't have any desire to be involved in this dispute."

After the man descended the steps, Miraldi saw one of the two young associates whom he had hired just before the Bennett trial. He asked the associate to come into his office and informed him about the adjuster's revelation. Feeling unwell, Miraldi told his secretary that he would be gone for the rest of the day. He got into his car and drove about fifteen blocks to his parents' house, a lone residential holdout sandwiched between commercial buildings on busy Broadway.

It was around four p.m. when he parked the car and walked into the small brick house. His father, a thin man with a full head of gray hair, sat in the narrow front hallway, smoking a cigarette through a yellow plastic filter. He was a retired tavern owner, eighty-four years old and still reasonably fit, although he seemed to spend most of his time in the living room watching Westerns such as *Bonanza* and *Maverick*. He had just recently awakened from his afternoon nap.

Miraldi's mother was in the kitchen, preparing the evening meal. She was a heavy-set woman, just approaching her seventieth birthday. As usual, she was talking to herself when Miraldi walked back to the kitchen to give her a peck on the cheek.

Over the next ten minutes, Miraldi exchanged small talk with his parents. He then told his mom that he had a headache and wondered if he could sleep for a few minutes on the living room sofa, a gray, worn piece of furniture that was probably thirty years old. She, of course, told him to go ahead.

About fifteen minutes later, his cousin's wife, Marguerita, arrived to visit with his mother. Marguerita and her husband, Alfredo, had come to the United States about twelve years earlier from Italy. Marguerita and his mom spoke to each other in Italian and usually talked about other relatives and friends. Seeing Miraldi lying on the couch, Marguerita walked into the living room. His eyes were open.

"What's wrong with you?" she asked.

"I think I just helped a man get away with murder," he told her.

"What are you talking about?" she asked in heavily accented English. "You're kidding, right?"

"Yeah, I'm joking," Miraldi responded.

About fifteen minutes later, Miraldi said good-bye to his parents and Marguerita. He drove straight home.

When he got home, he did not mention anything about his discussion with the insurance adjuster to his wife. In fact, he decided he would never tell his wife or his two sons about that meeting.

And he never did.

EPILOGUE

No one was more surprised by the ending to the Bennett story than I. Had I never written this book, I doubt that I would ever have known about the meeting between the insurance adjuster and my father. After I began this project, I talked with my father's partner, Ben Barrett Sr., about the Bennett case. "You know, your father always felt like Bennett duped him," Ben told me.

Ben joined my father's law firm in 1970, six years after the Bennett verdict. The two often began their work day in the office's tiny kitchen where they sat, talked, and drank a cup of coffee. One day my father told Ben about the meeting with the insurance adjuster and the disclosure of the recently-purchased insurance policy.

When Ben first told me this, I was skeptical and thought that he had misunderstood. No, he was certain and he remembered in detail what my father had told him. I still wanted more confirmation. I arranged a lunch with Richard Colella who had been an associate with my father at the time of the Bennett trial. He too recalled the meeting with the insurance adjuster.

I learned of my father's conversation with his cousin's wife, Marguerita, almost by chance. Although they spent many decades in the United States and became U.S. citizens, Marguerita, Alfredo, and their two children became homesick for Italy and moved back to their native village in the mid-1990s. In 2015, Marguerita and her daughter were back in Ohio visiting relatives. I invited them out to dinner. During the course of our meal together, I told them about the book.

"You know, I had a very strange conversation with your dad at your grandparents' house one afternoon about that time. He said something about helping somebody get away with murder and he was lying on the sofa, very tired and upset." The pieces fit.

After the Bennett trial, my father never rehashed the case with our family. In retrospect, this was unusual because we often discussed my father's cases at the dinner table. My brother and I were warned not to talk about "any of this" outside of the home and we never did. These discussions fueled our interest in the law and we both became attorneys.

After graduation from law school, I returned home and joined my father's firm. I practiced law with him for seven years, until his death from cancer in 1985 at the age of sixty-five. I feel very fortunate to have spent those years with him as a colleague as well as a son. I had the opportunity to see him try cases, depose witnesses, and deal with clients and other attorneys. He was, indeed, fun to watch in the courtroom. He was a great teacher.

Because I returned to Lorain County and practiced law here, I did get to know some of the attorneys and witnesses involved in the Bennett case. Paul Mikus later became a judge. I had a number of matters before him, including a bench trial. I initially felt intimidated by him—his forceful and demanding presence could be unnerving. However, he was always cordial to me and never treated me unfairly.

My older brother, Jim, also joined my father's firm and had his own dealings with Judge Mikus. Early in his career, Jim had several jury trials in front of Judge Mikus. In each of these cases, Jim represented a defendant who had been sued in a civil suit for personal injuries due to a car crash. Jim won his first three cases in front of Judge Mikus. Each time the jury found that my brother's client was not responsible for the auto accident. However, in his fourth case, the plaintiff sued two defendants, claiming that each caused the accident. Judge Mikus was decidedly hostile to Jim, roughing him up before the jury and making it obvious that he expected the jury to find my brother's client responsible and the other defendant not.

In the end, the jury found just the opposite, giving Jim another victory in Judge Mikus's courtroom.

Afterward, Judge Mikus explained somewhat sheepishly that he was trying to do my brother a favor. He recited an Eastern European maxim in a foreign tongue, probably Slovak, and then translated, "Sometimes you have to knock someone down with a big stick to keep him from getting a swelled head."

Although Judge Mikus maintained a civil tone with my father when he appeared in his courtroom, Mikus consistently ruled against him on every close question of law. The same was also true with Lon Adams.

Even my mother was not spared. Whenever Mikus saw her at a political gathering, he would come up to her, waggle his finger, and say, "He was guilty." He would then abruptly turn and walk away. Even without any context, my mother knew exactly who Mikus was talking about. Obviously, Judge Mikus took the defeat in the Bennett case very hard.

The same could not be said about John Otero. I defended several civil suits in which he was involved. Although a zealous advocate for his clients, he was always courteous and friendly. I doubt that the outcome in the Bennett case bothered him for very long.

I never tried a case in front of Judge Pincura, but he and his family lived in our neighborhood and his youngest son was a close friend of my brother.

I have one vivid memory of Judge Pincura that took place a few years after the Bennett trial. Judge Pincura was the featured speaker at a father-son athletic banquet at Irving Junior High School where both his son and I attended. He spoke about determination and never giving up. Being an impressionable seventh grader, I found his talk inspiring. My father, Judge Pincura, his son, and I walked home together from the event, and after the Pincura father-and-son duo had turned down a side street, I told my father, "Boy, I was really impressed by Judge Pincura's speech." My father seemed amused, and I sensed that he was going to tell me that the message was nothing out of the ordinary. However, he quickly changed his expression and said, "Yes, Judge Pincura is a good speaker."

Both my attorney wife and brother later had cases in front of Judge Pincura. After he retired from the Lorain County bench, he continued to hear cases in nearby Erie County as a visiting judge. He remained sharp and respected throughout his judicial career.

Of the Lorain police officers mentioned in the story, I knew two of them. In the 1950s, when my father was the Lorain city prosecutor, Bill Solomon, the tough sergeant, was always called to our house when we needed a plumber. I remember when Sergeant Solomon was forced to tear up the bathroom floor to repair leaking pipes. My mother was out of town at the time, and in her absence, he chose a predominantly black linoleum to replace the old one. She did not like the color and was upset that he had proceeded without her input. Defending his choice and blustering to my mother, Solomon told her, "It won't show the dirt, but it may show just a little dust." It is hard to believe that he and my father attacked each other several years later during the Bennett trial, each accusing the other of tampering with the bathtub overflow system. Bill Solomon never did any plumbing work for us after the Bennett trial.

I also knew Chief Frank Pawlak, my father's close friend. Although Chief Pawlak did not testify in the case, he did get involved in some of the investigation. As a five-year-old, I once drank a bottle of 7Up that was to be served at a party my parents were hosting that evening. I then filled the 7Up bottle with water and tapped the cap back into place. The 7Up was served to Chief Pawlak, who mentioned that the drink was "rather flat." I was the primary suspect and confessed to Chief Pawlak that evening. The chief accepted my apology, and I was neither arrested nor sent to jail, as I initially feared.

I also rode in a taxi with George Abraham a few years after the trial. When he found out who I was, he told me how he had almost single-handedly won the Bennett case for my father. When I got home, I told my father about this conversation with the taxi driver. Raising his eyebrows, he smiled and said, "Oh, he did, did he?" Now I understand his response.

Denied a pivotal role in the Bennett murder trial, George Abraham became the central figure in two other celebrated criminal matters. On

August 11, 1970, he went to Lorain detectives and claimed that one of his woman passengers had tried to hire him to kill another woman for five hundred dollars. Abraham was involved in a sting operation that later resulted in the woman's arrest and conviction.

Five years later, in 1975, George Abraham was at the center of controversy again. He contacted Lorain police after Dr. George Gotsis, a Lorain physician, allegedly approached him to kill the hospital's chief of staff, who had been involved in proceedings to revoke Gotsis's hospital privileges. An electronic recording device was placed under Abraham's clothing and he met with Gotsis to work out the details. Gotsis was indicted for conspiracy to commit aggravated murder. Abraham was the prosecution's chief witness; however, the jury failed to reach a verdict after it claimed the surreptitious audiotapes were often inaudible. After the hung jury, Lorain's county prosecutor at that time, Joseph Grunda, decided to no longer pursue the case.

Dr. Paul Kopsch continued to serve as Lorain County's coroner until 1972. The bullet Dr. Kopsch developed with several others, the KTW bullet, became the subject of a 1982 NBC prime-time news feature. Not only could the bullet penetrate hard objects, but some claimed that it could also pierce police body armor. The NBC special called the bullet "the Cop Killer." Bills were introduced in Congress to ban it. The NRA fought off several attempts, but in 1986, a watered-down version of the law restricting the sale of the KTW bullet passed.

After the Bennett trial, Dr. Kopsch never harbored any hard feelings toward my father. On occasion, he consulted with my father on legal matters as did other members of his anesthesia group.

Although Dr. Alan Moritz died many years ago, his treatise *Handbook of Legal Medicine*, published in 1956, is still available in used condition from Amazon.

Criminal law and procedure have changed greatly since the Bennett case. Two and a half years after Bennett's arrest, the U.S. Supreme Court handed down the landmark decision in *Miranda v. Arizona*. After the *Miranda* ruling, the police were required to inform a suspect of his or her rights, including the right to remain silent and to seek the advice of an attorney.

Today, the Ohio Rules of Criminal Procedure require each side to disclose expert reports to one another at least twenty-one days before trial. Under current rules, my father and Adams would have been required to submit to the prosecutor narrative reports in which Dr. Moritz and Dr. Kelly set forth their opinions. If the report is not submitted, the witness is not allowed to testify.

The Ohio Rules of Criminal Procedure also now require the prosecution to provide the results of any "experiments or scientific tests" to the defendant's attorney. If the Bennett case were tried today, the results of Sergeant Solomon's testing of the bathtub would have to be shared with the defense attorneys in advance of the trial.

As I wrote the book I was transported back to the Lorain of my youth. Lorain, indeed, was a melting pot where immigrants came seeking better opportunities for themselves and their families. I feel fortunate to have learned from these people. They were brave individuals who dared to dream of a better life for their children and then worked to fulfill that dream. If ever our country was a meritocracy and place of opportunity, it was during this part of the twentieth century.

Today, Lorain is a city plagued with problems and searching for an identity. Its manufacturers began to leave in the 1970s, along with good-paying jobs and opportunity. Lorain's schools, once the pride of the community, struggle to stay solvent and out of state control. The Polish neighborhood where Casper Bennett once lived is now one of the most drug-infested areas in the city, where violent crimes regularly occur. While writing this book, I drove through this neighborhood to reacquaint myself with the streets and houses; needless to say, I did not get out of my car.

When evaluating a city like Lorain, we unfortunately focus only on its current decline and forget about its vibrant past. Many cities go through cycles of deterioration and rebuilding. With its miles of lakefront, Lorain has the potential to regain much of its lost prosperity. We should not lose hope for Lorain and other cities like it.

Attitudes have changed about alcoholism and domestic violence since the Bennett case. Alcohol and drug dependency are now viewed as illnesses that require ever-vigilant treatment regimens. Fifty years ago, heavy alcohol use was condoned. For those who allowed alcohol to ruin their lives, the public viewed them as individuals with weak character whose conduct brought on their own addiction.

Of all the neighbors, friends, and family that the police interviewed, only Mary Mitchell, a next-door neighbor, reported that Casper was physically abusive to Florence. Although Mrs. Mitchell never saw bruises on Florence's face and body, she told police, "Florence told me that Casper beat her often." We also know that Irene Miller, Bennett's girlfriend, admitted to the police that Bennett slapped her around a few times but said he "never hurt her." Florence's other neighbors, friends, and relatives did not tell police about beatings or other evidence of domestic violence.

Today, domestic violence is no longer viewed as a private family affair to which society turns a blind eye. Professional athletes who abuse their wives and children find themselves suspended from their teams and, more importantly, vilified in the media. Now, more than ever, police and prosecutors are trying to take action to stop and punish those who physically abuse other family members. That being said, it remains a very significant problem and continues to destroy lives.

Whether or not Bennett was physically abusive to Florence, he was certainly verbally abusive to her. In divorce filings, Florence alleged that Casper threatened to kill her. Florence repeated this claim to her aunt, several neighbors, and her friends. One neighbor observed that Florence remained sober during the two periods when she and Casper separated. Each time Casper returned home, Florence took to the bottle again. Two neighbors believed that Casper was trying to kill Florence through "drink." The anonymous letter referenced in chapter 5 warned Florence that Casper intended to keep her "drunk until [she] sign[ed] off or *die*[d]." According to this unknown letter-writer, an intoxicated Casper boasted about this at several neighborhood bars.

At the very minimum, we can conclude that Florence and Casper Bennett had a toxic relationship. Casper's verbal cruelty likely fueled Florence's dependence on alcohol. Did Casper murder Florence on December 20, 1963? Despite my father's belated belief that Casper duped him, the reader can draw his or her own conclusion on that question. If, on the other hand, Florence's death was the result of a drunken, accidental fall, Casper created and fed the conditions that led to it. Of that latter proposition, there can be little doubt.

As for Casper Bennett, he gave interviews to reporters several days after the verdict. Meeting them at his brother's bar, Casper handed out this short press release:

> *Thank God for the just verdict the courts rendered. Only in this Democracy can we expect justice. God Bless America.*

Casper told reporters, "I prayed more in the last two weeks than I ever have in my life. My prayers were answered." He told the reporters that many people prayed for him, including three priests who visited him regularly and a first cousin who was a nun. Just before the trial began, his cellmate, Jimmie Meadows, slipped a handwritten prayer into Casper's prayer book. Casper shared his cellmate's prayer, spelling errors and all, with the reporters:

> *Oh Lord, be with this brother and his mouthpiece through this terable thing that has happened.*
>
> *Oh Lord, don't let these judges punish him for something he nos nothing about.*
>
> *Oh Lord, you no this thing happened to his wife was to be.*
>
> *Oh God, and our dear Lord and Father, kerect these mistakes that bad laws are doing to this good, innocent man.*
>
> *Amen.*

Although Bennett faced the prospect of death in the electric chair, he claimed that he held no animosity toward the Lorain police or the prosecutors. "That's their jobs," he said. He also told reporters that he would move back to the house at 1733 Long Avenue as soon as the police gave him the keys to it. As for the bathtub that was removed as a trial exhibit, he did not want it returned.

Casper survived Florence by thirteen years and died on December 18, 1976, still living at his residence on Long Avenue. His Ohio taxable estate was valued at close to $100,000. It included the two homes on Long Avenue, life insurance proceeds of about $30,000, and $10,000 in promissory notes issued to Bennett by Chet's Enterprises Inc. (presumably a corporation controlled by his brother, Chester). His will also mentioned two lots located in Florida, but the Ohio probate documents do not disclose their value. Casper Bennett did not marry Irene Miller. The bulk of his estate was left to another woman, one Martha Marsh.

My father practiced law until his death from cancer on August 15, 1985. He tried many civil jury trials and rarely lost. In the twenty-one years following the Bennett verdict, he tried only one other felony criminal case.

In 1971, he defended the former Lorain fire chief, Alfred Nickley, for assault with a deadly weapon. The retired fire chief owned a hobby shop and allegedly pulled a gun on a customer who was fingering and damaging balsa wood. The two had argued, and eventually the chief went behind a counter and emerged with the gun. My father once again won an acquittal after his client took the stand and explained that he had approached the victim with a plastic model gun made from a kit sold at the store. With dramatic flair, my father pulled the plastic gun from his briefcase, had it marked as an exhibit, and then showed it to his client, who confirmed that this was the "deadly weapon." The fire chief's case was a fitting end to my father's rare ventures into the criminal arena.

David Miraldi April 14, 2016

ACKNOWLEDGMENTS

I am indebted to a number of people who helped me as I researched and wrote this book. I cannot overestimate how valuable the police investigation was in recreating this drama. My public records request would have been a vain act without the help of retired Lorain police officer, David Moore, who somehow found the Bennett file in the basement of Lorain's city hall.

I talked with many people to gather background information about the characters and events. Thanks to my father's associates at the time of the Bennett trial, Richard Colella and Justin Lumley, for sharing their memories about the case. This story would have been incomplete without the revelation from my father's partner and later my partner, Ben Barrett Sr., who told me about my father's meeting with the insurance adjuster months after the verdict.

George Metelsky and his wife were two of the first people with whom I talked after I decided to write this book. Being the first officer at the Bennett home, Mr. Metelsky could return me to the scene as well as provide insight into the inner workings of Lorain's police department.

Orie Camillo, the court reporter, spent a lunch with me talking about the case. He later sent me an e-mail that documented many of his memories about the trial. Charles Adams shared stories about his father, Lon, and grandfather, Charles, while John Otero Jr. was equally helpful sending me newspaper articles about his father.

The newspaper accounts of the trial gave me an outline of each day's events. The *Elyria Chronicle*'s legal beat writer, Don Miller, was careful to include the highlights of a key witness's testimony and to write at least one sentence about the testimony of each minor witness. Both he and the *Lorain Journal* writer, Dick DiLuciano, vividly recounted the legal controversies that raged outside the presence of the jury.

Once I had completed the first draft, I received editorial assistance from my long-time friend, Dan Missildine, who raised thoughtful questions about the story. Next, my wife, Leslee, began editing and making recommendations as to style.

My copy editor, Aja Pollock, was extremely helpful. In addition to her editorial comments, she reviewed the story's timeline and checked various historical facts for accuracy.

I would be remiss if I did not thank my early readers: my brother, Jim Miraldi, my daughter, Emily Miraldi, my daughter, Virginia Miraldi Utz, my son, Daniel Miraldi, my cousin, John Miraldi, and my friend, Harriet Alger. Their enthusiasm encouraged me as I continued to write and rewrite the book.

Finally, after some joint brainstorming, my wife and son suggested the title to this book. I liked it from the moment they proposed it.

CPSIA information can be obtained
at www.ICGtesting.com
Printed in the USA
FFOW02n0422050817
38453FF